Dave
Rhoades

Altar

A Novel

Altar

Book design by Stormie Rhoades

For Jeanie,
You believed in me enough to understand
all the months I had to spend in the Netherworld.

To my children:
Tara, Dave, Stephanie, Tristan, Tredessa,
Rocky, Jovan and Stormie; thanks for always
being eager to turn the next page.

To my grandchildren:
Gavin, Hunter, Guinivere, Gemma, Averi and Amelie
your destiny is blessed and sure.

To the Tapper family, the
I hope you enjoy
Characters & story!
Blessings
Dave

Acknowledgments

My thanks to Jeff Gerke; your editing pen was swift and mighty, as always.
To Jim Bell and Bob Liparulo for the hours that I sat under your tutelage and your patience with my countless emails to pick your brains.

To all that have assisted me through this project with encouragement, proof-reading, opinion editing, critiques and saying: "ooh, that's really gross" in all the right places. If you are not public figures, I have protected your anonymity by not mentioning your last name, but you know who you are.
In no particular order...
The Brighton Writer's Circle: Pastor Al, Jo, and Floy. Mike Nappa, Chip MacGregor, Dave Lambert, Kathy Ide, Wanda Dyson, Angela Hunt, Nancy Rue, Dena Twinem, Nathan and the rest of the Nangies, Tami, Dan and Dawn, Heather, Leroy, Carolyn, Katherine, and mom.

Prologue

Just because something walks upright doesn't always mean that it was once human…

—

"You like the new edge?" Nathaniel asked.

"On my blade?" Michael asked.

"Yeah." Nathaniel whirled and lopped off a creature's arm. The beast shrieked and flailed against Nathaniel's chest catching its claws in his body armor. Nathaniel punched its snout sending it reeling to the ground.

Michael swung his sword and the head rolled into the dirt kicking up bloody jets after it. "I do," he said. "Back to back."

Nathaniel stepped behind Michael as several other creatures surrounded them in a circular dance, snarling and snapping at the two men.

"The new alloy seems to be quite strong," Michael thrust through the midsection of one of the beasts which were no more than rabid, dog-like mutants prancing on hind legs and swinging their make-shift weapons.

"It's the tempering that brings out its strength," Nathaniel stepped forward wielding two swords like a windmill and carved another creature into hairy chunks, then returned to his position behind Michael.

Nathaniel glanced to the family a few yards away, sheltered by an outcropping of stalagmites. "It's going to be fine."

A father, mother, baby in arms and a small boy and girl were huddled together in terror.

"We're going to get you out of here safely."

Michael and Nathaniel continued their death dance leaving the mutants in piles of bloody fur.

"Did you oil the blades?" Michael asked.

"Dipped like always," Nathaniel thrust into the eye socket of a creature that had not completed the mutation, more human than beast. "Do you think I'd forget the oil when we were coming here to fight?"

"No, just checking, little brother." Michael sliced through a midsection exposing the entrails as the creature hit his knees and fell face first into the dirt. "No wonder the cuts are so clean."

"Secret's in the oil," Nathaniel swung again and another head hit the cave floor. "I do what I can."

"What do you say we end this thing and get them out of here?" Michael motioned toward the family. "We'll leave Mel to clean up the rest of this mess."

"I'm all about that."

Michael and Nathaniel unleashed a torrent of slices and blows that sent the remaining creatures of the Netherworld lying in pieces all over the ground.

"These new blades will do fine," Michael said.

"I thought you'd like 'em," Nathaniel looked at the carnage around them.

"Calver!" Michael called.

A wiry man with a handle-bar mustache ran up to them. "Yes, boss."

"Take these people to the surface."

"Will do." Calver gathered the family and with several other soldiers he ushered the people away.

"Fall back!" Michael called to his men. "Head for the gates! We're done here!"

He and Nathaniel made their way along the huge cavern, sprinkled with bands of warriors still engaging the creatures.

"Mel," Michael said as they passed a short bald man with an inordinate amount of nose hair. "You, and your men, take care of the rest of this mess and meet us on the surface."

"Will do, boss," Mel puffed through his nose.

Michael and Nathaniel walked on, leaving the thrum of the battle behind them as they made their way down large rock corridors.

"The house of Haylel will rise again." Nathaniel said wiping his sword on the cuff of his armor.

"Not for several generations."

"But you know it will happen again."

"Of course it will happen again," Michael replied. "But that will give us time to find him."

"If he exists—"

"He exists," Michael said.

"Hope you're right."

"I usually am."

Nathaniel looked at his sword. "You know, we should manufacture these things."

1

She would die. It was unmistakable. Without doubt or mercy. These were her last moments on earth. All that she had been and all that she ever would be, ebbed away. Horror intensified up her spine until it short-circuited in her brain. The man's face peered through the river's surface. Distorted, muddled. Reality or apparition? Rescuer or phantom? She opened her mouth to scream but only sucked in water. Bubbles hissed in her ears, her skull throbbed and she choked up the filthy taste of the river. She gagged, trying to breath but only coughing up liquid.

Like some sadistic tango, the current pushed her away and then pulled her close again and she pawed for the surface.

The man smiled and extended his hand.

To drag her to safety or to hold her under?

Was it a welcome or a warning?

Relief or reckoning?

An asylum or an altar?

She reached for his large hand and muscled arm but the torrent held her; she would not be his today.

The river swatted her and its roar laughed in her face, arrogant condescension that pounded its amusement into her eardrums. It knew she was nothing. It would force *her* to know she was nothing; an insignificant speck on a planet that it would rip from her. The current hauled her back, away from the man and away from any chance of escape.

But she knew the man, a fleeting thought, a familiar stranger in a crowd. The water penetrated her nostrils and burned its way into her brain and her thoughts faded.

She collided with a rock and fastened onto its slimy surface, a last chance oasis in this hellish void. The suction relaxed, she clawed above the waterline and gasped for air.

The day had progressed without her and the clock tick paid no attention to her predicament. The emerald trees continued their shade ignoring her panic. The ebony crow sustained a cry of mockery from its perch on high. Yellow dandelions still punctuated the grassy field beyond her reach.

The man?

Gone.

Nowhere in sight.

She cried out for help but her voice was strangled and distant even in her own ears.

She put her foot into a crevice of the rock but slipped, plunging her back into the frothing rage. The suction seized here again and she thrashed against its hold.

Alone again.

Empty.

Void.

Buffeted in a million gallons.

She saw light through a curtain of bubbles but then tumbled into the darkness again as the sun gave way to the silt-mucked expanse of the river. It was deep, peaceful, like the passivity of a hurricane's eye.

Her lungs filled with water that felt as if it overflowed into her stomach. She became one with her tormentor. A splinter of time, a moment, a twinkle of the eye and she would never again escape death's grip.

The river whipped her headfirst into another rock and her scalp split without pain.

Was she already dead?

Incapable of feeling?

No more nerve endings to warn her of apparent danger?

No more blood?

Her blood had become the blood of the river. It pulsed through her veins like the banks that held the water captive. Her speech was only for its ears. Her breath now created the ripples on the water.

The pressure on her body subsided, the roar around her grew quiet and the man smiled.

She spiraled down like a whirlpool draining from a bathtub, sucked into the maelstrom through a vortex of current and she glimpsed a creature.

A fish?

A being?

A demonic, aquatic presence?

The man took a hold of her and tugged.

Life released her and she gave herself to him.

Yielding.

Euphoria mingled with trepidation.

Her muscles relaxed and she descended into serenity…

———

Zack Tucker walked along the dark street on autopilot until breaking glass interrupted his thoughts of the girl.

He slowed.

Murmured laughter.

Snickers.

Hushed words.

Three teenage boys darted from behind a hedge row. The first two missed, but the third struck Zack solidly; he hit the sidewalk seconds after his bucket of movie popcorn.

The third stopped. "Well, lookie what we got here."

Zack looked up and shook his head.

"I can't believe it." The third boy swore. "It's the poor excuse for a human being. The big boy that momma had a hard time pushin' out, right, Zacko Packo?"

Zack stood and picked up the empty popcorn container and turned to walk away. A rock hit him in the small of his back and made him recoil like a stray dog.

"Hey! What the-?" Zack spun, fist clinched. Bile churned up his throat and his stomach wanted to heave.

"Yeah, lardo, don't turn your back on me. I'm talkin' to you." The boy's voice was calm and deliberate. "Guess I rocked your world, huh, fat boy?"

The other two boys laughed.

Zack stared into Milton Drago's shadowed face and traced every feature from memory: Frigid, black eyes, void of decency; embedded beneath overgrown dark eyebrows. His straight nose started at a hate furrowed brow and ended above a pouty, rose colored mouth, better suited on a woman. Milton's square jaw was perpetually clinched, but when he showed them, his teeth were white and perfect.

Except for the rage that twisted his features, most would say that Milton Drago was a ruggedly handsome, outdoorsy seventeen-year-old.

"Cut it out, Milton, that was a long time ago," Zack massaged where the rock hit.

"Oh, my bad," Milton held up his hands in surrender. "Didn't realize the timeline between eighth grade and our graduation was so long ago, Zacko Facko—"

"Shut up, Milton." Zack said.

"Besides," Milton said. "You and me both know that you never *really* get over being FAAT." He pushed the word out from his gut. "That fat little freak is still waiting to squeeze out from under your extra-large belt. That voice is still messin' with ya, right? 'I'm a fatty, he's a fatty, wouldn't ya like to be a fatty too?'" Milton smiled.

Zack glanced behind him and stepped back.

"Gonna take off, heavy duty?" Milton asked. "Won't make it far—"

"What do you want, Milton?" Zack took another step back.

"Nothin' from you, fat ass." Milton stepped closer and brushed back his greasy black hair. "What'd you see?"

Kurt Clayton and Kevin Bauer stepped from the shadows to flank Milton. The Triune was complete.

"What are you talkin' about?" Zack asked.

"I -asked -you -what -you -saw," Milton gritted his teeth like an impatient English teacher.

"Nothin'."

"Nothin'? Not only are you fat, you're a liar too. A fat freakin' liar." Milton's eyes widened. "Hey, freak, what're you doin' around here anyway?"

"A movie," Zack excused himself.

"That porn flick? Zack, does your mother know?"

Kurt and Kevin laughed.

"Shut up, it wasn't…" Zack muttered.

"Oh, no?" Milton shrugged. "No, I guess not. Hey, what's the deal anyway?" Milton smiled. "Didn't want to drive down into Denver to get your rocks off? There's only kiddie movies playin' here."

"It's close to my house…" Zack said.

"Oh, right, right, I forgot." Milton stepped forward, Zack stepped back. "You and daddy have a place just down the street. Can't waddle too far from home, right?"

Zack stared at Milton for a moment. "The fat stuff's gettin' old, Milton."

"Is it?" Milton's eyes widened.

"Yeah, it is," Zack glanced behind him again.

A grin spread across Milton's face. "You wanna try and run? Go ahead, make a break for it." Milton waved. "Maybe daddy'll be standing there with open arms ready to give you a big sloppy kiss." Milton paused. "Or maybe, your sweet little mommy will—"

"Shut up, Milton." Zack clinched his jaw.

Milton turned away from him, nose in the air and folded arms. "Go ahead, freak. I'll let you pass."

Zack took another step back; his eyes darted from Milton to Kurt to Kevin.

"Come on man, let's get out of here," Kurt put his hand on Milton's shoulder and glanced up and down the street. "Someone's gonna see us."

"Shut up, Clayton." Milton knocked his hand away. "Nobody saw us do the house, you got another laptop out of the deal so shut-the-freak up. Nobody's watchin', except tubby piece-of-crap, here." Milton threw a thumb over his shoulder toward Zack.

He turned and faced Zack again. "So, how long you been watchin' us?"

Zack took a step back. "I was just walking by—."

"You heard breaking glass though, right?" Milton asked.

Zack took another step back. "I—"

"See, I knew it." Milton stepped closer. "What am I gonna do with you?"

"No, I didn't see—"

"Didn't see what?" Milton looked at him. "Now, Tucker." Milton took another step and slipped his arm around Zack's shoulder. "Don't try to lie your way out of this—"

"I'm not lying." Zack's voice cracked and he stepped away. "Why you hasslin' me?"

Milton slapped him in the chest. "What, are you gonna cry now?"

"No, I, uh—"

"That's right. I uh. I uh." Milton patted Zack's stomach.

Zack knocked Milton's hand away and shoved him backward into Kurt. Both tumbled into the hedge row. Milton fired off a volley of curses and Zack scrambled down the sidewalk toward home.

His legs pumped up and down like lead pistons and sweat poured from under his dark hair. But the hounds closed in on the rabbit easily. The collision forced Zack to his knees on the concrete sidewalk and the momentum drove him facedown into a hedge of rose bushes lining a rock wall.

Zack screamed. The impact drove thorns into his arms and face. A broken rose stem impaled his hand and his head hit the wall, skinning his cheek.

"What a piece of crap!" Milton's voice loomed over him. "You can't even run. You freakin' pig!"

Zack tried to right himself, unsuccessfully flailing his bloody arms.

"What's the matter can't stand up? Here, see if this helps." Milton kicked him in the groin and burst into laughter.

Zack coughed while excruciating pain exploded over his entire body. He tried in vain to free his hands to protect himself but all he could do was close his eyes. "Please. . ."

Zack thrashed like a fly in a web but tightened himself for the next phase of abuse.

"What the…" Kevin said.

Zack waited. No kicks, no fists. He slid his hand into the dirt and got a knee under him. He pushed and wiggled until he finally rolled onto the sidewalk and stamped it with bloody palm prints.

Through a crimson film, he squinted and watched the Triune run down the street. Milton, Kurt and Kevin appeared under the street light for an instant and then disappeared around the corner. Zack wiped the blood from his face with the heel of his hand and then onto his jeans. A few seconds later, car doors slammed, an engine turned over and tires squealed.

He drew an arm across his bloody forehead and scanned the dark street.

A man walked away from him.

"Hey!" Zack shouted.

The man continued to walk.

Zack yelled again. "Hey, sir? Could you help me?"

No response.

Zack blinked. The man's dark, shoulder length hair glistened in the moonlight and his ankle length duster flapped in the breeze like a renegade cowboy from the big screen.

"Well, thanks anyway…"

Zack closed his eyes. He heard the tap, tap, tap of the man's boots on the sidewalk and then silence. He opened his eyes. No one anywhere.

Zack put his head between his knees and slowed his breathing. He tugged at his torn shirt and saw his bloody knee caps that protruded through ripped pants. Zack rolled onto one knee, winced with pain, and hoisted himself up

Fall leaves rustled around his feet and Zack shook his head. Where's a cop when you need one?

In retrospect, the blonde at the movies was the best part of the evening.

2

The next morning, Zack reached his locker before the period bell sounded. He glanced at the large, black rimmed clock above the World History door.

Eight more minutes.

He sipped water from the fountain and looked down the hallway, no Triune.

"What are you doing out here?"

Zack whirled and notebook pages fluttered to the floor.

"Man, don't ever do that." Zack said.

"What?" John Welte bent to pick up the pages.

"Scare me like that," Zack let out a long breath.

"Sorry, man, I just had to get a snack and take a leak," John shuffled through the pages. "You were supposed to turn this in last week." He handed Zack a notebook paper. John's brown eyes twinkled under wire framed glasses that had only one lens. "Man, what happened to you?"

Zack watched John take inventory of his purple eye and the scratches on his face.

"Me?" Zack diverted the question by tapping on John's glasses. "What about this?"

"Popped out again," John squinted, looked up and down and then rolled his head like he had a neck ache. "It's not bad once you get used to it." John ran a hand through his auburn hair and then shook it out like a dog.

"So?" He eyed Zack's cheek again with one eye closed.

Zack fired his rehearsed answer. "I slipped and fell in the bushes on the way home from the movies last night."

John opened both eyes and handed the rest of the papers back to Zack. "Yeah, looks like you slipped a couple of times... again." John scrutinized the bandages on his hands. "Have any help?" He paused to scratch behind one of his oversized ears. "Slippin', I mean?"

Zack looked at him. "What are you doing in study hall anyway?"

"Had to help Mickey Martin again," John said.

"Geometry?" Zack asked.

"Course."

"What this time?"

"He has to figure the square footage of the Pentagon," John said.

"So? He couldn't do it by himself?"

"Well…" John hiked his pants over his sunken stomach. "I *am* sitting next to Staci Bransen while I help ole Mickey Mouse. Dude, she smells good."

"Ah, the fair Staci," Zack grinned. "And why is *she* in there?"

"Oh she's working on some graduation thing with one of those cute little freshmen chicks, also a lovely smeller." John shrugged. "Who knows? Us, seniors, don't need excuses to be where we are. We rock!" John thrust a fist in the air and then glanced around.

"Have you…seen Milton or Kurt yet today?" Zack scanned a notebook page.

"No, why would I? It's not noon yet and to my knowledge, this isn't a liquor store." John reached into his pocket, rooted around, pulled out a handful of Boston Baked Beans and popped them in his mouth.

"Just wonderin'," Zack shrugged, turning the page over. "How 'bout Kevin?"

"He'll be along," John said. "Daddy wouldn't want little Kevy's grades to drop."

John threw a few more beans into his mouth. "Hey, did I tell you? The yearbook committee voted those three "*most likely to serve time together*". He chomped and sputtered flecks of candy toward Zack.

"Hey, man, watch it," Zack brushed his pants. "How long you been waitin' to use that one?"

John munched like a cow. "A while." He popped another handful in. "What's your point?"

A nice looking girl passed them. "Hey Zack." She said and then nodded toward John. "Monkey."

Zack smiled. "Hey, Amber."

"Coming from you, Amber," John called after her. "I'll receive that as a compliment."

He turned back toward Zack. "Who started that whole, *monkey* thing anyway?" John finally swallowed the beans. "I really hate that."

"It was that one girl," Zack said. "Way back in eighth grade, what was her name?"

"I don't know, that's why I ask."

"Well, it does fit. Have you looked at your ears in a mirror lately?"

"Shut up," John said. "And to answer your first question, no, haven't seen any of the Triune." He opened his locker, took out a sandwich in plastic, unwrapped it and recoiled.

"Holy crap." John hooked it into the trashcan across the hall. "Score!" He thrust a fist into the air again.

3

The third period bell rang and Zack sat in his usual seat by the corner window. John slumped next to him and wiped someone's leftover cracker crumbs onto the floor.

A few seconds later, Ralph Fryberg traipsed through the door in baggy pants and wrinkled wool sport coat. The sleeves ended in the middle of his hands. He plopped onto the top of his desk, one leg cocked at the knee and the other touching the floor. Mr. Fryberg shoved his meaty hand into the inside breast pocket of his jacket, he extracted a plastic bag and searched his pants. He produced a pocketknife, opened the bag, sliced off a chunk of Limburger cheese and slid it into his mouth.

A girl gagged in the front row and then swallowed hard.

Mr. Fryberg peered over dark-framed reading glasses, that rested on the bulbous part of his nostrils.

"Now that I've cut the cheese and gotten your attention, we will begin." Fryberg's deep bass voice could have vibrated the windows.

"Who said: Those who cannot remember the past are condemned to repeat it?" Fryberg asked.

In unison, the entire class answered, "George Santayana." Some of the students rolled their eyes and others nodded their heads in rhythm with the answer.

Mr. Fryberg scanned the room and stopped on Zack's wounds.

Zack put a hand to the side of his mouth, "You should see the other guy."

Mr. Fryberg smiled and continued.

"The Romans were disciplined and proud. The Caesars expanded their kingdoms to the ends of the known world and were the greatest army that had ever existed up to that time, surpassing even the Egyptians in might and power. . ."

Zack stared at the Russell Crowe poster at the front of the room. *Gladiator*. Russell stood with determination, his biceps bulged, forearms hard, and he clutched the sword in defiance of Caesar, the Coliseum and Milton Drago.

Mr. Fryberg's voice brought Zack back from nirvana. "What do you think you would have done in ancient Rome, had you have lived back then?"

Silence.

"How about you, Miss Romero?"

"Sir?"

"What occupation would you have held in ancient Rome?" Fryberg repeated the question, sliced off another hunk of Limburger and sucked it between his lips.

"Well, maybe an artisan?"

"Ah, yes, a craftsman," He nodded and swallowed. "What type?"

"Uh, pottery maker, maybe?" Romero shrugged.

"A noble profession indeed. People have to eat and drink, right?" He scanned the terrified faces again and then pointed a finger. "How about you, Mr. Hinrady?"

Jake Hinrady continued to doodle on his notebook without looking up. "No doubt in my mind, Mr. F. An artist."

"Indeed, the margins, of your last essay, bear witness."

Several giggles escaped.

Mr. Fryberg sealed the plastic bag and stuffed the putrid cheese back in his pocket.

Fryberg turned his attention toward the corner window. "How about you, Mr. Welte," He paused. "Surely, a maker of spectacles?"

John closed one eye and peered at him through the single, smudged lens. "Oh, I'm sure I would have been an accountant, wielding an abacus instead of a sword."

The class laughed, John stood, bowed and sat back down.

"Anyone else?" Mr. Fryberg smiled.

More dead air.

Zack raised his hand.

"Mr. Tucker." Fryberg nodded.

"A gladiator, sir."

Zack heard snickers.

"Fat chance," someone muttered.

"Do you think so, Mr. Burgess?" Mr. Fryberg zeroed in on the insult. "Did you want to expound on Mr. Tucker's aspiration?"

"Uh, no, sir," Matt Burgess squirmed.

"Do you know anything about the gladiators, Mr. Burgess?"

"No, sir."

"Then perhaps you should let Mr. Tucker continue." He turned back to Zack. "Do you know anything about the gladiators, Mr.Tucker?"

"Uh, yes, sir." Zack sat straighter. "I know that they were usually slaves, forced to fight for their lives in the Coliseum and Circus Maximus. If they survived, there were great honors bestowed upon them, sometimes even their freedom."

"Impressive, Mr. Tucker. You *are* aware that most of them didn't reach the age of thirty?"

"Yes, sir." Zack nodded.

"And you would still seek to be enslaved in the arenas of Rome, knowing that a down-turned thumb would mean execution?"

Zack glanced at the tile floor then met Mr. Fryberg's eyes. "Yes, sir. I guess we all live and die in the arena of life."

"Very true, but at this present time, no one is chasing you around the room trying to lop-off your head with a sword." Mr. Fryberg eyed Zack's bruises. "Or are they?"

More giggles and Zack smiled.

The classroom door opened and Kevin Bauer entered.

Zack lowered his eyes and slid down a bit.

Mr. Fryberg pulled a pocket watch from his coat and held it up for all to see. "Well, Mr. Bauer, so nice of you to honor us with your presence 20 minutes into my lecture."

"Sorry, sir, I..." Kevin sat down.

"We are referring to page 285. Please catch up." Fryberg said.

Students around the room opened books and flipped pages.

"I assume that you did the reading that was assigned, Mr. Bauer?"

"Well...I... was sort of busy last night," Kevin glanced at Zack then back to Fryberg.

"Indeed," Mr. Fryberg said. "Am I to assume, then, that you will catch up tonight?"

"Yes, sir," Kevin nodded. "Most definitely."

For the rest of class, Zack sat at the feet of a master while Mr. Fryberg poured out his knowledge of ancient Rome.

A half hour later, Zack heard Matt Burgess whisper. "Five, four, three, two, one," and the bell sounded.

"Remember pages 300-350 for tomorrow." Mr. Fryberg scooted off the desk. "Ms. Wilson, can I talk to you a moment?"

Kevin was the first one out the door.

"What's the deal with him?" John grabbed his history book.

"Don't know." Zack shrugged.

"Are you sure you don't?" John stared.

Zack shrugged again.

4

Zack slammed his locker door. "Want to come over later and hang out for a while?" Zack glanced around.

"Sure." John followed Zack's gaze. "I don't have anything else on the burner today. Who you looking for?"

"No one." Zack paused. "Do you ever have anything on the burner?"

John squinted through the single lens. "What's your point?"

"Will you fix those things." Zack punched him on the shoulder.

"I kinda like 'em this way," John said. "Makes me unique—"

"It makes you weird." Zack said.

John bugged his eyes at Zack. "Are you alright?" He slammed his locker.

"Fine," Zack picked up his backpack and slung it over his shoulder. "I'll meet you by the trophy case at last bell."

——

Zack looked through the glass trophy case attached to the wall.

The Letterman Jackets received immortality on every shelf. Zack saw their smiles, accomplishment and confidence. He noted their raised index fingers in the photos indicating their place in line. The radiant beauties on their arms were no doubt destined for the homecoming court and promenaded their way to class, like Cleopatra riding on muscular, bronzed slaves. Kevin Bauer's photo stared at him from his perch on the swim team.

"Ready?"

Zack jumped.

"What's up with you today?" John asked.

"Nothin'."

Zack and John walked out a set of double doors toward the parking lot.

"The Female Flocking," John nodded toward a group of girls.
"Yeah," Zack grinned.

Janice Markum's jet-black spiked hair didn't waver as she approached. She took hold of Zack's chin with a black leather glove that had all the fingers cut out and eyed the cuts and scrapes.

"So, I hear the Triune got to you last night." Her black rimmed eyes looked like they were drawn by a sketch artist with too much ink in his pen.

Zack couldn't hold her gaze. "Uh, no, not really." He glanced down at the upside down skull on the front of her black T-shirt. Janice touched his face and then took hold of his hands and turned them to look at the palms.

"Don't know who got the worst of it." Janice said. "But since Kevin's the only one who showed up today-" She paused. "Hey, Geekster?" She took Zack's chin and guided it back up so that he was looking at her.

"If you did jack 'em," Her pierced tongue gleamed in the sunlight. "then rad!" She turned, rejoined her crew and they walked off campus.

Zack and John watched their black saggy jeans with safety pins, chains, and all things metal, attached to them.

"What was all that about?" John asked.

"Nothin' really." Zack started walking again. "We takin' your car?"

"Naw," John said. "Out of gas. We'll have to hoof it."

5

Zack and John rounded the corner by Delbert's Market just as the door opened and hit Zack in the chest.

"Oh, I'm so sorry." The blonde covered her mouth and dropped her plastic bag.

Zack caught it.

"Sorry," he handed it back. "I should've been watching—"

"Hey, how are you?" she asked.

"Uh, hello, again," he said.

She looked at his face.

"Are you all right?" Her green eyes widened.

"Yes, fine. I, uh, had an encounter with a bush on the way home from the theater."

"Last night?" She asked.

"Yeah."

"Looks painful."

She touched his face and Zack forgot about his wounds.

"Seen any good movies lately?" She smiled.

"Uh, no not really. I mean not recently. Uhh, not since last night." Zack winced.

John munched Boston Baked Beans and his head bounced back and forth, from face to face, like a line judge at a tennis match.

"This must be the Trekkie," she nodded toward John.

"We prefer, Trekkers," John said.

"Sorry," she said. "I didn't know it was—"

"You see," John continued. "*Trekkie*, denotes that we are but a passing fad…" He waved a hand. "A groupie, attributing our philosophy in life to a few 1960's actors who functioned amidst a set of cardboard consoles irrigated with Christmas lights." John took out a handkerchief, honked, wiped his nose several directions, fingered a nostril and then stuffed it into the back pocket of his jeans. "Instead of adopting an entire lifestyle bent on taking us where no man, or woman in your case," he nodded, "has gone before."

Zack and the blonde looked at John.

"Sorry," Zack said. "He doesn't get out much."

"Heyyy," John said.

She winked and smiled at Zack. "Thanks for your help last night."

Zack managed a John Wayne impression. "Well, I'll tell ya little missy, 'twas my pleasure."

She giggled. "Well, nice to see you again. Hope you're okay." She threw him a, *poor baby* look. "I'm always on the run, obviously. Nice to meet you, Dr. Spock."

"It's Dr. McCoy or Mr. Spock—"

"She gets it," Zack hit John in the arm. "Nice to see you again, too…" Zack called after her, then looked at John.

"What?"

He and John watched her walk toward her car and enjoyed every step.

"Man, she smells good," Zack said. "I—"

"Okay, Big Guy, spill." John hit Zack in the arm. "And what's with defiling my philosophy of life?"

"What?" Zack shrugged.

John held up a finger. "First, supposedly you got in a big fight and mopped the floor with Milton and Kurt; and now," John held up a second finger. "You meet some knockout chick at the movies and I haven't even heard about it? What gives, man?"

"Okay, okay, chill; it wasn't that big of a deal." Zack sighed. "What do you want to hear about first, Milton or the blonde?"

"Tough decision," John tapped his chin. "The doll baby, of course! Who cares about that skank, Milton?"

They began to walk as Zack explained.

"Well, I went to see Planet of the Apes—"

"With Wahlberg?" John asked.

"Heston."

"Oh, the original." John nodded. "Very good."

"So I'm sitting there with my popcorn, extra butter and Diet Pepsi, minding my own business—"

"Why do you do that?"

"What?" Zack asked.

"Get the popcorn with the extra butter and buy a *diet* soda?"

"I don't like to waste my calories on a drink—"

"Fine," John waved a hand. "Continue."

"Anyway, the movie ended and I was sitting there watching the credits—"

"Like usual." John nodded.

"And I gave myself a wedgie."

"What?" John stopped on the sidewalk.

"I didn't mean to, she was sitting there watching the credits too—"

"The Delbert's Market girl?"

"Yeah, she likes the credits too. And when they were over she got up and came toward me—"

"So."

"So, I froze, she's a knockout. You saw her? I didn't know what to do."

"So you decided, 'What the heck? I'll give myself a wedgie'?"

"Not on purpose, you idiot," Zack punched John's arm as they began to walk again. "I leaned forward and started to hike up my pants, and—"

"You grabbed your underwear instead?" John burst into laughter.

Zack shrugged. "Well, I was nervous."

"I'll say," John tried to stifle his laughter. "I guess I could see it. You're right, she *is* a knockout."

"Fortunately, her contact popped out."

"Lens?"

"Yeah. When she got next to me."

"Really? Next to you? Was she wearing the same cologne—"

"Yeah," Zack shrugged. "I guess so. I helped her find her contact, that's all."

"Well, I will say you do have sharp eyes," John nodded. "Like the time you found my contact at the Star Trek convention—"

"See, that's what I told her, the Trekkie thing—"

"Trekker—"

"Whatever," Zack said.

John closed the eye without the lens and then opened it again, craning his neck.

"I told her about the time we went and stood in line to get—"

"The Grace Lee Whitney autograph thingy—"

"Yeah," Zack said.

"So you called me, Trekkie?"

"I'm sorry, but I told you I was nervous. You would be too."

"We're not talkin' about me," John paused and smiled. "She is gorgeous though and those eyes. . . Holy…"

"See. You should have seen what she had on. This short skirt and some high heels, not too high, but high enough, they made her legs look… well, never mind. "

"Go on."

"Naw," Zack shook his head.

They walked a few more steps.

"Yeah, you're right." John took off his glasses and cleaned the lens. "So, what's her name?"

Zack didn't answer.

"You're kiddin', right?" John replaced his glasses.

Zack shrugged.

"All of that, and you didn't even ask her name? Dude." John cocked his head.

"I was nervous." Zack shrugged.

"You said that," John smiled. "So whatever happened with the wedgie?"

"I pulled it out when she looked down at the floor to find her contact."

"Smooth, man," John smiled. "Very smooth."

"So after meeting her, I just walked down the street in a daze. That's when Milton and the rest of the Triune jumped me."

"The scum," John said.

They walked a few more houses in silence.

"So, what's with Milton anyway?" John finally asked.

"Simple," Zack said. "He hit me and I hit the sidewalk, and then there was the guy."

"What guy?"

Zack related the rest of the evening and left out no humiliating detail.

—

"The thing that bugs me," John followed Zack onto his front porch. "is why didn't the guy say something?"

"Beats me." Zack fished in his pocket for his keys, slid it into the lock and opened the door. "I'm just glad he was there."

He let his back pack slip to the floor.

"Zack?"

"Yeah, dad."

Jeff Tucker walked out of the kitchen with a sandwich in a plastic bag.

"Hey, guys, what's up?"

"You headin' off to work already?" Zack noticed the open lunch pail on the hall chair.

"Hey, Mr. Tucker," John said.

"John," Jeff nodded and then turned back to Zack. "Mark's sick so I'm covering his shift." Jeff tossed the sandwich into the lunch pail and latched it shut.

"That's cool," Zack said.

"Yeah, we can use the extra cash," Jeff smiled. "Hold down the fort."

He hugged Zack, kissed him on the cheek, and then punched John on the shoulder.

"I love you, son. See you in the morning."

"Love you too, Dad. Have fun."

"Hey, somebody's got to." Jeff grabbed the lunch pail. "John."

"Yes, sir."

Jeff held up his hand with all five fingers spread apart. "Live long and prosper." And he was out the door.

"Come on, ya wuss," Zack grabbed John's shirt sleeve and pulled him toward the kitchen.

"Oh, yeah," John rubbed his arm. "He kisses you and punches me!"

"I'm sure he'd kiss you if you wanted," Zack grinned.

"He didn't do the Vulcan hand thing right—"

"I know," Zack said. "And *he* knows…"

6

The siren's rhythmic wail thrummed in Kurt Clayton's skull.

His lids opened and closed and his eyes rolled back in his head. The fire in his arm moved him in and out of consciousness. His belly ached and he lay in some sort of wet mass.

Kurt licked his dry, cracked lips. He searched for anything that resembled moisture. Someone lifted his lid, a bright light pierced his pupil, and he detected a faraway woman's voice muddled and garbled. The scream of the siren droned on. He needed to muffle the sound by any means.

She slapped his face and his cheek burned. Kurt tried to move his arm to squelch the pain but it wouldn't cooperate. His stomach was full of something, but an empty ache sucked on it like a vacuum hose.

He moved his tongue, something was in his mouth. A straw? A tube? The regular beep and systematic hiss ticked him off. He didn't know why. Kurt opened his eyes to bright lights and faces. He closed them again. The equipment shrieked and the ambulance jostled and his brain was about to explode.

Voices echoed, laughter intensified and color danced across his closed lids. He turned his head and spewed vomit onto the floor. Kurt saw the yellow mass on someone's shoes but his eyes rolled back and then focused on the white walls and tubes that swayed to the rhythm of the ambulance. Disproportionate, brightly colored balls collided with one another; he panicked and the woman paramedic slapped him again.

Why? Why did she hit him? They weren't supposed to do that…

Her red lips opened and closed, but no voice. He glanced around. She was the only one in the ambulance with him. Did they do that? He thought there were supposed to be two people.

The paramedic smiled, a large, tooth filled smile.

Her face.

Kurt found it attractive, captivating, like a runway model born with cheek bones that fit the current magazine era.

He tried to focus on her smile.

Her lips, her face, her features, her eyes, her makeup.

Her lips distorted and began to twist into a hideous, disproportionate, grin; the grin of one of those dolls who come to life in a horror movie. Kurt wanted to look away, he wanted to get up and run; if only he could lift his arms; but, straps held him to the gurney.

Her face twisted and those beautiful teeth faded yellow and her eyeteeth elongated into fangs.

Kurt was mesmerized, like when he'd come upon that accident that night on Highway 5, a head-on collision; flashing red and blue lights, cops everywhere, ambulances, fire engines and a body in the road covered by a white sheet. He wasn't supposed to look, out of respect, but there was a body in the road, you couldn't help but look. You wanted to stare at other people's chaos and tragedy. Sadistic, but true.

Like the Day of Muriel…

Kurt had to look at this paramedic, that beauty coupled with that hideous smile, he didn't dare look away.

The ambulance hit a pothole in the road; it jolted Kurt back and broke his concentration.

The paramedic's face had not distorted, her teeth were intact and he watched her perform her tasks: glancing at monitors, following the feed of the IV tube, checking her watch periodically.

He closed his eyes as his eardrums hammered him into a dream world. Kurt floated and then relaxed; the noises faded and he opened his eyes again, focusing on the paramedic's name tag for an instant, "Angie".

7

"Did you hear?"

"Hear what?" Zack asked.

"About Kurt Clayton?" John shifted from one foot to the other.

The first bell rang, and Zack bent to tie his shoe. "You've got to calm down, man," he said. "You're gonna wet your pants and—"

"He tried to commit suicide." John said. "They rushed him to the hospital!"

"What?" Zack stood.

"His little sister found him. Bunch of pills." John snatched a notebook from the locker and slammed the door.

"Is he okay?" Zack started down the hallway.

"Who knows?" John followed.

Zack pulled on the cafeteria door. "That's weird, man."

John sniffed the air. "Wonder what mystery meat they're sliding us today?"

"I don't care," Zack said. "I'm starved."

They entered the cafeteria, pulled orange trays from the bin and like Fords in mass production, shuffled down the line.

"Why would he do it?" Some girls behind them in line were abuzz. "I mean, he's such a doll."

Zack turned and noticed one's flaming red hair. He nudged John and rolled his eyes.

"That's for sure." The chunky blonde bent and grabbed a tray. "And Staci."

"Yeah, how's she doing?" The redhead asked.

"Who knows? It's tough for sure." The blonde said.

In front of Zack and John, two Neanderthals with letterman jackets had their own opinions.

"What about that new ride he bought, dude?" The muscular buzzcut asked.

"You mean, *daddy* bought for him," The other boy chuckled and his thick neck rippled.

"Whatever. Still, nothing I'd leave behind."

"Yeah, it's not like he's hurtin', or looks like you." Thick Neck erupted in a belly laugh.

"Yeah, very funny; you should be on TV," Buzzcut replied. "Ho, Ho." he grabbed his ample stomach.

Behind Zack and John, the girls rejoined the speculation.

"And that house—"

"You know it." the blonde paused. "It's beautiful."

"How do you know?"

"I've heard." the blonde said.

"But not *seen*," Red added.

"Well, no." the blonde said.

"The parents are worth millions." the redhead whispered.

"Really?" the blonde asked.

"I've heard." Red said.

"But not *seen*," the blonde said.

"Well, no," Red said.

Relieved the bread line had ended, Zack stood at the pay station. The heavyweight capped in a hairnet sat at a metal box and peeled off bills. Her disconnected gaze complemented her mundane smile.

"Thank you, have a nice day," she droned and slapped coins on the counter.

Zack and John emptied into the cafeteria and scanned some openings at various tables.

They approached a table of three freshmen. "Move over!" John said.

One acne faced kid with greasy hair looked up, picked up his tray and vacated the table. His two cohorts looked straight ahead and munched on burgers.

"You're harsh," Zack said.

"Nah, it's the pecking order." John waved his hand and sat opposite Zack. "They'll do the same thing when they've grown up." He stared at one of the freshmen.

Zack leaned forward ready to launch into full commentary about Kurt as a table full of girls erupted behind John.

"I don't know," Lisa George clutched her yellow binder. "I talked to Staci and she's going to spend the next few days at the hospital." She ran her acrylic fingernail down the spiral binding producing an annoying clicking noise.

"Here we go," Zack lowered his voice and watched the girls. "Now it's time for the yap session ."

John looked at the other two freshmen. "What are you lookin' at?" he squawked.

"Nothin'." one replied.

"Okay then, see that you don't." John grinned at Zack.

The two freshmen scarfed down the remainder of their burgers and left.

"Was it something I said?" John called after them.

"Rude, man." Zack grinned and shook his head.

John smiled and slurped down a French fry bathed in catsup.

"That's a real shocker," Karen Montoya's voice carried back to Zack and John. Her dark eyes sparkled. "Why'd he do it?"

Lisa piped in again, "Nobody knows. I heard it's something about last night."

"What happened?" Tina Moran plopped down next to Lisa.

"They were poking around Halstatller's Cemetery and they encountered something," Lisa said.

"Encountered?" Tina adjusted her skirt.

"It's a word that I use often," Lisa looked down her nose.

Tina rolled her eyes.

"Where'd you hear about the 'encounter'?" Tina used her fingers to put quotes around the word.

"From Del," Lisa said.

"Figures. Why the cemetery?" Tina asked.

"Are you kidding? That whole crew is out there every weekend havin' a good time." Lisa gave a knowing look.

Zack cocked his head to one side as the conversation unfolded.

"Well, I think…" John started to comment, but Zack held up a finger and motioned toward the girl's table. John turned around and looked, but then returned to his fries.

"Is that right?" Tina asked.

"Yeah, *that's* right," Lisa threw her a stern look and then resumed. "So anyway, I hear they were all out there startin' up when Kurt had to pee. Milton and Kevin decided to go into the woods with him. Strange boys." She rolled her eyes.

"And they get pissy about *us* and the bathroom thing." Tina leaned forward, giggling.

Zack smiled and glanced down.

"Shut up and let her finish," Karen put her hand on Tina's shoulder and moved her back.

Lisa continued. "So, Del says that she, Staci, and the other Stacey are sitting on the grass leaning against a couple of stones—"

"They were leaning against the gravestones?" Tina said.

"Will you let her finish?"

"They're leaning against the stones, lighting up, when all of a sudden," Lisa's eyes widened. "they hear Milton yell and he and Kevin come rippin' out of the trees."

"What about Kurt?" Tina asked.

"I'm getting to that." Lisa gave her a tap on the arm. "Del said that Milton and Kevin came running back yelling to them to get in the cars; she said their faces were ashen white!"

"Ashen?"

"Yes, ashen, you dink," Lisa squinted a dirty look.

"Do you really believe all this?" Carol Wannamaker scooted closer, joining the conversation.

"No, really; that's what she said." Lisa looked at her out of the corner of her eyes. "She said she'd never seen Milton look like that before."

"What about Kurt?" Tina asked again taking hold of Lisa's arm.

"I'm telling ya!" Lisa backhanded Tina's arm and then continued. "Del said at first they just thought that the guys were trying to scare them, you know, being in a graveyard and all. But then…" Lisa leaned in like they were around a campfire. "Kurt came out of the trees, half crawling and half stumbling.

Del said he was pulling up his pants and then stopped, dropped on all fours and puked a couple of times."

"Oh, gross," Tina shook her head. "That's just gross. Information overload!" She shook her hands, stomped her feet and blinked.

Lisa looked Tina up and down, waiting for her to finish her self-imposed seizure.

"Sorry." Tina regained control.

Zack strained as Lisa continued in a whisper. "So, he got up and all he could say was, 'Go! Go!' And he ran right by them."

Lisa sat back and took a bite of an apple, nodding her head and scanning the table.

"Well?" Tina held out her hands after a moment. "Come on. That's not all, is it?"

Lisa straightened and rested her elbows on the table. "Del said they grabbed their stuff and got out of there."

No one breathed until Tina broke the silence. "Why do you always call her the 'other Stacey'?"

"Will. You. Shut. Up!" Karen said.

 Lisa continued, "So, Del told me that all the way back to the house Milton didn't say a word. Not one word." She held up a finger to emphasize her point. "Del said Staci kept wiping the sweat and tears off Kurt's cheeks and asking him questions, but he wouldn't open his mouth either. They pulled up to Del's house and just sat there until the girls got out and the boys just drove away." Finally Lisa sat back, exhausted.

"Weird," Karen brushed her hair back from her eyes.

"Yeah, weird." Lisa nodded.

"So then, he goes home and takes a bunch of pills?" Tina asked.

"Looks like it," Lisa said.

The bell interrupted the commentary.

 Zack stood and picked up his tray. "I wonder if I should go and visit Kurt in the hospital?"

"Are you kidding?" John snatched his own tray. "You're no friend of his. Besides you'll be walking into a lions' den. *You know who* will be there, no doubt."

"I know. But now I'm curious," Zack nodded toward the dispersing girls.

"Well, you know what'll probably go down," John wadded his napkin and stuffed it into his milk glass.

"Yeah, I do," Zack said. "But I really want to know, especially after what happened to me the other night. Wanna come?"

They stepped toward the cafeteria door. "Ohh man, I don't know." John rolled his eyes. "Of course you know that's the first place I'd love to spend the evening, but—"

"Come on, ya wimp," Zack smiled.

They walked a few more steps. John turned and watched Tina and Lisa walk by.

"I guess I *could* tag along." He grinned at Zack. "But I'm staying in the waiting room. No cuts and bruises for me."

"Yeah, yeah." Zack put his dirty tray on the rollers and slid it toward the dishwasher. "I might be able to get the car," he said.

"Good, cuz I'm out of gas." John said. "At least the car kind." He made a fist, hit his chest and burped.

Zack slapped him on the back. "Pick you up around six."

8

John hung his head off the tattered couch watching reruns of Star Trek Deep Space Nine on the Sci-Fi channel. Zack's horn brought him back from Andromeda; he grabbed the remote, switched off the TV and jumped up.

"Be back later, mom, I'm going with Zack." he yelled and slammed the door of the modular home.

John opened the passenger door and slid into the seat.

"Hey," Zack said.

"To the hospital!" John pointed out the windshield.

Ten minutes later, Zack turned into the well-lit parking lot of Kimera General Hospital.

A remodel of the east wing necessitated three times around the lot to avoid the sea of blinking yellow lights. They pulled between two massive pickup trucks, jumped out and walked toward the entrance doors that slid open automatically.

"Yes, can I help you?" The young blonde behind the horseshoe-shaped Formica counter popped her bubble gum. She closed a supermarket tabloid and John snickered at the two headed alien baby on the front.

"Can you tell us where Kurt Clayton's room is?" Zack asked.

She flipped open a black notebook and ran her finger down the entries.

"He's on the eighth floor, room 818. Go to the end of this hall, there will be three stripes painted on the floor: red, yellow, and blue. Follow the yellow stripe."

"Like the brick road?" John asked.

She smiled. "Yes, like the brick road. The yellow stripe'll take you to the elevator. When you get off on eight, make a left, you'll see the nurse's station. Tell 'em you're here to see…" She looked back down at her registry, blew another bubble and popped it, "Mr. Clayton."

"Thank you," Zack said.

"No problem." She returned to her article.

John walked exactly on the yellow tape, all the way down the hall.

"You look like a DUI at a traffic stop," Zack said.

"Just trying to follow the cute blonde's instructions," John smiled. "I love to be bossed around by beauties."

The elevator doors opened on the 8th floor.

Zack approached the nurse's station. "Hi, we're here to visit Kurt Clayton. We were told downstairs that he's in room 818—"

"Yes, he is." The nurse snapped. "But *too* many kids are in there right now. You know what I mean?" Her eyebrows formed a "V" like she had just caught them sneaking out of math class.

"You'll have to wait until some others come out." She continued. "And if you've got any complaints about me," she tapped her name tag, "the name's Rita."

Zack paused.

"Uh. No, ma'am, no complaints. Is it all right to hang around in the waiting room?" Zack motioned to a couple of chairs tucked into a small room with a television.

Rita sighed. "Please. That would be fine." She lowered her shoulders. "I'm sorry, boys. I don't mean to be rude. It's been one of those days." She shook her head at the ceiling.

"Oh, that's okay. No problem." Zack smiled. "I know how that goes. We'll just wait."

John pulled a magazine off the waiting room end table and plopped down onto an arm chair. He froze on an article: *10 Easy Steps to Massacre Menopause*. He glanced at Zack enthralled in a comic book and slid the *Good Housekeeping* under a stack of sports magazines, then snatched *The World of Electronics,* opened it and cleared his throat.

The upheaval in the hallway disrupted John's inspection of bio-technology. Milton, Kevin, and Del came down the hall and rounded the corner wobbling toward the elevator.

"Wait, just a minute," Milton slurred his words and turned back toward the nurse's station. Zack brought the magazine up to his face. John leaned forward in his chair and peeked around the corner.

"Thanks so much for your hospitality," Milton spat across the nurse's station. "You've been so kind. If I ever need to commit suicide, I hope they bring me to this crap hole."

The nurse snatched the phone from its cradle.

"No need, Big Momma." He grabbed the receiver. "I was just leavin'!" Milton threw the receiver on the desk.

"Don't come back up here or I *will* call security!" the nurse yelled.

Milton responded with his middle finger.

Zack got up and peered with John around the corner of the waiting room. Milton, Kevin and Del climbed onto the elevator.

"Well?" He turned to John with arms outstretched like, *give me a hug.*

"I'm here for ya, buddy." John settled back into his chair and pointed to the floor. "I'm right here."

"Thanks a whole heckuva lot." Zack smirked.

"You are most certainly welcome," John went back to the magazine.

"I guess you're going to let me do this on my own, huh?" Zack hiked his pants and looked around the corner again.

"Yup." John didn't lift his gaze.

"Are you sure you won't…"

John pointed at the floor again and grinned.

9

Zack looked down at his shoes as they squeaked on the waxed floor. The disinfectant's smell reminded him of why he hated hospitals. He passed a room filled with bright balloons and grim relatives. The whir, of a floor buffer, interrupted the stillness.

Zack reached 818 and touched the door; it flew back and hit the wall.

Staci Bransen ran into him and shrieked.

"Oh, Zack, you scared the crap out of me!" She clutched her chest.

"Sorry, I didn't mean to…"

She took a breath.

"It's okay." She dabbed her red-rimmed eyes with a wadded tissue as the door closed behind her. "Sorry, I'm a mess these past few days."

"I…uh,came to see how Kurt was doing?" Zack said.

"Well, good luck. He's being a real a-hole right now."

"Sorry," Zack said.

"I can't get him to say anything." She threw up her hands and tears began to roll down her cheeks. "He just lies in that bed and stares out the window. Almost like he's succeeded in checking out, ya know?"

Zack nodded.

"I suppose it's all over school, what happened, huh?" She composed herself and sniffled.

"Yeah, it's a little hard to keep it quiet." Zack shrugged. "You know how school is—"

"Yeah, I do." Staci looked down at the tiled floor. "People are always looking for something to talk about, no matter who it hurts." She looked back at Zack.

"For what it's worth, I'm sorry." Zack patted her shoulder. "Hang in there, okay?"

"Thanks, Zack. That means a lot." She stepped close and hugged him. "It really does."

Zack's breath caught in his throat and all he could do was pat her again.

"This really makes you think…" she mumbled into his chest. "About how you treat people and," she released him and stepped back, "what they think of you. I…uh…well, could've lost him last night and I don't-" Her lip quivered and she sobbed into her hands.

Zack waited.

"Sorry." She wiped her nose on a wadded kleenex no bigger than a golf ball. "I should go to the bathroom."

"Sure," Zack said. "Go ahead."

Staci's tears dripped onto the floor. "Go on in if you want. Nobody's in there." She blew her nose. "James and Anna, Kurt's parents, went to the ballet. Can you believe it?" She shook her head. "Tough decision." She held out one hand. "The ballet?" She held out the other hand. "Or suicidal son?" She dropped her hands. "Sorry, better shut up."

She turned and hurried down the hall.

Zack slowly pushed the door open. Two beds sat opposite each other divided by a thin, white curtain. Kurt Clayton lay in the only occupied bed near the window, an IV snaked out of his arm.

"I heard you in the hall." Kurt stared at the dark window.

"Hey, Kurt, I…just wanted to…"

"No need." Kurt held up his left hand.

Zack took a step.

"Stay on that side of the room." Kurt's voice was a monotone.

"Oh, uh. Sure…" Zack stepped back. "I didn't —"

"The truth is, Tucker, you scare the hell out of me."

"What? I… Me?" Zack's eyes grew wide.

"Yeah, man," Kurt said. "I don't like you, can you get that?" He looked at Zack.

"Well—"

"Never have, Tucker. You're a joke, prancin' around like you know everything—"

"I don't…" Zack said.

"You've never been worth my time." Kurt sat up and looked past Zack into the corner. "Why can't you just leave me alone!" Kurt shouted.

Zack jumped. "I didn't say anything. I'll leave if…"

Kurt took a couple of deep breaths and relaxed, turning back toward the window again.

"Milton, Kevin and I…" He sounded like a dying man in an old western. "We had some great times…" He licked his cracked lips. "Those guys are the best friends…"

Kurt choked and then caught his breath. "You don't know how good you have it until…" He coughed up some phlegm and spat it on the floor toward Zack.

Zack moved to the empty bed and sat down.

"What?" Kurt yelled at the corner behind Zack. "No!"

Zack turned to stare at the empty corner. "Kurt, I—"

"You're so weak, Tucker. The other night…" Kurt wheezed and stared at the ceiling. "You ran, but it didn't matter. Milton was stronger. I was stronger. Milton is so much stronger…" Kurt gasped.

Zack jumped up and reached for the call button on Kurt's bed. Kurt grabbed his arm. "Why, Tucker?" he wheezed.

Kurt's bloodshot eyes darted around the room and then back to Zack's. "Immolo are captivitas atris f."

"What?" Zack's eyes widened.

Kurt screamed the words again, "Immolo are captivitas atris f!" His eyes dilated until only a sliver of white showed. "Immolo are captivitas atris f! Immolo are captivitas atris f!"

Zack wrenched his arm away and jumped back.

Kurt chanted the phrase, louder and louder, like a prayer to an unknown god. His head thrashed and tremors racked his body. The metal bed pounded up and down on the tile floor and Kurt convulsed from rail to rail.

Zack yelled and stumbled backward into the bedside table sending the water pitcher crashing to the floor. Blood and yellow puss exploded from Kurt's mouth and Zack ran for the door.

"Nurse!" He bolted down the hallway. "You gotta come!" Zack slid to a stop in front of the counter. "He's vomiting! Convulsing. Something?"

Nurse Rita jumped up, threw her ballpoint pen on the desk and yelled down the hallway, "Jackie!"

A rotund black nurse rushed from another room and John shot out of the waiting room.

"What's going on?"

"I don't know," Zack yelled. "Come on!"

"Stay there, boys." Rita ordered.

Zack and John hesitated, looked at each other and then followed the nurses down the hallway.

People peered out of neighboring rooms like a hallway of jack-in-the-boxes as the sound of shattered glass echoed down the hallway.

Zack slid into the nurses and John slid into him.

"Oh, my Jesus. Oh, my Lord Jesus, no!" Jackie covered her mouth. Staci appeared in the doorway behind them and screamed.

White curtains fluttered into the ebony sky through the jagged glass and Kurt Clayton was gone.

10

Zack stood in the hospital lobby and watched the parking lot fill with flashing red and blue lights. He replayed Staci's screams over and over in the back of his head.

"Here." John handed him a can of Diet Pepsi.

"Thanks," Zack popped the top and took a few gulps. "Did that Detective Nance guy get your statement?"

"Yeah, just finished." John glanced around. "Man, this place is crawling with cops."

"Yeah… Oh, crap." Zack watched a car roar into the parking lot and lock its tires. "Here we go."

"Staci musta' called 'em," John slurped from his root beer can.

Kevin, Stacey and Del burst from the car and ran toward the yellow police tape until two officers stopped them. Kevin wrestled away and fell to his hands and knees. Del and Stacey sobbed their way to the asphalt beside him and buried their faces in their hands.

Milton Drago emerged from the driver's side door and stood motionless.

He scanned the building until his eyes came to rest on Zack.

"Here he comes," John said.

Milton marched toward the entrance. He grabbed a side door and swung it wide, sending it banging against the concrete wall and rattling the glass.

"Back off, Milton!" John yelled.

"Shut up, Welte!" Milton lunged toward Zack. Two police officers rushed him and wrestled Milton to the floor.

"Calm down!" one officer yelled.

"Get off me!" Milton yelled. "It's his fault!"

"Stop yelling and settle down," the second officer said.

"He killed Kurt!" Milton cursed.

"What? You're nuts! I didn't…" Zack said.

"Cool it, man, just be cool!" The first officer yelled in Milton's ear. "If you can't, you're going to jail!"

"Do whatever you want, man!" Milton struggled against their hold. "You're going to pay for all of this, Tucker!" He kicked out toward Zack.

"Okay, pal, that's it." the first officer said.

They hoisted Milton to his feet and dragged him from the lobby; leaving behind a faint smell of cheap cologne, cigarette smoke and alcohol.

Zack slumped into a nearby chair and watched the ant trail of officers entering and leaving the lobby.

"This is crazy," John plopped into another chair beside him.

Zack put his head back and closed his eyes. "Yeah, I know. I just wish it was over."

"Where's Staci?" John asked.

"I think they have her drugged up and laying in the ER." Zack rubbed his eyes. "I've never heard anyone scream like that before."

———

"We tried to keep an eye on him," Nurse Rita Johnson leaned forward on the nurse's lounge sofa and put a Styrofoam coffee cup down. "but there were too many people going in and out of his room. I told them not to have so many in there, but they don't listen—"

"I'm sure you did," Detective Nance paused and flipped through his notes. "The eighth floor? For a suicidal patient?"

She moved her hair, behind her ears and then removed her glasses and rubbed the bridge of her nose.

"Not my doing, Detective. Psych is on first."

"So, why—"

"Because of Radiology."

"Excuse me?" Nance asked.

"The Clayton's donated a butt-load of money for radiology equipment, practically named the whole danged wing after 'em."

"Where are the Claytons?" Nance asked.

"Beats me. Breezed in and breezed out, in tux and see-through evening gown. We tried to call, but no answer."

"So, they weren't concerned with the throng in Kurt's room?" Nance searched for his cigarettes and pulled one out of the pack with his lips.

"You can't smoke in here—"

"I know. Sorry, I've got to have one between my lips at least once a day." Nance said. "Even if it's not lit."

"The Clayton's didn't seem concerned," Rita went on. "All the kids knew them and they seemed like buddies."

"Why do you say that?"

"I'd say mom and dad like to party with the kids, I guess." She shrugged and then dismissed it with a wave. "Just speculation, none of my business."

Nance shook his head, his unlit cigarette bobbed up and down. "Unrestrained, unmonitored, and a room with a view."

"Yup, you'd a thought he was in for a face-lift." She retrieved the steaming Styrofoam cup from the table. "A steady stream all day. I finally called security when I smelled the booze."

Nance scribbled on his pad.

"They cleaned out the nest, except for that demon and his friends."

"The demon?"

"That Milton." Rita gritted her teeth. "What a spawn."

"Was he in there when it happened?" Nance looked up from his notebook.

"No, he left a few minutes before, thank God." Rita replaced the cup. "If he'd have been here, I would have thought…" She shook her head. "Never mind."

"And no one else was in the room at that time?"

"Correct, just Zack," her eyes widened, "but he was down the hall with me when we heard the glass break. You know that, right?"

"Yes," Nance said, "we've verified all of that and he isn't a suspect."

"Nice kid," Rita said. "His friend John too." She stared at the floor. "Only ones that waited…"

———

Detective Nance stepped outside, fished the lighter out of his pocket and cupped his hands around the flame. He leaned against the concrete wall and exhaled, blowing a steady stream into the fall air.

"What a waste of a Friday night." He stared at the sea of flashing lights.

11

"I'll take care of you, you fat piece of…"

Zack bolted upright from the nightmare and squinted at the red clock numbers.

2:15 a.m.

That low-life piece of scum. Zack cursed Milton.

Kurt. Staci. All the cops. The lights. The nurses. The broken window. The sheet that covered the body.

John snored from a sleeping bag on Zack's floor.

Zack laid back and closed his eyes tighter, but Milton bombarded his brain.

Guess you're not so tough now? He smiled. I hope you rot.

John snored again.

Just a few more hours of sleep.

———

"I never could tie one of these things," John wrestled with a necktie.

"Well, don't," Zack said.

"I'm trying to show respect."

"There are easier ways," Zack said. "Besides, it goes so well with that red flannel shirt."

"Shut up, it was the only thing that was clean."

—

An usher seated Zack and John mid-way up Sacred Heart of Mary's sanctuary, which was filled to capacity. Zack stared at the massive oak beams, holding up the roof in an upside-down "V".

"Man," John scanned the congregation, "if you're in the balcony, you'd need binoculars to see the priest."

Zack grinned.

James and Anna Clayton, with daughters Tiffany and Kimberly, were on the front row. Staci Bransen accompanied her parents to the second row. Stacey Tuche, Kevin Bauer, Delrobia Huerfano and Milton Drago sat shoulder to shoulder in the third row.

"All the players are present," Zack mumbled.

"What?" John asked.

"Nothing."

"I've never seen so many people wearing black in one place," John whispered.

"What?" Zack asked.

"Nothing."

The massive organ played, *Softly and Tenderly Jesus is Calling,* while Zack and John watched the people file in.

"You've been made, man," John whispered.

"What?"

"The convict." John nudged him.

Zack glanced around. "Oh, yeah, I see."

Milton smiled.

Zack held Milton's gaze.

"What do you think?" John whispered.

"He's a frigin' idiot," Zack's stare was cold.

"No argument here," John whispered.

Milton scratched his temple with his middle finger so Zack could see and grinned.

Black, white, and red rose sprays covered the gleaming silver casket.

"Did you hear that Kurt's mom contacted everyone and told them to wear black or white?" John whispered.

"Where do you hear this stuff?"

"I get around." John grinned.

"I can believe the rumor." Zack glanced around. "It looks more like a wedding."

"Except for the people crying," John said.

"Well, yeah. Depends on who's getting married."

"He was a model son," the priest began. "A young life snuffed out and discarded…"

Zack stared at the silver coffin with its flowing black fabric hiding the carrier wheels. He looked at the folds of the fabric, reminding him of the fluttering drapes blowing out the broken hospital window.

"What's the matter?" John whispered.

"Nothin'," Zack said. "I was just thinking."

"Bout what?"

"Mortality."

"Big word," John said.

"Ever wonder what it would be like?" Zack asked.

"To die?"

"Yeah." Zack crossed his leg. "What do you think Kurt thought about?"

"What… when he went out the window?" John asked.

"Shh." A white-haired lady leaned forward. "Have some respect, boys."

"Sorry," Zack whispered. He looked at John and shrugged.

Did Kurt hesitate? Did it feel like soaring or did the fall literally scare him to death? He must have spiraled like an airborne dandelion seed. Did the lights of the city twinkle? Did Kurt remember insignificant dates? His fifth birthday? His 10th Christmas? The first time he tied his shoe? The first time he kissed Staci?

Did his subconscious faucet twist full on and overflow his consciousness? Did he finally regret chasing Zack that night?

What about pain? Afterward, when the dust had literally settled, what did Kurt encounter? Life after death? Heaven? Hell?

Zack snapped out of recollection as the congregation rose.

He watched the proper and upright Clayton family trail the casket, no hint of dignity lost. A single tear rolled down Anna's cheek. James followed, looking solemn and tortured.

The mammoth pipe organ sounded *Amazing Grace* and Staci and her parents followed the Claytons. She wiped her tears with a tissue and managed a brief, but distant smile at Zack.

Outside the church, like a morbid black beast at feeding time, the immaculate hearse sat against the curb, back door open. The pallbearers, a Who's Who of the championship football team, slid the container of Kurt Clayton's human remains into its mouth and closed the jaws.

12

John's Ford Fairlane resembled an automobile only in the truest sense of the word. Its rubber tires supported a body held together by Bondo. Without the body putty, John would have piloted a skeleton. Bringing up the rear of the funeral procession, he and Zack crossed under the archway entrance of Halstatller's Cemetery.

Half an hour later, on a green rise near a hedgerow, the priest spoke the familiar words from every big-screen graveyard scene that Zack had ever seen.

"Ashes to ashes, dust to dust. The Lord giveth, and the Lord taketh away. Blessed be the Name of the Lord."

"Amens" rang out through the gathering of bowed heads.

The bystanders approached and dropped handfuls of dirt on the descending casket.

Family, friends, and classmates filtered away from the gravesite. Milton Drago stood over the casket until he noticed Zack and John and started for them. Kevin grabbed for his arm, but Milton wrenched away.

Zack watched him approach and stick out his hand. He hesitated to receive Milton's handshake.

Milton leaned in close. "This is for you, Zacko."

He slid a folded paper into Zack's hand.

"Milton, who is this?" A white haired lady approached.

"Oh, I'm sorry, Mother. This is Zack, one of my close friends from school."

"Hello, Zack." She offered her hand.

"Hello, Mrs. Drago." Zack switched the paper to his left hand.

"I don't get to meet many of Milton's friends. I don't believe you've ever been over to the house." She shuddered slightly.

"No, ma'am, I, uh—"

"I've invited him, Mother, but he never comes over." Milton smiled. "He's always on the run someplace."

Zack didn't respond.

"I guess we should go, Mother." Milton put his hand on her back.

"Oh, yes," she said. "Well, nice to have met you, Zack. Wasn't it a lovely funeral?"

"Yes, Ma'am."

"Come over to the house to visit Milton any time you can." She turned away.

"Yes, I'm sure he will, Mother." Milton grinned. "See you later, Tucker."

They plodded off and Milton glanced back at Zack with a smirk.

"What am I," John asked, "chopped liver? How come he introduced you to Mrs. Dragon and I didn't get squat? She looks more like his grandma than mom."

"Late-in-life baby, I guess. Hey, she seemed nice though," Zack said.

"How could she *not* be nice? Milton sucks all the evil out of her house; all that's left is Grandma Goodie How old is she anyway?"

"Shut up, man, they'll hear," Zack whispered.

"Sorry."

Zack waited until they were a few yards away and then unfolded the note.

> *Let's settle this once and for all, man to wuss.*
> *Tonight, here, 11:30 pm.*
> *Only you.*

"He doesn't really think you'd be stupid enough to come here, does he?" John read over Zack's shoulder. "And even if you *were* stupid enough, he knows you wouldn't come alone, right? I mean, after him trying to attack you in front of the cops, I would think that Milton would have enough marbles rattling around up there that he wouldn't try anything *too* drastic. You know, in the fear that he would be a prime suspect, right?" John's voice shook.

Zack hesitated.

"Right?" John asked.

"Suspect?"

"Hey, man, I'm just saying, you'd be out of your mind if you did this." John pointed to the note and then looked at Zack. "You're going to do this, aren't you?"

Zack looked toward the grave where Staci stood alone. "Don't you ever get tired of being afraid?"

"Me personally or us collectively?" John pushed his glasses back up his nose.

"Sometimes, you've got to stand up for yourself, no matter the consequences."

"Well, I guess—"

"Milton Drago's been after me since junior high, jabbin', pokin', laughing at me, cussin' me out and I'm fed up with it." Zack stared at Staci.

"You're nuts, man." John put his hand on Zack's arm. "Let me give you a dose of reality, my friend. First of all, you *know* what Milton's capable of; and second, you know *he* won't be here alone. Kevin will be around somewhere." John glanced around as if it were 11:30 already. "Heck, Kurt will probably be floating around here, someway, somehow."

"Probably." Zack nodded as if in a daze. "But I guess if you come, then the odds would be even." He glanced at John.

"Me?" John pointed to his own chest. "Even with me coming it will still be two of them against just you. I couldn't even go down to Kurt's room with you the other night, and *he* was almost comatose."

"Well, I guess you gotta do what you gotta do then," Zack started toward Staci.

"Zack." John called. "C'mon, man."

13

Zack plodded up the grassy knoll.

"Hey, Staci," Zack said.

"Hi, Zack." She glanced up. "Nice service, don't you think?"

"Very nice."

"It's peaceful out here," she glanced at the falling leaves.

"Yeah, it is." He shuffled his feet. "How're you doing?"

"It just seems like a dream." She stared at the grave. "I know you always hear that, but it *really* does. How can your life change so quickly in just a few short days?" Staci paused and looked down. "We were engaged, you know?"

"Oh." Zack faltered. "I didn't—"

"It wasn't official or anything. My dad wants me to go to college first." She looked at Zack and then back down at the casket, now lowered into the ground. "It wasn't that they didn't like Kurt, they did, it's just that they think I shouldn't be dating *anyone* seriously yet."

"I guess." Zack kicked at the grass.

"So, Kurt asked me a couple of months ago, and I said yes." She lifted her left hand. "This is the ring."

"It's nice," Zack took her hand and examined the ring.

"It's not a big diamond or anything," she shrugged, "just a little stone. More like a promise ring…" She paused. "Until we could become official."

"Yeah."

She pulled her hand away and bowed her head, and Zack saw tears drop onto the grass as she continued. "I guess I won't ever have a chance to make it official now."

Zack wavered, then patted her on the shoulder.

"I'm so sorry, Staci. I really am."

"I know you are." She buried her face in his chest and sobbed. He held her .

"Sorry, Zack." She leaned back. "Thanks for coming up here with me. I don't blame you for anything that happened. You know?"

"Oh, I know. I—"

"No, really." She released him and took a step back. "Milton and Kevin…" she pulled a tissue from her purse and wiped her nose, "and Kurt, have really been tough on you the last few years. I *know about* what happened the other night when they chased you and roughed you up. When I found out, I was really pissed, and Kurt knew it too."

"You know, Staci, you don't owe me an explanation—"

"Yes." She touched Zack's arm. "I do. I'm not making excuses for Kurt; he could be a real butt-hole sometimes. But he had a lot of baggage that he carried from home." She wavered. "Did you know his older sister committed suicide?"

"No, I didn't. I thought Tiffany and Kimberly were—"

"His only sisters?" Staci asked. "Nope. Her name was Muriel Ann. Kurt was a fourth-grader." She wiped her nose again. "He found her."

"Oh, man."

"Kurt came home from school. His mom was out selling condos. His dad was at his office, like usual. The Sacred Heart of Mary bus dropped him off and Muriel was usually home by then, but when he called there was no answer. He used to tell me, 'I just had to go to the bathroom, that's all'; like it was some crime." Staci's voice softened. "He found her naked in the bathtub. It was half full of water." Staci paused. "She slit her wrists."

"Oh, man," Zack repeated.

"The coroner said she'd been dead since that morning. Kurt hated dripping water after that. He would always mumble, 'The Drips of Death on The Day of Muriel'. He was almost obsessive/compulsive about it. Although to look at him, you wouldn't know it." She paused to wipe her eyes again and then went on. "Tiffany and Kimberly were born later."

"Do you want to sit down?" Zack motioned toward the cloth-covered folding chairs that surrounded the gravesite.

"Yeah, I would, thanks." They sat and she adjusted her skirt. "I told myself that Kurt wasn't *that* bad. I knew I could change him if I was just given a chance, if I could only love him more... I know... sounds like a tormented rich kid story, right?" she paused, "But there's no excuse for just being mean."

Zack nodded.

"I suppose in one way I knew I shouldn't have been with him, but after he asked me to marry him," she looked down, "well, you know, we did it."

Zack shifted and glanced back down the hill at John sitting on the hood of his car.

"I know it doesn't sound like a big deal these days. But I *was* waiting. Since we were going to be married... My family is very religious and I was raised that Christians don't... And I guess I agreed with them but..." She looked at Zack. "Weird, huh?"

"No."

"I'm sorry." Staci said. "I just needed to tell someone." She touched Zack's arm again. "Del and Stacey don't even know, so don't tell anyone. Please? It really bothers me."

"I won't."

"My parents don't know either. God, I can't even imagine what my dad would say. I mean, they might suspect, but I don't know…" She wiped her eyes and then blew her nose. She took Zack's hand interlocking her fingers in his and looked directly into his eyes. "I might be pregnant."

The loud engine noise topped the ridge and Staci let go of Zack's hand. A plump, white-haired man wearing a farmer's cap chugged along on a bright yellow backhoe. When he saw them, he immediately cut the engine and the tractor rolled to a stop not far from the grave.

He climbed down off the hoe and removed his hat. "Oh, I'm so sorry, folks. I had no idea anyone was still up here; please don't let me disturb you." He waved a hand. "Take as much time as you need. I'll come back later." He turned to go.

"No, that's okay." Staci wiped a final tear. "We were just leaving."

"Are you sure? I didn't mean to-" the old man held out his hands.

"No, it's okay," Staci smiled. "Thank you."

She and Zack got up and walked back down the hill. Staci slipped her arm in Zack's as they stopped in the shade of a large oak and watched the old man.

The caretaker walked to the mound covered by an Astroturf blanket and pulled it back. He removed the apparatus that had lowered the casket into the ground. He climbed aboard the backhoe and turned the key. The engine roared back to life and puffed ringlets of exhaust into the clear, fall sky. He threw a few levers and the hydraulic bucket shook as it slid down to ground level. With one fluid motion, the hoe pushed the pile of fresh earth on top of the casket-shrouded body of Kurt Clayton.

Staci sobbed and trembled and Zack slipped his arm around her. They stood in silence watching the backhoe fill the hole. She finally composed herself and looked up at him.

"Thanks again for listening, Zack. This is going to be hell, but I guess what doesn't destroy us makes us stronger, huh?"

"Yeah." Zack nodded, releasing her. "Hey, Staci? I know we aren't really… Well, we don't really run in the same circles, but if you ever need to talk… I mean… I really enjoyed our conversation." He looked at the grass. "I just wish it could have been under different circumstances."

"Thanks, Zack, I'll probably take you up on that. I'll warn you though…"

Zack tensed for a brush-off.

"It's hard to get rid of me once I start buggin' you." She smiled and kissed him on the cheek.

Zack smiled and watched her walk back toward her car and slowly drive away.

John slid off the hood of his old Ford and sauntered next to Zack.

"Quite the conversation, eh?"

"Yeah, she's *really* nice," Zack said.

"I saw that," John raised and lowered his eyebrows.

They both turned and watched the backhoe finish its work.

"Really weird," Zack said.

"What?"

"Just a few days ago I was running from him. Now a ton of dirt is covering him."

"Yeah, don't look justice in the mouth," John popped a few Boston Baked Beans in his mouth.

"Like a vapor. . ." Zack mumbled.

He reached into his pocket and felt Milton's note.

14

A truck, with *Rudabaker Construction* painted on the side, came to rest at the same spot where John's Ford had been hours earlier.

Zack looked at his watch. *11:15 p.m.*

Zack's part time job, with his next door neighbor, Mike Rudabaker, had its privileges, namely a vehicle to drive when he needed it.

He glanced out the truck window, in the rear view mirror and then out through the windshield.

Full moon.

Rustling leaves.

Gloom.

He expected the theme from John Carpenter's *Halloween* to begin playing somewhere from behind a tombstone.

He turned off the lights and switched off the engine.

Halstatller's Cemetery was shrouded in fog, like every stereotype that Zack had witnessed on the big screen. Goose flesh rose on Zack's neck. Milton loved graveyards.

Hype or truth? Did Milton really prefer the dead? It didn't matter; Zack was out of his comfort zone.

He climbed out of the truck and the door slipped out of his hand and slammed shut.

"Crap."

The echo was enough to alert the dead.

He walked up the rise toward Kurt's newly covered grave. The mound smelled of fresh dirt and he could vaguely see the temporary metal marker in the moonlight.

"I didn't think you'd come."

Zack whirled.

Milton Drago stepped out of the shadow of the trees.

"Let's put this behind us, Milton, and get on with our lives." Zack fired his rehearsed opening.

"You killed my best friend." Milton said.

"C'mon, Milton, you know I never—."

"It's just like you pushed him." Milton spat. "You didn't, did you?"

"Of course not." Zack watched the grove of trees behind Milton for any other movement.

"So, what's the plan here, Milton? The note said you and me. So?" Zack's backbone stiffened. He peered at Milton's moonlit form over Kurt's grave.

Milton walked toward him, his right hand concealed.

"Look, Milton, you're upset about Kurt—"

"Freakin', right."

"We *all* are, but this is no way to take care of the problem."

"Oh, I think it is." Milton said.

"You're not going to get away with anything," Zack said. "Not after the hospital." He stepped toward the metal head plate.

"None of it matters." Milton's voice was low. "Kurt isn't coming back and I've got nothing to lose." Milton paused. "Might as well have a little fun." He brought a hunting knife forward. "Time to carve the fat Christmas turkey." He moved the tip back and forth and took a step.

Zack's stomach knotted. "Are you serious?"

"Afraid so, Zacko. I'm sending you to hell with Kurt. I figure that's where he went. So I'll do you here and he'll do you again there. Two for the price of one. Neat plan, huh?"

Zack's body tightened. He knew that to Milton Drago the plan made sense.

"I even brought a shovel." Milton said. "Always be prepared."

He smiled and Zack saw his white teeth.

"See," Milton went on. "It came to me today while we were sitting here looking at this hole in the ground. I'm going to dig this grave up, put you down there, and tuck you in again. Why would anyone *even think* of jackin' with the grave of a poor, suicidal kid in order to look for a fat piece of crap like you, right?" Milton asked.

"Are you nuts?" Zack asked.

"Maybe." Milton stepped forward.

Zack stood on the edge of full-out panic. In the back of the truck lay a myriad of tools that he could defend himself with; but, first of all, Zack couldn't run very fast, he had already proved that. And second, covering that distance with a knife-wielding Milton Drago on his tail, not happening. He scanned the trees and bushes for Kevin or anyone else to plead his case. He looked back and knew any sudden movement would trigger Milton's insanity.

"What about your mom?" Zack asked.

Milton stopped his approach. "What about her?"

"Well, she *did* invite me over to your house. If anything happens to me, won't she wonder why I haven't stopped by?"

Milton laughed and then shook his head.

"I'll say one thing, Tucker, you've got guts." He paused. "And I should be seeing them here soon."

Milton sprinted at him.

Zack faked to the left and then turned right, but his leg caught Milton's and both boys sprawled onto the lawn. The knife flew out of Milton's hand.

Zack scrambled to his feet and dashed toward the truck.

Milton cursed as Zack heard him searching for the knife.

Zack glanced back and Milton was on his feet coming full-on after him.

The bushes to his right rustled and Zack instinctively veered away, anticipating the ambush from Kevin.

A figure darted from the bushes and Zack whirled keeping an eye on it.

However, instead of coming after him, the person launched himself into the air hitting Milton high in the chest, like a cornerback clobbering a wide receiver.

Milton's feet flew out from under him and he hit the ground flat on his back. The knife turned tip over handle in the air and landed point first in the ground by Milton's leg. Milton lay gasping for air, clutching his throat and then blacked out.

"Oh, man!" Zack yelled.

The man rolled and then got up, brushing off a long, black leather duster. He walked over and stood over Milton's unconscious form. He ran his hand through long, dark hair that hung to his shoulders. Zack caught a tinge of beard stubble under blue eyes as he looked up at Zack. "You're okay."

"Yeah, thanks," Zack hung his head and closed his eyes. He leaned over with his hands on his knees, panting and trying to catch his breath as he realized how out of shape he really was.

"Where did you come from and how did you know…" Zack opened his eyes and raised his head. The man was gone. A gentle breeze rustled the trees and peace once again enveloped the cemetery.

Milton Drago lay next to the hunting knife still sticking out of the grass.

"How am I going to explain this?"

The engine rattle interrupted Zack's contemplation and he knew that John's old beater was behind the first pair of approaching headlights.

John jumped out of the car, left the door open and the engine running.

Zack held a hand up to shield the second pair of headlights

"What the— Is he?" John looked down.

"No, only the wind knocked out of him," Zack stepped closer into the beam.

The caretaker ran up from behind John's car. "Are you all right, son?"

"I think so." Zack said.

"John stopped down at the house and filled me in on what was happening up here tonight," the old man panted.

"You couldn't have done it about 15 minutes earlier?" Zack looked at John.

"You told me you wanted to do this alone." John punched Zack in the arm.

"The police are on their way," the caretaker said. "Are you sure you're alright?"

"I am now. Me and Milton were just having some words."

Zack turned back toward Milton. The knife remained, but Milton Drago was gone.

15

Muffled voices filtered through the thick underbrush. Kevin Bauer saw the flashing lights approach through the leaves and knew the police would comb the area. He turned and slinked away.

—

Zack glanced at his watch. *2:14 a.m.*

"Okay, Zack, I think we can let you boys go home. We have all the information we need." The barrel-chested police officer told him.

He keyed the microphone attached to his collar.

"Dispatch?"

"This is Dispatch, go ahead."

"This is 21. I need to call in an Attempt To Locate on a Milton Drago. Caucasian, age 18, approximately six feet tall, 155 pounds, long dark hair. Resides at 220 Meeker Road. Last seen in the vicinity of Halstatller's Cemetery, wearing blue jeans, hiking boots, and a red flannel shirt. Possibly armed and dangerous. Wanted for questioning on assault, battery, and possible attempted murder. This subject has been detained recently for similar charges."

Zack cringed.

"That'll get everyone's attention," the officer said.

"Yeah, I guess so," Zack said.

"We'll need the hunting knife for evidence."

"'Please, and take it with you'," John quoted the line from *The Wizard of Oz.*

Zack rolled his eyes and handed the knife to the officer.

"If Milton comes anywhere near you, call us." The officer took out a business card and handed it to Zack. "Don't mess with him."

"Okay," Zack said.

"You guys better go home and get some sleep, we're done here."

———

Zack tossed and turned sinking deeper and deeper into sleep.

The woman called to him through gushing water, he was back at the theater with Jamie but water rose over his ankles and knees until it reached his chest. He pawed at it, the woman swirled around him, calling him, reaching out to him.

Trophies from the case at school wrapped in letterman jackets joined the whirlpool and crashed into beakers from the chemistry lab with John's face smiling out of them. Zack looked up to the ceiling as curtains exploded out a window sending shards of glass raining down into the water around them. The Blonde bent at the waist spreading the water with her hands trying to look for her contact lens. The woman's arm swept past Jamie as she swirled in the torrent and tried to grab for her but Jamie shook free every time, preoccupied with the lens.

Zack tried to move toward Jamie but the current impeded him. He began to walk and then run, but it was as if he were trying to run in a swimming pool.

"Zack," a voice called. "You're okay."

"I'm not okay," Zack ran in place, out of breath.

He stopped and turned to see the man with the long hair behind him.

"You're okay, Zack."

Milton's knife, now the size of a sword, twirled end over end and struck the water sending a wave into the walls of the theater.

"You're okay."

"You're. Okay."

"You're okay!"

Zack bolted upright in bed, his head soaked with sweat.

"He didn't ask *if* I was okay." Zack wiped the sweat off his forehead. "He *told* me I was okay."

Zack smiled, turned his sweaty pillow over and finally drifted off into dreamless rest.

16

The next evening, Zack grabbed hold of the tarnished brass handle, bolted to Pizza Inn's oversized door. The door swung wide and he stepped onto dark maroon carpeting in dire need of cleaning. A well-worn path led to a counter cluttered in cardboard advertisements. Over the pickup station hung a grease-smudged sign that read "You toucha my pie, I breaka yo face!"

The crematorium-sized oven blistered the mozzarella and tomato sauce pies and the aroma of garlic and onions filled the air.

Zack stepped around a half wall separating the dining room from the pickup station and slid into his customary corner booth.

"Hi, Zack." The thin redhead approached.

"Hello, Terri." Zack smiled.

"What'll it be tonight?"

"I think the buffet." He tucked the menu back behind the salt and pepper shakers that were miniature Italian chefs. "John'll be here in a few and he'll have the same."

"What to drink?" Terri scribbled on her pad.

"We'll have a diet and regular soda."

"Hey, did you get that English essay done?" Terri asked.

"Yeah, finished it two nights ago."

"You don't suppose. . ."

Zack ginned. "Yeah, I could probably give you a few pointers."

"Okay, I'll get with you during study hall," Teri smiled. "Help yourself, you know your way around."

"You got that right," Zack returned the smile and slid out of the booth.

Moments later, he was back with two plates piled high.

He took a bite and glanced at the deserted half of the restaurant.

The man sat facing away from him. His shoulder-length dark hair was beginning to haunt Zack. Zack lowered his half-eaten pizza to the plate and rose as if possessed. He approached the booth by stealth and stopped a few feet in back of the man.

"I've been here waiting," the man spoke without turning.

Zack saw the steam rise from a coffee cup.

"What?" He stepped around to face him.

"It's been awhile since you were in here. Two weeks, hasn't it been?" The man brushed back his shiny dark hair from his forehead.

"How did you know—"

"Please." The man motioned to the seat opposite him. "John will be delayed this evening."

Zack lowered himself into the booth opposite him.

"Who are you?"

The man waved his hand and shook his head.

"Quite a turn of events the past few days, huh?" His blue eyes drilled into Zack.

"Yeah."

"Causes a person to think," he said.

"Yeah? About what?" Zack shifted in his seat.

"Life and death."

"I guess it does." Zack couldn't take his eyes off his defined cheekbones and rugged appearance.

This guy should be on a billboard with a cowboy hat perched on his head, sucking on a Marlboro.

"Too bad about Kurt." The man shook his head and took a sip of coffee.

"What do you know about it?" Zack asked.

"I can read," he said. "It's a tragic thing when a person gives up."

"Yeah, " Zack said.

"We think about suicide when we're lonely or upset or in despair, feeling like there is no other answer to our problems.

Sometimes it's a fleeting thought," The man brushed back his hair again. "but the ones who are obsessed with it, that's a different story—"

"I didn't know Kurt was—"

"It's an eager will to embrace the unknown and go where so many have ventured but never returned." The man paused. "You've thought about it from time to time yourself haven't you?" He took another sip.

"What are you talking about? I don't—"

"That night, scraped up in the bushes. You wanted to be in a more peaceful place, right? You just wanted the torment to stop."

"I don't want to talk about this." Zack scanned the restaurant.

"When Milton came at you with knife in hand, wasn't there a transitory thought of letting him accomplish what he intended?" The man paused. "What about the years since your mom left?"

Zack stood. His eyes welled and he clinched his fist.

The man looked up at him. "Kurt didn't jump—"

"Hey, Zack!" John stood by the corner booth.

Zack walked quickly toward him.

"What's up, man?" John glanced at the half-finished pizza. "You started without me—"

"John." Zack whispered.

"What?" John leaned in. "Why are you whispering?" John's eyes darted back and forth behind his glasses.

"It's him." Zack thumbed over his shoulder.

"Who? Milton?"

"No, that long haired guy, you idiot." Zack grabbed his shirt sleeve.

"What?" John looked over Zack's shoulder. "Where, I don't see…"

Zack turned and scanned the empty booths, then shifted his attention to the heavy front door as it snapped shut.

"Come on!"

17

Zack bolted through the door of the restaurant with John close behind; he looked left, then right, then left again.

A family helped an elderly grandma out of the car under the watchful eyes of the reproduction Victorian street lamps. Cars passed on the street. He heard no car doors slam, no engines crank and no tires squeal. He stepped to the corner of the building.

Nothing.

He walked the full breadth of Pizza Inn and peered around the opposite corner. No stone out of place. Like all of the other encounters, the man had vanished without a trace. Like a vapor.

"Zack! John!" Terri threw open the door. "Andy sent me out here to make sure you weren't stiffin' the bill."

"Naw, nothing like that," Zack waved his hand. "We just- Hey Terri, who was that guy drinking coffee in the booth tonight?"

"Which guy?" Terri glanced back and forth.

All three walked back into the restaurant.

"That guy back in the corner." Zack motioned toward the booths.

"No guy drinking coffee that I know of," Terri said.

"Come on, Terri? The guy down here." Zack walked down the aisle to the booth and stopped.

"What's up with you, man?" John followed his gaze to the table.

Pizza crusts littered the surface. A child's place mat was covered with crayon scribbles. Crumbled saltines were scattered amidst half eaten pizza crusts. Macaroni salad blanketed a booster seat. Partially filled glasses of soda sat next to a kiddy cup of milk and an ice tea glass, with a mutilated lemon in the bottom, resided in a puddle.

Zack walked slowly back to his booth and slid in. He looked at his heaping plate and pushed it aside.

"You're really starting to freak me out, man." John scooted in opposite him. "On a dark street is one thing, at midnight in a graveyard is a given, but now you're seeing people, that aren't there, in restaurants?"

Zack stared at John, but didn't see him.

"Hey, you guys." The voice made Zack jump.

18

"Oh, sorry, I didn't mean to startle you," she touched Zack's shoulder.

"Hey," Zack smiled.

"At the movies? I didn't really get to tell you thank you and you practically ran me over coming out of the store, so…" She offered her hand. "I'm Jamie Watkins."

Zack shook it.

"Zack Tucker."

"And I'm John Welte." John waved.

"Trekker," She nodded.

"You remembered." John grinned and glanced at Zack.

"Do you guys hang out here a lot?"

"Yeah, quite a bit." Zack relaxed. "Mostly Fridays."

John grabbed a piece of pizza off Zack's plate and ripped off a hunk.

"Appetizing." Zack shot a look at him. "How about you, Jamie Watkins?"

"First time. My friend Amanda'll be here any minute, Zack Tucker." Jamie smiled.

"Wanna sit?" Zack scooted over.

"Please." John sprayed pizza shards onto the table.

"Uh, yeah, maybe until Amanda gets here?" She slid in beside Zack.

He noted how nicely she fit into the tiny booth.

"That's nice perfume.cologne," Zack said.

"Thanks, it's Fresh Spray," Jamie said.

"Yeah, but what's it called?" John asked.

"No, it's…" Jamie stopped and laughed.

Zack watched her eyes twinkle.

"Hey, there's Manda," Jamie waved.

She spotted Jamie and waved. A pock-faced boy, and another girl trailed in after Amanda and they stopped at a large table in the middle of the restaurant.

"You guys want to join us?" Jamie asked.

"Uh?" Zack grunted.

"Hey, Manda, is it all right for Zack and John to join us?" Jamie called.

"Sure, why not?" She shrugged.

Zack picked up his plates and John headed for the buffet.

"I'm graduating this year from the Milford Academy," Jamie sat opposite Zack.

"Impressive," Zack said. "A private school. How do you like it?"

"Well, I'm not there yet. I'm going to start at semester break, in a few weeks."

"Yeah, that's pretty close to Summit Ridge High, where I go," Zack said.

"It's cool that we're not that far out of Denver," Jamie said.

"Yeah." Zack took a drink. "Small town feel, big city convenience."

"Impressive description," Jamie smiled.

"It's on the brochures from the Chamber of Commerce." Zack blushed.

They sat for a moment in silence listening to John's endless chatter with Jimmy Reardon, the other boy.

"Dad's a cop," Jamie broke the awkwardness.

"Really?" Zack asked.

"Yeah, he was a cop in Des Moines and now he's with Summit Ridge Police Department."

"Wow, that's great. Patrolman?" Zack asked.

"No, detective." Jamie picked at her salad.

"Wow, I guess Colorado's a little more exciting that Iowa?" Zack ginned.

Jamie smiled. "Yeah, my mom and I love the mountains. Missy and Charlie, my sister and brother, love it that we can drive a few minutes and climb rocks."

"How old are they?"

"Missy's eight, Charlie's ten."

"That's cool," Zack stared into her eyes.

"Yeah, I was an only child." Jamie said.

"Were you?" Zack sat mesmerized by every sentence.

"Then along came Charlie."

"Sounds like a good name for a sitcom," Zack said.

"Dad and Mom were so excited that they said, 'what the heck.' and Missy followed. At least, that's what they always told me." Jamie threw up her hands in mock surrender, *what are you gonna do?*

19

Zack glanced at the clock in the entry as he closed his front door. *11:30 pm.*

He sauntered down the hallway and noticed his dad sitting in the living room with only the television illuminating the darkness. Jeff sat in a tattered leather chair, sections of the arm peeled away, revealing the stuffing. Black-and-white images danced across the muted television.

"Hey, Dad. No work tonight?"

"No, since I covered the doubles the other day, they gave me the night off."

"Cool, what are you watching?" Zack stepped in to see the screen.

"Oh, just flippin' around right now. It was between that televangelist, the Right Reverend Daniel J. Blevins and The Sands of Iwo Jima with John Wayne."

"Really, which did you pick?"

"Sands, of course. That Blevins is a shyster," Jeff said. "Of course I'm so used to staying up all night, it's hard to fall asleep."

"Yeah, not me," Zack stretched and yawned.

"Where have you been?" His dad picked up a cup with a bank logo painted on the side and took a sip.

"John and I were over at Pizza Inn grabbing a little buffet."

"Must have been *some* buffet," he said in-between sips.

"Yeah, it was good but it was really the *company* that kept me." He grinned.

"Oh?" Jeff's eyebrows rose.

Zack watched the screen, lost in transition.

"Well?" Jeff asked.

"Well," Zack plopped onto the ottoman opposite Jeff. "Remember that girl?"

Jeff shook his head.

"The movies?"

"Oh, yeah," Jeff grinned.

"Jamie Watkins." Zack glanced up at the ceiling. "Just the name…" He moved the ottoman closer and related the expanded version and ended with "Wow! She's a knockout!"

Jeff smiled. "The love bug."

Zack nodded. "I guess. I don't know—"

"I remember…" Jeff trailed off.

Zack looked at his dad's strong cheekbones and sturdy nose. The man had been steam-pressed by life, and angst pierced Zack's heart because they rarely broached the subject of his mother.

Through grade school and puberty, Zack had compensated for the lack of maternal contact with a knife and fork. But somewhere in his mind-vault hung the fragrance of perfume and the memory of freshly baked cookies.

"Don't stop. Go on, Dad. Tell me."

"I'm sorry. I don't know, son. It's just… difficult for me to talk about it. You know." Jeff sipped from his cup. "I've told you before." Jeff waved his hand.

"Some." Zack hesitated. "I was really young, though. And now—"

"Yeah, I know." Jeff looked down.

"Help me remember, Dad. Please?"

Jeff glanced at the television, then back at Zack and sighed. "All right. I'm not promising anything."

Zack stretched back into the chair behind the ottoman, his head propped against the back.

"When you were 5, I took you to the zoo."

Zack nodded.

"You loved it, especially the lions," Jeff said. "I remember it was a Saturday."

"Good memory from when I was 5."

"It's with me always. I bought you cotton candy, and you got it in my hair…you were riding on my shoulders." Jeff looked at his son and Zack smiled back. "We had hot dogs, and you slumped over on the top of my head. I said something to you, and all I could hear was snoring. I figured it was time to go home. So I laid you in the back seat of that old Toyota we had—"

"I remember that car. Smelled like rotten eggs a lot."

"Yeah, those catalytic converters... You were so tiny."

"Not anymore," Zack patted his stomach.

Jeff smiled. "By the time we got home, I guess the jostling of the car woke you. You had to tell Mom about the lions. I couldn't get the door open fast enough and you ran into the house. Your voice still haunts me…" Jeff closed his eyes. "I heard you running through the house, into the back yard and upstairs."

Jeff opened his eyes and tears rolled down his cheeks.

"I went in after you and I remember your little legs coming down the stairs, a look of curiosity on your face. 'Where's mommy?' "

"I do remember a little." Zack said. "The lions, back and forth in their cages. On your shoulders. I don't remember going home."

"Suppressed memories." Jeff pulled a tissue out of a box on an end table and wiped his nose. "I've done the same thing.

"My memories," Zack swallowed, "I think, are just pictures in our photo albums." He paused. "I don't remember her other than that."

Jeff leaned forward and patted Zack on the knee. "It's okay, I'm up at night sometimes wondering. Dead? Alive? What's she doing? What's she look like?"

"Why'd she leave, Dad?"

Jeff leaned back and stared at Zack before he spoke. "She was *just* gone." Jeff paused. "And I was the prime suspect."

"What?" Zack's eyes widened and he sat up. "I thought she left. Dad, what the—"

"She vanished," Jeff said. "Like some magician's trick. I don't know *how* and I don't know *where*…"

"But they suspected you?"

"They always do in cases like this. Husband's the first one they think of—"

"But—"

"But it wasn't me," Jeff reached for another tissue and blew his nose. "They went through the house with a fine toothed comb. Everything. Kitchen, living room, bedroom; there were cops everywhere. Nothing."

"She just vanished?" Zack was incredulous.

"No evidence. No blood. No fight. All of her clothes were here. No suitcases gone." Jeff wiped his nose again.. "there were even carrot peelings in the sink and a pot on the stove, but not turned on. She just vanished."

"Like a vapor," Zack said.

"Yeah," Jeff said. "I did everything I could. After a few weeks the cops chalked it up to a runaway—"

"A runaway?"

"We were kids, Zack, not much older than you," Jeff said. "They thought she got home sick or found someone else. Later… I wondered myself."

They sat in silence watching John Wayne and his men dig into the beach.

"I stopped looking," Jeff said.

Zack glanced at him.

"But I never stopped wondering." Jeff blew his nose again and then took a deep breath and smiled. "I passed a travel agency window the other day and it had this huge poster of Australia. She always wanted to go to Australia. What a firecracker she was."

Zack smiled.

"She would talk with an Australian accent and we would talk about a trip 'down under' for hours on end; of course *she* would do most of the talking." Jeff's eyes gleamed. "I watch women's faces whenever I go to the store or the mall. I wonder what she would look like now." Jeff stopped. "I loved her, Zack, I'll always love her."

"Is that why you never remarried?"

"I'm still married, son." Jeff brushed his wedding ring with his thumb. "I'm thinkin' one day the door bell will ring and there she'll be. Won't have changed, still the knock-out I married seventeen years ago."

"Nineteen," Zack said.

Jeff hesitated. "No, son, seventeen."

"But it was two years before I was born."

Jeff looked at him. "Your mom was pregnant when we got married."

Zack looked down at his shoes. "So, I was abandoned and illegitimate."

"No, Zack..."

Zack looked up. "Why didn't you ever tell me—"

"Zack, I—"

"Is that why you got married?" Zack's voice tightened.

"No—"

"Because you *had* to?"

"No, Zack."

Zack stared at Jeff. "Dad?"

"No, that's not the reason; we got married because we were madly in love. We didn't know for sure she was pregnant—"

"What about grandpa and grandma? What did they say?"

"They had no idea; they probably don't to this day."

"They can count, can't they?" Zack's voice rose. "They can add up nine months, can't they?"

"Yes, they could. But they never said anything about it, and neither have I—"

"Oh, Dad," Zack shook his head and looked back at the floor.

"I'm really sorry to tell you like this, Zack."

They sat in silence. Jeff staring at Zack and Zack staring at the floor.

"No big deal," Zack finally muttered.

"Zack, I'm sorry. I kept it from you, but I want you to realize something." He straightened up. "Look at me, son."

Zack's face tilted toward him.

"There's never been a moment that I didn't love you with all that was in me…"

"I know that, Dad," Zack's face was wet.

"No. Really." Jeff continued. "You have always been my reason for living. I couldn't have made it through life without you being here. I can't imagine life without you now." He leaned forward and put his hand on Zack's shoulder. "I didn't marry your mom *because* she was pregnant. I *married* her because I loved her."

Zack nodded slowly.

"People call children born before marriage 'a mistake'. I look back now and wish that the circumstances had been a little different, but I don't regret bringing you into the world. You were *no* mistake. You were part of the plan."

20

Northwood Community Christian Church sat on the edge of town nestled in the foothills and desperately needed a coat of paint. The gravel parking lot corralled the cars in uneven rows; and, Zack and Jeff parked accordingly.

Mavis Springer, a hefty, black woman, met them at the front doors.

"Good mornin', my boys!"

The only thing broader than her smile was her bear hugs and she latched onto Zack. "How you doin', honey?"

Sister Mavis outweighed her husband, Harry, by at least 250 of her 375 pounds. Together they had six kids: Jeanie, Joey, Timmy, Tammy, Sammi, and Dana whom they called *"Caboose."*

"I'm great, Sister," Zack wrapped his arms part way around her. "How about you?"

"Oh, I'm blessed today and every day, sweetie. Praise Jesus Almighty!"

"The kids?" Zack asked.

"Doin' fine. They're runnin' around here somewhere." Mavis released Zack and latched on to Jeff. "How you doin' today, Brother Jeff?"

"I'm good, Sister. Wonderful to see you."

"Better get you a good seat up front." Mavis said. "I'm lookin' for great things from the Lord Jesus today! You don't want to miss out on that outpouring."

"Oh, don't worry about that." Jeff smiled and released her.

The traditional church pipe organ had been abandoned for another style of music pounding the walls from the front stage.

Gus Jenkins' wiry fingers plucked a Les Paul guitar while Raymond Garcia kept a syncopated Latin beat on a blue sparkle drum set with a hole in the kick drum. Sister Donna, Pastor Presence's wife, banged out the sound of a honky-tonk piano.

Twin brothers Larry and Gary played trumpet and saxophone, and Stanley Winston III, from "NewAwlans, Loose-iana", plucked an acoustic standup bass. When the "Holy Ghost came on him," his fingers were a blur.

Pastor Presence's 110-pound frame darted back and forth across the stage like an African American hummingbird.

"Come on and hep me preach!" he yelled a rhythmic beat.

"I've got hope in my soul and it burns like fire!"

"Yes, say so!" the congregation responded.

Zack sat on the second row with his arm on the back of the wooden pew. Pastor Presence lay flat out on the platform, animating Jesus' encounter with the demoniac in the graveyard of Gadera.

Zack flashed to his own graveyard experience with Milton Drago.

Zack glanced down the row of people and watched Lydia Welchel's six year old son push himself under the pews on the heavily waxed floors.

Zack scanned colorful dresses and men decked out in dark suits with brightly knotted ties. Joey Chisom sat a few rows from the front. His leather vest with an enormous cross embroidered on the right breast revealed huge biceps ripe with tattoos of the risen Lord. Joey arrived that morning on his "Bless-ed Hog," and if he wanted to talk to you about Jesus, you were inclined to listen.

"And that demoniac smiled!" Zack saw the splatters of sweat as Pastor Presence's voice blasted through the microphone. He glanced up at the preacher and nodded his head.

The hairs on Zack's neck bristled.

Man, Milton's really getting to me.

He tried to shake the feeling, but goose flesh broke out.

Zack turned and his eyes froze on the far corner. "Oh, God…"

He saw the hair and the beard stubble that framed the man's rugged face.

21

The man stood at the rear of the sanctuary. His tweed sport coat over faded blue jeans, appeared to never have been taken off the hanger before. His open-collared, white shirt was neatly starched. No floor-length leather duster this time.

Zack felt blood leave his face; his heart faltered, but he couldn't pry his gaze away. The man's blue eyes followed Pastor Presence. He nodded and smiled, engulfed in the sermon and then turned to look at Zack.

Zack glanced away. When he summoned the courage to turn around again, the man was gone.

Crap! Not again.

Zack saw the double doors separating the sanctuary from the foyer close and he got up and walked quickly to the back.

Seconds later, Zack bolted through the outer doors and into the parking lot. The man stood by a grove of trees across the sea of haphazardly parked cars.

Zack shielded his eyes from the sun.

Well, I guess that rules out a vampire, he thought.

"We have to stop meeting like this." Zack approached him.

"Good sermon today, huh?" The man smiled but didn't offer his hand.

"Yeah, it always is. Do you come here often?" Zack nodded toward the church.

"Occasionally."

"Funny. I've gone here most of my life and never noticed you." Zack said.

"Guess you're not very observant." He looked at Zack.

"Guess not."

"You're with people every day," the man said.

Zack shrugged.

"You don't really notice them either, right?"

Zack looked down kicking at the gravel, like a scolded five-year-old. "Yeah, I guess," he said.

"Mrs. Murphy's a prime example," the man said.

"Who?" Zack looked up.

"Mrs. Murphy. The woman who takes your money for the fried piece of shoe leather between two slices of bread that you and John chug down every day."

"Yeah?" Zack shrugged.

"She lost her cat."

"That's too bad," Zack said.

"Is it?" The man made eye contact again and Zack couldn't turn away as he continued. "She's 50 pounds overweight and lives alone, not of her own choice. Amber had been with her for eight years. She has no living children and her sole purpose in life is to take dollars from teenagers who have more in their wallets than she makes in a week."

"That's not me," Zack said.

"How about Jenny Montgomery?" The man asked.

"Jenny Mont—"

"She sits behind you in English." the man said.

"Oh, Jenn M. I never knew her last name—"

"My point exactly, Zack. Every morning she looks in her bathroom mirror, sees the haircut that she chopped herself and the face looking back at her and mouths the words, 'You're hideous. You're not worth the air that it takes to fill your lungs. The world would be a better place without you.'"

"How do you know these things?"

"Her dad molests her on a regular basis."

"What?" Zack's gaze tightened. He looked into the trees and then back at the man. "Why are you telling me all of this?"

"She tried to tell you one time," the man said. "Do you remember?"

"No, not really, I don't…" Zack stammered.

"A few weeks ago. After class. You asked her how it was going. It was a passing comment to you, just something to say to be polite."

"Well, I—"

"You didn't really want to know."

Zack looked at his feet.

The man continued. "She was ready to tell somebody about the horrendous night she'd had. She wanted to scream it out. Do you remember what you did?"

"John called me…" Zack mumbled from memory. "As she was beginning to speak, I turned and walked away from her." Zack looked back at him.

The man stared back. "Journals, crumbled pieces of notebook paper, conversations; we can pick up a lot of information if we'll pay attention. *You,* of all people, must understand that, Zack; the feeling of being alone with no one to understand?"

Zack nodded.

"I didn't come here to preach you another sermon; the one inside was good enough." The man nodded toward the church. "Do you want me to stop showing up like this?"

Zack looked at him. "Well, I guess…"

He took an ivory colored envelope from his inside jacket pocket and handed it to Zack. Zack's name was embossed on the outside; he ran his finger over the raised letters.

"If you're interested, follow the instructions. If not, throw it away."

He turned and climbed into a convertible Mercedes sports car, started the engine, and drove slowly out of the gravel lot and onto the roadway.

22

"I want to open this… but I don't want to." Zack looked across the restaurant table at Jeff after church and laid the envelope on the table.

"This is nuts." Jeff said.

"I know, dad, but I didn't tell you what's been going on so that you don't worry."

"I realize that, son, but I am concerned about your safety—"

"Dad, I'm almost eighteen You gotta stop worrying sometime."

"Is that the rule?" Jeff took a sip of his coffee.

"Well, at least Milton's gone," Zack said.

"That's true, but he could be back," Jeff said.

"I know, Dad, but…"

"Zack, this whole thing's really bizarre and you don't know *who* this guy might be. He said he's been at the church? I've never seen—"

"Yeah, me neither," Zack paused, "but if he wanted to hurt me, he's had plenty of opportunities. Why show up at our church?" Zack grabbed the syrup and soaked his order of pancakes.

"Yeah, or maybe he's baiting you—"

"Dad."

"You never know, Zack."

"I know he's not." Zack stared at the envelope. "Somehow, I know."

"Then I guess you'd better open it," Jeff said.

Zack took a few more bites of the pancakes, sat back, wiped his mouth, and took a sip of his drink. He pulled the envelope toward him, opened it, and took out two pieces of paper and scanned the words:

Zack, on Thursday next, please come to Golden, Capadocia Parkway, address 250.
I will meet you at my place of business.
Your arrival is anticipated at 7 p.m.
Feel free to bring anyone with whom you feel comfortable.
I trust your judgment.
Regards.

On the second piece of paper was a map.

Zack passed the papers across the table to his dad.

Jeff took them and scanned them. "What do you think?" he asked.

"Well, it's better than Milton's letter." Zack grinned. "At least this one doesn't say 'come alone.' "

"Are you going to do this?" Jeff asked.

"I've got no choice. I've *got* to see what's going on." Zack waved the paper.

"I'm going with you." Jeff said wiping his mouth on his napkin.

"Dad—"

"No." Jeff shook his head. "You're still my son. I lost your mom. I'll be *danged* if I'm going to lose you to some maniac—"

"What about work?"

"I'll figure something out," Jeff waved his hand. "I'll take a personal day or-"

"I don't know yet, Dad. He said bring anyone. Doesn't that mean he's got nothing to hide?" Zack pointed to the letter.

"Maybe that's what he wants you to think." Jeff's tone was final. "No. I'm going,"

"I don't know…" Zack said.

"Well, you've got nearly a week to decide if you want to go, but I'm there." Jeff tapped the envelope.

"Thanks, Dad." Zack resigned to Jeff's coming along. "I've got to tie up some other stuff first."

23

Milton's brick house, near the school, sat on several acres of pasture land in unincorporated Weld County.

Zack turned off the engine of Rudabaker's truck and scanned the yard for any sign of Milton.

The cracker box two-story, occupied a disheveled lot with a detached garage. A small barn adjacent to its dilapidated back porch needed a great deal of attention.

The weed-encased window wells indicated a basement, but lack of a weed trimmer or anyone to man it. The sagging wooden siding desperately needed paint. The brick pillars on each corner of the porch supported the overhang and Zack wondered how long it would hold up the sagging roof, with several bricks coming loose. Visibly repaired patches in the roof contrasted decaying shingles.

Zack climbed out of the truck. The breeze from the neighbor's cow pens reinforced the rural feel.

Zack walked up the uneven sidewalk onto the porch and rapped on the flimsy screen door. After a moment, the faded, flowered curtains in the front window rustled. Zack heard the door latch and the woman poked her face through the crack.

"Mrs. Drago?" he asked.

"Yes?" She squinted shielding her eyes from the bright day.

"I'm Zack Tucker." He paused. "A few days ago, at Kurt Clayton's funeral, we met?"

Her vacant stare faded finally into recognition.

"Oh, yes. Milton's friend! Have you seen him?" She launched into a run-on dissertation. "Do you have word of him? The school's been calling, the police are looking for him, you know. They stopped by several times and said if I saw him or heard from him to let them know immediately, they wanted to ask him a few questions. They say that, but I think what's *really* happening is that Milton is working *with* the police. Yes, he's working with the police on a case. I just know it. I don't know though, whether it has something to do with Kurt's death. He has such a great mind and is *so* intelligent... Milton I mean, not Kurt. Kurt is gone," she gulped a breath then continued to ramble.

"Of course *you* would already know that because you go to school with him... well with them both, Milton and Kurt. Of course, you *wouldn't* go with Kurt anymore because he died. Have you seen Milton? I don't know where he could be, he hasn't been home. I suppose that he might be hungry... I don't know if he took *any* food with him Maybe he might be at a friend's house... He doesn't always check in. He's not at your house is he?" She finally stopped.

"Uh, no, ma'am." Zack shrugged. "I don't know where he is, either. In fact, that's the reason I stopped by, to see if you had any information?" Zack took a step back. "But I guess you don't..."

"Oh, no, why would I have any information? I'm *only* his mother; why would he tell me anything?" She shrugged in exasperation.

Zack couldn't tell if he was part of her ongoing conversation at this point.

"Won't you come in? I just baked chocolate chip cookies." She calmed and returned to semi-coherency. "They're Milton's favorites. I thought I would have them ready in case he came home. I'm Katherine." She swung the door wide and offered her hand.

Zack shook it.

"Thank you, Mrs. Drago," Zack hesitated. "Katherine."

The interior contrasted the unkempt exterior. To his left Zack saw the steps leading upstairs, a maroon and gray runner folded its way down each tread.

Zack trailed after Katherine and around an oval dining room table with neat stacks of letters and bills arranged on top. The aroma of the cookies overlaid the smell of a roast in the oven.

Zack's saliva glands began to hurt as he followed her into the living room.

Zack sat in a plush recliner, as Mrs. Drago disappeared into the kitchen. The rattle of china echoed from the kitchen until she returned with a plate of cookies and glass of juice in hand.

"Here you are. I hope you like orange juice."

"Thank you," he took the glass. "I do."

Zack scanned the room, pausing on the mantle cluttered with pictures. Milton in a suit and tie.

"Nice pictures." He got out of the chair and stepped to the mantle.

"Ahh, yes, many wonderful memories," she followed him.

"That one is of me and my husband before we were married." She pointed. "And next to that is a photo of Milton's sister, Camaria."

"I didn't realize Milton had a sister." Zack picked up a silver frame.

"Two, actually. Cammie is married and lives in Maryland with her husband and two children. Ronnie's 4 now and Rennie is 5. We don't get to see them as much. They're busy, you know. Henry, Cammie's husband, is an elementary school principal, so we only get to see them during the summer."

"That other picture, in the gilded frame, is our other daughter, Becky. She isn't married yet. She and her roommate live across town. Becky is an assistant manager of a savings and loan. We see her a little more often now, since Merle..." she stopped.

Zack lifted a heavy frame. Milton, with pained expression, stood next to a rugged, quite obese man.

"Your husband?" Zack angled the frame toward her.

"Yes, that's my Merle, God rest his soul. That picture was taken a few months before he passed on. An accidental fall took him. Of course you probably remember about that tragedy, I'm sure Milton told you."

"No, actually, he didn't." Zack said.

"Yes, went out to the pen in back of the barn and stepped in a gopher hole, of all things. Fell and hit his head on a rock. Lay there for some time, the paramedics told me." She walked over and sat down.

"Oh, I'm sorry," Zack said. "I didn't know. I thought—"

"Yes, it happened three years ago now." She continued. "It's still hard for me to go out in that pen even now, after all this time."

She stared at the wall. "Of course, we don't really keep too much out there anymore anyway." She mumbled. "Milton had left for school early that day, and he didn't find out until later. It was hard on him I think." She paused. "He always had guilt over his father's death."

24

She looked up as if just realizing that Zack was there. "Yes, Milton was going through a rebellious time, you know how kids do?"

Zack nodded.

"He and Merle… had words before he left for school about some silly thing; Milton was *so* angry. It's funny how those things seem so monumental at the time, but now, I can't even remember what they were fighting about. They hadn't gotten along for some time."

Her gaze began to wander and then came back to Zack.

"Anyway, Milton left in a huff, slamming the front door, and Merle went to the garage, slamming the back door. I thought at first maybe they would go outside and talk about it. I saw Milton circle around the house and head toward the barn, but I guess they never got a chance to iron things out." She stood. "Would you like some more to drink?"

"No, ma'am, I'm fine, thank you," Zack waved her off.

She sat back down. "Merle could be pretty tough on Milton at times, the only son and all. Merle always sulked in the garage when he was upset. I guess most men do. Yes, he was off his regular job that day; he helped with the grain elevator over in Elbert you know. That's about 30 miles away from here, east. He loaded the box cars full of grain."

She rambled on again, looking past Zack.

"The rest of the time, he mostly filled in with odd jobs around the neighborhood and always seemed to have something he could do around here." She looked Zack in the eyes.

"He spent a lot of time in that garage, doing whatnot. There and over at Mrs. Franklin's. She was a widow you know; had two young girls that were very fond of Merle. Sort of like making up for their dad being gone and all. He would go over for hours and do odd jobs around her house. Helping her out with the chores and whatnot…"

A teakettle's whistle interrupted her musing.

"Could you excuse me for a minute?" She got up again.

"Sure." Zack walked over and took another cookie and a drink of the juice.

Katherine returned a few moments later with a cup and saucer in her hands, the steam from freshly brewed tea rising.

"Now, where were we?" she asked.

"You were telling me of the fight that Milton and your husband had had the day that he…" Zack hesitated. "Died."

Zack walked back to the mantle looking at the photos again.

"Oh yes." Katherine waved her hand. "Well, Merle stayed out there a couple of hours. As I said, it wasn't unusual. We had an unspoken rule, when he was in that garage, I didn't ask and he didn't tell."

She slurped her tea, winced and then continued. "It was getting on near lunchtime, so I called him a couple of times and he didn't answer. Merle was always such a depressed sort; I didn't think that much of it, so I let it go for a little while."

She dunked a cookie in her tea and then sucked the moisture out of it before biting down.

"I hadn't fixed anything fancy, some bologna sandwiches or something, I don't recall. I do know that I sat down to eat without him and I had forgotten the pickles. Merle loved sweet gherkins. I knew that if he came in and those sweet gherkins weren't on the table, he would… Well, miss them; so, I went into the kitchen to get them, and I thought, 'I wonder where he is?'"

She put her finger to her temple as if reliving the moment.

"How ridiculous it was that he was sulking that long, so I decided to go to the garage and find him."

She paused and pulled a hankie out of her dress pocket, blowing her nose.

"Excuse me," she said. "Where was I?"

"The pickles," Zack turned to look at her.

"Oh yes, the pickles. Well, Merle wasn't in the garage. I called for him, but no answer. I went to the barn and looked inside. By now I was getting a little worried, so I went around the barn and I noticed that a part of the fence was down and one of the cows was off a ways away. I walked around the corner of the barn and didn't see anything." She shrugged.

"Now, I was really worried, so I went back in the house and called the police. I didn't really know what to tell them, but I explained as best I could."

She looked at Zack.

"Do you know that it took them almost 45 minutes to send a car out here?" She tapped her wrist. "I mean, we are not that far off the beaten path. Did you think it was that hard to find?"

"Uh, no." Zack walked over and took a sip of juice again and sat down.

"Well, then, there you have it." She nodded, rocking back and forth. "Anyway, the officers finally arrived and they combed the same areas that I did. I told them I'd already looked in those places, but I guess they just thought I was a crazy woman or something." She shook her head.

"But when they went a little farther into the cow pen." She paused. "They found Merle."

Her eyes welled with tears.

"He was lying in the weeds. He had fallen and hit his head on a rock and his tools were strewn about. By the time the ambulance arrived, there was nothing they could do. I overheard them talking; they said it was quite a mess." She looked past the wall again.

"They wouldn't let me see him until the viewing a few days later. Imagine that." She shook her head slowly. "My *own* husband of 40 some odd years and they wouldn't even let me see him."

"Yes, ma'am." Zack shifted in his seat and glanced at the clock on the wall listening to its steady tick, tick, tick.

"All I saw was a sheet-wrapped body being loaded into the back of the ambulance."

Katherine paused taking a sip of tea and then continuing. "I guess it was for the best though. I called the girls, and they came right over. Becky and her roommate, Nancy. They have been together for a while now, did I tell you that?"

Zack nodded.

"I mean, Cammie obviously didn't arrive until a few days later. *They* got here quicker than the police did and they live across town! Becky that is, she lives across town, not Cammie. She arrived a few days later."

She sipped again.

"Milton finally came home. We tried the school, but he wasn't there. I thought that was strange, but he finally came home. My little boy was finally home."

She stopped for a long moment and began to hum like she had finished the story. After a few minutes of listening to the clock tick and the chorus of *Shall We Gather at the River*, Zack finally spoke.

"So, Milton came home, from school?"

"Yes, he came home alright. I don't know whether he was ever the same after that. He just had this dead look about him. Yes, that's what I would call it, a *dead* look. I don't really remember him crying about Merle. Oh, I'm sure he did, but I don't know what he was thinking. He moved down in the basement not too long after that, said he needed his 'space.'"

She paused again.

"We left things the way they were out back for a while. I sure couldn't go out there and do anything. The kids went out and looked around, but it was too much for me. I didn't need to see that," Katherine looked at Zack, "you know?"

Zack nodded.

"Finally, I think Milton went out and did some cleanup and the weather took care of the rest of it." She waved her hand in dismissal.

Zack turned and looked at a photo sitting on the end table beside him. He saw the round eyes, the childhood twinkle and the wholesome smile.

How could this little boy turn into the monster that was now Milton Drago?

"We take so much for granted." Mrs. Drago began again. Zack turned back toward her.

"One day is like any other day, we get up and dress and fix breakfast and we're off to school or puttering around the house and, in an instant, your entire life changes." She dropped her head and then finally looked back at Zack.

"I was married to Merle for forty-two years and seven months." She wiped a tear with the hankie.

Zack glanced down at the picture, and something caught his eye. Milton, decked out in fishing vest, with pole in hand. Merle grasping a rod, reel and tackle box, and hanging on Merle's belt was *the* knife.

"Wow, this is quite a knife your husband has here." Zack said.

"Yes, that was his favorite." Katherine snapped out of her contemplation. "He used it for hunting and fishing and whatnot. I always thought it was a bit dangerous to leave lying around when Milton was little."

She threw up her hands. "But what did I know?"

Zack watched her.

"Merle said that Milton had to learn respect for things." She shook her head. "Knives and guns and whatnot. Merle was Merle. I haven't seen that thing for a long time now. I'm sure it's around here someplace." She glanced around as if it could be hiding under the rug.

I know where it is, Zack thought.

The ringing phone jolted them out of their conversation. Katherine pushed herself up and shuffled across the area rug. Zack stared at the photo.

"Yes, oh, Mildred," Zack heard Katherine in the kitchen. "Wait for just a minute." She pulled the phone away from her ear. "Zack?"

"Yes, ma'am." Zack walked to the kitchen doorway.

"It's my sister, long distance." She covered the receiver as if letting him in on a secret. "Thanks so much for taking the time to stop by. Milton's other friends never come to see me." She glanced at the phone. "Could you show yourself out?"

"Yes, I will." Zack turned to leave.

"Oh! I just thought of something. Mildred, hang on." She laid the phone down. "Can you help me with something?" She motioned for Zack to follow her.

"I'll be glad to if I can," Zack said.

"The school library called me. Milton had a book that needed to be returned to the Biology class. It's a copy of *Gray's Anatomy*. Could you return it for me?"

"Sure." Zack nodded.

"I don't know exactly where it is. Would you look down in Milton's room?" She picked up the receiver. "Mildred, yes, I'm back."

Zack looked at her.

She pointed toward a corner door, off the kitchen.

"Through that door and down into the basement," she whispered.

25

Zack walked to the basement door and stepped down three steps onto a landing. On his right, the door leading to the back yard was unlocked. To his left was a long set of cluttered stairs. He started down.

Exposed two-by-four studs with makeshift shelving housed jars of peach preserves and canned tomatoes along the wall. His labored steps on creaking stairs caused his jaw to tighten until finally his foot slid onto the basement concrete slab.

Zack stood enveloped in darkness. He searched the wall, no light switch. He stepped forward into a cobweb, causing him to paw his face. Zack shuffled on the concrete, sliding his feet along one after the other, fanning his arms for a pull string on any light. A few more paces and Zack kicked a soft, heavy heap. Terror shot through him and he froze expecting hands to latch around his ankles at any moment. Faint light illuminated the stairs behind him, but he couldn't focus. His mind raced. He was a fool to come here. He thought of the unlocked back door and panicked.

In a last-ditch effort, he swung his arms wildly. His hand hit a weight on the end of a string. It apparently ricocheted away from his hand and swung back, hitting him in the face. His head instinctively recoiled as he fumbled again, grabbed the string and pulled. The string broke in his hand, but the bulb glowed white, blinding him and he rubbed his eyes.

He exhaled as he saw a pile of clothes lying in front of the washing machine.

Zack scanned the basement and focused on a door in the corner, standing partially open. He pushed through it into more darkness. The pungent odor of dirty socks and sweat invaded his nostrils and he hoped that Milton wasn't lying in wait. He inched along the wall finally making contact with the switch and flipped it.

The single, clear bulb threw a yellow hue around the room.

Zack froze staring at the walls.

Two walls were black, two were blood red. Posters of hideous mythical creatures from the Netherworld hung askew. Painted flames licked the ceiling as if Zack stood amidst the brimstone of hell. At the head of Milton's bed, like a Gothic headboard was an uncompleted mural of a great winged dragon. Its decapitated victims hung in blood soaked talons, and flesh and blood dripped from its fangs.

Zack picked through piles of dirty clothes on Milton's bare mattress and then through the clutter on his bedside table.

Nothing.

He ran his fingers across the spines of books on a shelf; death, occult, true crime were amidst some Louis L'Amour westerns.

Zack slid a book off the shelf and opened it.

Fun With Dick and Jane.

He flipped the pages of the first grade reader with a child's hand writing in the margins.

Mommy, daddy, Cammy, Becky, Milty.

Zack closed the reader and slid it back on the shelf. No *Gray's Anatomy*.

He stepped to a corner desk and shuffled through the stacks of papers on top. He slid open the drawer. Papers, pens, a pocket knife, and stacks of photos of Milton and Delrobia. Zack took the stack and flipped through until he ran across several semi-nude pictures of Del. He glanced behind him and then shoved them back into the drawer like he had been caught coming out of an adult bookstore.

He opened the bottom drawer and lifted a few textbooks. A tattered spiral notebook lay underneath with winged creatures drawn on the front. "Milton", in quotes, was scribbled in Magic Marker across its cover.

Zack glanced behind him again. He grabbed the notebook and backed up, sitting on Milton's bed. His hands trembled as he flipped the page.

> *These are the personal manuscripts of Milton Drago, what follows is the essence of what I am and what I did here on earth.*

Zack flipped through pages of disconnected poems and intricate pen drawings of creatures and demonic faces. He glanced at assignment due dates and notes to Del scribbled in the margins.

Zack paused on a pen drawing so intricate that at first he thought it was a photo.

It was three boys laughing at an overtly exaggerated fat kid in a bush. Zack was immortalized and violated simultaneously. Then something else caught his eye and he shuddered. A faceless man, clad in black trench coat with hair down to his shoulders lurked behind the event. The caption under the picture read: *Darkness Comes!*

Under the words, in smaller print, an afterthought:

> *Immolo are captivitas atris f.*

"Did you find it?"

Zack slammed the notebook shut and jumped up, stepping into a pile of dirty clothes and hitting something hard.

"Uh-" Zack stammered and stooped to uncover *Gray's Anatomy*. "Yes, ma'am, I did. Be right up."

Zack replaced the notebook and made his way back toward the stairs like a 6-year-old fetching a toy from a dark basement.

"I wrapped up some cookies to take with you. I hope you like them," she said.

"Thanks, Mrs. Drago. You didn't have to—"

"Nonsense, no trouble," Mrs. Drago said. "It's too bad Milton wasn't here."

"Yes, it was," Zack said. "Thanks, Mrs. Drago."

Zack threw the copy of *Gray's Anatomy* on the seat of the truck and looked back at the house.

He shook his head. Only a mother's love.

26

"You did what?" John opened his locker door.

"I asked her out," Zack said.

"Just called up and asked her out."

"Yup," Zack said.

"Wow, where you takin' her?"

"The movies, retro night." Zack opened his locker and peered in.

"That's monumental, dude!" John slapped him on the back. "A real live girl. You're a legend—"

"Hey, I almost forgot," Zack interrupted. "I went to Milton's house yesterday." He dug through his locker rearranging the stack of books from largest to smallest.

"You what?"

Zack extracted a book on the history of Rome and grabbed his favorite pen out of an empty soup can.

"Yeah, I had to see what I could find out."

"Are you nuts? What's come over you? Going to killer's houses, asking girls out! Who are you and what have you done with my pudgy friend?"

"I'm tired of being afraid." Zack scribbled circles on a piece of notebook paper, testing the pen's ink.

"So, what did you find out?" John shut his locker and stepped closer.

"Well," Zack stopped priming the pen and they turned down an empty hallway, "our friend, Milton, has quite the weird habitation going."

"Oh, really? Who would have guessed?" John rolled his eyes.

"Yeah, pretty horrific stuff. It's not hard to figure out *why* he is like he is. I really feel sorry for his mom, though," Zack said.

"Oh?" John's eyebrows rose.

"She's nice, but clueless when it comes to Milton. Get this…" He punched John's arm. "She said she thought that Milton was helping to solve a case and that's why the police wanted to question him."

"What an upstanding citizen," John snapped to attention and saluted.

"You know it." Zack glanced down the hallway.

"Hey," he hit John's arm again.

"Will you cut that out!" John massaged his arm.

"Kevin just went into the locker room." Zack's focus was set. "I need to talk to him."

"What?"

Zack brushed past John and started for the locker room.

"After you're over your schizophrenia and you revert back to your normal personality, will ya let me know?" John called after him.

27

Zack pulled on the locker room door and a stringent potpourri of chlorine, sweat socks and rubber mats hit his nostrils; he stood still. A locker door slammed and Zack walked toward a row of lockers and peeked around the corner. Kevin sat on the bench, adjusting a sock.

"Hey, Kevin."

Kevin jumped and then swore.

"You scared the piss out of me!"

"Sorry, didn't mean to." Zack said.

"What do you want?" Kevin scowled.

"Let's talk," Zack said.

"Not now, I haven't got time. I just had to grab something; besides, I've got nothing to say to you, Tucker." He stood, gathered his books and shoved passed Zack.

"What happened that night at the graveyard?" Zack followed.

Kevin stopped without turning toward Zack. "What do you mean?"

"Well, I know about the night you, Milton, Kurt and the girls went there."

Kevin let his breath out slowly. "How do you know?"

"*How* doesn't matter," Zack said, "but there *are* a lot of weird things going on lately."

He paused. "Give me some answers."

Kevin turned toward him and stared for a moment in silence.

"Why should I?" Kevin asked then hesitated. "No. I don't think so." He shook his head and turned back toward the door.

"Were you there the night Milton came after me?" Zack asked.

Kevin stopped. He launched himself and grabbed Zack by his shirt lapels, shoving him against the lockers.

"Don't make trouble for me on this, man, or I'll bury you! You freakin' hear me?"

Zack saw the despair in Kevin's eyes and raised his hands in surrender. "That's cool, man—"

"Listen," Kevin softened. "I never meant any of that bullcrap. I didn't want to hurt you, man, you gotta believe me!" Kevin's eyes pleaded.

"That night, I didn't know what Milton had in mind. He asked me to go with him and he had some booze in the car, so I thought we were going to party, that's all; I didn't know he had the knife. I don't want something like that on my record, you got me?"

Kevin loosened his grip.

"You've gotta swear that you won't go to the cops with this." Kevin's eyes widened. "Did you already?"

"No," Zack shook his head. "I didn't even mention your name."

"Good, man, let's keep it that way." Kevin released Zack's collar. "Please. I'll tell you, Tucker." He looked around the locker room. "Kurt's dead and Milton's a goner too. He's already checked out."

"Dead?"

"No, you idiot, he's just split. I don't know where. And frankly, I don't care. I haven't heard from him." Kevin stepped back, glancing around. "Come with me."

He motioned Zack away from the door next to Coach Swanson's empty office. They pushed through a back door and into the swimming pool area.

"We don't have much time," Kevin said. "Swanson will come in for his morning swim and kick us out of here. He usually spends a few minutes in the teacher's lounge first thing to grab his morning coffee."

"How do you know?"

"Swim team, doofus." Kevin paused. "Listen. That night at the graveyard, the first night, I mean. The girls and us decided to have some fun. It's Milton's favorite spot." Kevin shook his head. "Me, I just go to party with my girl and for the liquid refreshment. I don't care where we go.

"So Milton brings the beer. He gets it off some friend of his that's 21. But this night he not only had the beer, but also shows up with a bottle of Jack Daniels. Who knows why? I don't ask."

Zack nodded.

"We had the music on and Milton breaks out the booze. I'd never had whiskey before so I drank some, but it tasted like crap. Stacey and I were mostly going with the beer. For some reason, Milton had a butt load. The usual things start up. Kurt and Staci are outside the car. Milton and Del climb in the backseat. Me and Stacey are sitting on the ground by one of the headstones.

"Well that crap whiskey is doing a number on me. By this time we've been there a while and we were all blitzed. You wouldn't know."

"Go on." Zack ignored the putdown.

"Well, I gotta puke. So I told Kurt. By this time Milton's done with Del, and he climbs out of the car and says he's gotta pee, too, so we start to stagger toward the trees. Kurt says he better keep us safe from the Boogie Man, so he's laughing and falling all over himself. We walked a little ways into the woods until we were out of sight of the lights of the car, you know, we didn't want things illuminated."

Zack nodded again.

"I'm out there and I gotta heave. So I let go, which disgusts Milton. He says, 'Hey, Bauer, can't you take it?' I told him to go to hell and I hurled again. He says, 'Already on my way, buddy!' and laughed while he started pissing trying to write his name with the stream. Kurt's a little ways away from us cuz he had to take a dump." Kevin winced.

"I didn't want him anywhere upwind from me. I already smelled, you know? I mean, crap! So I told him to go off in the bushes somewhere.

"By now, I'm down on all fours with the dry heaves but at least my stomach's feeling better. Man, I hate whiskey!"

Zack grinned.

"I felt this weird calm." Kevin continued. "Just the sound of the breeze in the trees and we heard Kurt's voice. Milton yelled, 'Hey, Clayton, we can't hear you, speak up!' But no answer, just Kurt's muffled voice.

"Man, I can hardly stand. But I started walking toward the sound of Kurt's voice. I pushed back the bushes and fell into this clearing. Kurt's a few feet away with his pants around his ankles, hanging his butt over a fallen tree trunk and he's sitting there talking to some girl!"

Zack's eyes widened.

"At first I thought Staci followed us into the woods, but then I thought she wouldn't be talking to him while he was taking a dump. That's disgusting; not like they're married right?"

Zack shook his head.

"So, Milton found us and bursts through the bushes, almost falling over me. We start walking closer to them. The chick's back is to us and Kurt's talking away. We walk in close enough to see the girl, you can tell she's not bad-looking, you know? And Kurt looks up and says with this dry, matter-of-fact voice, 'Guys, I'd like you meet my sister, Muriel.' And she turns and looks at us."

28

Kevin stopped and closed his eyes while sweat ran down his temples. Zack's neck hair came alive.

"She looked at us and said some words that I didn't understand, some "imolo" crap or something like that and then smiled. She smiled this hideous smile, this demonic smile and raised both arms."

Kevin caught his breath.

"Black blood gushed out of deep gashes in her wrists! It was like motor oil running down her arms and pooling on the ground!"

Kevin reached out and grabbed Zack's arm in fear. He leaned in and whispered, pushing every syllable out in short breaths.

"I'm telling you the truth, Tucker. I'm not lying to you... Do you understand?" Kevin's eyes darted back and forth as he stared into Zack's face.

"I haven't told anyone about this; I don't know why I'm telling you." He sounded as if he would hyperventilate. "I was too scared to say it before now, but she keeps me up at night. It was like a freakin' horror movie."

He relaxed and dropped his head.

"I lock my door every night, my windows too. I'm not religious, but I found my mom's old Bible and I keep it and a butcher knife on my bedside table. I can't eat." Kevin clutched his stomach. "I had to tell someone, Tucker. I think I'm going crazy." He wiped the sweat off his forehead.

"What happened then?" Zack put his hand on Kevin's arm. "What happened after that, Kevin?"

"I freaked, man." Kevin almost yelled. "We all did. It sobered me up fast! I turned and ran in the direction of the car with Milton right behind me. We all saw her. All three of us. I remember it was like running in a bad dream, I didn't think I could make my legs move fast enough."

Zack looked at him. Ironic how running from those guys felt the same way.

Kevin forced the air out again.

"We finally cleared the trees, and I fell onto the lawn. We started yelling for the girls to get in the car and a moment later Kurt came through the bushes behind me. I could hear him sobbing. I never heard him cry like that, but I couldn't stop running. He kept saying, 'It's her! It's Muriel. It's my dead sister!'

"When we got in the cars, Milton couldn't find his stinkin' keys." Kevin glanced around at the floor like he was looking for the keys again.

"The girls were yelling at us to tell 'em what was wrong." Kevin looked at Zack. "Milton kept cussing them and then finally hit Del across the mouth and kept screaming for her to shut up. We had to crawl around on the ground to look for the keys. Kurt huddled in the back seat with Staci, like a little kid. He looked like one of those unborn babies in the science pictures."

Zack nodded.

"Yeah, just like that." Kevin nodded. "The freakin' keys were under the driver's side tire. We had to rock the car back and forth to grab them! I don't know how we got them and I don't know why they were there."

Kevin palpitated as he spoke.

"We finally took off and hit one of the headstones on the way out."

Kevin swallowed.

"I looked out the back window." He paused. "She was standing there. Right there, Zack." Kevin motioned as if reliving it. "In the trees, partially hidden by the bushes; she was just watching us, her dress blowing in the breeze." He paused again. "And she had that smile."

Kevin turned his wrists outward to show Zack the stance. "She stood like this. I saw that black blood again."

Kevin turned toward Zack. His face was pale and his breath formed short puffs.

"You've got to believe me. I've got no reason to make any of this up."

"I do believe you." Zack put his hand on his shoulder. "Calm down, Kev, you're going to hyperventilate. I believe you."

"Hey, you guys!"

Zack jumped.

"You're not supposed to be in here; it's time for class," Coach Swanson said.

"Yes, sir," Zack stood.

They walked past the coach into the locker room and then toward the door.

"One other thing, Kevin," Zack said.

"Come on, Tucker. Don't you think you've milked enough out of me?" Kevin sighed.

"What about the man?"

"What man?"

"The night you guys chased me?"

Kevin paused. "I don't know *what* he is."

Kevin opened the door and stepped into the hallway. "All I know is that he scared the hell out of us that night. I looked up and he was *just there*." Kevin motioned with his hands. "And his eyes; even in the dark I saw 'em." Kevin's eyes widened. "They looked right through me. It was terrifying. I got out of there."

Kevin closed his eyes and then opened them again staring into Zack's face. "Why's all of this happening to me?"

Before Zack could answer, a girl passed them. "Hey, Keevviinnn." She smiled.

Kevin didn't look at her.

The class bell rang and like water from a floodgate, the halls swelled with students.

"I've gotta go," Kevin said. "I can't talk about it anymore."

Kevin didn't speak for a moment, looking down at his feet, but then he raised his head and looked at Zack one last time.

"Remember man, the other night at the cemetery when Milton came for you?" He paused again and grabbed Zack's shirt sleeve. "I wasn't there. You got that?" He turned and the wave of students swallowed him.

29

Zack stepped from the shower and toweled off. He looked over his shoulder into the mirror, and pulled the towel back and forth like a television commercial for a vibrant new soap. Tiny whiskers met their demise as he slid the razor across his face. He gave the mirror a goofy grin.

"Hey there, buddy. You're going out with Jamie Watkins tonight. You, lucky Buck." He winked.

He combed his hair in different styles.

Straight back, the Bogey look.

Swooping forward, the James Dean.

He tufted the back so it stuck straight up, the Alfalfa.

Definitely not.

He combed his hair like normal and left it.

What if I show up and she turns off the porch light and I hear her friends snickering in the distance? Zack stared into the mirror. *Naw, she wouldn't do that.*

He dabbed on his cologne. Gotta leave room for the popcorn smell.

He checked his watch. Right on time. *They should be there to secure the good seats.*

He thumbed through the shirts in his closet, XL's, good. No more XXL's for me.

The blue shirt, that's the ticket. A declaration of casual masculinity. She will think of me as velvet steel.

He smelled the armpits. "Good, it's clean."

He pulled on his slacks and looked at himself in the mirror remembering his eighth grade year: Taunts and jeers and trying to squeeze into the same black double knit pants every day because he thought they made him look smaller. Zack shook his head and grinned. More like sausage casings than pants.

Not tonight though. Who cares? Jamie's waiting.

Zack checked his shoes, wallet, keys, and breath mints. Just in case.

He was ready.

Ready for a date with Jamie Watkins.

Harold's truck sat in Zack's driveway, washed, waxed, and vacuumed. The dashboard was clear of petrified sandwiches and all nonessentials were scraped from under the seat. The construction tools in the truck bed were stowed in Zack's back yard and he had transformed the vehicle into a princess's carriage.

A few minutes later, he pulled to the curb outside 4995 Roosevelt Place, switched off the lights, and cut the engine. He checked his watch. Early. If he went to the door, the uncomfortable visit would overtake him or, worse yet, Jamie might feel rushed.

Zack looked at the house and then glanced at his watch. He took a coin out of his pocket and flipped it. Tails. He would sit outside for a few more minutes.

The street lamps popped and then glowed, chasing away the blue sky. Jamie's neighborhood grew quiet, interrupted by an occasional barking dog or passing car. A young man, in a gray sweat suit, jogged past opposite the parked truck. Zack watched him and then switched to the side mirror to follow his progress.

Jamie's porch light came on and a mountain of a man stepped onto the porch and walked toward the truck. Zack leaned over and rolled down the passenger window as the man bent down to look in.

"I'm Jason, Jamie's dad." His bass timber nearly rattled the door frame and he thrust a tree-trunk sized arm through the window.

"I'm Zack." He pumped Jason's hand knowing there was a real man attached to the other end. "Nice to meet you, sir. I'm a little early. I didn't want to disturb—"

"Nonsense. Jamie sent me out to get you. Come on in."

Zack climbed out of the truck and followed the six-foot-four, three-hundred-pound wall toward the house. Zack was no ninety-five-pound weakling, but he felt like a place-kicker dwarfed by a linebacker.

Inside, Zack sat on a leather couch.

"So, a retro movie tonight, eh?" Jason asked.

"Yes, sir. Rock Hudson and Paula Prentiss. *Man's Favorite Sport*?"

"I know it well. Great movie. Jason, please. *Sir* makes me seem so old." He smiled.

Zack laughed, "Okay."

An attractive woman entered.

"Zack," Jason said. "This is my lovely wife, Jenni."

"Hello, Zack." She smiled.

"Nice to meet you, ma'am." Zack partially stood and shook her hand.

"Jenni."

"Jenni." Zack grinned.

"Would you like something to drink, Zack?" Jenni asked.

"Uh. No, that's okay." Zack said.

"Zack, do you date much?" Jamie's dad asked.

"Uh, no sir. I, uh-."

"Here's what I know, Zack." Jason continued. "When you're waiting on a woman to get ready for a date, you might as well make yourself comfortable, because it's going to be a while." He laughed. "Have something to drink."

"Well, alright then." Zack relaxed. "I'll have something,"

"Water, lemon-lime soda, root beer, milk, orange or cranapple juice?" Jenni listed.

"Cranapple, please," Zack settled back into the squeaky leather. "So Jamie says you just moved here?"

"Yeah, I've always loved Colorado."

Jenni returned with the drinks.

"Here we go."

"Thank you, Jenni." Zack tried to seem casual using her first name. "So, a detective, huh?"

"Thanks, Baby," Jason took the soda and turned back to Zack. "Right now, robbery. They'll be moving me into homicide soon, but Summit Ridge is small compared to Denver PD, so we do all sorts of things."

Jason popped the tab on his can of soda.

"Wow, that's exciting," Zack said. "I don't know if I could handle it, though."

"Yeah, it's interesting, to say the least. I remember this one patrol —"

"Oh, Daddy, you're not boring Zack with one of your cop stories, are you?"

Jamie entered behind Zack.

"Hi, Zack," she said.

"Hi, Jamie." He stood.

Her well fitted sweater and blue jeans made the blood leave Zack's brain.

"You look wonderful." He glanced at the huge cop sitting opposite him.

"Thank you. You're sweet," she said. "I just threw something on."

"She's been 'throwing' for about two hours now," Jason grinned.

"Oh, Daddy, that's not true!" She giggled and slapped Jason's arm. "Well, I guess we better go. Zack doesn't like to walk into a movie late."

"A man after my own heart," Jason rose. "If you aren't there in time for the trailers, then what's the point?"

"My sentiments exactly," Zack smiled. "We won't be out too late. The movie's over around nine. We may get something to eat afterward, if Jamie wants to. Is that cool?"

"Yeah, that'll be fine. Enjoy yourselves," Jason said.

Zack held Jamie's jacket as she slipped into it.

"See you in a little while," Jamie said and they were out the door.

30

Cigarette smoke cascaded out the Jaguar's window, illuminated by the blinking marquee. A man and woman sat motionless, watching the theater parking lot.

"Where is he?" James Recent asked.

"Coming around the corner now," Angie said.

The construction pickup pulled next to the curb and Zack jumped out, bounding around the bed of the truck to open the door.

"That's sweet." Angie blew a cloud into the windshield.

"I think it's pathetic," James said.

"Ready?" She reached for the door handle.

"No."

He grabbed her arm. "Wait."

"For what?" Angie slumped back into the soft, leather seat. "I found him and proved what I'm capable of so let's take him out."

"Not quite yet." He reached over, snatched her cigarette, took a drag and blew it into her face.

"Are you kidding? There won't be a better time, he's off guard and vulnerable."

James squeezed her arm until she winced. "I said, I'm not ready yet."

"Okay, okay," Angie wrenched out of his grasp and began rubbing it like a third grader with an Indian Rope Burn. "What do you suggest, your majestic, grand high, PooBa?"

James went for her throat digging his long nails into her neck until little beads of blood formed. "I suggest you watch your mouth before you are talking out of a hole in both cheeks."

"Sorry," Angie gasped. Her eyes darted back toward the theater. "What do you suggest?"

He released. "We wait until we can really foul up the entire plan. We wait until we have them right where we want them."

"I wish you would let me in on things," Angie said.

"In due time." He reached over and stroked her cheek, wiping her own blood across her cheek. "They'll involve you, don't worry."

"I certainly hope so." She rubbed her neck.

"They will," James smiled. "Poor baby."

"Don't leave me out of the loop anymore," Angie said. "Please?"

"I'm not, but I also expect you to think for yourself. Come up with a plan."

"Me? A plan? I thought you were going to—"

"Shh, not now, my dear. In due time." He put his finger across her lips. "Relax; let them watch their little movie."

31

The Broadway theatre, a refurbished dinosaur, held the opulence and grandeur of celluloid days long gone. Large pillars blossomed into ornate vine and leaf designs at their crown and framed the entrance. The pink and black color palette screamed 1930's Hollywood.

The marquee lights chased each other around the poster frame reading: *Retro Night - Man's Favorite Sport.* The glass-encased poster was an original. Paula Prentiss's hand touched the smiling face of Rock Hudson as she whispered in his ear. The encounter was highlighted by a mustard-colored background and below the drawings of the faces, it read: *A Howard Hawks production – Man's Favorite Sport – in Technicolor – Music by Henry Mancini.*

"Two, please," Zack extracted his wallet from his back pocket and slid the money through the glass hole.

"Here's your change, enjoy the show," the girl droned. She pursed her lips and popped her bubble gum.

Zack yanked the huge porcelain handle capped in gold and held the door open. They stepped onto plush, freshly vacuumed carpet. Like the runway at the Oscars, a burgundy fleur-de-lis pattern set on a dark gray background stretched ahead of them. A gentleman, in white gloves, tails, and top hat, greeted them.

"Welcome to the Broadway. How are you tonight, Zack?" he said, taking their tickets and tearing them in half.

"Thank you. I'm great, Mr. Duffy. We're really excited to be here," Zack said.

"Well, *we* are excited to have you with us tonight."

Zack leaned in close to Jamie when they were a few feet away from Mr. Duffy.

"He owns the place and lives for these nights. He told me once that this is what Hollywood was all about, 'when going to the movies was an event'."

"I'm impressed that he knows you by name." Jamie playfully tapped Zack's arm.

"I spend a lot of my hard-earned moola here." Zack grinned as they stepped to the concession counter.

"Ahh, the smell of fresh popcorn." He inhaled, tilting his head toward the ceiling and closing his eyes.

He then turned to Jamie, shielding his mouth with one hand as if telling her a secret. "Not like the places that bring it out in big garbage bags and warm it up. Do they really think we don't know?"

"Guess not," Jamie shrugged.

"Mr. Duffy wouldn't hear of it." Zack said. "What do you want to drink?"

"Uh, I'll take a medium raspberry tea," Jamie said, scanning the menu board.

Zack hesitated, "Do you want your own popcorn?"

"No, I'll just share yours, if it's okay," she smiled.

"Certainly," Zack masked his apparent enthusiasm. "My pleasure."

"Oh, thank you, sir," Jamie said.

"Rick." Zack nodded to the dark-haired boy behind the counter. "We'll have a large Diet Pepsi , a medium raspberry tea, and the Bucket-O-Corn."

"Comin' right up. How ya been, Zack?" Rick turned to grab the paper cups with a red, white, and blue logo on the side.

"Doin' good. This is Jamie Watkins. Jamie, Rick Hernandez.

"Hi," Rick waved.

"Hi," Jamie replied.

"Ole' Zack and me go way back. A couple of years now?" Rick asked.

"Yeah." Zack nodded. "Rick started here when he was 14, been here ever since. We can't get rid of the guy." Zack gathered up the tray with the two drinks and the popcorn.

"Hey, the place couldn't function without my expertise," Rick said stepping back from the counter and stretched his arms out. Then he turned to Jamie with a slight bow. "It was nice to meet you, Jamie. And, as always," he paused for effect, "enjoy the show!"

The lights faded and Jamie snuggled in close. Comical moments triggered her touch on his arm. Zack found everything about her intoxicating. He could smell her shampoo, clean and fresh.

He loved sharing the popcorn with her, their hands brushing against each other in the bucket. He laughed at the screen, but his mind was wrapped around her. He noticed every time she shifted in the seat, every time she crossed her legs. He loved to hear her giggle. He would whisper comments throughout and she would snicker and slap him on the bicep.

The night was perfect, peaceful and her company dissolved any nervousness. Zack watched her as she watched the screen and wished that she would turn toward him for a kiss.

When she did look at him, his head snapped back to the front. He was glad for the dark as the blood rushed to his face.

Finally the lights peeked from behind the shell-shaped porcelain fixtures and the credits rolled up the screen.

As the other movie-goers filed out, Zack and Jamie remained until the Motion Picture Association logo came into view. Like clockwork, the cleanup crew entered with brooms in hand and pushing a rolling trash can. Zack stood and smiled at Jamie.

"Ready?" he asked.

"Yeah." She took his arm.

They moved from the auditorium and for the first time exiting the Broadway Theater, Zack had no thought of self-consciousness, pretense, or angst.

"That was great!" Jamie said as they threw their trash away. "Thanks so much."

"I had a good time too," he said. "Thanks for coming with me." He held the door. "Hey, are you hungry?"

"Yeah, a little. In all the excitement today I didn't really have anything since lunch." She paused. "Except for the popcorn."

"All the excitement." He liked that phrase.

———

Later that evening, they strolled up Jamie's sidewalk and as her hand brushed Zack's, with one smooth motion he took hold and she intertwined her fingers in his.

"Thanks again for the movie and supper." She stood facing him and holding both of his hands now. "It was great, Zack." She caught his eye. "I really had fun."

"Yeah, nothin' like a *huge* burger before bed." Zack smiled. "I really had a good time too. Maybe again?"

"I'd like that. Call me tomorrow?" She asked.

"It would be an honor, m'lady." He let go of one hand and raised the other up, bowing before her like royalty in King Arthur's court.

She giggled and curtsied. He turned and walked a few paces and turned again.

"Good night." He backed down the sidewalk.

"Good night," she said.

He watched her open the door and go in, stifling the urge to leap into the air.

In the truck, he sat momentarily watching her house. Zack started the engine and the truck guided itself away from the curb. Her house grew smaller in the rearview mirror. When he turned the corner, he bellowed a war hoop and thrust his arm out the window.

———

The Jaguar pulled to the curb a few houses down from Jamie's and cut the lights. James lit up a cigarette and exhaled the smoke as they watched Zack's truck disappear around the corner.

"So, is the plan coming together in your mind?" He asked.

"Yes." Angie nodded.

"What have you come up with?"

"Simple," she said. "Exploit his vulnerabilities."

"Do you know how you're going to do that?" James took another drag.

"Are you kidding?" She smiled. "He's so insecure, a visit from Milton should do it."

"What if it doesn't?"

"I've got some other ideas." She winked.

"I hope so, I don't want to have to take care of this." He slid his hand up her shoulder and grabbed the nape of her neck squeezing. She let out a yelp and then snarled.

"You can't fail on this one." He shot her a demonic grin.

She pawed at his hand.

"Stop it!" Angie growled. "You're hurting me."

"Am I?" James Recent relaxed his grip and exhaled. He held the cigarette out in front of him. "Ya know, I really like these things."

32

Expectation overwhelmed John and Zack as they scrutinized the gleaming rows. Zack's mind raced. He had been chased, beaten up, pushed into bushes, had seen people who weren't there, been startled, surprised and scared. He had a classmate jump out of a window, was now possessing insight into the spiritual realm with dead girls sitting on fallen trees, had an attempt made on his life, and now a potential girlfriend. It was time to dump Rudabaker's truck and buy a vehicle of his own!

"How you boys doin' today?" The salesman's southern drawl boomed as he shuffled toward them. The rustle of his polyester pants seemed to fill the car lot.

"Big Mike's the name, and makin' folks happy is the game!" Mike's plump hand shot out of a tweed sleeve. He pumped Zack's arm until it felt numb. "What can I do ya for?"

"Well, I was looking for a vehicle." Zack stifled the urge to answer back in a southern drawl.

"Two door?"

"Well, I, uh—"

"Four door? Sports car? Truck?"

"Yeah—"

"Sporty model? Convertible? We have a variety of colors and price ranges." Mike didn't take a breath. "I'm sure we can fix ya up proper."

"Well, I was sort of looking at these trucks over here," Zack said pointing to a row.

"Good choice, good choice." Mike slapped Zack on the shoulder. "I'm not thinkin' you'd fit in one of them little European jobs anyway. You'a big boy!"

Mike's beer belly rippled as he cackled, the single black button on his tweed coat would explode if he didn't calm down.

Zack glanced down at the zipper on Mike's candy apple red slacks; he couldn't help but notice. It was just as stressed, the metal tangs barely interlocked and Zack wanted a place to run if they gave way.

"Now, I got a nice model over here." Mike grabbed Zack by the elbow and guided him toward a midnight blue Ford.

"Now, she needs a little TLC, but she runs good and the price," Mike clucked his tongue and pointed his finger toward Zack like a gun "is just right."

Zack opened the driver's door and poked his head in. "Mileage seems a little high—"

"Oh, she's just getting her second wind." Mike slapped him on the back nearly knocking him into the front seat. "Why this engine ain't good-n-broke in yet." Mike winked at John.

Zack stood and closed the door looking at the sticker on the window.

"Well, the price *is* a little high," he said, "and there are a few dings here and there." He squatted and closed one eye, looking down the bed of the truck.

"Character," Mike slapped the side of the truck. "A little Bondo and it'll be smooth as a baby's bottom!"

After a few minutes of haggling and Mike making repeated trips in and out of his tiny, glass enclosed hut, the price stuck.

"Course, you'll have to call your dad," Big Mike said. "We'll need his John Hancock that it's okay for me to sell this baby to a minor—"

"Already on his way," Zack smiled.

And the deal was done.

The phrase "We can fix that for ya" was forever imbedded in Zack's brain as he waved goodbye to Big Mike and drove off the lot in a "previously owned," $1200 truck. John followed in his old beater.

A few miles later, John peeled off toward home squealing his tires and giving Zack a thumbs up out the window.

Zack pulled up in front of Jamie's house holding the horn down. He jumped out, came around to the passenger side and leaned against the truck with his arms crossed over his large chest, one foot crossed in front of the other on the sidewalk. James Dean wouldn't have looked cooler.

Jamie opened the door, hair mussed and wearing a worn Iowa State University sweatshirt over fitted blue jeans. She padded onto the sidewalk, her brightly painted toenails accenting her bare feet.

"What's this?" she asked, her eyes wide and a smile spreading across her face.

"Like it?" Zack asked.

"Yeah, it's great!" She stepped closer and ran her hand along the body of the truck.

"I just bought it."

"Wow!" She opened the passenger door and peered in.

"Want a ride?" Zack asked.

"Of course. I'll tell my mom I'm going and get some shoes on."

Zack looked down at her feet. "You don't have to wear shoes on my account." He grinned.

"Oh, a foot man, huh?" She looked back over her shoulder and smiled.

Zack blushed, remembering Big Mike's words, "You gonna love that bench seat!"

Zack agreed as Jamie slid in next to him.

33

Zack remembered the words on the note the man had given him, *Thursday next*, as he drove to Golden, forty-five minutes away. He glanced in his rear view mirror. Jeff Tucker was right behind him at every stop light and curve.

The lights on the Coors brewery illuminated the clouded sky. Coors, a city unto itself, was nestled in the foothills near Clear Creek Canyon. Zack rolled down his window and inhaled the smell of the hops and barley cooking that saturated the air. The reflections of the lights cascaded down Zack's windshield and the slow, rhythmic sound of his tires rolling over the expansion joints nearly lulled him to sleep.

Capadocia Parkway was a well-lit throughway that wound for several miles into the foothills and up into a heavily wooded area departing Golden.

Zack's headlights finally illuminated large brick pillars supporting a black, wrought iron arch across an entrance. Ornate iron gates opened automatically as Zack pulled under the arch. He glanced at the enormous copper numbers free standing on the manicured lawn outside the gate. It read *2503*.

The broad, tree-lined blacktop reminded Zack of Cherrywood Country Club and he found himself watching for golf carts to come darting across in front of him. His truck, followed by Jeff's car wound up the driveway finally emptying into a massive parking lot.

Zack stopped at a tiny brick shack which he supposed held a guard and stared at his own reflection in the window. He leaned forward in the truck and then back trying to see anyone.

No sign of activity.

He checked the rearview mirror then the side mirror. No movement. He poked his head out the driver's window and looked up. No guard towers with high-powered rifles. He looked back at his dad, shot his hands out the window in a "who knows?" gesture and hit the gas.

They drove down a frontage road flanking the parking lot and Zack parked in the space marked *Visitors* in front of the building. Jeff held back a few rows with the car idling.

Spotlights illuminated three, thick metal flagpoles securing the Colorado state flag, a flag that bore a logo that read: *Gideon Manufacturing*, and the American flag. They rustled gently in the breeze as Zack peered through the windshield. Like the bow of a great ship, a semi-circle of glass windows overshadowed him. Above them were mounted gold letters that gleamed like a beacon in the night sky, *Gideon*.

Zack got out of the truck and shut the door. The sound echoed against the emptiness of the parking lot with only a few cars dotting the pavement. He looked up at the large building and then back at his dad and then walked to Jeff's open window.

"Be careful, son, and if you need me, I'll be right here. You've got your cell phone."

"Right here." Zack tapped his pants pocket. "Are you sure you want to hang around? I'll be all right. I can call if—"

"Just until we see," Jeff said.

Zack turned and walked toward the building noting the faint light shining from inside a few of the smoked windows.

A cat meowed, an eerie screeching cry, like it was being tortured in a Bella Lugosi movie. He pulled on the glass double doors and they swung effortlessly toward him. He stepped through another set of interior doors and onto a thick lobby mat bearing the seal of Gideon. Zack stood momentarily scanning the vast lobby. An oak reception enclosure with a black marble counter capping it stood to his right. He peeked over the counter watching the deserted switchboard blink red and green lights like a mini Christmas festival. He noted the high-end computer and several small television monitors changing scenes in sequence as closed circuit cameras scanned the hallways and parking lot. He saw Jeff's car, still and alone in the night and was relieved that his dad had stayed.

The *In* basket was empty, while the *Out* basket was arranged in neat, paper clipped piles, no doubt waiting for the boy from the mail room to scurry past. Zack turned the sign-in book around and ran his finger down the list. Nothing unusual. The book rested next to a row of walkie-talkies with tiny red lights blinking off and on as they recharged in their cradles. A small banker's lamp with a dimly lit bulb burned on top of the counter while its twin across the desk was dark. Around the perimeter of the large lobby, the floor's highly polished marble edges framed an island of plush carpet.

Like a flying saucer invasion, enormous round lights, with muted wattage, loomed overhead while a three tiered balcony ascended to the ceiling of glass and steel, framing the moon and stars like a giant movie screen. Polished oak posts topped with shiny brass spheres provided entrance to zigzagging staircases which accessed each balcony.

Large built-in bookcases, with crown molding, housed volume after volume of expensive-looking leather-bound books. In between the shelves were solid double doors with brass kick plates and fancy name placards labeling meeting and conference suites. Dark hallways led to destinations unknown, and plants and trees grew like a jungle out of large pots.

Small round tables spotted the lobby edged by tufted leather chairs. A rock fountain gurgled in the corner next to a wall donning numerous photos, awards, and plaques. Zack squinted seeing phrases like "In Honor of," "In Recognition for," and "In Good Standing" as he stepped forward.

"Does it meet your expectations?"

Zack's heart skipped.

34

"Oh, God! You scared the crap out of me." Zack clutched his chest. "Yes, very much." He took a deep breath. "This is really a nice building."

"Why don't you go out and tell your dad that he can come in and wait in the lobby? The temperature is dropping and there is no need for him to sit there with the car running." The man smiled.

"Oh, well, I—"

"It's all right, Zack." The man began fastening his dark hair back into a ponytail. "I told you to bring anyone with you. If you were my son, I would feel the same way."

Zack went back out the set of double doors to the car.

"Hey, Dad, the guy said you could come inside and wait in the lobby if you want to."

"So much for covert operations, huh?" Jeff shrugged. "We wouldn't make very good spies." He grinned as he shut off the car and climbed out.

"Hello, Mr. Tucker," the man stuck out his hand as they walked back into the foyer.

His muscular hand swallowed Jeff's and his large bicep rippled under a white T-shirt. "I'm John M. Abbeer, pleased to make your acquaintance."

"Jeff, please. Thank you, you also," Jeff shook his hand.

"Feel free to accompany us," Mr. Abbeer pointed toward a hallway.

"No, that's all right. I'll wait here in the lobby. I'm a little embarrassed."

"Nonsense. I told Zack I would feel the same way. That door," he pointed across the lobby, "leads into a hallway and a well-equipped break room with fresh coffee. We keep the pot brewing 24-7. Help yourself. We're going upstairs. We won't be long."

"Thanks, I think I *would* like a cup." Jeff walked toward the door and disappeared down the hallway.

"We've been at this location for about three years now," Mr. Abbeer said as he turned to Zack. "It affords us much more space than our last place. This building alone has over three million square feet of manufacturing space."

Mr. Abbeer waved his hand around the room. "The tour guides tell people that it's about half the size of the Pentagon. We've got recreational facilities, including a golf course and pool. Meeting areas, picnic areas for the employees, and a heavily wooded buffer zone separates us from the rest of Golden."

"An entity unto yourselves," Zack said.

"Exactly, and all of this set on a 1500-acre complex which suits our purposes well."

"Wow! I would say so." Zack glanced around. "And what purpose is that?"

"Let's go to my office, shall we?" Mr. Abbeer directed him.

Zack followed him down a hallway lined with windows exposing unoccupied offices. Through a doorway they entered a glass-enclosed walkway like an enormous gerbil tube, spanning a factory floor.

"This area runs only five days a week from 6 a.m. to 8 p.m. They're getting ready to close down in a little while."

Mr. Abbeer pointed to metal presses and kilns burning in the distance. Scattered workers roamed the floor bringing another day in the trenches to a close.

"What do you manufacture?" Zack tried again.

Mr. Abbeer smiled, but didn't answer.

The tube deposited them into a small atrium. Mr. Abbeer walked to an ornately engraved elevator with swirls of gold leaves and vines and pushed the illuminated button. They stepped in and Zack felt gravity pull on his stomach as they ascended to the 11th floor.

A marble runway led into a foyer connecting several short hallways, like spokes on a wheel. They walked onto plush carpeting and down a wide, burled wood corridor that dead-ended with a massive set of quarter-sawn oak doors.

Gold leaf letters spelled "J.M. Abbeer."

Mr. Abbeer pushed open the doors.

"Have a seat." He motioned to a high backed, leather chair.

"Impressive." Zack glanced around Mr. Abbeer's office.

Ebony library shelves stretched floor to ceiling on two of the walls. A winding wrought iron staircase serviced a matching catwalk that accessed more shelves of leather bound volumes.

An ornate bar grew out of one corner and in front of it, stood a Louis XIV pool table that Zack remembered from a magazine that his dad had shown him once.

Opposite him, affixed to the wall, was a collage of weaponry swords, knives and shields of varying sizes, shapes and eras.

"How high's the ceiling in here?" Zack looked up.

"About thirty-five feet," Mr. Abbeer said.

"Holy crap!" Zack said. "And the battle scene painted—"

"Like it?" Mr. Abbeer followed Zack's gaze to the ceiling.

"Yeah," Zack said. "Alexander the Great and the Battle of Granicus."

"You know it?"

"I have a model of it in the basement of my house."

"Really?" Mr. Abbeer said.

"1/35th scale. It's one of my favorites in history. My friend, John and I work on it almost every week. Alexander stepped ashore with his 35,000 Macedonian warriors and about 7,600 Greeks thrown in for good measure; and declared that all of Asia would be won by his spear—"

"You *do* know it," Mr. Abbeer said.

"He clashed with King Darius III at the river Granicus, near Troy, of Trojan Horse fame." Zack glanced at Mr. Abbeer then back to the ceiling and continued. "Alexander defeated an enemy that numbered 40,000 and according to legend—"

"Only lost 110 men," Mr. Abbeer finished his sentence.

"That's right," Zack looked at Mr. Abbeer. "This is weird that you have the same battle—"

"It's a constant reminder to me—"

"Of what?" Zack asked.

"Battles are won through strategy."

"Yes, they are," Zack said.

"And casualties can be kept to a minimum, don't you agree?" Mr. Abbeer asked.

"I guess so."

"Zack, let me get to the point of why you are here." Mr. Abbeer leaned against the front of his massive, hand carved oak, desk. "As I told your dad, I am John Michael Abbeer. Around here, everyone calls me, Mick. My brother, Nathaniel, and I own this company, and that's the reason I have asked you here tonight." He paused. "I want you to come work for us."

"I'm sorry?" Zack looked back at him and then scooted forward in the chair.

"Zack, we are looking for quality people who display good character." Mick held up one finger at a time to emphasize each point. "We value excellent moral fiber and people who are not afraid to tackle a challenge. I need people who work well when faced by adversity, able-bodied men and women who are not easily discouraged." Mick smiled. "I've had my eye on you for a while now."

"Is that why—"

"We recruit only the best of the best," Mick continued. "Interested?"

Zack sat and stared at him for a moment.

"Well, I don't know what to say. How do you know that I'd fit here- And about my character? Well, I do like to think of myself as loyal, but… What do you make here?"

"All of this for a job interview, right?" Mick smiled. "You need us, Zack. And we certainly need you." He paused. "Now, here's the deal..."

Mick walked to a tidy bar and placed two glasses on top. The ice clinked as it hit the bottom of the glasses.

"Juice? Soda?" He asked.

"Orange juice, maybe?" Zack said. "Thanks."

"Yes. A favorite of mine as well."

Mick walked back around the bar and handed Zack the glass and a small can of orange juice.

"I will start you at a salary that will more than support you and your dad. He wouldn't need to kill himself all night long at the bottling plant—"

"How do you know?"

"He could spend more time tying flies and hunting, or planning to open his business." Mick smiled. "That's his dream anyway, right?"

Zack stared at him. "Yes."

" Rocky Mountain Bait and Tackle?" Mick shrugged. "I do extensive background checks on those I'm considering."

Mick poured juice into his glass and took a sip. "Zack, I hand-pick my people." He sat the glass on a coaster on his desk and leaned back against the front. "We don't advertise in the want ads. Our positions are by invitation only, and most of our employees are lifers, retiring with a substantial pension." He took another sip. "We take care of our own."

Mick stepped to a cabinet and pulled out several catalogs, laying them on Zack's lap.

"Look through these for a few minutes. I've been summoned to the manufacturing floor; I'll return shortly."

Zack glanced around. No page over an intercom, no cell phone ring, no beeper.

35

Zack thumbed through the first catalog of industrial, construction and automotive hand tools. The second was more a manual than a catalog. Bound in leather with the medieval crest of Gideon on the front, it caused Zack's palms to sweat. Glossy page after glossy page of armor, swords and medieval axes gave way to daggers, sabers and claymores. His heart raced the further he moved into the battle armament.

Zack's fascination with history bordered on obsession at times and in his hands he held the greatest visual representation of the past. Manufacturing framing hammers was one thing, but manufacturing swords was quite another.

"Hey, Mick?" The door opened and a blonde man poked his head in. "Oh, sorry. Seen Mick?"

"Uh, he said he was called to the manufacturing floor?" Zack shrugged.

"Cool. I'm Nathaniel, Mick's brother." He crossed the room with his hand outstretched. "You must be Zack."

This gene pool is well maintained, same blue eyes and extremely muscular forearms and biceps.

"So, did Mick give you the pitch?"

"He did." Zack nodded.

"Hey, Nate?" A young brunette girl knocked on the door.

"Hey, Dess," Nathaniel said. "What's up?"

"Calver says Number 8 is acting up again and needs you to take a look and see if it needs an overhaul."

"Again?"

"Hey, I'm just the messenger." She shrugged.

"Zack." Nathaniel turned back toward him. "This is Tredessa Huntington, she works the weaponry manufacturing floor."

Zack brightened. "Really? That's so cool." He stood and shook her hand nearly spilling the catalogs.

"Yeah," Tredessa said. "Those blades would be dull as butter knives without me." She smiled.

"Man, that would be a great place—"

"It's a lot of fun," Tredessa said. "Sorry, though, gotta go. I just came up to give Nate the bad news." She looked at Nathaniel.

"Well, thanks a bunch," Nathaniel said. "A ten thousand dollar message."

"Hey, what can I say. Merry Christmas. Nice to have met you, Zeek—"

"Zack."

"Sorry. Zack. See you around?"

"Maybe so," Zack said as she whisked out of the office.

"Tell Calver I'll be down in a few minutes," Nathaniel called to Tredessa's back. "So, Zack, sounds too good to be true, right?"

"Well… Yeah."

"The fact that you're even sitting in this office indicates that you've got what we're looking for." He paused. "And Mick doesn't blow smoke."

"Well, well, little brother." Mr. Abbeer reentered the office.

"Hey, Mick. Did you check on press number 16? Sam said it's giving him fits."

"Yes. I sent Del down to look at it. He should be on it now."

"Okay," Nathaniel said. "And Dess just told me Number 8 is out and Calver is having a fit and needs a new—"

"Which will cost me twelve thousand dollars," Mr. Abbeer said.

"Ten" Nathaniel said.

"Still," Mr. Abbeer shrugged. "Lot of money, but I guess that cowboy knows best."

"And Calver knows that we can't afford for the machine that hones the blades to go out—"

"Give Calver what he wants," Mr. Abbeer turned toward Zack. "And now you've been introduced to the black sheep of the family?"

"Yes, we were just getting acquainted," Zack grinned.

"Not hardly," Nathaniel said. "And don't believe a word of it, Zack. Mick thinks all musicians are bums and never get any work done. Which, in my case, isn't true." He winked.

"What do you play?" Zack asked.

"Little bit of everything, mostly brass and woodwinds. We've got a group that plays on Saturday nights at a club here in town. The Jazz Emporium over on 6th?"

"I've driven past," Zack said. "Never been inside."

"We should remedy that. Bring a date. Great atmosphere and a killer T-bone steak," Nathaniel said.

"Man, I love jazz," Zack said.

"We've got a gig Saturday. You should pop on over and hear me play trumpet. My treat."

"Your treat?" Mr. Abbeer asked. "There's no cover charge. Everyone gets in free, you musical bum. I guess that would make *you* a cheap date, Zack."

"Yeah, whatever," Nathaniel smiled. "Better go down and keep Calver happy. Nice to finally meet you, Zack. I hope you find a home here."

Nathaniel walked to the door.

"Thanks, you too." Zack paused. "I mean, to meet you."

"Zack," Mr. Abbeer started again. "Why don't you think about all of this for the next couple of days, say, until Monday? Talk it over with your dad and see what he thinks."

Mr. Abbeer handed him a business card. "That's my private number. Have your dad call me if he has any questions. I want you to be at peace with your decision. Talk to some of our employees. Get a lay of the land. I know that you are right for Gideon." He paused staring at Zack. "Hey, if you don't like it, you can always quit, right?"

"Thank you, Mr. Abbeer. I'll certainly think about it." Zack rose and offered his hand.

"Everyone calls me Mick." He shook Zack's hand. "And Nathaniel is, Nate. Anything we can do to alleviate any angst, let me know."

"Could I take the catalogs? To show my dad?"

"Certainly."

"Even the leather—"

"Most certainly," Mr. Abbeer said.

He showed Zack back through the maze to the lobby.

Jeff sat reading a manufacturing magazine with a steaming cup of coffee at his elbow.

"If you wouldn't mind showing yourselves out, I have some pressing matters. Thank you for taking the time to come and meet with me and I will look forward to speaking with you again on Monday, either way." Mick shook Jeff's hand as he rose.

"Mr. Tucker, good day to you, sir. You have a fine son; he is a testament to you rearing him alone." He smiled.

"Thank you," Jeff put his hand on Zack's shoulder. "I'm proud of him."

"I'll be in touch, Zack." Mick turned and disappeared down the hallway.

"How'd it go?" Jeff asked.

"Fine," Zack paused. "Sort of strange though."

"What do you mean?"

"I didn't tell him that you raised me alone." Zack shrugged. "Who knows? He offered me a job."

"Really?"

"Yeah, can you believe it?" Zack asked. "Weird, huh?"

"A little eccentric, I'd say," Jeff said as they pushed toward the doors, "but everyone does things differently I guess."

They both stopped.

Hundreds of cars occupied the parking lot.

"What the…" Jeff said.

Zack looked at Jeff and shrugged. Jeff nodded in agreement. They drove past the guard station and a white-gloved guard saluted. Zack returned the wave out of reflex.

36

Milton Drago opened his eyes and brushed the greasy hair off his face. He stared at the lump of clothing with the man inside, lying next to him. The old duffer was passed out stone-cold drunk. His once-exquisite suit, from a bygone era, was caked with mud, dried blood and stank of urine.

The Wall Street financial wizard, Milton shook his head.

The bum's scraggly, matted beard clung to filth and leftover food. His meshed locks of gray hair protruded from under a soiled red stocking cap. His head rested in a puddle of his own milky, yellow vomit.

Milton hadn't remembered the man being there when he found the semi-dry piece of cardboard beneath the overpass, but now he snuggled into Milton's territory. Milton instinctively glanced at his wrist. The twenty dollars he had gotten for his watch at the pawn shop hadn't lasted long. He squinted. The bank clock was two blocks away, but he could make it out, *2 a.m.*

Milton sat up and stretched sore muscles and rubbed the circulation back into his legs. He rolled his head to one side and then the other, trying to alleviate the tension in his neck. A light mist magnified his depression. The traffic overhead a few hours before had served as white noise to dissipate the night sounds but now it was annoying.

He rolled over to one knee and looked at the snoring heap, then searched the man's jacket. He slid his hands into the man's pants pockets until his fingers touched soft, wet paper. Milton gagged and pushed the thought out of mind. He extracted three dollars.

"Too bad, you old fart," he whispered, his mind reverting back to the childhood taunting of his sisters. Finders keepers.

He stood up and slipped the money into his jeans and looked down at the old bum.

It's your own fault.

—

The 55-gallon drum burned a few yards away.

"How's it going?" Milton moved into the firelight.

"That's a pretty friggin' stupid question." The unshaven face recoiled. "How'd you think it's going? I'm standing here trying to keep from bein' frostbit and warming my hands over a cauldron of trash! I'd say we was walkin' in tall cotton now, boy!" The man swore.

Milton didn't answer; he knew it wasn't that cold out. He put his hands over the heat as a tall black man approached.

"Jess." The black man nodded to the unshaven face.

"Mason," the man replied.

"I found some day-ole stuff yesterday morning in back of the bakery on 8th," Mason said. "It was decent, a few mouse turds, but—"

"Beggars can't be choosers!" Jess and Mason both laughed.

"You reckon they might put it out again this morning?" Jess asked.

"Maybe." Mason smiled showing several missing teeth and those that hung on were black with decay. "They start baking around four. That's when they throw out the old stuff."

"Tell anyone else?"

"Naw," Mason said. "Thought maybe just you and me would go. No one's goin' to bother us."

"Oh, I don't think nobody would have a mind to try and take it away from me." Jess produced a switchblade from his coat pocket.

Milton looked at it and then looked down at the ground.

"Yeah, that's right, boy, you better look away," Jess spat. "You can bet I've used this before, and I'm not afraid to use it now!" He swiped at Milton, who shrank back.

Jess and Mason cackled.

"What you out here for anyway, you pissant?" Jess leaned in close to Milton. "What's the matter? Daddy cruel to ya and you thought, 'what the heck, I'll just go live on the streets?'"

"Shut up!" Milton snapped.

Jess taunted. "I'm a big boy now; I can take care of myself!" He paused and brushed up against Milton. "Or maybe your daddy loved you a little too much, is that it, cutie?"

"Get off me, you freak!" Milton pushed him away.

Jess swore again and then laughed. "You don't know life. A little skinny runt like you won't last long out here without your mama's teet to suck on, believe me." Jess coughed up phlegm and spat. "I'm a friendly dude—."

"You got that right," Mason chimed in.

"Compared to most round here." Jess continued. "If you're lucky, you'll only get beat up and robbed." He smiled. "It's amazing what one human being can do to another."

Jess folded the blade and shoved it back into his pocket. With one smooth motion he came out with a flask, unscrewed the lid, and took a swig. He passed it to Mason who gulped heavily then handed it back to Jess.

"You want some?" He tipped it toward Milton.

"No, thanks." Milton shook his head.

"Ain't man enough yet, huh?" Jess said, taking another pull.

"I could drink you under the table." Milton muttered.

"What's that, boy?" Jess cupped his hand over his ear.

"Nothin'."

"He just don't know where those lips of yours have been." Mason hit Jess in the shoulder and laughed.

"You got that right," Jess said taking another swig and then wiggled his tongue like a snake. "Maybe this boy ain't so stupid after all." He laughed again.

The clip clop of the high heels on the sidewalk interrupted the banter.

The lady strutted over to the fire.

"Hello, boys," she said.

"Hellooo, Angie," Jess's eyes widened and he wiped his mouth with his sleeve.

"What's happening?" Angie purred.

"Looks like *you're* happening." Mason said looking her up and down.

"And who might this fresh one be?" She ignored the remark and eyed Milton from head to toe.

"Somethin' the cat choked up!" Jess laughed.

"Now, I doubt that." She smiled.

"What are you up to tonight?" Mason asked.

"Oh, I thought I would take a stroll while my chauffeur was washing the limo. Then it's back to decorate the country house," she said with a wink.

"Yeah, I thought I'd just relax here in the sauna until my broker calls about those stock options." Jess laughed.

Milton stood expressionless.

"How's Puffinking getting along?" Mason asked.

"Oh, they're fine," she said. "They've gone dancing some tonight." She paused. "Well, just stopped by for a minute. Guess I better get back to work, can't leave Puffinking alone too long."

Angie got a few paces away and turned back around. All three men stared at her. She pointed to Milton and beckoned with her finger in a *come hither* motion.

He looked surprised and pointed his finger at his own chest. "Me?"

She nodded and he slowly walked toward her. Jess and Mason looked at each other as she slipped her arm into Milton's.

"Come with me, Milton," Angie said.

"How did you know my name?"

She put her finger to his lips and they strolled down the street, disappearing into a doorway.

37

Milton lay on the lumpy mattress. A 40-watt bulb cast irregular shadows on the cracked plaster walls. The sheets reeked of cigarette smoke masked by perfume. Milton glanced at the clock radio screwed to the pressboard nightstand. *3:33 a.m.*

The bare bulb illuminated the red heart and pious smile of the plastic framed Sacred Heart of Jesus; he stared straight at Milton.

A pressed back chair, with a broken leg, stood propped against the wall as if it had no missing appendage. Milton's filthy pants lay in a wad on the chair; his once-white pockets, now black, stuck out like ears.

Angie sat up in bed, the sheets falling off her as she rose. She walked toward the bathroom, the curves of her body silhouetted against the backdrop of the light.

"Interesting tattoo," Milton said, watching her naked back.

"Puffinking," she said and closed the door slightly.

"Puffinking?" Milton asked, propped on one elbow. "Hey, it's sorta like a painting I did on my wall; it's not finished yet, but...."

The little brick house, with the broken wood slats on the porch, seemed so long ago. The brick pillars, out front, supporting the overhang and the aroma of fresh baked cookies wafted into his mind. His mom stood on the porch with her arms open toward him and tears of joy seeping onto her aged cheeks.

Milton lay back on the stale pillow and closed his eyes. He knew that even though this dump had sporadic hot and cold water pressure, he could never again take a shower for granted.

He heard the toilet flush and opened his eyes, scanning the dingy room.

"Ya know, I have something like your tattoo painted on my wall at home," Milton started again. "Mine doesn't have a snake, though. Might not be a bad idea to add one." A sliver of light shone out the partially closed bathroom door.

"Hey, Angie, you want to get something to eat? If you could buy me something, I'm sure I could pay you back later."

No answer.

"Angie? I'm starved. I haven't eaten anything decent for a while," he called again.

He gathered his jeans, put them on, and walked toward the light. He pushed the door open and peered into the windowless little room.

"Angie?"

He saw the swirl of the water as it filled the filthy toilet. The showerhead, that just a few hours before had provided him relief from his filth, dripped incessantly. He smelled the mold and saw his own muddled reflection in the cracked mirror. He quickly looked behind the door as if playing hide and seek.

No Angie.

38

The following Wednesday, Zack turned into the parking lot and pulled into the third row. Through the double set of doors, he approached Ms. Gibson, the Gideon receptionist.

"Hello, I'm Zack Tucker. I'm here to fill out paperwork and go through orientation?"

"Hello, Zack." She scanned an appointment book.

"Yes, here we are. Please have a seat and I'll call Mr. Pinkerton in Human Resources."

She pushed a few buttons on her telephone console.

"Mel, a Zack Tucker to see you."

Zack thumbed through a magazine noting her monotony: "Gideon Manufacturing, how may I direct your call?" and "Gideon Manufacturing, please hold."

A squat, five-foot, bald man with an inordinate amount of nose hair padded through a side door.

"Mr. Tucker, I presume," his pudgy hand shot up to meet Zack's.

"Yes, sir." He paused. "Zack Tucker."

"Nice to meet you, Mr. Zack Tucker." He grinned and his cheeks looked packed full of nuts.

"I am Mr. Mel Pinkerton." He puffed through his nose hair and seemed to whistle as he spoke. "Welcome to Gideon." Mel turned and walked away. "Let's go to my office. Where else would we go, right?"

Like Milton's mom, Zack wondered if he was a part of this conversation, as Mel muttered along, but he followed him anyway.

"You do want to get paid, am I right, or am I right?" Mel cackled then turned to the receptionist. "Ms. Gibson, hold my calls."

He grabbed the handle of the door he had come through earlier and swung it wide. He turned toward Zack and wrinkled his nose. "I just love saying that..."

Zack followed him through the side door and down a bright corridor to a carpeted, compact office that looked like a landfill of paperwork. He surveyed wall after wall of shelves piled high with books, folders and paperwork that hadn't been straightened for months or maybe even years; not a filing cabinet in sight.

Mel plopped down behind a low desk and shuffled through a few folders before finding the proper forms. He shoved aside a couple of stacks like Moses parting the Red Sea and smiled up at Zack.

"Please sit down, Mr. Zack Tucker."

Zack turned to look at the two chairs in front of Mel's desk that were piled with more folders, books and papers.

"Oh, just move them aside," Mel looked back down and thumbed through the forms.

"Throw 'em… on the floor. Well, I don't really mean 'throw'; *place them* is more like it. Well, you know what I mean."

Zack picked up a pile, placed it beside the chair, and scooted some books to the back, finally resting on the edge of the seat.

Mel cleared a place on the front of his desk. "Scoot a little closer, Mr. Zack Tucker. Here's a pen." Mel handed him one.

Form after form. W dash this and 10 dash that. Line after line of history and next of kin. The pen spit Zack's signature numerous times on photocopied lines. Mel watched Zack from across the desk, puffing through his nose hair and whistling while he breathed. Finally Zack signed the last sheet and handed it back to Mel.

"That'll do ya."

Mel snatched a pair of reading glasses and perused the documents. He took a few sheets and tossed them onto a pile of disheveled papers.

"Don't need those." He stapled a few of the sheets and took a rubber stamp to another few. With a whump, whump, he hit the pages, scribbling furiously. He licked his thumb and pushed the pages back until he saw the pink sheet.

"Oh yes, here we are. Medical history." Mel looked up at Zack through the bifocals he had perched on the tip of his nose.

Zack was back in fourth grade at Fillmore Elementary.

"Zack, has your mother or father ever had chicken pox?"

"I. Uh. Don't know. I think my dad has."

"Well, I certainly hope he has because if not, he's going to get them." The white uniformed school nurse turned and looked into his red-dotted face.

"I'm surprised that your mother didn't take you in for a shot."

"He doesn't have a mom." The blond girl, clad in a plaid skirt, sat on a large wooden chair across the room, swinging her crossed legs back and forth, back and forth.

"Angie," the nurse said. "Be quiet now."

"Well, it's true," Angie insisted. "His mom ran off."

Zack's ten-year-old eyes filled with tears.

"Now Angie, that's enough." the nurse said. "What are you waiting here for anyway?"

Angie smiled and pointed at Zack. "I'm waiting for him."

She slid off the chair and walked to the door of the nurse's office, swinging her skirt. She paused in the doorway and grinned.

"Be seeing ya around, Zacko Packo…"

"Mr. Tucker?" Mel's words brought Zack back to the office.

"Uh, no, sir. My mom hasn't lived with us since I was very young and I don't know her medical history."

Mel paused. "I see. Well, these are just standard questions anyway; who pays attention to these files, right?" He waved off his own question.

"We'll take care of that later." He laid the papers on the stack and they slid back onto the desk.

"Everything else looks good," Mel said. "How 'bout the 95-cent tour, Mr. Zack Tucker?"

"Yeah, that would be great." Zack rubbed his eyes.

39

Kevin Bauer sat on the couch with a phone in one hand and the remote control for the plasma television in the other.

He stared at the screen, repetitively squeezing the channel button listening to Stacey drone on about something she was pissed about.

Daddy Dearest and third wife, Karen, were gone to host yet another benefit dinner: Save the whales, save the rainforest, save the ozone, save the freakin' kitty cat down the street. Karen didn't care; it was an excuse to slink around in a low-cut gown, spend the lion's share of Kevin's inheritance and show off her diamonds to the Saturday morning spa buddies, that not only worshiped the ground her stiletto heels touched, but the allowance that her Sugar Daddy paid her.

Daddy Dearest and Mommy Dearest.

Kevin shook his head as he watched the guy yell at him from the screen about some new enzyme that would get blood out of carpeting.

Thanks for the hint in case I ever murder somebody.

Mommy Dearest.

Kevin scoffed.

Only ten years older than me.

It wasn't that Karen resembled Joan Crawford, that relic of an actress in that old movie, but he *would* vote her most likely to beat him with a clothes hanger, given half a chance.

What a gold digger.

Kevin glanced around the room. Every light in the house was on.

So what? If Daddy Dearest could buy Karen the latest model Beemer then he could fork over the dough to keep his son from reliving the cemetery experience.

"Yeah, Fryberg said it had to be in tomorrow," Kevin said into the phone.

"No, Stacey, I don't have it done yet." He paused. "I was busy, okay?"

Another pause.

"No, not with that Angie girl." He switched TV channels. "Will you get off my case about her?"

He buzzed past one of the home shopping networks.

"I'm not going to discuss this with you right now. Later." He switched off the phone and threw it on the couch beside him.

"Who watches this infomercial crap?" He switched again.

A baby cried.

Kevin muted the television.

Only the distant hum of clothes in the dryer.

He un-muted and pressed the channel button again.

Gilligan's Island reruns.

The baby wailed.

"What the-?"

He pressed the mute again. A few seconds later the cry came and another answered.

Two babies?

He slowly got up from the couch and parted the curtains.

Only darkness.

His own muddled face stared back from the window pane.

Kevin cupped his hands around his eyes and pressed his face against the glass.

Shadows danced across the lawn and it cried again; he recoiled.

The cemetery had marred him for life, but he knew his only course was to switch off the lamp.

The TV automatically un-muted in time for Ginger to scream at the sight of a headhunter and Kevin jumped, knocking the lamp onto the floor.

He grabbed the remote, switched the television off, and threw the remote back on the couch only to see it careen off a pillow and thump onto the floor.

Kevin cursed.

He turned back to the window.

Still too much light.

Still too much glare.

The cry came again, low, hungry, waiting to be fed.

Kevin rubbed his eyes.

Neighbors?

Several acres away and besides, that old hag didn't have any kids left at home and no grandkid in their right mind would visit her.

Kevin scanned the darkness.

It wailed.

It yearned for him.

It wanted to possess him, to drive him mad.

Kevin cursed again.

Get a hold of yourself, Bauer, you're not some wuss. Be a man, turn out the lights and get a good look.

He hesitated.

Go ahead, turn them out.

He switched off the recessed lighting around the parameter of the large family room, then the hallway and the kitchen. One by one, the illuminated blanket of safety began to unfurl until finally, with one last flip of a switch, Kevin stood vulnerable in the blackness.

He stepped to the window and looked across the lawn.

That was better, no glare and…

It stared back at him.

Kevin's arm pits moistened and his head pounded. Terror rose from the depths of his stomach, up his throat, ready to explode out his mouth in either that hot dog he had for dinner or a scream.

"Oh, God," Kevin whispered. "She's come for me."

Kevin watched her standing on the lawn beside the great oak that held the tire swing of his childhood. The giant limb held the swing until his mom bought Betty.

"Betty," Kevin said.

He swallowed the terror.

"That stinkin' Betty Boop." The possibility of a scream came out in a giggle.

That stupid Grecian statue that he had nick named, Betty Boop, stood near their in-ground pool.

He exhaled.

Betty moved.

Kevin gasped.

No she didn't! Did she?

He stared at her. Only the shadow of the trees dancing across her moonlit face.

The moan began again.

Kevin tensed.

One horror movie after another flooded his head; unquiet coffins, zombies with half eaten faces peering in windows, dead cats clawing their way out of early graves.

Was it the cemetery again?

Was she out there?

Calling him? Wanting him?

"Shake it off, man," Coach Swanson's raspy, cigar ridden voice echoed in his head. "Let it go, Bauer. Shake it off."

He stood upright and glanced around the room the huge, dark room. A faint light leaked from under the laundry room door.

The dryer still whirred.

The clock: tick, tick, tick, matching his heart beat for beat.

Tree shadows fell in waves, an Aurora Borealis through the windows and across the carpet.

The wailing cry sounded louder and closer.

Kevin Bauer shuddered.

The gun.

His dad kept a gun down the hallway.

He turned and would have bolted down the hallway, but for the darkness.

Everything would be fine if he could get that gun.

Kevin opened the darkened closet.

The smell of leather jackets stuck in the back of his throat.

He reached for the top shelf, rooting around. His hand moved over hats and gloves and in and around boxes, but he was too short.

Concentrate, focus on the purpose.

His shoulder ached; he strained, batting at the boxes.

The cries grew louder.

Kevin's heart thumped.

It was a haunting cry, a despondent cry, a cry for help.

He couldn't see.

But whatever was out there couldn't see him either.

The playing field was even.

The stool.

There was a stool in the closet.

He moved a hand under the coats and they parted. Stirring and swaying back and forth on the hangers.

He touched something.

The vacuum cleaner.

No stool.

Kevin swore.

Mommy Dearest.

Kevin swore again.

Mommy D. always took it to reach her booze on the top pantry shelf.

That drunken-

He couldn't protect himself now because of that manipulative, conniving, drunken slob.

Kevin glanced down the hallway.

Was it in the pantry?

He wasn't even sure. It could be anywhere. Her booze were everywhere.

The cry lashed at him, that moan, that constant thump in his brain. He clasped his hands over his ears.

Get a hold of yourself, Bauer. You've got to do this.

He lowered his hands and inched back down the hallway, across the family room, with hands outstretched, and into a short hallway that ended at the pantry door. He slid his hand down the smooth wall, like a blind man, until it hit the doorjamb.

Kevin's hand trembled as he turned the knob. No natural light from inside and if he turned on the light now, it would give away his position.

He pushed the door open, stepped inside and closed the door behind him. Kevin fumbled for the switch; *up and down and all around*, some part of that nursery rhyme droned in his head.

It wasn't there.

No switch.

No light.

No safety.

And no gun.

MacEvoy Construction.

"What a bunch of idiots!" his dad had ranted.

When MacEvoy Construction built the house, the door to the pantry was a left-hand door. It should have been a right-hand door. A person had to open the door, step into the dark pantry and reach behind the door for the switch.

He heard the cry again.

Muffled inside the pantry, but still there.

He was safe, but was not.

Kevin inhaled the scent of spices, garlic and onion powder, coupled with coffee and sugar.

Blackness, thick enough to taste, smothered him, incapacitated him. He had to find the switch.

He ran his hand along the edge of the molding and a sliver caught his finger and buried itself deep.

"Crap!" He screamed and then flailed for the switch. He found it, hit it and the light blinded him.

The dark spots faded and he rubbed his eyes.

Kevin gasped.

40

Its form loomed from the corner of his eye.

Fear wrapped its arms around him in a Heimlich maneuver and squeezed until the scream exploded out his mouth.

The baby cried.

Acid churned in his stomach and his throat burned.

Kevin closed his eyes and bowed his head, awaiting a blow to the skull.

Nothing.

No thunder in his ears.

No brain-splitting crack.

No jaw wrenching crush.

Nothing.

Kevin opened his eyes.

The black kitchen apron hung from a hook on the shelf and under it sat the stepstool.

He grabbed it, threw back the door, left the light on and ran back for the hall closet. He slammed the stool down and jumped up on it rooting around on the top shelf.

"Why is there so much crap up here?" He cursed.

He knocked things from the shelf. A thin cardboard container housing light bulbs hit the tile floor and shattered.

The baby screamed on, the sound deafening in his ears.

"Where is it!" he yelled.

Gloves and hats hit the floor.

A box toppled off the shelf spilling magazines across the floor.

He touched cold steel.

Kevin clutched the handle of the pistol and toppled off the stool. He hit the floor and then tried to right himself against the wall.

Focus.

Any movement?

He swept the gun back and forth like he was a detective sneaking down a dark alley.

Flashlight.

He needed one, he had to have it.

Under the phone in the kitchen.

Kevin started down the hall until he reached the doorway. The tiny green light on the phone charger beckoned to him like a shipwrecked sailor to a light house.

He slid the drawer open and an alarm sounded.

Kevin dropped for cover, hitting his head on the drawer.

The buzzer on the dryer told him his jeans were ready to wear.

Kevin cursed.

He touched his throbbing head.

No wetness? No blood.

He pulled himself up using the partially open drawer and heard it crack, but it held. He found the flashlight and turned it on. A faint beam hit the wall.

"It just figures," he said. "Freakin' old batteries."

The cries penetrated his brain.

He glanced at the microwave clock. Daddy and Mommy Dearest wouldn't be home for hours, no help from them.

He walked to the double French doors leading into the back yard and pushed down on the handle. It swung open.

It wasn't even locked? Some mutant babies, with glowing eyes, no doubt, were stalking him and the freakin' doors weren't even locked!

The patio tile felt cool against his bare feet.

He splayed the beam across the lawn until the bushes swallowed it.

The light passed across the in-ground pool; Kevin hated that pool at night.

He stepped toward the black water.

The abyss, a water grave, maybe even a bog of blood. He thought he could see a body submerged in 10 feet of water, but only for an instant. He shook his head to loosen the horror movie images.

The low cry came from behind the pool house.

Kevin swept the light across the tiny cottage that was an oversized doll house and back along the tree line.

He stepped from the brick patio onto the cool grass and then back to the cement of the pool walkway, until his toes touched the Mexican tile around the pool. Kevin peered into the heated water, steam rising from the ripples as they lapped against the side. Two feet or a thousand and two feet deep, he still couldn't see the bottom; and, the thought of the body still submerged made him weak.

The wail screamed at him from behind the pool house.

He jerked the light back to the edge of the wall. The beam hesitated, lessened, and died.

Kevin Bauer stood on the edge of murky depths, a .38 caliber revolver in one hand and a flashlight with no beam in the other. The wind whistled through the trees and across the water. The babies called to one another. Terror gripped him. He felt like wetting his pants, but squeezed and held it back.

He tapped the flashlight on the gun barrel and the bulb glowed white. Kevin scanned to the left and then back to the right, his knuckles white around the handle of the pistol. Images of mutant babies came into focus. Their demonic smiles, their bulbous eyes, their crooked, tiny fangs. The images melted into the girl at the cemetery, her arms oozing blood.

"Oh God," he whispered.

In that moment, the thing that he feared the most sprang to mind and he came face to face with the possibility.

Is it really her?

Fear paralyzed him.

The shriek came from the left of the pool house piercing the night. He whirled and the faint beam illuminated its red eyes.

41

He followed the red eyes darting across the lawn. Revelation came like someone hitting him with a baseball bat. Kevin wanted to laugh and then cry and then throw something.

He cursed, "Two cats!"

They bristled, backs arched and fangs bare.

"Two freakin cats!"

They hissed, cried, and screamed at each other. A throaty thrum came from deep inside their bellies. Kevin closed his eyes and listened.

"Like babies crying," he said softly.

The cats were ready for a full-fledged fur ripping.

"I hate you!" he screamed. "I hate your hairballs and the stink that you spray! I hate everything about you!" He shook the flashlight in a maniacal rant.

The two Tomcats collided, growling, and leaping and scratching. They leapt through the bushes and were gone.

The "baby cries" dissipated.

"I ought to shoot you just for the hell of it!" he yelled, waving the pistol.

The movement came from his right.

Kevin whirled and brought the gun to bear, instinctively squeezing the trigger. The cylinder rotated.

The hammer clicked.

The pistol was silent.

"Hey man, it's me."

Kevin directed the light into Milton Drago's face.

42

"I could have killed you, you idiot." Kevin lowered the gun and staggered backward until he slumped into the cushion of one of the pool chairs.

"Killed me with what, air bullets?" Milton plopped down opposite Kevin. "You were never that good of a shot anyway."

Kevin looked at the gun. "It was always loaded before." He looked up at Milton. "Where've you been, man? Everyone's asking." Kevin pointed with the barrel of the pistol.

"To hell and back," Milton replied looking up at the stars. "You can't imagine what you miss until it's gone." Milton paused. "Parent's home?"

"Do you think I'd be walking around on my patio with a gun and flashlight if they were?"

"I don't know your family habits." Milton shrugged. "Why didn't you just turn on the patio lights?" he asked. "I remember, this place lights up like the North Pole at Christmas."

Kevin stared at Milton dumbfounded. "I, uh, didn't think—"

"Yeah, you never think," Milton laughed. "You could've just hit the floodlights!" Milton slapped his knee. "What an idiot. I thought that was you sneaking back and forth in front of the window, but I didn't know for sure." Milton nearly fell out of his chair with laughter.

"Shut the hell up." Kevin snapped and then grinned and rubbed his eyes. "My dad and the drunk had some fund raisin' piece of crap to go to so I was 'babysitting myself' as Mommy Dearest put it."

"She's still around, huh?" Milton asked.

"She'll never leave as long as daddy keeps depositing into her bank account." Kevin got up. "Come on, I've had enough excitement for one night."

Milton hoisted himself out of the chair with a great deal of effort and followed Kevin toward the house.

"Man, you stink," Kevin said. "What, are you wearing sweat and garbage cologne now?" Kevin fanned his nose. "Stay down wind of me."

"Shut up."

"How long have you had those clothes on?"

"Three weeks." Milton brushed back his greasy, matted hair with hands caked with filth.

"That's three weeks too long. I've never seen you like this."

"Never been like this."

"You really need a shower," Kevin reached for the patio door knob.

"How soon are your dad and mom going to be home?" Milton took a hold of Kevin's arm.

"She's not my mom," Kevin pulled away.

"Sorry, I didn't mean to get your panties in a wad."

"They'll be boozin' until dawn, man. Your stink is getting to me. Get in the shower, will you?"

"Which one?"

"Any one, we've got seven." Kevin covered his nose with the back of his hand.

"And my clothes?"

"If burning were legal…" Kevin blew out a breath. "There's no way those are touching my washing machine." Kevin grabbed a garbage bag out of a drawer. "Put them in here and seal it, I don't want any of your stank leakin' out."

—

Forty five minutes later, Milton walked bare-footed back into the kitchen drying his long hair with a towel.

"Where's the clothes?" Kevin asked.

"Left them in the bathroom—"

"In the bag?"

"Of course, in the bag." Milton tossed the towel on a chair. "Chill, I'll get them in a minute."

"You better, I don't want Mommy Dearest finding them—"

"Chill-lax, man." Milton eased down onto a counter stool.

"Here." Kevin set a steaming plate of spaghetti in front of him. "I nuked some leftovers in the microwave."

Milton said nothing and grabbed a wad with his hand and shoved it into his mouth slurping it up like a dog digging in trash.

"God, man, use a fork." Kevin slid a fork across the counter. "When was the last time you ate?"

Milton paused, staring at the counter. "Couple of days ago."

Milton took the fork in his sauce covered hand and began to gobble and slurp again, his face nearly in the plate. "Don't ask what it was."

"I won't."

Milton mopped up the last of it and licked all the sauce off the plate. He slid the plate across the counter to Kevin.

"More?" Kevin asked.

"Stupid question." Milton let out a long belch.

"Disgusting," Kevin said.

"Always was." Milton said. "How about letting me stay here?"

"Here?"

"Yeah, just for a few. I can't go home cuz of the cops."

Kevin spooned more spaghetti and sauce onto the plate and put it in the microwave punching several buttons. He stared at Milton.

"Come on, Kev."

Kevin paused. "I don't know…"

"Please."

The microwave dinged and Kevin removed the plate and slid it across the counter to Milton.

"I guess."

Milton began to inhale the second plate.

"My dad can't know; he'd probably turn you in."

"I won't tell him." Milton licked the plate again.

"That's disgusting."

"Can't help it." Milton belched again.

Kevin snatched the plate and scoured it with hot water and disinfectant soap.

"The pool house." Kevin said, as he placed the plate in the dishwasher rack, added soap, closed the door and turned it on.

"Pool house?"

"Yeah, we never use it this time of year anyway." Kevin dried his hands on a towel. "If Karen wants to take a dip, she's usually in and out of the house, she doesn't bother with it."

He threw the towel aside. "It's got a bed and bathroom in it, what more do you need?"

"Nothin'."

"You'd have to stay out of sight though. If she's catches a glimpse, she'll freak and call the cops."

"No problem, I'll sleep for days anyway."

43

Several nights and several conversations later, Kevin and Milton sat in the kitchen again, both nursing a beer while dad and Karen enjoyed a long spa weekend.

"Told Del you're back yet?"

"No, tramps blab too much." Milton took a pull from the long-necked bottle. "Besides, I've got Angie now."

"That hooker you met?" Kevin took a swig.

"Yeah."

"That's nasty, man. You never know what kind of crawly things you're going to get from those skanks."

"Angie's not like that." Milton gulped the beer.

"You sure?"

"Yeah. Better than that tramp, Del."

"At least Del doesn't get up in the middle of the night and make off with what little bit of money you have."

Milton stared at Kevin, looking past him or through him.

"Yeah, when I woke up, she was gone alright." Milton took another sip and then seemed to come to. "But Del's history, man."

"Speaking of history," Kevin took one last drink, "I've got homework."

"Ah, history..." Milton grinned. "I remember the days," he took his last drink, "but not too fondly."

He glanced at the clock: *12:30am*. Milton got up and shoved his bottle deep into the garbage bag.

"I'm tired anyway. Later."

"Good night." Kevin followed him to the patio door and locked it after Milton left.

—

Milton flopped onto the sheets and rolled up in his blanket. The whir of the space heater and waft of warm air comforted him unlike so many nights sleeping on concrete and asphalt.

He stared up at the shadows on the ceiling.

"Angie." he whispered.

He could still smell her hair.

He could still see her smile.

He could still taste the gloss on her lips.

He could still hear her voice.

"It's not your fault," She had told him.

Milton began to fade.

—

"Then whose fault is it, Katherine?" Merle shouted. "Certainly not mine!"

"You didn't lock the door," Katherine said.

"The little pervert shouldn't have come into our bedroom." Merle gritted his teeth.

"He didn't know we were in there."

"He should have, it's *our* bedroom."

"He needed toothpaste," Katherine said.

"Yeah, right. The perv wanted to watch—"

"Merle!"

"You're always coddling him—"

"You're always yelling at him." Katherine said.

"Somebody needs to." Merle finished his beer. "*You're* certainly not going to. He's always hiding behind your skirt. The stinkin' little pervert."

———

Milton rolled over, clutching his pillow in the warm pool house.

"Pervert. The stinkin' pervert…"

———

"They're not mine, mom!" Milton's 12-year-old voice cracked, as he stood with one hand on the open cardboard box.

"What kind of sick, perverted things were you doing with these?" Katherine held up a fist full of skin magazines.

"They're not mine. I thought this was my comic book box." Tears ran down Milton's face. "Please believe me." He wiped the tears. "Don't tell dad."

"These young girls," Katherine pointed to the front of the magazines, "are not objects for your perverted ways."

They heard the car stop in the gravel driveway and the door close.

"Mom, please."

Katherine threw the magazines back into the box and tried to quickly close it up as Merle entered the open garage door.

"What the-" He looked at Katherine, then at the box and finally settled on Milton.

"Leave us, Katherine."

Katherine's anger faded to fear. "Merle, I—"

"Leave me to tend to the boy, Katherine, or I'll deal with you later."

Merle's eyes were slits. He walked over to the box and gently rearranged the magazines and methodically folded the flaps shut.

"Mom?" Milton's eyes were filled with terror. "Please…"

"Leave us, Katherine or you'll get some of the same." Merle turned toward her. "Fix me a chicken pot pie."

——

Milton turned onto his side in the pool house and pawed his pillow.

He saw his dad's belt slide out of the loops of his pants.

His huge belly jiggled as he drew back.

Milton turned to the other side on the pool house bed.

He saw Merle's belly ripple as the first stroke of the leather caught him across the shoulder and wrapped around his neck and head.

Milton screamed.

He sat up in bed.

Had he screamed? Or did he just remember?

Again and again, lash after lash, Merle screaming curses at him as he cowered on the cold cement floor.

Merle's chest jiggled; Milton's old man needed a bra.

His gut rippled like the rise and fall of the ocean.

A catsup and mustard stained ocean.

A sweat soaked ocean.

He could still smell it.

The smell of sweat and blood was still in his nostrils, now even five years later, and Milton pulled his knees up and cradled them around his chest just like he had done that day on the garage floor.

A kaleidoscope turned through his mind.

Snapshots.

Images.

Colors.

Sweat and blood and panting and screaming.

The crack of the belt.

The pain.

The sobbing.

Over and over and over.

"Girls are so much easier to raise!"

"Girls are so much easier!"

"Girls are so much…"

Milton stared at the ceiling of the pool house.

Girls are easier.

So much easier.

You would know, Dad.

44

"Kevin?" Milton awoke to cabinet doors opening and closing. He heard the water running in the bathroom sink.

He slid to the edge of the bed and staggered to the doorway.

"Hey, Kev, would you mind throwing these pants in the wash when you go back to the house?" He pushed the bathroom door open, jeans in hand.

Angie stood over the sink, her back to him. Excitement rushed his heart, but quickly turned to panic.

"Angie?" he asked.

She turned slowly and her hair swung around her shoulders. Milton saw Angie's forehead and eyebrows, the ones that he had kissed many times in their passion, but like a hideous Picasso painting, her nose and right eye were Kurt Clayton's. Muriel's left eye and cheek cascaded into Kurt's three-day-old beard stubble and then back into Angie's chin. Blood trickled from her right ear forming a necklace that dripped into the collar of her shirt. Her lips, cracked and bleeding, melted into her chin from which grew long, protruding hairs that curled back into her neck and embedded into the skin, forming pustules.

Her open blouse revealed black, matted chest hair, protruding over her breasts.

Milton inspected her once-muscular, tanned legs; but, as he watched, the muscles receded and metamorphosed into misshapen puffs of saggy skin draped over bone. Milton stared at blackheads forming on her legs. They erupted into black, thick hair that twisted and writhed like earthworms pushing toward the surface in a downpour.

Milton recoiled, covering his mouth and gagging.

Her lips curled into a gruesome smile and she spewed the words, "Immolo are captivitas atris f."

Her teeth grew to carnivorous length and she lunged at his throat, fangs laid bare.

45

Kevin flipped on the light in the pool house just as Milton sat up and flung the sheet off the bed. Milton was a mass of sweat and his stench filled the room. Kevin watched as a yellow puddle formed under Milton and saturated the sheets.

"Oh, God." Kevin turned away.

"Sorry, man." Milton's voice trembled. "I feel like crap."

"Well, don't do that." Kevin turned back toward him.

Milton looked down at the mess. "I'll, uh, clean it up. Sorry."

"Yeah, sure." Kevin grabbed a towel off a chair and threw it to Milton. "How am I going to explain—"

"I said I'd clean it up. Give it a rest." Milton wiped himself like a toddler, tucked the towel between his legs and walked bowlegged into the bathroom. Kevin gagged as he heard the shower come on.

Milton spoke over the rush of the water. "I don't know, man. This all started the night we chased that tub of lard! If it weren't for him…"

Kevin approached the partially open door. "What do you mean?" he called above the sound of the water.

"Are you kidding?" Milton asked through the curtain.

"Which part is Tucker's fault?" Kevin asked.

"All of it! Me leaving home. The cemetery. Everything."
Milton turned the shower off and climbed out.

"Hand me a towel." he said.

Kevin handed him another towel and Milton covered up, but not before Kevin saw the seeping, yellow lesions on his inner thighs and groin.

"You see, man." Milton motioned toward his genitals. "All because of that piece of crap—"

"Zack?"

"He ruined me."

"Zack did that to you?" Kevin motioned toward Milton's crotch.

"No, you idiot." Milton swore again. "He drove me out, made me have to leave home. He's ruined my life—"

"Zack didn't—"

"Sure he did! What, are you on his side now?"

"No, I'm just sayin'—"

"I'll never be the same." Milton looked down and inspected himself.

Kevin turned to go.

"You don't know."

Kevin stopped with his back to Milton. "Know what?"

"What I had to do just to survive."

"I don't want to—"

"Just to get food."

"No, I don't and I don't want any gory details either." Kevin turned back toward him.

"You don't have a clue," Milton turned toward the mirror and began combing his long hair.

"*I* don't have a clue?"

"No, you don't." Milton's voice was calm and even.

"You're pathetic, you know that?" Kevin said.

"What?" Milton stopped combing his hair and looked at Kevin. "What did you say to me?"

"I mean really, the great Milton Drago." Kevin's lips tightened. "Life of the party. Milton the Hateful. Leader of the Triune. Nasty—"

"Are you kidding me?"

"Ready for a fight any time. Used up girls and threw them out like so much garbage—"

"You're garbage." Milton's eyes turned into slits.

"The Mighty. The Conqueror." Kevin paused as Milton crossed the room and stood inches from his face.

"What are you talking about—"

"About you," Kevin said holding his ground. "You and I got together stealing liquor and porn from that old fat guy on the edge of town, remember?"

"Yeah, I remember. So, what's your point, Bauer?"

"My point is that you were once "the Man". I looked up to you. Now look at you." Kevin looked Milton up and down. "You're 15 pounds underweight, you got some sort of venereal disease from some skank you met while pawing through trash cans—"

"Angie's not a skank—"

"Whatever. My point is that you just got done pissing your bed, like some little girl. When are you going to stand up for yourself? Get back in the game—"

"Right now." Milton took a swing at Kevin, but he blocked it and shoved Milton backward onto the bathmat.

Kevin smiled and offered a hand to him. "Now that's the Man!"

Milton's embarrassment faded and he grinned. "You piece of crap."

Milton started laughing and took Kevin's hand, pulling himself up. "You had me going."

"Seriously," Kevin said. "It's been weeks now. What are you going to do to come back?"

"I'm takin' out the garbage."

"Yeah?"

"Yeah, police or no police. Jail or no jail. I'm taking Tucker out. He's going to pay for driving me to this." Milton motioned toward his crotch. "That fat tub's gonna pay big time."

46

"So what's up with the convict?" John nodded down the school hall. "I hear he's doing time in study hall right now."

"Milton's mom needed him home, I guess." Zack shrugged, closing his locker and bending to tie his shoe.

"Figures," John said.

"Did you hear anything about him staying at Kevin's house before he came back?" Zack asked.

"Yeah. Fact or fiction?" John shrugged. "Who knows?"

"I guess, Milton's all she's got." Zack scooped up his books and stood. "She's a nice lady. Too bad she's cursed with a son like Milton."

"That son-of-a-Milton," John grinned. "So, that's it, huh? No more legal spankin' for him?"

"Yeah, guess not," Zack said. "I hear a year's probation, 500 hours of community service, and the judge told him to stay away from me."

"Yeah, that always works." John rolled his eyes.

"A hundred yards—"

"You carryin' a measuring tape now?" John patted Zack on the shoulder.

"Unless we're in the same class," Zack continued as they walked down the hall.

"Then the tape," John flicked his wrist, "might as well be out the window."

"I didn't make the rules."

"So, what if Mr. Upstanding Citizen: 'Of Course I Wouldn't Even Think of Bothering Zack Tucker, Your Honor' violates the order?"

"Then he goes to jail," Zack said. "Do not pass go; do not collect 200 dollars."

"Before or after he kills you?" John fixed his gaze on the blonde passing by.

Zack shrugged. "Either way."

"Did he, or did he not, come after you with a machete?" John began marching back and forth like a prosecutor in front of the grand jury.

"Knife." Zack said.

"Whatever." John waved his hand. "Did he, or did he not, lunge at you—"

"Fell, really—"

"—to do you bodily harm?" John shook a skinny finger under Zack's nose.

"I didn't fight it." Zack held up his hands. "His mom needs him. Maybe he's changed?"

John paused for effect and covered his mouth. "Bullcrap."

"Yeah, that's what I thought, too." Zack smiled.

———

Zack walked off the elevator onto Gideon's eleventh floor.

"Hey, Rita." He waved to Mick's assistant.

"Well, hello, Zack. You're looking good." Rita's smile wrinkled her fifty-six-year-old cheeks.

"Thanks."

"Been working out, I see," Rita curled her arm, displaying a skinny muscle.

"The work around here will do that to you." Zack patted his stomach. "I've lost twenty pounds—"

"Well done," Rita said.

"Eat right, move right, live right. That's what I always say."

"You took our motto literally." Rita's green eyes sparkled.

"Of course. Mick busy?"

"Let me check." She pushed a button on the phone.

"Mr. Abbeer, Mr. Tucker to see you, if you're not busy?"

"I'm always busy," Mick's voice came from the speaker. "Send him in anyway."

Zack opened the office door.

"Mick?" Zack found it awkward to call the owner of a multi-million dollar company by his first name, but he had insisted.

"Zack. How are things?" Mick looked up from a pile of spreadsheets.

"Great, thanks." Zack's voice cracked. "Can I ask you something?"

"Shoot." Mick leaned back putting his hands behind his head, his blue eyes making contact with Zack's.

"How am I doing?"

Mick looked at him. "I'm getting excellent reports. Carlos says he couldn't do without you."

"Carlos lies," Zack smiled, "but thanks."

"You got your promotion, right?"

"Yeah, Carlos told me. Thanks for that also." Zack paused. "I was wondering…" He lowered himself into the overstuffed leather chair across from Mick. "Remember when I first started? You said I could suggest someone to work here—"

"I remember." Mick leaned forward with his large forearms on the desk. "John?"

"Actually, yes—"

"Done." Mick picked up his pen again and marked on the spreadsheet. "How soon can he fill out the paperwork?"

"Don't you want to talk to him?"

"Are you recommending him?" Mick didn't look up from the spreadsheet.

"Well, yeah," Zack said. "He's a good worker, very reliable."

"That's good enough for me. Have him stop by. I'll send Mel a memo right now."

Mick swiveled in his chair and began punching keys on the computer keyboard.

47

The streetlights reflected off the newly washed and waxed truck as they pulled to the curb.

"Nice," Jamie looked out the window at the restaurant.

"I decided to go someplace without paper-napkin holders on every table," Zack smiled, "and I love the foothills. Get out of the city and breathe some fresh air."

Zack climbed out, smoothing his black suit pants and adjusting his tie. He opened Jamie's door and watched her long legs precede her form-fitting black dress. She handed him her black bag, as she adjusted her spaghetti straps and stepped onto the sidewalk.

A gloved doorman, in a red waistcoat, opened the restaurant door.

"Good evening, folks. Welcome to the Ole Grist Mill."

The entry glowed blue-green from the 500-gallon fish tank bubbling in the corner. Large, flat fish glided effortlessly from one end to the other.

"Good evening to the both of you. May I have your name?" another red coat asked.

"Yes, Zack Tucker."

He scanned a large leather-bound book. "Ah yes, Mr. Tucker, right here." He pointed to the page. "Party of two?" he asked.

"Yes," Zack replied.

Red pushed a button on his station and another red coat came around the corner.

"Phillip, show Mr. Tucker and his guest to their table, please." He pointed to a map of the restaurant on the podium.

"Follow me, please." Phillip led the way down a small wood-paneled hallway.

"First time with us?"

"Yes," Zack said.

"Well, let me tell you a little about us." Phillip turned a corner and Zack and Jamie followed. "The Ole Grist Mill, founded by James A. Brooks Esq., was, at one time, a turn-of-the-century mining camp, complete with dredge and plume."

Zack noted a mine shaft stretching back into the mountain as they rounded another corner.

"He and his son, James A. Brooks II, extracted what little bit of remaining gold there was around the 1920's and decided to turn it into a restaurant. We sell gold nuggets extracted from it in our gift shop." Phillip pointed vaguely.

"It has been passed down from son to son ever since. Our present owner, James A. Brooks IV, has it now. Here we are." Phillip opened the door to a mining office, with floor to ceiling windows overlooking the Denver skyline.

"Your waiter will be with you shortly. Enjoy."

"Wow, Zack, this is great." Jamie said as Phillip walked away.

Zack looked around. "Yeah, I always wanted to come here. We were on a waiting list for this table, but I figured, 'hey, it's my birthday.'"

"Good choice." Jamie smiled and touched his arm. "And happy birthday."

"Yeah, the big eighteen," Zack said. "Guess I'm a man now." He exaggeratedly poked his chest out and curled his bicep. "I can vote, have my own bank account, and join the army."

Jamie laughed as the waitress approached.

"Good evening, folks."

Zack exhaled.

"May I interest you in something to drink and an appetizer before dinner?" She handed them the menus, holding onto to Zack's slightly longer as he tried to take it.

Zack nodded for Jamie to go first.

"How about lemonade?"

"Very good, ma'am." She turned toward Zack and smiled. "And for you, Zack?"

Zack paused.

"Uh, a diet, whatever you have…" He looked at her.

"You don't remember me, do you?" The waitress smiled.

"I'm sorry, I don't." Zack returned the smile.

"Angie? You know, from Mrs. Hanrady's homeroom. Junior High?"

"Oh." Zack nodded with reservation. "How are you?"

"I'm fine."

She smiled down at him, pausing for a long moment. "You certainly have changed."

She looked him over then turned toward Jamie and wrinkled her nose. "I used to have the biggest crush on him."

Jamie wrinkled her nose back and then rolled her eyes.

"Well, I'll get those drinks." Angie touched Zack's arm.

"That's weird." Zack poured some water from the carafe sitting on the table.

"Yeah, I suppose it is." Jamie gave him a knowing look. "So she had a crush on you, huh?"

"No, I mean," Zack took a sip, "the weird thing is that I *do* remember her."

"Oh?" Jamie tilted her chin down and looked up at him as if to say; *tell me what that's all about.*

"She hated my guts."

"Really?" Jamie raised her head.

"Yeah. She was always in my face laughing and puttin' me down." Zack looked in the direction that Angie had gone. "She spread some pretty bad trash about me. Even in Junior High."

"That *is* weird."

"I don't know what she's talking about," Zack picked up his water glass and took another sip, "but there's no way that she had a crush on me. I was crap as far as she was concerned."

"She obviously thinks you're cute now," Jamie said. "And so do I, don't let her get any ideas."

Zack shook his head. "No way. I know what I've got and I don't need her."

Jamie smiled.

He fumbled in his pocket and produced a tiny white box with a red ribbon tied around it. He pushed it across the table in front of Jamie's china plate.

"What's this?" Jamie's eyes brightened.

"I've wanted to give you this for a little while now."

She looked into his eyes.

"You know what this week is?" Zack asked.

Jamie nodded. "Our five-month anniversary."

"Yeah," he smiled. "Five months since I laid eyes on you at the movies. I just wanted to say thanks."

"Thanks?" Jamie asked. "It's *your* birthday and you're giving me presents?"

"I... didn't have a lot of confidence before. Sometimes I think I still don't, but the past few months... Well.," he took another sip of water, his hand shaking slightly, "they've been the most exciting of my life."

"Oh, Zack."

"Open it, please." He nodded toward the box.

She pulled the ribbon and lifted the lid. She removed a ring box and opened it.

"Zack, it's beautiful." Her eyes welled with tears.

"Do you like it?" Zack asked.

She nodded as the tears, now too many to be contained, trickled down her face. She slid her delicate finger into the ring and held it up in the light.

"It's a ruby. See?" Zack pointed. "And those are real diamonds around it."

"I don't know what to say, Zack. No one's ever given me a present like this before."

She scooted her chair back and came around the table, bending to put her arms around him. She tilted her head and kissed him.

Zack's hunger was gone as he watched her sit back down.

"I guess things must be going well at Gideon?" She looked at the sparkling ring again.

"Yeah." He could hardly talk. "I got a raise and I've been moving up the ladder."

She waited for him to continue.

"Moving up?" she prodded.

"Yeah." Zack was still dazed.

"Zack?" She leaned forward waiting for him to continue.

"What?" Zack shrugged.

"Moving up, like how?"

"Sorry, my mind was somewhere else." He grinned. "Yeah, Nate is showing me a few things. I have been wrapping hilts and putting the pommels on. That's the little knob on the end of the handle, for you non-Gideonites." He winked. "Wouldn't want those things flying out of your hand in a battle."

"Of course not." She smiled.

"I'm unloading steel sometimes. Keeps me in shape." He curled his arm, revealing his bicep through the suit jacket.

"I can tell." Jamie looked at his sleeves.

"I just got John on and he's going to be working with our computer network," Zack said. "Of course."

"Naturally."

"But now they've promoted me." Zack took a sip of water.

"Cool."

"Sharpening station." He leaned back, putting his hands behind his head like the meal had already come and gone and he was enjoying the satisfaction.

"That sounds interesting." Jamie prodded.

"It's actually a big deal." Zack smiled. "At least at Gideon."

"That's cool. Working with the blades?" She smiled and admired her ring again.

"Yeah." Zack sat up. "And this month starts Heritage Month."

"Oh, really?"

"Yeah, it's some intense training period that we work on our mind, soul and bodies. Learn the history of the company, stuff like that. It's like a company boot camp to improve ourselves, for the good of Gideon. Happens every year I guess—"

"That sounds cool." Jamie took a sip of water.

"We even get some kind of martial arts training."

"Really, why?"

"Beats me," Zack said. "But hey, if it's free, I'll take it."

Jamie smiled.

Zack looked around for their drinks. "Hey, Monday's teachers' in-service and I won't have to work until later. Want to hang out?"

"Oh, I would, but I still have school and then I've got to get right to work."

A white-coated waiter approached.

"I sincerely apologize, folks; we had a mix-up in the seating chart and I didn't realize that this was my table. May I start you out with something to drink?"

"Well, Angie already took our order for the drinks."

"Angie?"

"Yeah, the waitress." Zack pointed in the direction of the kitchen. "She was here a few minutes ago."

The waiter paused. "I don't know an Angie. We only have male waiters here."

48

"Man, am I glad to see you!" Carlos wiped the sweat off his forehead as Zack approached.

"Mary was sick last week and won't be in today. Orders are backing up. Do your thing, man."

"We'll bust it out," Zack started toward his station.

"And hey, Zack?"

Zack turned around.

"This one's a special order." Carlos pointed his finger at Zack like a gun. "So, do it right."

"Hey, it's me," Zack shrugged. "No problem."

On page thirty-six of the Gideon catalog, it was called Baraq, the Lightning Sword. Zack took hold of the handle and lifted the blade out of the trough of oil.

He pointed it toward the floor, watching the oil run down the blade and drip off the tip.

Zack sat down, clamped the sword in a vise, lined with a thick leather pad, and adjusted a work lamp.

He took a smooth round sharpening stone and worked it lightly against the steel, down the blade and back up, feeling the gentle grinding.

Zack closed his eyes, to feel for any inconsistencies. He bent close and listened as the stone did its work, up and down, back and forth, taking raw metal and bringing it to an edge that would slice through paper, cleaner than a razor blade. He caught light dancing across his closed lids, the mirror shine of the blade reflecting the lamp as he pushed and pulled the edge into submission.

The chaos of the manufacturing floor transformed into the roar of the Roman Coliseum.

He opened his eyes and peered at the elegant weapon from a bygone era. Gladiators and knights, lords and ladies, and damsels in distress paraded themselves before him. Peace engulfed him and tranquility wrapped itself around him as he felt the slippery oil soak his fingertips and run down his knuckles.

He stared at the pummel, with the gold plated crest of Gideon on it. His gaze moved to the red-leather wrapped handle, past the thick hilt and onto the wide, double edged blade, where he stared back at himself in the mirrored finish.

Nate had instructed him well and he placed the back of his thumb nail perpendicular to the blade and dragged it across the edge, leaving small shavings of nail on the blade.

It's perfect.

Complete.

A finalized piece, ready for whatever collector would pay the price.

He wiped the blade with a soft cloth, soaking his hands with oil, and then mopped the excess onto a porous towel. Zack slid open a drawer and extracted a pair of white, cotton gloves and worked his hands into them. Gently, with both hands, as if it were blown-glass, Zack carried it to a crimson-velvet lined case and laid it in position. He folded more crimson velvet over the top and lowered the polished, Madagascar Rosewood lid into place. He latched the brass clasps and removed the white gloves, throwing them in an unmarked porcelain container.

He glanced over at the bumper sticker affixed to his toolbox.

Become One with the Blade

And Zack Tucker had.

49

Another school day ended and John followed Zack into the Gideon parking lot, pulled into a slanted parking space, and climbed out of his car.

"You've got to get rid of that thing," Zack approached and watched smoke puff from the tailpipe, like an old man lighting up a stogie. The car let out one last cloud and then stopped convulsing.

"Hey, man, it's a classic," John said.

"A classic piece of crap."

"Shut up," John followed Zack toward the building. "I think me working here is going to be interesting. Thanks for putting in the good word for me." John glanced up at the Gideon logo.

"What can I say?" Zack stooped to tie his shoe and John jumped sideways to avoid tumbling over him.

"Hey!" John yelled, regaining his balance. "Hit your brake lights next time."

"Sorry," Zack said.

"Are you really sure about all this? Me working here?" John asked.

"No, I'm not," Zack stood. "But I do know that you don't have anything else going on in your life."

"I've got things."

"What, reruns of Star Trek?"

"What's wrong with that?" John shrugged. "It's not like *you* have anything else going."

"I've got a feeling that some of this is bigger than both of us." Zack looked up at the massive building. "But it's a cool place to work." He smiled.

"Well, maybe bigger than me," John punched his arm.

"Very funny," Zack stepped onto the sidewalk. "I guess I just felt like something was missing in my life, you know?"

"Well, if it's anything like that night at the cemetery, it'll be your head." John said.

"I'm not worried," Zack grinned. "You'd catch my head before it hit the ground."

"That's what I'm afraid of, my friend."

Zack pulled on the handle of a side door marked *Employees Only*.

—

Angie watched Zack and John disappear through the door. The loud rap on the Jaguar's window made her jump.

She pushed the button and the window slid down.

"Yes, Officer?" She used a demure, southern drawl.

"You can't park here. This is private property." The heavily muscled black guard motioned with his white gloved hand.

"Oh, really?" Angie smiled, scratching her knee and then delicately adjusting her skirt higher on her thigh.

"Yes, really." the guard said.

"I was just passing by and thought that this might be a nice place to stop, and," she paused for effect "relax."

"This is not a place to relax," he said. "You'll have to move on."

"Oh, but, Officer, I'm really tired." She yawned and then stretched, showcasing her low neckline.

"Couldn't I just stay a little while? You could keep me company." She patted the seat beside her.

He put his massive hand on the door frame and leaned closer, staring into her eyes. "Mick told me to tell you to move on, Angie."

She spat at him narrowly missing his cheek and cursed.

Angie slammed the gearshift into drive, as the guard stepped back and she floored it. The tires squealed and they roared further into the parking lot. She cranked the wheel, threw the Jag into a power slide and headed straight back toward him. He did not flinch. Angie turned the wheel slightly, her outside mirror dusting his jacket, as she exploded past him and down the winding driveway.

He turned, watching her speed away and smiled, keying the microphone clipped to his shoulder strap.

"Sir, this is, Dexter, at the front gate. She's gone."

50

"He's like this encyclopedia of war!" John said a week later, as he and Zack walked out of a Gideon classroom. "There wasn't one question that anyone threw at him that he didn't have some sort of answer for."

"You got that right," Zack said. "I'd bet Fryberg would love to pick Mel's brain. Who'd have thought that short little guy with all that nose hair would know—"

"Don't you think it's kinda weird though? How he talks about the battles?" John asked.

"You mean the Caesars and the Napoleonic War?"

"Yeah," John stopped to use the glass in the fire extinguisher door to straighten his hair. "Like he's been there?"

"No, I don't think *that's* strange at all." Zack rolled his eyes and continued down the hall.

"He's a bottomless pit of historical warfare." John ran to catch up. "The World Wars and Vietnam—"

"Yeah, he knows his stuff," Zack said.

"Hitler's strategies—"

"I know."

"Yeah," John said. "Really weird."

They paused in front of a large cork bulletin board, on the wall, and Zack ran his finger down a schedule fastened by a smiley-face thumbtack.

"Come on," he said. "We're supposed to be out on the golf course next."

"Oh, joy." John bent in half and grabbed his ankles to stretch his hamstrings.

"Why do they make us run miles around the golf course? Do they know what the golf course is supposed to be used for?"

"Come on, ya wuss." Zack grabbed his sleeve and pulled him toward the door.

"You, guys, enjoying Heritage month so far?" Nate walked out of a classroom.

"Man, this is great." Zack gave Nate a high five.

"Reminds me of the Olympics," John said. "I'm not really that much of an athlete—"

"Hey, you're getting paid to sword fight and learn martial arts." Zack punched him in the arm.

"Well, at least we *are* getting paid," John said, rubbing his arm.

"Yeah," Nate said. "It's a great way for us all to get together every year and learn the craft. See where we've come from and where we're heading." Nate looked at both the boys. "By the way, where are you heading?"

"Well," John began. "I'm trying to get things straight in my life right now and I was contemplating Star Trek Episode 64, the Tholian Web? Whether it was an energy weave or some sort of matter/anti-matter laser projection—"

"No, I mean where are you heading right now?" Nate rolled his eyes.

"Oh," John said, "Golf course. Gotta do some laps."

He began running in place then stopped. "Hey did you guys ever think that golf courses should be used for—"

"Are you guys coming to my seminar this afternoon?" Nate asked.

"Yeah," John hesitated. "What's it called again?"

"Lethal Weaponry," Zack piped up before Nate could answer.

"Right," Nate pointed at Zack.

"Oh, yeah," John nodded. "Wouldn't miss it."

"You almost did," Nate grinned. "We'll be practicing."

"Practicing what?" John asked.

"Killing each other with swords." Nate walked away.

51

Zack watched the second hand sweep across the clock's face.

Thirty more seconds.

Another twelve hour day.

"You bout ready to go man?" John approached, with an industrial sized bag of Boston Baked Beans.

"What are you still doing here?" Zack took a handful out of the bag and laid them on his workbench.

"Oh, had some server problems in Human Resources and Mel wanted it taken care of after all the office staff left." John rubbed his right shoulder.

"How come I have to run laps and all that physical workout when I'm just sitting on my behind in front of computer screens all day?"

"Because you're special."

"Well, that's true." John cranked his neck from side to side. "What are you doing?"

"Hey, watch this," Zack's eyes sparkled as he pulled a double-edged battle sword from its sheath.

"Now be careful," John said.

"Not to worry, man," Zack gripped the leather-wrapped hilt in both hands. "This is what we do here."

He began slicing the air with the razor-sharp blade.

"Hey," John stepped back, "just because we were in Nate's class a few weeks ago doesn't mean that you can…"

The most formidable weapon you possess is your mind. Zack remembered Nate's words that day. *It's all a game of chess. Anticipate your enemy's next move and use it to your advantage.*

The enemy before him was a seedless watermelon, resting on a football kicker's tee, atop a four-foot-high pillar.

Zack spun 180° and brought the sword to bear, slicing horizontally across the melon's rind.

"Holy crap, man!" John jumped back, his Boston Baked Beans scattered across the concrete floor.

"What are you doing!" He looked down. "Man, that was a brand new bag of beans. Cost me six bucks!"

John looked at the melon. "Oh, that's too bad, chief." He skated across the pond of baked beans and patted Zack on the shoulder. "A little more practice and you'll hit it next time, buddy."

Zack stepped to the melon and touched the top. It halved, falling to the floor and splattering John's shoes.

—

"I really miss you."

Zack leaned with one hand against the break-room wall, an hour later. He cradled his cell phone between his shoulder and his ear, as he took another bite of what was left of a Granny Smith apple.

"Yeah, me too," Jamie said. "You've really been working some hours lately." She paused. "Still like me?"

"Of course." He straightened.

"It's been tough on me, not seeing you," she said.

"Yeah, I know, babe," Zack sighed. "I've had a lot to do." He paused, and then brightened. "Hey, this weekend though?"

"What?" Jamie asked.

"We've got this weekend off," Zack said. "Nate said we needed some time."

Jamie hesitated. "That's great, you need the rest. Going to just stay home and take it easy?" She fished.

"No, I want to spend it with you." Zack reached out, tracing the mortar between the bricks with his finger.

"Oh, really?" Her voice brightened.

"Of course."

"I was hoping you'd say that." Her voice was coy. "Are you sure, though? You've really been through it the last few weeks."

"No."

"No, you're not sure?" She hesitated.

"No, I don't need the rest," he said. "When I'm with you, I'm adrenaline-pumped. I don't need the sleep."

"Is that a fact?" Jamie asked. "So, want to go somewhere?"

"Nah. I was thinking of maybe hanging around your house, if that's all right with you? Will it mess up any Friday night plans?"

"Well, I'd have to cancel that appointment I have with the Secretary of State about that new foreign policy, but…No, shouldn't. Want me to fix food or something?"

"Hmm, I wouldn't want to mess up the state of the country." He paused.

"Mac and cheese?" she asked. "I could bake a pie or… spaghetti?"

"The blueberry pie sounds good, but how about pizza? I'm buyin'," Zack said.

"Yeah, we haven't done that for a while. Around seven?"

"I'll be there." Zack fidgeted. "Hey, Jamie?"

"Yes."

Zack drew in a breath. "I love you."

The phone was silent for an instant. Zack nervously surveyed the floor and drew lines with the toe of his shoe.

"I love you too, Zack."

Zack grinned.

"Okay then. Now that we've got that settled, I guess I'd better go. Talk to you later."

52

Zack's truck rolled to a stop at the curb outside 4995 Roosevelt Place. He climbed out and stepped onto the street. A pug-faced dog, with a jogger attached to the other end of the leash, trotted past.

"How's it going?" the jogger asked.

"Pretty good. How 'bout you?" Zack answered.

"Doin' well." The man never broke stride.

It's amazing how much we communicate in a series of clichés. Zack shook his head. Must be the species.

Zack rang the doorbell and Jamie answered in jeans and a sage cashmere sweater, with buttons up the front.

"Wow! You look great, Zack." She hugged him. "Have you lost more weight?"

"Yeah, last time I checked I was down almost 35 since I started working there." Zack beamed. "They've been killing us at work."

He buried his nose in her soft hair and then gave her a kiss. They stood in the doorway holding each other.

"I've really missed you," Zack said.

"I've missed you, too." She snuggled into him.

She reached up and felt his bicep and Zack flexed instinctively.

"Wow!" She wrapped her arms around him.

"Hey, you two," Jason rounded the corner smiling, "let's not have too much of *that* while we're gone."

"Uh, no sir," Zack took a step back.

"Only kidding, Zack." He patted Zack on the shoulder as he went by. "But not really."

Jason kissed Jamie on the cheek. "Have a good evening, Sweetheart."

Jason walked out the door, jingling his keys.

"Are they going—?"

Zack didn't finish as Jamie's little brother, Charlie bounded down the stairs.

"Hey, Zack!"

"Hey, Charlie." He gave Zack a high five.

"Where you going tonight?" Zack asked.

"Dad's taking us to Go Cart Speedway!" He was out the door. "See ya later!"

Jenni came down the stairs, followed by Missy.

"Yeah, best polish sausages in town," Jenni rolled her eyes, "and Jason's a sausage fanatic."

"Bye, Missy," Zack said.

"Bye, Zack." She spurted past.

"You, guys, have fun." Jenni kissed Zack on the cheek and then Jamie.

"You too, Mom," Jamie said.

"Oh, I will, if I can squeeze into one of those little go-cart seats." She smiled.

"That shouldn't be any problem," Zack said.

"I like this guy." Jenni nodded to Jamie. "Better keep him."

"I intend to." Jamie smiled.

Like watching the in-laws leave after Thanksgiving dinner, Zack and Jamie stood in the doorway, as the car pulled out of the driveway.

"They didn't have to leave." Zack looked down at her.

"Oh, yes, they did." Jamie smiled. "I wanted you all to myself tonight."

She closed the door and kissed him.

"Did you get it?" Zack asked.

"Follow me." She took his hand and led him down the hallway to the family room.

"Right here."

She walked over and reached for the movie. *The Quiet Man* was printed across the top. John Wayne's and Katherine O'Hara's pictures painted on the front.

"I love the classics." Zack plopped onto the couch with the box in his hand.

"I'll order the pizza; what do you want?" Jamie stood in the doorway.

"How about a large supreme?"

"Minus the onions." She smiled.

"Definitely, no onions." Zack winked.

"Here, you can go ahead and start. I'll be right back." She took the movie from him, put it in the player and turned it on.

"I'll go order," Jamie stepped into the hallway toward the kitchen.

Zack settled back on the couch and closed his eyes, enjoying her lingering fragrance.

"Do you want something to drink, babe?" Jamie's voice was sweet, but far away. "I've got Diet Pepsi."

"That's great," Zack yelled in a half sleepy tone. "Want some help?"

"No, just relax."

I think I will.

She returned moments later with two Diet Pepsi cans and a large glass filled with ice.

"We'll share." She popped the top and poured the bubbling liquid into the glass.

"Ah, the sound of refreshment." Zack sat up and rubbed his face.

Jamie produced a straw and slid it into the glass.

"Do you want your own straw?" she asked.

"No, that's all right. I'll guzzle from the side." Zack took a sip.

"You know, I have to have one." Jamie said. "I don't like the clink of the ice against my teeth."

"They're nice teeth." Zack said. "Wouldn't want anything to happen to them."

She settled in next to him, snuggling into his chest. Images danced across the screen, as Zack's arm was around her shoulder, caressing her hair. He leaned in and kissed her forehead.

"Thanks for tonight." He intertwined his fingers in hers.

"Thanks for coming over." She looked up and smiled.

Zack leaned back on the couch and faded into silence until the movie music awakened him.

"Man, what's taking the pizza so long?" Jamie looked at the Felix the Cat clock on the wall, its tail swishing back and forth as it ticked off the seconds.

"That guy said it would be less than an hour or it's free."

"Sorry, I dozed off." Zack shook his head.

"It's okay, I know you're tired."

"How long's it been?" Zack tried to focus on his watch.

"More than an hour," Jamie patted Zack's tummy, "and I know you're hungry; your stomach keeps growling."

"Really? Sorry."

The doorbell rang.

"Finally," Jamie jumped up.

Zack pulled a twenty from his wallet.

"Will this be enough?"

"It should be." She snatched it. "It'd better be free."

She marched out of the room on a mission.

Zack scooted forward on the couch, watching John Wayne's manly swagger coupled with his masculine confidence Zack mouthed the lines along with John Wayne and smiled as he took Katherine O'Hara in his arms and kissed her.

"Hey, Jame? What did you order again? I *am* really hungry," he called.

"I guess that lard gut of yours will just have to wait." a male voice said.

Milton Drago stood with one hand over's Jamie's mouth and the other around her waist, holding her against his body.

53

Zack leapt up hitting the coffee table and spilling his drink. "Milton!"

"Well, well, Wally and the Beaver home tonight without Mr. and Mrs. Cleaver," Milton said. "I saw them leave, just waiting for the right moment." He smiled.

The movie droned from the small screen as Zack sized up Milton.

Milton snuggled into Jamie breathing heavy on her neck. "Don't worry, sweetie, by the time the cops get here, our little party will already be done."

"What are you doing, man?" Zack said. "This isn't—"

"Something I should've done a long time ago." Milton sneered.

"Milton," Zack stepped toward him and then stopped as Milton flinched, "this is between you and me, leave Jamie out of it."

"Leave her out of it?" Milton asked in a mocking tone. "Oh, no, she's in it up to her pretty, young neck," he said.

He began to run his hand under her shirt and up her stomach. Zack moved around the coffee table.

Milton stopped and slid his hand back down to her waist.

"That's really it, isn't it, Milton?" Zack took a deep breath.

"What?"

"Always hiding behind something, right?" Zack took a step. "Kevin, Kurt, your little knife and now a girl."

"Now, Tucker." Milton snuggled into Jamie and gave her a peck on the neck. "Me and the babe, here, are just having some fun."

Zack took another step. "That's why you always had to run with Kevin and Kurt, they were out of your league on the social ladder, but—"

"I don't need them!" Milton said.

"That night in the cemetery was a fluke, right?" Zack asked. "Kevin was around someplace, right? Just in case you got in over your head with me? He could pull your bb's out of the fire?"

"Wow, Tucker," Milton exaggerated a blink, "out of that fat finally grew some backbone."

Zack's jaw tightened and he stepped forward.

Milton backed into the hallway, dragging Jamie with him.

"Well, I tell you what, Milton," Zack said, "let's not get *your* blood on Jamie's carpet—"

"My blood?" Milton scoffed.

"Front yard," Zack said, "or will you need Jamie as a shield?"

Milton shoved Jamie forward into Zack's arms.

"Are you okay?" he asked.

"Yeah," she gasped. "Are you sure—"

"I'll be okay." Zack hesitated. "Stay in here."

Milton stepped backward down the hall, as Zack walked toward him. Milton danced through the open front door, taunting Zack to follow, as they both crossed the porch and ended up on the lawn.

"I should've finished this at the cemetery," Milton reached behind him.

"Guess you were a little distracted, huh?" Zack took a step.

"Maybe, but not this time," Milton spat and pulled a knife.

Zack stopped.

"I don't know what that was about, Tucker, but no one's going to come out of the woods tonight to save your sorry lard ass!"

Milton shifted the knife from his right hand to his left and then back again.

"Always got something up your sleeve, don't you?" Zack hesitated. "Afraid to use what you got?"

"Tough talk," Milton said.

"Milton, what's it like?" Zack asked.

"What's what like?"

"When you're alone at night and the demons come?"

Milton stared at him through dead eyes. "You have no idea."

Milton lunged.

With one fluid movement, Zack blocked the knife and grabbed onto Milton's wrist as if to tango. With the other hand, he latched onto Milton's throat lifting him onto his toes.

"I'm not the lard butt I was last year!" Zack said.

Zack moved close to Milton's face.

"Here's the deal, I'm going to do all the talking here." He squeezed Milton's voice box a little harder.

Milton's eyes bulged.

"You're going to drop that knife because all I have to do is apply a little more pressure and you will not only piss your pants and pass out, but you'll never be able to speak again without the aid of an electronic device. Do you understand?

"A simple nod will do." Zack said.

Zack saw the terror that had previously been on Jamie's face, now on Milton's.

Milton's face began to turn red and Zack heard the knife hit the ground.

"Guess, you're losing knives right and left." Zack loosened his grip. "Now, isn't that better?"

Milton brought his free arm up and Zack forearmed Milton in the face. Milton's nose bone snapped and blood exploded from his nostrils. Milton screamed and fell on his back in the grass, clutching his face.

Zack grabbed him, flipped him over and put a knee in his back. He forced Milton's face into the grass.

"Did you really think I would be so stupid?"

Milton didn't answer.

A patrol car squealed to the curb, with its lights flashing, and two officers jumped out as Jamie ran onto the front lawn.

"Okay, get off him!" One officer shouted, shining his flashlight into Zack eyes.

Zack released his grip and stepped back, showing both palms.

Milton scrambled to his feet, but the officers had Milton cuffed just as Jason and Jennifer Watkins roared into the driveway. Zack saw the magnetic police light flashing from the roof of Jason's car. Charlie and Missy, wide-eyed, were glued to the back windows like suction-cup dolls.

"I'm Jason Watkins," he flipped open his wallet as he approached, displaying the gold shield, "out of Robbery Division. I live here."

A second police unit pulled up, also with lights flashing.

Jenni opened the back car door and herded Charlie and Missy up onto the porch, as sirens filled the subdivision's streets.

"I'm Matherly," the first officer said, as the second hauled Milton to his feet.

Milton swore. "He broke my nose! I want to press charges!"

The officers paid no attention.

The paramedics stopped in the middle of the street just as a huge lime-green fire engine rounded the corner, lights ablaze.

"Your daughter impressed our dispatcher when she called." Matherly said.

"Oh?" Jason asked.

"Yeah, gave the right 10-code for what was happening." Matherly said.

"The curse of growing up in a cop's home." Jason smiled.

"She said the suspect had an assault charge on him from before?"

"That's right," Jamie said, as she and Zack approached, "and he assaulted me, tonight—"

"We'll definitely be pressing charges," Jenni said.

"I'm pressing charges too!" Milton yelled. "You're going to pay, Tucker! You're going to get yours!"

"Stop talking!" Matherly said and looked at Jason. "I can tell this will be a great ride to the jail."

Jason grinned and then walked over to Zack. "Are you alright?"

"Jason," Zack's voice trembled, "I'm so sorry, I feel so stupid—"

"It's okay, Zack," Jason said. "You were in hand to hand combat with someone with a knife; we, cops, don't even do that."

"Really?"

"Unfortunately, that's how suspects get shot, not dropping the knife."

"Jamie, I'm sorry it came to this," Zack said.

"Zack," Jamie kissed him on the cheek, "wow! You were great! I'm just glad you're okay, but you wiped the ground with that moron!"

"Jamie," Jason said.

"Sorry."

Jamie and Zack watched while Milton sat in the rear of a patrol car and a paramedic administered first aid.

Porch lights snapped on all over the block.

"Oh, man." Zack glanced up and down the street. "I'm so sorry, Jason. I really caused a mess.

"Don't worry about it." Jason smiled. "It's a little dull around here anyway." He glanced at Milton. "So, this guy is a real piece of work, huh?"

"Yeah, Milton Drago; we've been fighting since eighth grade. Not like this, of course." Zack shrugged. "He's just one of those guys that has to stick it to ya all the time, you know? I guess it finally came to a head. I'm really sorry. I don't want you to think that I'm the type of guy—"

"Not at all, Zack." Jason smiled. "I checked you out."

"Jason?"

"Dad?" Jamie said.

"Well, you're my first born," Jason shrugged, "and rank hath its privileges." He turned back to Zack. "If I didn't think you were decent, we wouldn't be having this conversation."

"Thanks." Zack watched the patrol car leave the curb with Milton in the rear.

"Uh, excuse me," a boy dressed in a red, white, and blue uniform said. "Did someone here order a pizza?"

He scanned the squad cars, ambulance, and fire engine with wide-eyed curiosity. He glanced at the ticket on the box, up at the front porch numbers, and then back to the ticket on the box.

"Yeah," Jason said, "and you didn't come for so long, we had to call the cops!"

—

Nate and Mick stood on the sidewalk a few houses down.

"Are you sure about this?" Nate asked.

"He has to battle his own demons first," Mick said.

"I guess, but what about when the real thing comes at him?"

"That's where you come in," Mick said.

"Yeah, I sort of guessed that."

"You have to make sure he's ready. We can't lose him."

"We won't," Nate paused. "Hey, pizza doesn't sound half bad?"

"For you maybe," Mick said.

"Come on." He punched Mick's arm. "Pizza Inn?"

"I'll just have the salad bar." Mick smiled.

"Suit yourself."

54

John grabbed the cordless phone off the coffee table and muted his DVD remote.

"Welte's Mortuary, you stab 'em, we slab 'em. Hello?"

"Hey."

"Well, if it isn't the Terminator." John said.

"Funny." Zack's voice came over the phone. "What are you doing right now?"

"What do you think?" John asked.

"Cataloging your Star Trek episodes?"

"Of course," John said.

"Which episode are you up to now?"

"43: Bread and Circuses." John said.

"You know," Zack said. "It's really scary that you already know all of the episodes by heart and can recite almost all of the lines—"

"Scary? Scary, my friend?" John leaned forward on the couch. "That I know all the episodes of the television show that changed American culture as we know it?"

"Well, that too," Zack said, "but more than that, why would they actually name an episode: *Bread and Circuses?*"

"Yeah, well I think it's a cool name too." John's voice rose. "You, of all people, should know it well. The Enterprise crew beams to the Roman history planet with the modern television technology and the commercials in-between the fights—"

"I know which one it is," Zack said. "Never mind. Do you want some overtime?"

"Yeah, man" John sat up on the couch, "of course. By the way, how's our little friend doing in jail?"

"Who cares? It's only been a day. So, what about the overtime?" Zack asked.

"I said, *yeah*. When?"

"Tonight, around seven. You'll be on the floor with me," Zack said.

"Manual labor?" John raised an eyebrow.

"Better than that closet you're stuffed into with all those monitors and hard drives."

"Hey, hey, that's my domain, man." John pushed his glasses back up his nose. "Don't be criticizing us Phaser Heads for what we contribute. If it weren't for us, geeks, the place would go down the drain." John smiled, picking at a spaghetti spot on the couch cushion.

"Yeah, right, forget about all of us that *actually* make the product," Zack snickered. "See you tonight."

"Live long and prosper." John hung up.

———

Gideon was in full-blown night-shift production when Zack toweled oil from the blade.

"Oh, man."

"What?" John stood a few feet away from Zack's workstation. Zack glanced at his black T-shirt: *Never put all of your ranking officers in one shuttle-craft.* And shook his head. "Oh, I'm out of finishing oil." Zack put one eye over the opening of a metal container, shaking it back and forth.

"There's some over here." John picked up a can.

"No, it's that imported stuff," Zack said. "It looks like olive oil, but more red. I just hate to stop —"

"No, problem, I'll get it," John said.

Zack paused. "Thanks, man. Do you know where it is?"

"No." John turned to look at the cute blonde working on some custom cases.

"Hey, focus, man. Forget about Mindy." Zack said.

Mindy smiled at John.

"Hey, she smiled at me first, man," John said. "What can I say? All the girls like the intelligent ones."

"It's because you're funny lookin' and she pities you." Zack smiled. "It doesn't mean anything. So, you gonna get the oil or what?"

"Yeah."

"It's the imported stuff in the gold can." Zack said.

"Yeah." John stared at Mindy.

"John!" Zack said.

"Sure, man." John's eyes met Zack's. "How hard could it be if *you* do it every day?" John's eyebrows twitched up and down.

"John?" Zack tried again to bring him back from blonde heaven.

"Yeah, no sweat." John waved his hand. "Don't give it another thought."

He tipped an imaginary bowler hat to Mindy as he walked past.

55

John pushed through a set of swinging doors and into the hallway, whistling into the darkness. The dim lighting catered to images of Mindy and he ambled right and left, down corridors, through doorways and up stairs. He skirted stacks of crates and peered at arrowed signs as if they were written in brail.

Finally he stopped.

He was lost.

—

Zack glanced at the huge hands of the clock on the manufacturing wall.

It's a good thing that I'm not a surgeon waiting for a kidney to transplant.

—

John pushed on a door.

Locked.

He walked down the hall. Another lock.

He proceeded, shoes squeaking on freshly waxed tile.

He stopped at an intersection of several hallways.

Left, right or straight?

Like a bloodhound on a killer's trail, John cocked his head and then walked toward light shining from a door, propped open by a mop bucket.

Pizza?

The faint aroma made the glands in his jaws ache. He stepped into the industrial kitchen that was wall to wall stainless steel. John walked to a large refrigerator and pulled on the door.

Leftover pizza was covered with leather buttons. Pepperoni.

John shrugged.

"Don't mind if I do," he muttered and shoved a piece into his mouth.

John wound through a maze of pots and pans hanging from ceiling racks and waved at the custodian exiting the walk-in freezer.

The man gave him a *right back at ya*.

John skirted a stainless steel counter and pushed through a door marked *IN*. Its twin, marked *OUT*, hung silently under a sign warning: *ENTERING A HIGH-TRAFFIC AREA, PLEASE PROCEED WITH CAUTION*.

He shuffled across the empty cafeteria seating area, with its expanse of tables and straight-armed chairs, through another set of doors.

John stopped in front of the elevators.

Finally, at least now I know where I am.

Fifth or fourth?

Mindy flashed across his screen and then Zack crowded back in.

Are you listening John?

John shook his head.

Focus.

John punched the lighted button on the gold elevator and the doors slid back with a ding. He climbed aboard and pushed number five.

The doors slid shut, but no movement.

"Come on."

He looked up at the numbers above the door, back at the buttons and pushed five again.

The elevator stood motionless and the doors remained closed.

"Oh, crap!"

He pushed number four. Nothing.

He pressed several other buttons.

No good.

"This is all I need." He hit the door with a balled-up fist.

"Hello!" he called. "I'm stuck on the danged elevator!" He slapped the doors again.

"Oh what the—"

John randomly hit buttons until the elevator lurched and began a descent.

56

Zack glanced at his watch.

Nearly half an hour.

Should've been ten minutes.

He finished the sword he was working on and stepped near John's station.

"Hey, Tredessa, have you seen John?"

"No, I'm sure that skinny little thing had to take a break," she grinned.

Zack glanced around, no Mindy either. Zack shook his head.

Zack rode the service elevator to the third floor and walked down a wide hallway speckled with metal carts and hand trucks. A forklift sat in the corner, the battery-charging light glowed red in the shadows. He pulled the handle of Storage Room Three.

"John?" Zack called.

Hundreds of metal speed racks loomed overhead as he stepped inside.

Good thing I didn't send him to the warehouse.

Zack looked down the neatly categorized shelves, like he was shopping for cereal. A thrumming bass guitar and a syncopated drum beat made him pause. A few more rows and he poked his head around a rack of shelves.

A man sat cross-legged on the floor, checking labels on small boxes and scribbling on a clipboard. A blaring silver boom box, with huge round speakers, was tethered by an orange extension cord, stretching into oblivion.

"Hey, Hector!" Zack cupped his hands around his mouth.

Hector jumped and turned the volume down.

"What's happenin', Zack?" Hector asked.

"Have you seen John?"

"Who?"

"John Welte, one of the new guys?" Zack glanced at his watch. "I sent him down to get some finishing oil about 45 minutes ago."

"Nah, man, haven't seen any dudes in here, just little ole' me puttin' the boxes away." Hector bobbed his head.

"Okay, thanks. Don't work too hard," Zack said.

"Hey, you know me," Hector shrugged, "I'm chillin' like a villain."

On the way out, Zack stepped down an aisle and grabbed a gold, metal can of finishing oil.

—

Zack rode the elevator back to the manufacturing floor and set the can outside the door. He glanced at his station. No sign of John. He stepped back into the elevator and looked at the worn buttons, the numbers barely readable.

"What a space cadet." Zack shook his head.

The doors closed and Zack pressed a button.

After another half hour of searching, Zack stood in front of the gold elevators.

Eeny, Meeny, Miney, Mo and he chose the third elevator and stepped inside. He scanned the black panel with the white buttons and pressed B1.

What the heck, never been to the basement.

He heard the mechanical whir and felt his stomach rise as the elevator dropped. After a long moment, the elevator braked and the doors slid back.

Darkness climbed aboard.

57

The musty odor stung his nostrils.

He leaned out, holding the door and trying to focus. A single dim bulb encased in metal mesh, threw a yellow tint on the damp walls.

"That doesn't seem to be 100-watts!" he yelled. "All I need now is a chainsaw wielding hockey player!" His voice echoed into the void.

Zack looked up in time for a large drop of water to hit him in the forehead and his heart skipped.

"Yeah, that's what we need… 25-watt bulbs and dripping pipes," Zack mumbled. "John!" His voice ricocheted back at him.

He looked on the wall. No fire extinguisher to prop the door open.

"Well, *that's* against OSHA regulations." He said.

He scanned the dimly lit floor. A metal mop bucket sat in the corner.

"That'll do!" he cupped his hands around his mouth.

He stretched out, wiggling his fingers, one hand still holding the door.

No good.

He propped his foot against the door and stretched like a first baseman going for a low throw.

Still couldn't reach.

I'm not chancing that this stupid elevator will leave me stranded.

Images of his skeleton slumped in the corner, for lack of food, flashed across his mind.

Zack? Zack Tucker? Yeah, he was working one night and just disappeared. Didn't find him until two weeks later. Had attempted to chew off his own finger to stay alive, poor fella.

"John!" Zack shouted again, wiping the sweat from his forehead. "I *am* going to kill him."

He straightened up and gave himself a count, rocking back and forth like he was at the starting blocks of an Olympic 100-yard dash.

Zack bolted toward the bucket.

He heard the door hesitate behind him and start to slide shut.

He smiled, success within his grasp.

Zack skidded through a water puddle from the overhead dripping and sprawled shoulder first into the concrete wall, knocking the breath out of him.

He rolled into the metal bucket, sending it ricocheting off into the darkness, as the interior light of the elevator faded and the doors snapped shut.

Zack put his aching head down on the cool concrete momentarily and then slammed his fist against the floor.

"I'm going to wring your neck!"

He pulled himself into a kneeling position. "The evil spirits are nothin' compared to what I'm going to do to you."

Zack smacked his forehead with the heel of his hand.

What an idiot, I am.

The red *Hold* button on the inside of the elevator door, he could have just pressed that.

He got up, brushed off his dirty, wet jeans and walked over to the elevator door. He pushed the call button, but no response. By now it had returned to the first floor.

Why didn't Mel tell me about these elevators? Why would he? I shouldn't be down here.

He looked around, shielding his eyes from the bulb in an effort to adjust his vision, and then started down a concrete hallway spotted with more dim wattage.

He passed several locked metal doors and caught movement out of the corner of his eye. Zack Tucker froze.

A newspaper headline flashed through his mind: "Rats in sewer pipes appear in toilets". Even now, he always checked before sitting down.

Another mass darted across the floor.

It's an *entire* rat army.

Then the legion paused in the dimness, stood on one set of hind legs and sniffed. Zack smiled at a single mouse.

He stomped his foot, kick-starting his own heart again and sending the mouse scurrying into the blackness.

The hallway dead-ended at a door which opened into a stairwell.

As he started down the stairs, his foot caught a metal edge and he clamored against the railing, grabbing hold before he plunged face first into the wall. He opened the first door he came to and stepped into a chain-link cage.

A massive chain and padlock secured a gate to steel posts, that were affixed to the ceiling and floor. Its wire mesh protected a dark room littered with equipment and crates. Zack rattled the gate.

"John!"

He scanned the darkness.

"Okay, this is beginning to get freaky," he muttered. Returning to the staircase and descending another flight he pulled on the last door.

Huge overhead pipes dripped condensation, as a steady hissing steam created humidity like a Louisiana swamp. A sulfuric smell assaulted his nose as he walked a few yards down a service tunnel and onto a suspended concrete landing, jetting off into space. He took hold of a guardrail surrounding the platform and gasped.

Zack's blood rushed to his head and he tightened his grip on the railing as he peered into a massive subterranean cavern illuminated by powerful lights, like a football stadium. Zack closed his eyes, intentionally sucking in and blowing out in long, exaggerated breaths. He opened his eyes again and looked down, shuddering and almost losing his balance.

It has to be twenty stories to the ground, his throbbing brain told him.

Zack slid down the rail and sat on the concrete, shifting his gaze upward. And at least the same distance to the ceiling.

He breathed in and out deliberately.

This must be the foundation of Gideon.

"We affectionately refer to it as 'the Netherworld'." Mel's word's echoed in Zack's memory. "Don't worry about it; you won't need to go down there anytime soon."

58

Zack steadied himself and looked back toward the tunnel. No turning back.

Fastened to the wall was a chain-link gate allowing access to metal stairs. He crawled to the gate, pushed it open, and started down on shaky legs.

Zack inched his way down, making deliberate contact with every tread.

Story after story, each landing led to more stairs.

Get a grip. One step closer to the ground. Don't look down.

Ten stories later he stopped and stared at the cavern floor.

They look like amphitheater seats.

He descended a few more stories and stopped, gripping the railing.

"Johnnn!" Zack cupped his hands. The echo faded with no response.

More stairs and landings. Periodically Zack would peer down another dark tunnel.

Zack stopped, leaning against the railing and panting.

Jamie. Her hair, her skin.

He smiled.

Zack laughed as Jamie faded into John's face and his hands around John's neck, throttling him until his eyes bulged.

His legs ached and his feet burned, but he started again.

Only a few more stories.

Zack planted his foot firmly on top of a concrete pillbox that looked fresh out of World War II. He expected the Guns of Navarone to be sticking out of the front.

He walked to the edge and grabbed hold of a rail.

Only about another thirty feet to the ground.

He walked back toward the stairs and stopped at a hatch in the concrete.

Zack took hold of a handle in the hatch and lifted.

"Oh, crap," he mumbled, "more stairs."

Zack sighed, as his feet touched the ground and he looked back at the incredible distance. The stairs wound a tiny ribbon upward that disappeared at the top.

He stood in a concrete tunnel large enough to drive two eighteen wheelers down, side by side.

Behind him, a tunnel, threaded with large, steaming pipes overhead, stretched into darkness.

Zack walked the opposite direction toward the mouth of the tunnel.

"John?" he called through the whisper of the steam.

No response.

He cupped his hands again, louder. "John!"

Two large iron gates stood ajar at the tunnel opening. On one side, a keypad beeped in time with a blinking red light. Below it was a huge bank of industrial levers obviously controlling the flood lights.

Zack pushed through the gates and into the cavern.

He walked a few more yards and stood on the brink of a massive amphitheater, with long flat seats descending away from him and steps dividing the rows.

Stone pillars lined the sides, reminiscent of ancient Rome.

John Welte sat in the front row, a dot in the vast expanse of the cavern. In front of him was an enormous carved-stone wall.

Zack bounded down the steps two at a time. "John!"

He reached John huffing and puffing and punched him in the arm. "You, idiot! Where have you been?"

John didn't respond.

"I've been looking all over for you, you…"

Zack followed John's gaze.

"What the—" He turned toward the massive granite wall and looked up.

"It's got to be sixty stories to the roof!" Zack said.

Zack walked the length, of half a football field, to the wall and ran his hands along the smooth, cool granite. His fingers danced in and out of the cuts and polishes and he closed his eyes as if hypnotized, running his palm over inlayed gold. Zack laid his cheek against the even surface, allowing the chill to sooth the sweat running from his temples. The floodlights illuminated the carvings of horse and rider, shields and swords and crests from some ancient time.

Zack opened his eyes and stepped back, staring at the center of the wall. Affixed by heavy pins, larger than his body, were two polished marble gates.

"Holy—" Zack recoiled at the sheer expanse of the marble slabs. "And these have to be four stories at least!"

His eyes wandered down every vein and cut in the gates.

"And no handles." Zack looked up.

Over the doors, huge golden letters spelled out: *SHEH-OLE*.

"This is incredible!" Zack said. "This all has to be worth a fortune!"

He turned and looked at John.

"John?"

John stared past Zack at the gates, chewing on something. His jaw muscles tightened and relaxed as he pulverized whatever was in his mouth.

"John?" Zack approached him again and touched his shoulder. "John? Buddy?" He shook him.

John looked up. "How long?"

"How long what?"

"Have I been sitting here?" John asked.

"I've been looking for you for almost two hours now. What gives?" Zack threw up his hands. "I send you to get some oil and you end up praying in front of the altar of King Kong?" Zack chuckled. "What are you eating?"

He put his hand on John's shoulder and John shrugged it away.

"I eat these when I'm nervous." John picked up a small bag of Boston Baked Beans.

"What are you talking …What *is* this place?" Zack glanced around.

John stared at him through blank eyes. "Do you remember sophomore literature?" he asked.

"What?"

"Sophomore Lit." John adjusted himself on the seat, pulled out another handful of Boston Baked Beans and threw one into his mouth.

"We talked about ancient Hebrew history, remember?"

"No, not really. Well, I remember the class." Zack shrugged. "But no details off the top of my head. Man, that was two years ago, I didn't have to—"

"There was a particular passage in one of the scrolls that mentioned a word. Sheh-ole. You don't remember?"

"No, I don't remember." Zack exhaled. "I already told you I didn't. What's this, a history quiz? Why are you being so weird—"

"It fascinated me," John interrupted. "The term, I mean. We buzzed over it so quickly and obviously no one cared."

"Yeah, so?" Zack said. "Obviously I didn't care either—"

"But I went home and researched it." John said.

"Okay?"

"It means 'The City of the Dead.' " John paused, looking back and forth at the massive wall. "Also 'HELL.'"

John swallowed and drew in a breath, his eyes pierced Zack. "What have you gotten us into?"

59

Milton Drago walked into a long, narrow room with smudged glass lining the wall to his left. Several orange-clad men sat in cubicles talking on heavy black handsets. The guard led him to a round iron seat in front of the Plexiglas.

"You've got 20 minutes, Drago. Watch your temper and your language."

Milton sat down and motioned toward the receiver.

"What took you so long, Mom?"

"I couldn't get here any faster." She paused. "You know I got a speeding ticket coming over here the other day." She paused again, staring past Milton. "The last time I got a speeding ticket was—"

"You should've come sooner, mom, now I'm not going to have enough time—"

"Well, I just didn't know about that speed limit sign." Her gaze returned to him. "How's your nose?" Katherine touched the glass. "Looks better. Are they treating you alright?"

"No, they're not, Mom." Milton glanced around. "This is jail, not a freakin hotel."

"I don't like you to talk that way, Milton. Do you need anything?" Katherine asked.

"Money." Milton replied flatly.

"Well, I'll try…" Katherine shook her head and looked down.

"Don't try, just do it, Mom."

"It's just so tight right now, Milton, and now with this ticket." She glanced at her purse.

"I've got to have it!" Milton hissed. "It's not my fault *you* got a ticket."

Milton glanced at the guard standing by the door and then lowered his voice almost to a whisper.

"It's different in here, Mom. See, if I have money, I can make deals and get things."

"What things?"

"Just things, Mom." He ran his hand through his greasy hair.

"What things?" She stared into his eyes.

"Cigarettes, okay?" Milton spat back.

"I don't like you smoking, Milton."

"Mom! It's not about that! It's about surviving!" he shouted.

"Booth seven! Quiet down!" The voice exploded over the loud speaker.

Milton glanced back at the guard and softened again.

"See, " he drew on the glass with his finger, watching it make circles, "I just need it, Mom. Please." He stopped drawing and looked up. "If I have money, I can pay for things and it will help me not to get…"

Katherine sighed. "Okay. I'll leave it for you out front. There's not much." Katherine paused. "Milton, why haven't you talked to Del?"

"That's over, Mom. I don't want to see her anymore—"

"But, Milton, you could work it out—"

"I'm not interested in *working it out*, Mom. We're history." He waved his hand dismissing her comment. "She's a slut."

"Milton. I don't like you using those sorts of words—"

"I'm just telling you what she is, Mom. She'll sleep with anybody. Dad always called those kind, 'damaged goods.' Don't you remember?"

"I remember, Son." Katherine stared at him. "But still—"

"Forget it." He brushed his hand over his hair again. "Forget her. Listen, there're more important things right now." Milton glanced around as if telling a secret. "You gotta get me out of here, Mom. Whatever you've got to do."

60

The cell door slammed behind Milton. He looked at the walls, crusted with graffiti.

Jesus Saves, Diablos Rules!, Jerry was here, When you're out, call Tina for a good time-555-8747, Be it ever so humble, there's no place like hell.

Jailhouse prose. Milton shook his head.

At least I'm in here alone.

"Kiddy Bait," the guards called him.

"We got to make sure you make it to the judge in one piece." A large guard had told him. "You won't last five minutes in with the heavies. We better keep you hidden away."

10:00 p.m., straight up.

The buzzer sounded and the lights snapped off, plunging Milton into hated darkness. The yard light shone through the shoe-box-sized window, which didn't help.

He rolled over on the wool blanket and inhaled the scent of the institutional detergent.

Well, at least my smell is returning. He touched the bandage on his nose.

61

Darkness engulfed Milton and he turned over on a pillow barely larger than his head. He bounced his legs up and down, trying to work out the boredom. Squirming, wiggling, and flopping like a carp on a river bank. Milton stared at the shadowed wall until his eyelids grew heavy and he drifted off.

—

Milton combed through tall, crimson grass, speckled with tiny yellow-orange flowers. He saw the two people beside the barn, a mile away and with every step squished blood between the toes of his bare feet like he was wringing out a rag from a butcher's shop.

One foot in front of the other for what seemed like hours but the barn was still a mile away. He moved his empty hands to his eyes, like a child, pretending that he held binoculars and twisted his wrists, zooming in.

The magnification startled him and he blinked.

I'm in too close.

He cranked his hands the other direction and saw a young man, in black jeans, pacing back and forth in a blur.

He removed his hands from his eyes and broke into a run, but the barn remained in the distance. He panted to a stop and adjusted his hands over his eyes again. The man wore denim overalls and was engrossed in a heated argument with the young man in the black jeans.

Black Jeans shoved Denim Overalls away and he stumbled. Milton peered through his hand-binoculars at Denim Overalls' grimy cuffs over the muddy boots. He raised the focus to a huge belly stressing a thread bare long-john shirt.

Like looking through a rain soaked window, Milton couldn't quite focus.

Denim Overalls suddenly recoiled, holding his head.

What's happening?

What is it?

Another blow came and Denim Overalls tried to block it, but Black Jeans took aim again.

Black Jeans swung.

What was it?

What did he swing?

Denim Overalls' arms went limp and he stood motionless. Milton watched as blood drenched the base of Denim Overalls' collar and turned the creases of his white long-john shirt into crimson streams from the inside out.

Milton's legs began to tremble and he looked down, seeing blood flow from under his own pants and onto his bare feet.

He looked back at the blurred images.

Like a faucet had been twisted to full on, the blood flowed over the tops of the overalls and ran down into the pockets.

Milton tried to focus again blinking back the sweat.

He watched the pockets fill with blood and spill out like a gasoline nozzle when the automatic shutoff fails. The blood cascaded down the folds and lines of the overalls and onto the muddy boots, turning them dark brown. The blood gushed out of his pant legs, like a circus clown shoving a garden hose down his pants. It soaked his white tube socks and bubbled over the laces into the dirt.

The man slumped to his knees and then toppled face down in the weeds. He lay motionless.

Milton lowered his hands and stared at them.

Blood red binoculars were fused to his hand as if melted on a hot griddle. He put the binoculars back to his eyes, running up the blood-spattered torso of Black Jeans, as he stood over the body, and zoomed in on his face. The nostrils flared with every breath, and the eyes darted back and forth like those of a little boy caught behind the barn with a dirty magazine.

Milton took one step and stood next to the smiling young man who looked up at him.

Milton Drago stood face to face with himself.

62

Milton bolted upright in his bunk, his sweat-soaked undershirt clinging to his chest. He rubbed his eyes, trying to focus on the dark cell's interior. The form in the corner didn't register in Milton's mind until he rubbed his eyes again. It crossed one long leg over the other, gently swinging a stiletto high heel.

Terror seized him, like a tumor growing from his stomach and clawing its way up his throat until it exploded over his vocal cords and out his mouth.

"Guard!" But it only came out in a squeak.

Angie leaned forward into the light that dribbled through the window and laid a finger across her ox-blood colored lips.

"We don't need anybody watching us, Baby," she said.

"Angie? What are you doing here?" Milton closed his eyes, winced and then opened them again.

"Yes, Baby, I'm real," she said.

"Guard," Milton whispered. "How did you get in here?"

His heart thumped and his face flushed, as sweat ran down his temples. He balled into a fetal position on the blanket. The silence framed the peck of her high heels, on the concrete, as she crossed the cell.

Clip. Milton winced.

Clip. The echo sent his stomach into spasms.

Clip. He cradled his knees.

Clip. He jumped as Angie slid her hand down his thigh.

"Angie." Milton breathed.

"Relax, Baby," Angie climbed onto the bed and stroked his forehead. "Puffinking is here."

She kissed him, long and deep, as if possessing his being, then blew into his mouth.

Milton felt her hot breath burn down his throat and into his lungs, like the first time he inhaled a cigarette.

"Angie," Milton managed, "where have you been? Why did you leave?"

"Not to worry, honey," she touched her belly, "you'll always be with me."

"Angie, I've needed you—"

"And I, you," she said. "I will become a part of you and you, a part of me."

Milton put his arms around her and held her to his chest, feeling the rise and fall of her breath. He closed his eyes and felt her lips against his ear. Every pour alive. Every hair follicle groaning for her touch, aching for Angie's whisper to brush against them. Milton felt no pain as the tip of the dagger penetrated his chest.

Angie released him and he looked down at the front of his orange jump suit. It was like a child's toy, a retractable blade on a pirate's knife. He felt the steel, cold and hard penetrating his rib cage and the walls of his lungs.

Milton grabbed the front of the orange cloth and pulled it open. He saw beads of blood beginning to form around the black blade, like a crimson, pearl necklace, they flowed around the razor edge and dribbled down his stomach.

He opened his mouth to scream, in that instant between when a toddler smashes his finger and when the sound actually leaves his mouth, but he couldn't. The pain was dull, almost non-existent. Far away; a monotonous thud, pounding away in another room. He felt it touch the sack of his heart. He sensed the tip, as if a doctor's syringe pierced the flesh.

Terrifying, yet soothing.

Horrifying, but exciting.

Milton watched as Angie's delicate hand twisted the handle of the dagger and it began to pump clear liquid down the brilliant ebony edge until it reached his chest and slipped inside past the beads of sweat and blood.

He sensed it, sliding down the blade to the tip and infusing his heart. Inoculating him against anything and anyone that would try and oppose him. No one could harm him. No one would dare try. His mother's worries had no effect on him. His father's abuse could not detour him. Zack Tucker could not stand against him. He would possess Zack. He would conquer him. He would annihilate him.

The oil coursed into his heart, penetrating the cells, replacing them, strengthening them, rejuvenating them. He felt it. The hatred. The rage. The revenge. That burning from deep down in his carnal soul that bubbled up and encased his being.

Milton watched the black blade slide back out of his chest and the wound frothed as if acid sealed the gash.

He looked up at Angie and closed his eyes, feeling the pulse, her pulse inside him. He opened his lids again in an amber haze. His pupils magnified the faint light streaming into the cell and he saw, as if it were a sunset on the horizon.

Angie turned and sat on the edge of the bunk while Milton stroked her hair and back. She pulled her shirt off over her head to reveal the dragon and snake tattoo on her back.

Milton tried to speak, his voice raspy and low. "Why do you call it Puffinking?"

"Puff the Magic Dragon and King Cobra, honey. Puff and King." Angie smiled and lay back down beside him. "Be quiet now, darling," She kissed him. "Give yourself a few minutes rest; we have a job to do."

63

The county jail's policy mandated that a veteran jailer, like Manny Cranztuber, be paired with a rookie deputy, which in this case was Trevor Janish.

"No way?" Janish blurted out as they sat in what the guards affectionately called, "the Cage". "Do you really think that Green Bay will let Kendrick Washington go?"

"All I'm tellin' ya is that Macavoy would be a fool if they didn't give Tyrell Smith the ten million to play for them next year and dump Washington. I think—"

"Who the hell is that—" Janish moved to the bars and peered down the corridor at the woman walking away.

Milton Drago's laughs erupted through the ventilation system until they reached the Cage.

64

"What?" Zack turned and looked at the wall and then back at John. "What do you mean, the Gates of Hell?" He forced a grin.

"Who are these people?" John's eyes filled with dread. "And what sort of company has this underneath it?" He opened his arms wide toward the wall.

Zack's grin dissolved.

A hideous scream echoed through the cavern and Zack spun. Like being birthed from the stone, a black form wiggled and squeezed from a fissure in the granite wall.

Zack took a step back, bumping into John. They watched black, fur covered arms pry free. It panted and pushed, puffing its way out of the crevice. Further and further it squirmed; chest first, then waist, then hindquarters. With a final heave, it fell into the dirt.

"Is that a man?" John whispered.

"I don't know." Zack took another step backward.

It stood upright and shook itself, like a dog with a horse's mane, and rustled the long hair on its back. The creature stretched long, hairy fingers and flexed sharp, dirty claws. It dropped to all fours and scratched its shoulder with its hind leg producing a cloud of dust mites, and then peered at Zack and John growling through yellow fangs.

The creature sprang toward them on powerful hind legs, covering the distance quickly and screamed human curses with undertones of rabid snarls. John froze as the creature launched itself and knocked him to the ground.

They both tumbled onto the amphitheater floor and the creature rolled into the first row of stone seats with a thud. It bounded onto all fours again, hissing and wagging its head, squinting red slits for eyes. It lunged again closing in on them. Zack whirled and slapped it away. The creature folded in a heap and then shook its head.

"Stop it, that hurts," the creature hissed, in a woman's voice.

Zack recoiled seeing the gnarled features of a woman.

"It's female." He turned to John.

The creature leapt again, sinking her teeth into Zack's shirt and shaking it like a dog with an old rug.

Zack felt searing pain in his chest and grabbed her mane, forcing her to bite harder. He screamed and punched her head frantically until she loosened her grip. Zack grabbed her by the mane and pulled her off, holding her away from him.

Zack gagged and vomited into her long hair at the sight of his own blood on her fangs.

The fangs snapped inches from his face and Zack shrank back, smelling her sour breath and feeling the saliva splatters against his cheek. She swiped at him digging her claws into his arm and then his neck, opening lines of bloody flesh. Zack pummeled her again and again, trying to make the creature release.

John kicked the creature in the side, finally dislodging her. She hit the ground and rolled into a pillar with a piece of Zack's bloody shirt stuck in her teeth.

Zack whirled as he heard another scream, and a second creature flopped into the dirt from the crevice.

"Run!" Zack yelled, and he and John bolted toward the steps.

The beasts were on them, the first latching onto John's foot.

"She got my shoe!" John called, wiggling out of it.

"Keep running!" Zack yelled in panic.

"Easy for you to say, you've got both shoes!" John squawked and stumbled, falling onto the steps.

Zack scrambled to the top of the amphitheater and glanced back, catching his foot and sprawling into the dirt. She bounded after him three steps at a time and lunged toward him.

He balled up in a fetal position and covered his head.

Zack heard her scream and then a *whump* as if someone hit a ripe melon with a baseball bat. He opened his eyes and saw half her head hit the ground and throw up puffs of dirt and blood as it rolled. The torso flopped next to him, one dark eye twitching as it looked at him. He gasped as the body broke into spasms and then lay still.

Zack rolled onto his back and looked up.

Nate's gleaming blade drooled blood. Mick flanked him, sword also unsheathed, as Mel trotted up, out of breath.

"I guess you took a wrong turn somewhere, aye?" Mick said. "We usually don't introduce you to this level for a few more months."

Nate pulled Zack to his feet.

"Probably better clean up the remains." Mick turned to Nate.

"I'm on it," Nate nodded.

"I'm sorry, Mick. I was down here looking for John—" Zack doubled over out of breath.

John limped up, one shoe on, the other off.

"Are you okay?" Zack asked.

"Yeah, the other thing took off when Nate split this one's head." John pointed to the heap on the ground.

"Mick?" Zack asked. "What's going on here and what are these things?"

"We need to get you to the infirmary and get that wound looked at," Mick said, "then explanations are in order."

65

Jamie sat in her queen sized bed, propped up by five goose-down pillows and wearing her favorite gray T-shirt, with *Properties of the St. Louis Cardinals* scrawled across it, written in what looked to be a large piece of sidewalk chalk.

"Let's see what the Dashwoods are up to tonight."

She flipped the pages of *Sense and Sensibility*. The colorful descriptions of the English aristocracy fascinated her, even for the third time through.

She glanced at the clock, almost 10:00 pm.

Weird, no call from Zack.

She scanned the pages.

Jane Austen, what a classic.

Jamie reached for the glass of juice, nearly knocking it off the nightstand. Her eyes darted back and forth across the description of the English countryside, as she took a drink. She replaced it and then wiped the sweat from the glass on her blue jean cutoffs.

Jamie glanced at the double French doors that opened onto her balcony.

What was that?

She stared out into the darkness.

Nothing.

She returned to Jane Austen.

There it was again.

What was that movement? Was she just imagining...

The trees.

Jamie sighed.

The sway of the trees opposite the balcony came to mind.

It's just the wind, gotta be. Did she lock the doors though?

It's the second floor. But still.

Jamie laid the book face down on the comforter and slid to the floor, then inched along the area rug until her feet touched the hardwood floor. She reached for the deadbolt and twisted it home.

Something outside moved and Jamie jumped back.

What was that?

She moved back to the door and cupped her hands against the glass.

Jamie traced the outline of the balcony railing, the trees beyond and the form in the blackness.

It moved again.

She screamed and stumbled back toward her bed.

Weapon?

Nightstand.

What could she use?

Letter-opener?

She doubted it.

She glanced toward the window again and knocked the half-full glass to the floor, spraying sticky juice onto the rug and across her bare feet.

Milton Drago's face appeared in the window. He looked at Jamie and blinked yellow eyes shaped like a cat's.

"Dad!" She screamed.

One French door exploded, raining glass onto the floor. He peered through the jagged glass, like looking out of the maw of a Great White Shark.

"Daddy!" she screamed again.

"Daddy!" Milton screamed after her.

Milton pushed through the glass and looked down at the deep gashes cut by the shards. He watched the black blood run down his arms and turn black as it reached his wrist, then looked back up at Jamie and smiled. His long hair was wet and the tangles reached nearly to his shoulders. His whiskers were in-grown throughout a face erupting with pimples that festered and were ready to pop. His arms were thin, like a drug addict's, but had the start of a thick mat of hair like a dog's front legs. Milton bowed at the waist like an old man with back problems.

"I've missed you," he said.

The bedroom door flew open nearly imbedding the doorknob

in the sheetrock. Jason Watkins glanced around and then leveled a .45 caliber semi-automatic pistol at Milton.

"Police! Stay where you are!"

Milton leapt at Jason like a cat, as he squeezed the trigger.

The bullet hit Milton in the leg, spraying black puss against the broken door, as he landed a few feet from Jason. He looked down at the hole, raised his head and smiled. The gun had chambered another round and Jason squeezed again. The second bullet hit Milton in the side and spun him to the floor.

Jenni ran in behind Jason and screamed as Milton rose.

Jason dropped the pistol and his six-foot-four frame closed the distance instantly. He hit Milton like a linebacker and they both slammed into the wall, buckling the sheetrock and sending a spider web of cracks shooting off in all directions. Milton snarled and pushed Jason back.

Jason stumbled, grabbed a wooden chair covered with Jamie's clothes, and swung.

The chair caught Milton in the head and sent him sprawling toward Jamie's bathroom door. Milton pawed at a pair of jeans caught on his head and then shook himself like a dog coming in from the rain.

He smirked at Jason.

"It's not that easy, Daddy," Milton hissed.

He lunged for Jamie, caught her by the arm and pulled her in front of him.

Angie appeared in the broken window and stepped through.

Jason started for Milton and Jamie again, but Angie held up her hand. "No, Daddy, it's not that easy—"

"Who *are* you?" Jason yelled as Jenni ran to his side.

"We're the ones that are going to take your daughter," Angie smiled.

"Like hell you will—"

"Exactly." Angie began to swirl her arm and dust and dirt appeared to come from it.

"Daddy!" Jamie screamed.

Jason started for her, but the clothes were picked up in the vortex joined by notebook pages and shoes. Jane Austen's novel flew off the bed and joined the other debris now beginning to swirl as if in the midst of a Kansas tornado. The chair left the floor and Jason and Jenni dropped to the ground, as the nightstand shot past them in the torrent. Pencils embedded themselves in the wall; the glass flew across the room and smashed into the bathroom mirror, shattering it and spraying liquid and glass onto the sink.

"Jamie!" Jenni screamed. "Jamie!"

"Mom! Help me!" Jamie reached out from the middle of the maelstrom, her arm scratched by the dust and dirt coming from the center.

"Jamie!" Jason yelled above the roar of the storm, as the chair ripped along the wall like a can opener, cutting the sheetrock and sending framed art flying in all directions. The chair whirled and hit the French doors, exploding them in a shower of glass and wooden shreds. The chair continued its buzz-saw destruction, as it left the wall and struck Jason in the shoulder and head, driving him to the ground unconscious.

Jenni screamed and pulled herself next to Jason as the nightstand trailed the chair, one leg striking her behind the head and sending her into the wall in a heap.

"Mom! Dad!"

Jamie reached out, but the violent surge and centrifugal force sucked her closer to Milton. She looked at Angie, whose hideous smile never changed.

"Sorry, sweetie," Angie yelled, "but we need you."

The storm picked up speed and destruction, like being caught in the middle of a vacuum cleaner, and sucked all three of them out the shattered door, off the balcony and down into a crater that opened in the lawn.

66

"Gladys, we had a problem on one of the lower levels," Mick said as they reached the infirmary.

"Oh, dear me." Gladys's silver hair glistened in the fluorescent lighting, as she padded across the floor.

"Come right over here, Zack." She put a wrinkled hand on his shoulder. "We'll get you fixed up good as new."

"Thanks, Gladys," Zack said.

He slowly removed his shirt. He looked down at his open flesh, chunked, like prying grapefruit loose with a spoon. The blood on his chest had begun to dry. He felt his neck, and dried blood flaked onto his hand.

Zack lay down on the examining table. Gladys inserted a hypodermic needle into a small clear, glass bottle filled with green liquid and then held it to the light and flicked it.

"You may feel a little pinch," Gladys said.

Zack knew what "a little pinch" meant: brace yourself. He was neither surprised nor disappointed.

The heat crawled through his veins and the buzzing in his head overcame him. The pictures on the wall swam and his focus blurred. The voices in the room grew garbled and muffled. He looked at Nate's face. It was round and enlarged, like blowing up a helium balloon. Zack felt himself laugh, but heard it moments later. The curtain was falling and his eyelids closed. Then, blackness.

———

Zack floated, rising and falling with a current driving him from one river bank to another. He felt the surge and heard the roar.

A river?

A torrent?

What was this place?

He felt a hand on his forearm. A small hand. A child? A woman? It tugged at him, pulling him from one direction and then another. What did she want? Why would she not let go?

Fatty. Or Patty. Or Mattie? Who was she? She latched onto him, digging her nails into him. He remembered when he was young and one of those big grasshoppers would accidently land on his leg, digging into the flesh. Was she a huge grasshopper clawing for survival in all this water?

The surge pulled him.

Tumbling him end over end, head over foot; down, down, down, ever downward until he touched bottom and then silently, with no force, roar or torrent, he began to rise back to the top.

Sunlight.

Water depth: shallow.

But she wasn't with him. She had let go or been thrown clear of him.

The voice was muffled, bubbly like Zack was only submerged in a bathtub full of water.

"He's coming to."

"Zack?"

Zack fluttered his eyes, light then dark then light again.

"Zack? You doin' alright?"

Zack opened his eyes.

The clock blurred into focus.

"An hour?" he asked, or he thought he did.

Mick, Nate, and Mel clustered together in conversation while Gladys pumped up the blood pressure cuff around his arm.

John's face appeared upside down over his.

"How ya doin', buddy?"

Zack blinked again and smiled.

"Wow, that was a wild ride," he mumbled.

"He's going to be fine, Mr. Abbeer." Gladys looked at her watch, holding Zack's wrist.

"A couple of days and he will be as good as new. I salved the wound and it will do the trick." She released the rubber bulb and unwrapped the blood pressure cuff.

Gladys leaned close to Zack and whispered. "The secret's in the salve."

He smelled like fresh peppermint; and, like draining water from his bathtub, the drugs wore off and his mind returned.

"How are you doing, Zack?" Mick asked.

"A little stiff, but alright, I guess." Zack sat up and stretched.

"You should have very little side effects," Mick said.

"So this has happened before?"

Mick stared at him. "You'd better get home. John, you drive him."

"10-4," John said. "Come on, man."

He took Zack's arm and steadied him as he slid off the examining table.

67

"What do you mean, taken?" Zack said into his cell phone, a few hours later. Cobwebs spun in his head as he tried to wrap his mind around the wake-up call.

"We don't know all the details yet, Zack." Mick's voice was calm and even.

"Jamie? But I don't understand. Taken from what? Taken *to* what? What are you talking about?"

"Zack, you will want to come in right away. I'll explain."

Mick hung up.

He bolted out of bed, stubbing his toe.

"Oh crap!" He stumbled toward the bathroom.

Zack glanced in the mirror, as he frantically searched for the shirt he had thrown on the side of the tub the night before.

A slight scab covered his gash from the creature.

He moved closer to the mirror and reached down rubbing the scab. It fell to the floor exposing a fresh scar.

"What the—"

He ran his finger over the virgin skin.

We could make a fortune from this stuff.

Less than forty-five minutes later, Zack ran through the doors of Gideon.

"Zack!" Mel motioned as he scurried past. "Go to the war room!"

"War room? Mel, what's happening? Mick called and said

Jamie—"

"Mr. Abbeer will explain it to you when you get to the war room." Mel gathered paperwork off the reception's desk. He turned back to Zack.

"When you get there, watch and listen, but don't ask any questions yet," he paused with compassion in his eyes. "It'll be alright, Zack; trust us."

"But Mel—"

He turned and hurried across the lobby. "It's on the third floor, at the end of the hall, you can't miss it." He disappeared through a doorway.

"I've been missing it the whole time I've worked here!" Zack said.

Zack ran for the elevator.

"Hey, hold the elevator." The man rounded the corner and stepped onboard.

"You got called in too, huh?" the man asked.

"Yes, my girlfriend—" Zack paused remembering what Mel had said. "Never mind."

"Are you going to the war room?" the man asked, punching the button marked three.

"Yes," Zack looked up at the light console, indicating which floor they were ascending to. He glanced at the elevator door then down to the floor and back up at the numbers. The elevator finally slowed and stopped and the doors parted. He turned to the man.

"I'm Zack Tucker." He offered his hand. "You look really familiar, have we met—"

"Ever get down around accounting way?" The man shook his hand and hung on.

"No." Zack pulled his hand away.

"Probably not then." The man grinned. "My name's James Recent. You can call me, Jim."

68

Zack hurried into a massive auditorium filled with thousands of people.

"Holy—" Zack glanced at his watch, *3:30am.*

"Zack." Nate stood near the door like a Marine guard at parade rest, his hands clasped behind his back and elbows sticking out to the side.

"Nate, what's happened? I—"

Nate stepped toward him. "In due time. We know where Jamie is and—"

"But Nate, I—"

Nate placed his hand on Zack's shoulder and tranquility flowed like warm honey over him, beginning at the top of his head and ending with the soles of his feet.

"Nate, I don't understand."

"You will. Trust, Zack, trust."

Zack swallowed hard and cleared his throat. He looked toward the auditorium. "How'd you get this many people here at this hour?"

"They're all here for you."

"Me?" Zack asked. "But—"

"Welcome to the night shift," Nate smiled.

Zack looked at Nate. He wore a tight black t-shirt with the crest of Gideon embroidered in gold stitching on the left breast. His massive biceps were hardly contained in the armholes. His black paramilitary style pants, with numerous pockets, were tucked into black combat boots.

"You look like you're ready for war," Zack said.

"Something like that," Nate smiled.

"Where do you want Jim and me?" Zack asked.

"Jim?"

Zack turned around and realized James Recent hadn't followed him out of the elevator.

"Well, I guess… Where do you want me?"

"Follow me." Nate started down the aisle and then stood at the end of the front row like a theater usher.

"Sorry, Zack," he said as he motioned for him to sit. "We were going to ease you in slow, but under the circumstances—"

"Hey! Wait for me!" John ran down the aisle out of breath.

"It's about time," Zack said, as John slid into the seat beside him.

"You know me," John said, "late to my own funeral."

"I hope this isn't it," Zack said.

John smiled and then turned somber looking up at Nate. "What's going on?"

Mick stepped onto the platform.

Nate turned as everyone in the auditorium stood and came to attention, as if the President of the United States had just entered. Zack and John came to their feet and stood erect, watching Mick walk to the center of the massive stage behind a white marble podium. He was dressed similarly to Nate, with black t-shirt, gold crest on the left breast, black paramilitary pants and boots.

Behind him was a massive wall of purple drapes, spanning from the 50-foot ceiling to the floor of the stage.

"Be seated." His voice boomed over the auditorium from a cordless microphone head set.

Everyone sat down.

"A chain of events has been set into motion in the last 24 hours that affects not only the future of Gideon, but all of mankind."

Zack glanced around at the intent faces of his co-workers and colleagues.

"What's he talking about?" John whispered.

Zack shrugged.

Mick held up a remote control and the purple sea behind him parted, revealing a topographical map, the likes of which Zack had never seen. Brilliant colors cascaded over mountains, streams and continents, but Zack could not recognize any of the landmasses.

"There has been a disruption in Tartaroo."

The crowd murmured.

Mick held up his hand for silence.

"Echthros has summoned Abaddon back to the throne room."

Zack noticed more whispers, but Mick did not quiet them.

"Echthros?" Zack turned to John.

John shrugged. "Sounds major."

Mick stepped closer to the colossal map.

"Echthros has massed his forces again, here." He moved a laser pointer back and forth on the map. "His plan is to move up the Basin of Death, storm our gates and overrun Gideon. This, of course, will create the domino effect that he has always hoped for."

The auditorium fell silent and Zack looked at John.

"Zack Tucker."

Zack's head snapped back up front, as if he had been caught talking in study hall.

"Please stand," Mick said.

Zack rose slowly.

"Zack's girlfriend, Jamie Watkins, has been taken."

More murmurs swept the crowd, eyes on Zack.

Mick waited for the wave to subside.

"Some of the Charis have also fallen into Echthros's hands."

A rumble of whispers again moved through the auditorium.

Mick held his hand up again. "They will be used as shields against us, as always, or be executed before he marches."

"Like always," a man behind them said.

Mick stepped back to the podium and looked directly at Zack.

"We will get her back."

The auditorium erupted in applause; and, tears welled in Zack's eyes. He turned to the crowd and mouthed the words: "Thank You," and then returned his attention to Mick.

Mick turned back to the audience.

"*And we will not*," he emphasized, "allow him to reach this city." He paused. "You remember the chaos that it caused last time."

Zack looked around, thinking it resembled a convention of bobble-headed dolls.

"I don't remember," John whispered.

"Shh," Zack turned to him.

"Thank you, Zack, you can sit back down."

"This operation," Mick scanned the audience, "is mandated *covert*. A full frontal attack, and Echthros will execute the Charis. He cannot know we are coming; no matter how anxious we are." Mick met Zack's eyes.

"Better that way." The man patted Zack's shoulder. "Don't let the freaks know what hit 'em."

Zack wondered what he meant by *freaks*.

"We will enter the City of the Dead here." Mick pointed the laser dot at the map. "Our forces still hold the position."

"Well, at least that's something to be thankful for," someone else said.

"We will then proceed toward Tartaroo," Mick said. "According to our intel, the passage to the south is largely unguarded and Echthros is not aware of our information. A forward team, led by Nate, will be inserted to penetrate Tartaroo and recover the captives. The events that have transpired concerning Jamie Watkins will complicate matters, but nothing that they can't handle." Mick looked at Nate and nodded.

Nate stepped in front of the stage and turned toward the throng.

"I need the following people to join me up front: "Tredessa Huntington,—"

"From weaponry," Zack whispered to John as Dessa came forward.

"John Welte,—"

"Me?" John's eyes widened as he got up slowly and left his seat.

Nate didn't miss a beat. "And Zack Tucker."

Zack stood and walked toward Nate.

"These people are the tip of the spear," Mick said. "They are our first line of defense and intelligence."

The entire auditorium erupted in applause and was on their feet with whistles and shouts.

"People of Gideon!" Mick shouted. "We are the chosen remnant!" His voice grew intense on the backs of the shouts.

"The guardians of peace. The protectors of mankind!" His voice grew more forceful with every word. "This night, we march! For the protection of your families, for the safety of our homes, for the liberation of Jamie Watkins!" Mick paused again. "And all of mankind!"

The multitude roared with chants of victory.

Mick shouted. "Prepare your weapons! Pneuma be with us!"

Like the swelling of the ocean surf, they surged throughout the auditorium.

"Okay, you guys!" Nate shouted over the roar. "Zack, you come with me, the rest of you, go with Calver!"

Nate motioned for Calver to join them.

"Be with you momentarily!"

69

Zack followed Nate to a service elevator, large enough to accommodate a bulldozer. He flipped the switch to hold the doors until Mick rounded the corner and climbed aboard.

"Gentlemen," Mick said.

Mick flipped the switch back to the *ON* position and then glanced around the elevator.

"It looks like we've just accelerated your training, Zack."

"I'd say so," Zack said.

Mick was now wearing a type of utility belt that Batman would have envied, complete with compartments and rectangular sections that looked like ammo pouches. At Mick's side hung Baraq, in a stainless steel sheath. In Gideon's catalog, it was deemed *The Lightning Sword;* lightweight, maneuverable and sharp enough to shave the fuzz off a peach.

"Wow," Zack exhaled. "Nice sword."

"Thank you," Mick looked down at it. "Nate did a pretty good job on it earlier this week," Mick paused, "for a musical bum."

Zack glanced at Nate who was grinning.

"I know my speech didn't give you a lot of information, so let me briefly bring you up to speed.

"Up until now, in your life, time has been a constant. When we cross the threshold into the Region of the Dead, past, present and future will coexist in equal time slices. Up here, it will be business as usual. Down there, we will accomplish in an hour what normally takes us a month. Because of the time continuum, your dad will see this day as any other workday. You were called in to work early today. You'll be home, *hopefully,* by supper."

Hopefully? Zack thought.

The elevator stopped, and the doors slid back, depositing them on a level that Zack didn't recognize.

"Questions?" Mick asked, as they stepped off and began to walk down the passageway.

"Echthros?" Zack asked.

"Ultimate evil," Mick said. "We've been at war with him for centuries, and like all tyrants, he's bent on world domination." Mick looked at Zack. "We can't allow that."

Centuries? Zack thought, but didn't ask.

"Mick, I know you said upstairs that Jamie... Well, was that all just for my benefit—" Zack's voice cracked. "Or will we *really* get her back?"

Mick stopped and turned toward Zack so suddenly he was sorry he asked. The blue eyes bored a hole into Zack's soul.

"Do you trust me, Zack?"

A barrage of imagery flooded Zack's mind: lying face down in the bushes, the cemetery and Milton on the ground, the table at Pizza Inn and the meeting at church. At any one of those moments, Mick could have harmed him or even killed him if he would have wanted to; but, instead he brought peace to his heart. Gideon had become a second home to him and Mick's and Nate's friendships were invaluable. His mind flashed finally to Jamie.

"With my life," Zack said.

Mick smiled. "Then think of us like a National Guard unit. We are going to defend our borders and obliterate this invading army bent on the destruction of mankind," Mick paused, "and we *are* going to get Jamie back. You are one of the keys to do that. Do you understand?"

Zack paused and then said. "I guess so."

"Then for now, you will carry out the mission and more intel to follow."

Zack's eyes narrowed. "I will."

"Alright then," Mick said. "We go."

They proceeded down the corridor and stopped at a large vault door. Nate pressed his hand against a sensor pad and then punched in a series of commands on a computer keyboard.

Zack heard the rush like an airlock in a submarine movie and Nate pushed on the door.

"Here's our little armory," he said.

70

"Holy crap!" Zack said. "What a military paradise!"

"That it is," Nate grinned.

Rack after rack of battle armament stretched into a room the size of an airplane hangar. On their left was a row of assault vehicles, armor plated, camouflaged, four-wheel drive, with large knobby tires. They were lined up as if sitting on some arms dealer's car lot.

Zack took note of the machine guns mounted on the top. Past them sat several larger vehicles, that Zack could only describe as small tanks with a large canon jetting from the front.

"Are those helicopters?" Zack asked, looking into the distance, past the tanks.

"Yup," Nate smiled. "A few little things we picked up cheap."

"Oh, really?" Zack said.

"They're a modification of the Apache attack copter. We don't get to use them very much, fortunately and unfortunately." Nate grinned. "But when we do…"

"So, we get to take some of those—"

"No, we're not going in with that fanfare; covert, remember?" Nate said.

"Oh, yeah," Zack nodded.

"We're going to rely on a little less conventional, but highly effective means." Nate led him toward the opposite wall. The racks held body armor and row after row of more personal weapons.

"This is like Toy-R-Us for guys." Zack said.

A large staging area was in the center and people scurried back and forth.

Nate led Zack to a row of velvet-covered tables in the center of the great hall, where Tredessa and John stood.

Zack gave John a high-five then turned toward Tredessa.

"Hey, Dessa," Zack smiled.

"Zack." She nodded. "So, we're rockin' and rollin' together."

"Looks like," Zack said. "Only the best, I guess."

"No doubt." Dessa smiled as she examined the equipment on a table before them.

"Okay, guys," Nate said, "are we ready to get after this?"

"Yeah," John glanced around. "So, is this it? Us, four, and no more?"

"You're all we need for now," Nate said. "Calver and Mel will join us at the rendezvous camp underground and have a crew with them. We're the advanced team and we'll be moving quickly."

"That's what I like." Dessa picked up a small, but deadly looking knife off the table and swiped it a few times in the air. "Speed and agility."

"Well, lady and gents." Nate looked at Dessa, who smiled back. "We put you through a little bit of hell during Heritage Month, and now you'll have the opportunity to see the real thing—"

"I don't like the sounds of that," John said and was met with Zack's elbow in his side.

"But it did prepare you for our little excursion," Nate continued, "even if you didn't realize it."

Zack grinned. "I should have known something was up."

"Since none of you have been through one of our *little assignments* before, I need to fill you in on a few things," he paused, "to keep you alive."

"Once again," John said, "I don't like the sounds of that."

71

Nate slipped into his instructor's voice.

"You'll carry three main offensive weapons. I believe you've already met Mr. Baraq, the Lightning Sword of Destruction."

He held up the gleaming double-edged sword, with the ebony handle wrapped in leather, the golden Gideon crest in the pummel.

"Wear it proudly," Nate said. "Many who have carried this down through the years have given their lives for this cause."

Zack looked at the gleaming sword.

He was an eighteen-year-old high school senior, a man by all rights; but, he didn't feel like a man. The United States military would say he was a man, a soldier, maybe even *An Army of One*, but he didn't feel like a soldier. He was a boy. He had tests to take, projects to finish, models to build and term papers to hand in.

He wanted to retreat, to hide, to flee and forget he had ever stepped foot across the Gideon threshold. Who was *he* to be marching into the bowels of hell? Was this all real?

He glanced around. Thousands of people readying themselves, for what? Battle? War?

With some unknown enemy that Zack had never heard of before, and could barely pronounce, that had snatched Jamie,

He shook himself.

Jamie.

The young, beautiful girl that had become the love of his life; she was his reason for existence, the one he worked hard for so that some day he could… marry?

Yes.

He would do this.

He would march.

He would fight.

Whatever it took, whatever it may cost him, Zack was willing, he was able and he was mentally capable if need be. No greater love has a man than to lay down his life for a friend.

Friends.

He looked at John and Dessa, and then his eyes went back to Nate, still moving his lips, but it was like no sound came out.

Nate.

And Mick.

He couldn't let them down. They had rescued him, saved him; they had salvaged his pathetic life and he could not back out now. No, there was something that kept him here.

A need.

A desire to do something that mattered.

A validation of a life spent playing the victim.

Zack Tucker could not let *himself* down.

"This one," Nate's commentary brought him back, and Nate slid a short sword with a pearl handle from its leather scabbard, "you know as Mekayraw. It's swift and deadly. And this little fella, Dessa, you'll love." He pulled a dagger from the sheath on his boot and hurled it to the opposite wall, driving it through a Dairy Queen coupon tacked to a bulletin board.

Dessa grinned.

"Let's just say this comes in handy in a pinch." Nate smiled.

"Nate?"

"Yes, John."

"Well. I was just wondering," John turned to scan the massive hangar, "with all this military hardware surrounding us—"

"Why swords?" Nate finished the thought.

John shrugged. "Well, yeah. Wouldn't it be better to use some Terminator rocket-propelled grenade launcher and just blow them all to, excuse the pun, Hell?"

"Normally," Nate said, "but where we're going, standard ammo won't get the job done. Remember, most of the things we will encounter are already dead or weren't alive to begin with, in the sense that we understand it—"

"I definitely don't like the sounds of that," John mumbled.

"Okay, follow me." Nate left no room for further discussion and led them to another table arrayed with battle gear.

"Zack, I need a mannequin." He pulled Zack closer.

"Take off your shirt. I'm going to show you how to outfit yourself. If your body armor is out of order, it won't fit comfortably or do the job well."

Zack pulled off his shirt to a number of hoots and whistles and cat calls from passersby.

"Here, put this harness on."

Nate handed him a collar with a long tail running down to a waistband. The collar was affixed with two medallions, which were inscribed with the crest of Gideon.

"What are these?" Zack asked as he slipped them over his head and tightened them around his throat.

"Your voice mic. With some added features."

"Really?"

"It is very important that it touches your skin."

Nate helped him run the tail down his spine and Zack fastened the waistband in place. Nate pressed a button on the collar and the medallions sucked in slightly to his throat.

"Is that an okay fit?" Nate asked. "Not too tight?"

"Yeah, that's fine, but… Weird," Zack moved his head from side to side. "I expected the metal to be cold."

"Nope, believe it or not, this rig running down your spine will keep your body temperature at a constant rate also, no matter the elements."

"Fascinating," John said.

"Also, this little guy," Nate held up a plug coming from the back of the harness, "plugs into your ear piece so we can hear each other. Tap it once and whoever you're looking at can hear you. Tap it twice and everyone wearing one of these within about a fifty yard radius will pick up the signal."

"Only fifty yards?" John asked.

"Because we're underground, "Nate said.

"Makes sense." John grabbed his throat microphone and slipped into it. "These are so cool!"

Nate handed Zack a linen T-shirt. "And this next."

Zack slipped into it.

"And this." Nate reached under the table and pulled out a black, sparkling mesh vest.

"Mail?" John was tapping on his throat mic. "As in King Arthur?"

"Black Diamonds," Nate reached over and pulled John's hand away from his microphone. "As in, a girl's best friend."

Dessa snickered.

"You're kiddin' me," Zack said. "I thought black diamonds were extremely rare?"

"They are." Nate smiled. "We have most of them. It's something that our armament department whipped up a few years ago—"

"Looks like a bullet-proof Kevlar vest," Zack said, "only shiny."

"We call it Kevline." Nate said. "A marriage made in heaven, Kevlar and black diamonds—"

"And worth a fortune, I'll bet," John said.

"Worth saving your life," Nate said and helped Zack pull on the vest and buckle it in.

"You'll find it quite comfortable. Slick, so as to thwart direct blows, waterproof, and lightweight for catlike moves." Nate danced like a prizefighter shadow boxing. "It'll take just about anything they will throw at you."

"Who's going to throw at us?" John asked. "And what will they be throwing?"

"Getting the rookies ready?"

Dexter, walked past, slapping Zack on the back and nearly toppling him. Dexter was arrayed in full battle armor, and his huge biceps glistened with sweat under the shoulder caps of his Kevline vest.

"Hey, who's guarding the front gate?" John asked.

"Don't worry," Dexter said. "We got it covered. You guys ready to kick some serious butt?"

He pulled a huge sword and slashed through the air.

"Would it matter if I said *no*?" John asked.

"Don't worry; I'll be right behind you." Dexter said.

"I'd prefer in front of me." John said.

"That'll work, too." Dexter laughed and walked on.

"I'll let *you* put this on yourself." Nate handed Zack a flexible, Kevline groin protector and he pulled it on like a pair of shorts over his black fatigues.

"I think the rest of this is self-explanatory."

Nate motioned to items on the table including elbow and knee pads, shin guards, traction-soled combat boots, leather gloves, with the fingers cut out, and headsets that fastened into one ear.

"I'll be back." Nate said. "I think they're struggling. He walked to another group trying to get ready.

Zack, Tredessa, and John helped each other buckle on their armor and then began to flex and stretch to test its elasticity.

John picked up a molded helmet lying beside the other equipment.

"You can put that on if you want," Dessa said, "but I'm not wearing one."

"You're supposed to." John sounded like a first grader.

"How do you know?" Dessa said.

"Because it's here," John said.

"It looks like someone just left it lying here," Dessa said. "Besides, I like my head to be free." She grabbed her hair and whipped it into a ponytail.

"Well, if you're not wearing one, then I don't have to either." Zack shook his shoulder length hair.

"Wow!" Dessa said. "Was your hair always that long?"

"Not when I first came here," Zack said. "I don't know, it's something about this place. Makes it grow incredibly fast."

"I like it," Dessa said.

"Thanks, so does Jamie." Zack paused for a moment and glanced at the floor.

"And she will again." Dessa slapped him on the shoulder.

Zack looked up and smiled. "Yes, she will. Thanks."

"Don't mention it." Dessa grinned.

"What are you guys talking about?" John asked, trying to pull the helmet over his head. "You're nuts if you don't wear one of these."

"I think it's a little small," Zack grinned.

"So what, let those who ride decide," John said.

Nate walked back over, grinned at John and shook his head.

"Zack, can I see you a minute?"

"Nate," John said. "They won't wear their helmets."

"That's okay, I'm not wearing one either," Nate smiled.

Dessa smirked at John.

"Well, I'm wearing one." John mashed it on his head.

"We're marching into the Netherworld and you won't even wear a helmet…" he muttered. "Diamonds or no diamonds, I'm wearing it."

Nate led Zack to another table.

"Listen," Nate started. "I know that this thing with Jamie is tough."

Zack looked at him.

"But you've got to keep your head in the game," Nate tapped the side of Zack's head with his finger. "You've got to believe we're going to get her back."

Zack nodded.

Nate's gaze pierced him. "Do you know what I mean?"

"Yeah."

"Mick thought it might help for you to carry this." Nate stepped aside revealing the Madagascar Rosewood case.

Zack's eyes widened.

"Nate?"

"This will be a lethal weapon in your hands." Nate said.

Zack unlatched the brass buckles and pulled the crimson velvet cloth off the Baraq. His hands trembled as he clutched the leather wrapped handle and held it up to the light. The blade's reflection gleamed in his eyes.

"This is awesome. Thanks so much, Nate." Zack's eyes were wide.

He buckled on the belt and slid the Baraq into its sheath.

Nate and Zack rejoined the others. "We're part of three forward teams. Mel will lead one and Cal the other, but we're the first ones in. Questions?"

"So, these will work when guns won't?" John held up his Baraq sword.

"They're dipped," Nate paused, "in the imported oil."

"The oil—"

"That you never came back with," Zack said.

"Well, exccuuuse me for becoming preoccupied with the Gates of Hell," John said.

"Only the battle blades are dipped," Nate scanned their faces, "and they work extremely well." He paused. "Are we ready?"

"As ready as I'll ever be," John said. "I sure would like a .45 automatic though. Don't you think I could—"

Nate shot John a look.

"Never mind," John finished buckling his vest. "This thing just doesn't fit right—"

"We've got a small backpack that buckles into your rig," Nate said. "Pick it up as we exit; it's got some more provisions in it."

They left the armory, climbed onto a service elevator, and descended to the third level basement. Zack gazed down the large tunnel that he remembered being big enough to drive two trailers down, side by side. Throngs of men and women lined the walls readying themselves for battle. Murmurs of support, and pats on the back, ushered them down the tunnel until it finally emptied into the amphitheater where Zack and John had been attacked.

They walked down the steps and stood in front of the massive marble wall.

Nate looked at them. "We're the tip of the spear, the first ones in."

"Is that a good thing?" Zack looked around.

"It's an honor," Nate replied. "And all of them know it." Nate waved his hand toward the congregation. "Mick doesn't usually send rookies in first, but this is special, *you* are special and it shows he has confidence in all of you."

"Ok, then," Zack straightened.

"This'll be a search and destroy mission," Nate said, "and we'll engage the enemy while we gather information."

Nate strapped on two Baraq swords, fastening them to his back in an X. Under them he fastened a small waste pack.

"Quite the swords," Zack said.

"Hey, what can I say," Nate replied. "I'm ambidextrous."

Nate approached a heavily muscled blonde man in the midst of a few dozen warriors.

"Stay here until Mick coordinates with you."

"Yes, sir," the man replied. "Success, Nathaniel." He shook Nate's hand.

Nate walked to the gates, slipped his hand in a depression in the marble, searching for the handle. He took hold and twisted it. Air belched from the crack, spraying dust onto his forearm and a small door popped open. A panel, housing a scope, keypad, and microphone, slid forward.

A hush fell over the crowd as Nate looked into the viewer. He spoke slowly and deliberately into the microphone, his voice barely audible. Finally, Nate punched in a long numeric code on the keypad and took a few steps back, looking up at the huge gates.

Metallic scraping echoed as the tumblers fell into place and the steel bolts released.

Nate walked to the center of the double marble gates, grabbed the golden handles and pushed.

The Gideon army, of several thousand, stood silently as they watched Nate, Zack, Tredessa and John transcend time and cross the threshold into the Region of the Dead.

72

The massive, marble gates snapped shut behind them, plunging them into total darkness.

Zack stopped. "Nate? Are you sure—"

"Give your eyes time to adjust." Nate's voice was calm and even over their headsets.

Zack felt the medallions vibrate on his neck and they threw a red cast around them.

"Yeah, I can make things out now," John whispered, "but won't the light give us away?"

"We're the only ones who can see it," Nate's voice boomed in the silence. "And it only glows in the total absence of light."

"Oh, okay," John whispered, his eyes darted back and forth.

"There's really no reason to whisper, John," Nate said.

"Oh, okay," John whispered again.

Their red beacons threw shadows on moist, granite walls as they began to walk.

"I've already had one shower today," Zack said.

Sweat and the humidity mingled on their skin. Zack's hair relaxed and began to drip moisture, as a warm, dank breeze whistled from the cavern depths.

"What a pleasant smell," John sniffed.

"What exactly did you expect a place called *The City of the Dead* to smell like?" Dessa asked.

John shrugged. "I don't know, *maybe* like dead people?"

A bubble of red light surrounded them, like a force field in a child's cartoon, and they tramped down a mile long path amidst stalagmites that, a millennium before, had forced their way through the dirt to sentry the secrets of the underworld.

The path began a rise and just over a slight ridge, they emptied into another massive cavern, with light filtering from the surface, and their tiny red bubble dissipated. Gnarled rock formations, worn from eons of erosion, were sandpapered down to nubs. Above them hung thousands of stalactites, like an inverted bed of nails from a giant's torture chamber.

"Holy…" John said.

"That about says it," Zack said glancing up at the sheer magnificence of their newly discovered surroundings.

Multi-colored light reflected off shadows and crevices to form a haunting glow of a place that was far outside the scope of their control. Holes, dug in the side walls, gave Zack an eerie sense of being watched by some behemoth that was about to swallow him like an appetizer.

Several miles further on down the path they were halted by seven-foot man-made walls that stretched off into the shadows.

"Looks like the Great Wall of China," John said.

"Only shorter." Zack glanced in both directions.

"This is the last line of defense before they would reach the gates," Nate said. "If all else fails—"

"Hopefully, we won't need them." Zack reached out and patted the wall.

"Hopefully," Nate took a few strides, jumped up and hoisted himself to the top. "Only six more to go."

"Six?" John said.

"Yup," Nate said. "Seven total. Number of perfection. Let's go." He dropped out of sight.

"I hope perfection is in our favor." Dessa grabbed a handhold, stepped into a concave and began to climb.

"Okay, that's easier," Zack said as he scrambled over the first wall, leaving some of his skin on top. He turned and pulled John up.

After scaling the seventh wall, John collapsed at Nate's feet.

"I think you ought to look into some gates," John panted. "It'd be easier."

"I think the whole idea is to make it hard," Zack stood beside him, winded.

"Well, they succeeded." John reached up for Zack.

Several hundred yards later, light dawned on a crystal clear river and they stopped.

"Wow!" John looked into the sparkling water. "It's so pure."

John moved closer. "And I can see the bottom. How deep is this?"

"Pretty deep," Nate said. "What, did you just think water came out of a faucet?"

"No," John smiled, "from bottles."

"We'll follow this for a few miles to the falls." Nate turned to follow the river bank.

"This is great." Zack glanced around. "Just like summer."

"A constant seventy-eight degrees down here," Nate said.

A couple of hours later, they stood on the precipice of an underground valley. The river ended in a waterfall, which ran off a plateau and into a rainbow-encased pool, several hundred feet beneath them.

"Caves on the surface let the sun filter to the valley floor." Nate yelled over the roar of the falls.

"I see," Zack yelled back, looking at the roof of the cavern.

The river continued from the pool and into the distance, toward a small cluster of lights.

Nate stepped over the edge and onto a narrow, rocky path.

"Watch yourselves. If you slip, it'll be a long fall," Nate yelled pointing down. "Just a little further and we can stop and rest."

"If we don't die first," John slid a shaky foot over the edge. "Did I ever tell you I'm scared of heights?"

The roar of the falls pounded in Zack's ears on the way down, but his feet finally touched the mossy carpet at the bottom and he wiped the spray off his face and arms. The water that had resembled a small pool from above turned out to be a small lake as they reached its light laced surface.

"Holy!" Zack jumped back as a sofa sized, transparent fish with huge, dark eyes swam near the bank.

"Are those catfish?" Dessa asked.

"Maybe?" Zack leaned closer. "They're like those giant ones over in the rivers of India. But look at the tentacles." He pointed.

"They're like a squid." John ventured near the bank.

The fish searched the bottom for food and periodically stuck a tentacle out of the water to test the air. They watched them meander back and forth with no fear of humanity.

"That freaks me out," John said, gazing at the enormous fish.

"They're like albino Koi or something, but I can see their bones."

"Well, they don't need protection from the sun down here." Nate walked on. "Enough with the aquarium, come on."

Another mile and the river crossed their path, separating them from the lights. A wide, rock bridge spanned the river and emptied them into a torch-lit community of tents and campfires.

"I'm starved. Is that meat?" John inhaled.

"Smells like it," Dessa said, "but down here? What kind?"

"Hey, us growin' boys gotta eat!" John licked his lips.

"It's better than some of the smells of the last few miles, that's for sure," Zack said.

Two columns of fully armored soldiers, their swords and spears glistening in the torchlight, snapped to attention as the little band crossed the bridge.

The ranking officer approached.

"Nathaniel." The soldier extended his hand.

"Jordan," Nate embraced him. "Good to see you, man. What's our status?"

"All quiet here. We haven't encountered anything that should concern us." He paused. "A troglodyte or two once in a while. They smell our food and wander into camp, but we make short work of them." Jordan pointed to a bloody heap a few feet away.

Zack walked over and looked at large, furry beasts, cuddled together as if sleeping. The smell was overwhelming, like a toxic combination of sulfur and ammonia.

"How secure are we?" Nate asked.

"Two hundred and fifty five soldiers strong, four hundred personnel all together."

"Excellent," Nate turned. "Zack."

Zack rejoined Nate as he continued. "This is the *last* line of defense. If *we* fail, it's up to them." Nate slapped Jordan on the shoulder.

"Don't worry about that." Jordan smiled.

"I don't." Nate grinned.

"If we fail?" John whispered to Zack. Zack shrugged.

"Nothing will get past us, sir." Jordan said.

"We'll rest here for a while," Nate said. "Provisions?"

"More than enough. We made a run to the surface yesterday to stock up." Jordan said. "Make yourselves at home." He motioned toward the fires. "They've got some supper on too."

"Go ahead, guys," Nate said. "Jordan and I need to strategize."

Nate and Jordan walked into camp while Zack, Dessa and John gravitated toward the boiling pots.

—

An hour later, their stomachs were full and they settled into a large tent.

"This is really weird." John arranged a sleeping bag on an army style cot.

"What?" Zack muttered from the soft pillow.

"We're napping in The Region of the Dead."

"Well, *some* of us are trying to take a nap," Zack said and turned over.

"I was just thankful that the pots turned out to be USDA prime beef, from the surface." John fluffed his pillow.

73

Zack's own snoring woke him. He sat up, stretched and instinctively looked at his wrist. No watch. He rubbed his eyes.

"Did you sleep well?"

Zack jumped and turned to look at the form sitting on the opposite cot.

"Sorry, I didn't mean to startle you." He offered his hand. "We met in the elevator?"

"Oh," Zack's heart began to slow. "Yes, Jack?"

"James…Jim."

"Oh, right, sorry," Zack said. "Jim, and I," Zack shook his

head, "don't remember your last name either, sorry."

"Quite alright, Recent, Jim Recent."

"Right. Sorry, I'm a little disoriented. I'm not used to this," Zack smiled. "Where's John?" Zack glanced at the rumpled sleeping bags.

"I believe he and the girl are out with the others." Jim said.

"Man, did I sleep." Zack yawned and stretched again. "I didn't realize how tired I was."

"Yes, all of this trekking will wear you out," Jim smiled.

"So, you made it down alright?" Zack asked.

"Yes, I came in on the same wave as Calver."

"Oh, Cal's here?" Zack smiled. "What a nut."

"Yes, he's quite interesting."

"Reminds me of one of those skinny gunslingers from the westerns," Zack said. "Handlebar mustache and all."

Jim stood. "Indeed, quite the wry wit.

"He gave us an entire hour lesson on sharpening blades one day."

"Well, guess I'd better be going," Jim said. "I know you're moving out in a short time. I saw you in here as it were and just wanted to give you a shout."

"Thanks, yeah, what a wild ride," Zack said. "You're obviously coming with us?"

"Yes," James Recent said. "I'll be watching your back, as they say. If I can assist you in any way, just let me know."

"Thanks, Jim," Zack turned and grabbed his boots from the other side of the cot and when he turned around, James Recent was gone.

—

"Hey, guys." Zack approached Nate and the others around the fire.

"Well, we were wonderin' when ya'll would get up." Calver

reached out.

"Yeah, I was really tired." Zack yawned as he pumped Calver's hand.

"Good. We wanted you well rested, we'll be moving out soon," Nate said.

"Still hungry?" Mel held up a plate.

"No, I'm good thanks." Zack patted his stomach.

"Restock your provisions. That tent has supplies in it." Nate pointed. "But don't overstuff your pack. Remember, *you're* carrying it."

An hour later they were on their way again, Nate, and the scouting team, leading the way and Calver and Mel with their fifty soldiers bringing up the rear.

—

After ten miles of putting one foot in front of the other, they collapsed beside another stream. Zack shrugged out of his backpack, letting it slide to the ground. He breathed a thankful sigh for the hours of training on the treadmill.

"The water here is not *only* fit to drink," Nate said, "but the best you'll ever taste."

"It's gotta go some to be better than back at camp." John smacked his lips.

"Try it and see." Nate motioned toward the stream. "We'll stop for a while and eat. Zack, build us a small fire and, Mel, break out some of that beef, will ya?"

John plopped down on a small boulder and pulled off his boots, scratching his legs. He pushed both socks off his feet and began to rub in between his toes.

"Well, at least no blisters," he said, waving his socks over his head like a helicopter blade.

John Welte didn't see the creature until after it pounced.

74

John tumbled backward, as claws tore through his shirt and screeched against the diamond webbing. The creature was on all fours, on top of him; its talons pressing into his ribs. John winced at the hot, stinking breath and gagged as its slimy tongue squirmed across his forehead.

The creature reared its head and howled like a wolf at a full moon. Dessa's sword sent a warm gush across John's body and knocked the creature into the dirt. It flipped and rolled, bounding onto three legs with the fourth dangling from a crimson sinew. It snarled at the bloody sword. The beast lunged toward John again, the bloody tendon trailing after it, but Dessa caught it with a deathblow and sent the creature's lifeless weight on top of John's legs.

John screamed like a little girl and kicked the creature off him.

"Now, you owe me," Dessa wiped her bloody blade on the creature's pelt and replaced her sword in the sheath.

"Only my life," John panted.

"By the way, Troglodytes have a keen sense of smell." Nate stood behind her with blade drawn. "I wouldn't give them anything to hone in on." He nodded toward John's bare feet.

"Troglodytes? Like back at camp? Did we go over that in orientation? I don't remember that? Do you remember that?" John asked Zack, who shrugged.

John finally let go of the sock, still clutched in his hand. "This might've been good information a couple of hours ago," he mumbled as Nate walked away.

"Well, *we* don't like the smell," Zack grinned "why should they?"

"Well, excuuuse me." John picked up his socks and sat down, pulling them back onto his feet. "Mister Never Let's Off Any

Disgusting Odors Of His Own!"

Zack grinned.

"Sure, pick on the kid with the chronic foot odor," John said as Zack walked toward the dead creature.

Zack poked the hairy carcass with the tip of his sword and watched the fur for any movement. He peered into the glassy black eyes and the face, with the snout of a bear, but with shark teeth that protruded from under a flap of lip that could have been canine. Its whiskers were long like a jungle cat's, but under its chin was a tuft of blood-red and white hair like a goatee.

Four digits, serving as fingers, and a thumb sported bloody bear claws. Its front paws had mutated like a man with rough pads on the insides of his hands. Zack examined the stomach. It looked like the underside of a dog, but the Troglodyte had a small, red bag with three nipples not unlike a dairy cow, that all dribbled a bloody-yellow puss out of the holes.

Zack gagged, thankful that they had eaten hours before. He turned away and rejoined the others around the fire.

"Hey, Nate, can I ask you something?" Zack plopped down cross-legged near the warmth.

"Shoot." Nate pulled a hunk of beef off a skewer that rested among the coals.

"So, what's the deal with this, Echthros?"

A slight grin spread across Nate's face.

"What, you're not happy wandering around down here in the dark? Now you want to know what we're doing?" He passed the meat around.

"Thought it might help." Zack took the meat.

"Gather round, children, while ole Uncle Nate tells you a bedtime story." Nate swirled the coals, liberating sparkles of floating light.

"Echthros, of The House of Haylel, once inhabited the dynasty of Lord Pantokrator. They co-existed in a kingdom of peace." Nate's eyes narrowed in the firelight. "That was before Abada came."

John plodded over and plunked down next to Calver, snuggling his bare feet next to the flames.

"Queen Abada was the wife of Beel." Nate went on. "Who reigned over a third of the earth, abusive and ruthless. Haylel desired her beauty and his fascination turned to obsession as he devised a plan to seduce her, but before he completed the plan, he had to ally with Beel."

"For what?" Dessa asked, sitting down next to John. She looked at his feet, wrinkled her nose, and scooted next to Zack.

"The rebellion." Nate stared into the fire, "against Lord Pantokrator."

Nate sat silently, poking a glowing stick and watching the scarlet-rimmed ash peel away.

"Aaannd?" John hunched forward, cradling his knees with his arms.

"It was a horrendous blow to the kingdom," Nate said.

"Guess he wanted it all." John reached for a hunk of meat.

"He always does." Calver spit tobacco to one side and leaned back on both elbows.

"That's right." Nate poked at the coals and then snapped out of his trance. "So, the House of Haylel and the House of Beel decided to play their hand against Lord Pantokrator."

"But we took care of 'em," Mel handed meat to Dessa.

Zack glanced at the old man.

"That we did." Nate nodded, a slight smile on his lips.

"Yeah, we really rearranged his nads." Cal turned his head and spat.

"Lord Pantokrator banished them and *this* is where they ended up." Nate flicked at the sparks.

"Down here?" Zack pointed to the ground.

"Yup." Nate said.

"Wait a minute." Zack's eyes glazed as he searched the recesses of his mind. "How long ago was that?"

"Oh, it was a while." Nate paused. "Of course, with Haylel and Beel occupying the same space, they eventually came to blows."

"Put two wolves in a room and they gonna fight every time," Cal said.

"Exactly," Nate pointed his glowing stick at Cal. "Echthros of Haylel defeated the House of Beel and Abada became the prize."

"The witch." Calver said.

"The banishment altered her beauty and she became Abaddon, a seductress filled with hate and destruction; and, Echthros, of the House of Haylel, possessed her."

Nate handed the stick to Zack. "So, there you have it."

"So, where are they now?" Zack tossed a twig into the fire.

"The Netherworld." Nate said.

"Is that Tartaroo?" Zack asked.

"Yeah, they wreak havoc in the hearts of men, feasting on their souls," Nate paused, "and bodies."

"Oh, man." John shook his head. "More things I don't like the sound of."

"Like it or not, that's where it's at. When Haylel fell, death and destruction exploded into creation. He hates the inhabitants of the world of light and is hell bent on revenge."

"And that's where *we* come in?" Zack nodded looking into the fire.

"That, and to rescue Jamie." Nate threw another small log on.

"Of course," Zack said.

Mel finished pulling the last pieces of meat off the skewer and then tossed his stick into the fire.

"Well, I suppose…" He stood stretching his back.

"You're right," Nate said. "I hate to break up this little party when you're all about to fall asleep, but we'd better be off."

"Ohh, man." John hoisted himself up. "There's never any rest in this man's army."

"Not a bit'" Nate smiled. "Better put your shoes on though."

"That's a good one." John squinted sarcastically.

"Cal, dowse that fire," Nate said.

75

Several miles further, the rock formations narrowed and the ceiling lowered.

"I'm not too fond of tight places," John said, as the light faded and his medallions began glowing.

"You okay?" Nate noticed his labored breaths.

"Yeah." John scanned the ceiling and then the walls. "This is sort of like that episode, *Devil in the Dark*, with the Horda that ate through solid rock? And I fell into—"

"Which episode number was it?" Dessa asked.

"25," John said without breaking stride. "As I was saying, I fell into this well once—"

"Was that at your Grandpa's farm that time?" Zack asked.

John paused and looked at Zack. "Yes, it was. Never have liked that closed-in feeling since then."

"I can see why." Dessa glanced around and grinned. "Is it just me or is it getting closer down here?"

"Stop that!" John glanced back and forth and up and down.

"Just kiddin'." Dessa smiled.

"I think I'm okay though." John said.

Nate put a hand on John's shoulder. "Just about a hundred more yards. Okay?"

"Hey, you know me, all guts and no glory. Except for the closed quarters," John ducked like a bat might swoop down and snatch him at any time.

"He'll make it." Tredessa grabbed his arm. "Repeat after me. There's no place like home; there's no place like home."

"Thanks," John smirked. "Just call me Dorothy."

"Okay." Dessa said.

"Kidding."

John concentrated on his shoes, until a hundred yards later they came out the mouth of the tunnel and stood in front of a dead end dirt wall.

"I thought you said we'd get out of this soon?" John put his hands on his knees and started to hyperventilate.

"Nothing to worry about," Nate said. "Just a little trick."

"Tricky? I don't like tricky!" John puffed short, deliberate breaths.

"Calm down, Dorothy," Zack grinned.

"Don't even go there." John chided. "Besides, it's easy for you to say. It wasn't *you* in the well." John eyes widened. "As I recall though, *you were* standing at the top."

"Hey, I'm innocent." Zack held out his hands.

"I said *trick*, not *tricky*," Nate corrected.

Zack approached the wall of dirt.

"What are you doing?" John asked.

"It's just weird," Zack reached toward the dirt. "It's skin."

An arm, still attached to a body, folded out of the wall.

76

Zack jumped back, colliding with John.

"What the—"

"It's alright." Nate steadied him. "Lay two fingers on both the medallions on your neck at the same time and breathe steadily."

Zack looked at Nate and then slowly touched the medallions on either side of this neck with his right hand. His eyes watered. His vision blurred. He rubbed his eyes with his left hand. Zack cocked his head and peered harder at, what he knew now to be, a man encased in the dirt. He focused on the dirt and it dissolved into a gel and then into clear liquid. Zack gazed into acres that stretched in front of them.

"I see them." Zack's voice was near panic. "Oh, I see them!"

"Don't let it freak you out." Nate's voice was calm and low.

"It *does* freak me out, man! They're dead!" Zack cried. "They're all dead!"

"What're you talking about?" John peered at the solid dirt wall, trying to fumble with his own medallions.

"Zack!" Nate snapped him out of panic mode.

"Sorry, man, it's just—"

"Remove your hand off the medallions." Nate said.

Zack did as he was told and the images remained. He moved his fingers into the dirt and drew them back as if touching something hot.

"It's like jelly sand," he said. "This is *really* creepy."

"Jelly sand?" John asked. "What's going on? What are you—"

Zack touched it again, pushing his arm deeper into the transparent dirt and then drew back.

"Why are you able to put your arm into the dirt?" John asked.

"What is this?" Zack asked.

"It's one of the Cities of the Dead," Nate said. "A graveyard."

"I still don't see—"John said.

"Put your fingers on your medallions and hold momentarily," Nate said.

"How do we pass through this?" Zack asked.

"We walk through like normal." Nate said.

"This isn't normal." John now stood next to Zack, looking into the dirt.

"Well, it's the norm down here." Calver, Mel and their team had caught up with them and he stepped next to Nate. "We do it all the time."

"You walk through dead people?" Zack was incredulous.

"Nah." Cal pulled out a can of chewing tobacco, took a pinch and planted it between his cheek and gum. "Round 'em."

"They're real bodies." Mel reached into the jelly sand and poked at the body. It swung back and forth as if suspended on rubber bands. "And they're buried in rows just like normal. We are quite close to the surface here." Mel's breathing came out in whistles. "About nine feet under."

Zack glanced up.

"We simply walk around them like we would if we were up on top and you were walking through a graveyard."

"My dad always told me to *never* step on anyone's grave, out of respect for them, but holy crap!" Zack exclaimed.

"Sort of a different perspective, huh?" Nate asked.

"I'll say," Zack said. "Where're the caskets?"

"Look close," Nate said. "They're still there. The medallions allow you to view the dead in their purist form."

Zack angled his head as if looking at a 3-D picture on the back of a cereal box. He tilted his head. One way he simply saw the body, the other way, the casket around the body.

"This is crazy," Zack said.

"And we're going to do this?" John stepped back.

"Not if we stand here gabbin' about it all day." Calver smiled and spit. "You'll like it; it's a trip!"

Calver walked into the wall like it was normal and his crew followed him.

"Just pass through them like walking down a corn field row," Nate said.

"It's a corn field of dead people!" John piped up, looking from side to side. "Hey, man, you know I'm down with this, and I don't mean to be a pain, but what about breathing?"

"Just like normal," Nate said. "It's only a different dimension."

"If you say so." John rolled his eyes. "But then again, you said we would be out of the tunnel soon too and—"

"I've never felt anything like this before." Zack said.

He had both arms extended into the jelly sand. Zack pulled back and then eased his body in, inch by inch like descending into a hot tub. First an arm, then a leg, then his torso until, with one final act of courage, he poked his face through the mucus.

They watched Zack's chest heave in and out quickly and then slow to normal breathing.

"Weird, it's like liquid." Zack's voice was muddled as if talking through a throat full of phlegm, but he waved his arms like swimming. "But not, and I can actually breathe just fine. John, it's cool!" He cupped his hands around his mouth and shouted. "Can you still hear me?"

"Loud and clear," John poked at the wall.

"Okay, let's go," Nate said.

"I don't know if my claustrophobia will like this—"

"You'll be fine, John," Nate patted him and stepped into the wall.

"It's really sort of fun," Zack called, "once you get used to it."

"Come on, Dorothy," Dessa shoved him into the wall and then stepped in behind him.

"I didn't mean for you to really call me Dorothy." John made swimming motions.

Mel and the rest of his crew joined them.

They walked through a sea of bodies that seemed suspended, like marionettes from a puppet master's strings.

Thousands of bodies, in different stages of decay, some all but faded into dust. Zack moved through the dirt, adjusting to the sound of warm liquid in his ears. He brushed against bodies that jostled back and forth, as he passed.

Some of their little bodies were in pristine condition, as if napping, arrayed in miniature suits and frilly dresses.

They're so young, Zack thought.

He choked back the tears as he passed by their tiny, dead faces, eyes closed in final peace.

He skirted corpses whose faces were weathered and wrinkled as if mummified. There were Victorian women, ensconced in velvet, and cowboys laid out in leather chaps, bullet holes in their heads or rope burns around their necks. He saw the mangled and deformed that exited the earth under tragic circumstances.

77

"Wow! You were right Cal, what a rush!" Zack shook himself like a dog after a bath and combed through his hair. "Feels weird to be back out in the air again; at least, cave air." He glanced around.

"Hey Nate," John said. "I—"

"Shh," Nate whispered. "Get down." Nate motioned for them to drop.

The entire band scattered for cover among the protrusions and crevices. Zack hit the ground and rolled behind a large stalagmite next to Nate.

"What is it?" he whispered.

"A scouting party," Nate whispered back. "The Daemons are on the prowl, looking for food or trouble. Either way, we don't need the publicity."

Nate tapped his mic twice and whispered, "Everyone wait here until I make my move. Mel, you know when."

Mel nodded.

Nate snaked his way between stalagmites and smooth rock projections.

Mel tapped his mic twice and looked at Zack.

"Zack, move forward slowly to cover Nate." he whispered. "Wait until Cal and the others are in position."

Cal's handlebar mustache could not hide his smile.

Zack inched his way forward under cover of a rock wall. He peered above the wall and froze, focusing on what lay on top. His breath came in shallow gulps and he felt like passing out. Zack closed his eyes, shook his head to clear the sudden rush of blood, and then reached out and snatched one of Jamie's slippers from the top of the wall. He looked at it momentarily and rubbed his eyes; he then slipped it inside his vest and looked back up to the creatures coming down the path.

Nate had called them, *Daemons*. Unlike the Troglodytes, these creatures walked upright on crooked, canine hind legs and Zack wondered how they balanced, as their leathery feet padded the dirt.

They snarled and drooled, periodically snapping at each other with fangs laid bare. Their strides were mismatched and random like the undisciplined march of zombies in a B-movie. One creature swiped at another, leaving deep, bloody gashes, but the second creature seemed unaffected by the injury and continued to plod along.

Zack watched their hands swing back and forth at their sides like a gorilla's, grimy and scarred, with fingernails that were now more like talons, caked with black filth. Their hair, which was a matt of fur, was moist and filthy.

Polished black marble eyes, with no white rims, were set deep in their skulls. Heavy, overgrown brows, like Neanderthal's, hung over the eye sockets, but with a pointed bone in the middle of their forehead that looked as if, at any moment, it would break free of the leathery skin that covered it.

Through noses, that resembled pigs' snouts, they snarled and squealed while mucus ran down their stubbly beards, that covered protruding chins.

They marched along, heads down and swaying from side to side, similar to a herd of elephants. Oversized flies and gnats buzzed around the pack, as a death stench hovered around them like a cloud from putrefying rubbish.

Nate stepped from cover, in front of them, and limped across the path. His head was down as if searching for something and he dragged one foot behind him.

The lead creature stopped and several other creatures ran into one another. They panted, turning their heads like inquisitive dogs. The leader stepped forward. A nervous spasm made its arm tremble. With the other arm, it slowly slid a weapon, resembling a makeshift sword, from its scabbard.

A low, guttural tone resonated from deep inside the creature's throat, like a person who had been smoking for forty years combined with a dog's snarl; Zack thought he heard it cough out the word: "Food."

Zack felt the heat on his neck and glanced around. Everyone's throat medallions glowed red.

Nate stood in the clearing, bobbing up and down and wheezing like dying road kill. The creature stepped forward poking him lightly with the tip of his blade and Nate slashed through its mid-section so quickly that the shock barely had time to register on the creature's face. It turned to look at its cohorts and the top of its torso slid off at the stomach and hit the ground solidly, spilling blood and intestines into the dirt.

The creatures scattered in a flurry of confusion.

Mel and Calver closed in from the sides and Zack attacked from the flank.

A creature leapt toward Zack, ricocheting off a boulder like a jackrabbit. Metal collided with metal as Zack swung the blade in the first real battle for his life. The creature's scream shook Zack's teeth. With swift reflexes and powerful strokes, the creature sliced at Zack's armored wrist cuff and the Baraq flew out of Zack's sweaty grip. He stumbled backward, caught his heel and sprawled on his back in the dirt.

The creature circled Zack like a tiger, its eyes aflame. A broad smile spread across its face, revealing pointed, yellow teeth seething with mucus. The creature raised its sword high for a final deathblow just as Zack buried his Mekayraw sword to the hilt in the creature's stomach. Cold liquid gushed from the midsection and the creature's face twisted in defiance. Its sword hit the ground a moment before its body collapsed in the dirt.

Zack saw Dessa pull her sword from the lifeless chest of another creature.

"How great was that?" Dessa ran toward Zack.

"Yeah, great," Zack said. "I dropped my sword."

"That's why you have two." Nate walked past and slapped him on the shoulder.

"What do you think, Mel?" Nate wiped his blade on one of the dead creatures.

The little man looked from carcass to carcass with a huge chipmunk grin on his face.

"Oh, I'd say we're okay." Mel puffed through his nose hair. "We haven't been detected." Mel glanced around to see if what he had just said rang true. "These fellas were an isolated group out for groceries. Not a bit organized, you know?"

"Let's clean up the mess and hide the carcasses," Nate said.

Zack walked over to Nate and handed him Jamie's slipper.

78

"At least we know were on the right track." Dessa took the slipper from Nate.

"Or at least, path," John said. "Man, her feet are really small."

Zack glanced at him.

"Sorry."

"Okay, you guys," Nate said. "Gather round." He squatted, unfolded a map in the dirt and looked up. "Zack, we *will* find her, but first things first." He looked back down at the map.

"This cavern that we're in will lead us to Tartaroo." He pointed to a gray area. "This sector to the west is Hahdace, the place of deposited souls. That's where the captives are."

The others looked over his shoulder.

"So you're saying that Hell is somewhere under the Rocky Mountains." John said.

Nate continued without responding to him. "We're going in unnoticed."

"How?" John asked.

"Do you really want to know right now, or later?" Nate smiled.

"Will I be able to handle it *now?*"

"No."

"Later will do just fine." John shrugged.

"We'll need to move the captives into a safe zone. Mel, I'll have *you* do that." Mel nodded. "Mick will take care of the assault on Echthros until we get there, then—"

Movement from above their heads cut off his instructions and they all ducked for cover again.

"This is getting to be a habit," Zack whispered to Dessa.

High above them, a man encrusted in a transparent placenta, struggled. His arm split the membrane and clawed through the film. Zack watched as he wiggled and stretched until he ripped the sack and dropped head first to the ground.

From the same place, a woman kicked against another sack, her leg splitting through, and she screamed as she dropped. Immediately behind her, a little girl wailed as she tumbled like a stunt double in a movie, but unlike a stunt double, she didn't land in a huge air mattress; she hit the ground with a thud and bounced.

"It has to be a hundred and fifty feet to the top of this cave,"

Zack whispered, "and it doesn't seem to affect them?"

The man scanned the cavern through blackened eyes. His once blond hair, now matted with dried blood, clung to his forehead. The dark haired woman wore a blue cotton sundress, with bright fuchsia Hawaiian flowers, that formed a border around the hem. Her shoulders were stained with the blood from her ears, but the little girl seemed unharmed.

"Nate?" Zack whispered.

"Sudden death." Nate whispered. "Something happened up there to send them down here unexpectedly. From their condition, probably an auto accident. They've become the Charis and that's who were rescuing."

"They just drop in?" Zack asked.

"Some, but at least they come in peacefully," Nate paused. "Not everyone does."

"What do you mean?" Zack looked at him from the corner of his eye.

"*These* people are in a holding pattern." He pointed toward them. "There are others who stay permanently."

"Others?" Zack questioned.

"The Rawfaw." Nate stared. "Ghosts. Damned forever to Tartaroo. *They* come in kicking and screaming—"

"No ghost stories right now, okay?" John crawled up beside them, glancing back over his shoulder. "I'm nervous enough."

Nate continued anyway. "And once in a while, the Rawfaw escape Sheh-ole."

"To where?" Zack asked.

"The surface."

"You're kidding?" Zack's eyes widened.

"Nope. They find their way up long staircases, hewn out of the rock, and wander the streets of the cities, like Denver, for a while—"

"No way!" Zack whispered.

"Imagine serial killers, murderers, rapists that are no longer human." Nate gave Zack a sideways glance.

Zack watched the man and woman trying to orient themselves, as Nate continued.

"We try and catch them," Nate said, "before they make it to the surface, but when they elude us, we're forced to deal with them."

"Oh, really?" John whispered.

"It isn't pleasant." Nate shook his head.

"Like the creatures we met on the trail?" Dessa asked.

"No, those were mutant Daemons, pretty stupid actually. They've never been men or women on the surface. The Rawfaw are much more intelligent." He paused. "And lethal."

"Wonderful," John poked his head close to Zack. "We're dealing with worse than Daemons now?"

"Well, they're damned already," Nate said. "Nothing to lose and they've already pledged their allegiance to Echthros."

"Great," John said.

Zack glanced at the family on the road. "But the Charis?"

"Harmless," Nate said. "They'll mindlessly drift toward Hahdace. Not really sure *why,* but at least there, they'll be protected and nourished."

"Forever?" John asked.

"No, until final departure," Nate said.

"Departure to where?" Zack asked.

Nate ignored the question. "Unfortunately, some of them will be scooped up by Echthros and used for other purposes," he paused, "but that's what we're going to stop."

They watched the little girl cling to the man's hand like a frightened animal.

"Where are we, Daddy?" she asked.

"I don't know, baby, but don't worry. Everything will be all right."

"All I remember is looking up at the grill of that truck," the woman said. "Good thing you swerved."

"I know," the man said. "I thought we were goners." He glanced around. "Obviously not."

They began to wander down the trail.

Nate's group held cover until the Charis were down the path

about a hundred yards.

"Come on," Nate motioned to them, "but keep out of sight."

They followed the Charis through the twists and turns of the underground, going deeper and deeper into the earth.

"What about the other captives we're rescuing?" Zack asked.

"Periodically," Nate said, "people are trapped in transition and the House of Haylel intercepts them. They try and bully or bargain their way into the World of Light by taking them hostage."

"That's where *we'll* come in," Calver said.

"You've done this before?" John asked.

"Some," Nate said. "Most of the time the underground forces keep them at bay, but every once in a while there'll be an uprising. Hasn't been one like this for a while though. Something must be up."

"They must have something in mind," Zack said.

Nate looked at him and paused. "I agree."

For a few miles they walked in silence.

Auto fatalities. Everyone dead in the car.

Zack shook his head.

Life accelerates in a constant and then finally hits the wall, death. The veil is lifted, or maybe people lift it for themselves, and then they step through and close it behind them forever, like Kurt. All that you were and all that you would ever become, vanished.

Like a vapor.

"These people don't even know they're dead," Zack finally whispered.

"Weird, man," John said. "Makes you wonder." He paused. "Hey, you don't think?"

"What?" Zack asked.

"We're not dead? Are we?"

Zack paused.

"No." He hit John's arm. "You're starting to freak me out, man. Stop it."

"Keep it down, you guys," Mel whispered.

"Sorry," Zack said.

"Don't be sorry, just be quiet."

The Charis ambled along, like homing pigeons, through roughshod canyons, over rocky inclines and past steaming pools that belched sulfur. They disappeared around a heavily entangled row of stalagmites.

Zack wiped the back of his neck, with his hand, as the air turned clammy and warm.

He heard the little girl scream.

79

Nate and the others ran to the point where the Charis had turned the corner and peeked around, careful not to give their cover away.

The little, dark haired girl clung to her mother's skirt, staring at the massive pile of intertwined bones and body parts. They lay naked on top of each other, knotted together like a tangle of Christmas lights, with so many arms, legs and severed torsos that it was impossible to identify one person from another.

Some were mere skulls while others decayed with their mouths open in screams of horror. Decapitated heads, with bulging eyes, sat alongside others who clasped their hands over their ears in an attempt to drown out the horror. All of them entombed together for all eternity.

Zack watched the faces, old and young, all meeting the same horrific fate. Violent death.

"Nate?" Zack asked.

"The Rawfaw have been feasting." Nate said.

"Oh, God," Zack whispered.

The dad shielded his daughter's eyes, pretending to play *Peek-a-Boo*, until they were past the carnage.

Zack scanned the horizon. Like the blaze from millions of

fires, red tendrils danced in front of them from a few miles away.

The Charis slowed and then disappeared over a rise as a massive explosion rocked the underground. Zack heard screams, and a mushroom cloud climbed upward, followed by the smell of rotten eggs that drifted toward them. Zack's eyes watered and he gagged.

"Oh, God!" Zack covered his mouth and swallowed to keep from throwing up.

John began to dry heave.

"What *is* that?" He sucked in air and held it.

"The surface air creates a breeze," Cal said. "Kinda-like blowing a fan into the hole of an outhouse—"

"Great analogy." Dessa held her nose.

"Thanks," Cal said. "And its dinner time for the Rawfaw. They're feastin' tonight."

"On what, the city dump?" Zack covered his mouth and nose, remembering the pile of bodies.

"Something like that." Calver pulled a bandana from his pocket and tied it around his head like an outlaw from the old west.

"I don't want to know, do I?" John asked.

Cal shook his head.

"Never mind." John turned his head and gasped for air, pinching his nose.

"You'll get used to the smell," Nate said.

"I doubt it." John spit on the ground. "I remember this one Trek episode—"

"Let's hold up a little," Nate interrupted. "We're coming to the outskirts of Hahdace."

They skirted some boulders, the size of houses, and stopped at the base of a granite incline.

"Hahdace will be well guarded by thoroughly trained Rawfaw and Daemons. We can't alert them." Nate said.

"Oh great, Special Forces Rawfaw." John wiped the sweat. "Just what we need."

Nate looked up, scanning the granite walls.

John followed his gaze. "We're going up there, aren't we?"

"Yup, with an elevated position we can better size up the situation."

"Walk *down* the hill, so that we can climb back *up* a mountain." John shrugged. "Makes sense to me."

"What, is the climb going to kill you?" Dessa patted John's stomach.

"No, I'm just not particularly fond of heights," John said.

"Claustrophobic. Acrophobic." Dessa said. "It's a wonder you leave the house."

"Yes, it is," John said. "It's a wonder *you* know such big words! But somebody's got to keep your butt out of the fire."

"*My* butt?" Dessa smiled. "We'll *see* whose butt gets hot."

"You sound like an old married couple." Nate shook his head.

"Please." Dessa rolled her eyes.

"I suppose we won't be using any ropes?" John skirted the remark.

"Ropes? Come on, Dorothy, you can make it." Dessa started up the incline.

"Hey," John said, "I told you not to call me—"

"Nope, no ropes, just us," Nate said. "There's a bit of a path, but—"

"I don't see any path." John looked up the mountain.

Nate paid no attention. "When we reach the summit we'll rest, Dorothy."

"See what you started." John called to Dessa who was already several yards ahead.

Zack grinned and started climbing.

80

Like a centipede curling its way up the mountain, Nate's group led, with Mel's and Calver's groups bringing up the rear. Forty-five minutes later, they reached the plateau and crawled to the edge of a rock overhang.

Thick walled earthen dwellings peppered the landscape in the distance and row after row of narrow dusty streets cut across Hahdace.

"It looks like an adobe subdivision." Zack wiped his sleeve across his forehead and peered through a set of small binoculars. "This is really weird."

Chimneys puffed smoke, as men carried water to people washing clothes on washboards. People milled around a town square surrounding a large fountain bubbling crystal water. As if it were a Sunday after church, children played *Ring-Around-the-Rosie,* while grandpas dozed in chairs, propped in doorways. Dads carried children on their shoulders past small, weird looking dogs, some with three ears, nipping at their heels. People embraced and laughed with friends around tables of food.

"It could be a first century movie." Zack adjusted the focus.

"Keep watching," Nate peered through his binoculars, "for our opportunity."

Zack scanned over the city of Hahdace. Dual mud walls were separated by an expanse that looked like the kill zone of a World War II concentration camp. The outer wall kept a company of Daemons and Rawfaw at bay, patrolling the perimeter; while, in-between the walls, a band of Charis patrolled, in a loosely organized squad.

"There're our little people." John adjusted his binoculars on the family of Charis that they had followed in.

"They're still milling around?" Dessa turned her binoculars on them.

"Looks like," Zack said.

The Charis family hesitated, in confusion, near large stone pillars, at the entrance to Hahdace.

"This is not good." Zack watched the Daemons immediately respond.

"But here comes the cavalry," Calver said.

They watched the Charis guards pour out of the gate, wrestle the family away from the Daemons and bring them safely behind the walls.

"Feisty little fellas, ain't they?" Calver scratched under his bandana.

"Why don't the Daemons go in after them?" Zack scanned back and forth from the Daemons to the Charis and then inside the walls.

"The Daemons are ruthless, but pretty stupid," Nate said. "They only cross into Hahdace when Echthros puts the call out for more souls and their power is very limited once inside. It's mostly snatch and grab."

"What does Echthros do with them?" John asked.

Nate glanced at him without responding.

"That's good enough for me." John turned his binoculars back toward Hahdace.

"How come the Charis don't just rush them?" Zack asked.

"There are only a few hundred Charis in Hahdace at any given time. Too few," Nate said. "Besides, where would they go?"

"True," Zack agreed.

In the distance, flames belched into the sky, illuminating the entire underground. Smoke followed and within minutes, the pungent smell of sulfur-scented rot drifted toward them.

"Man." John fanned his nose. "If that was a fart, I don't want to see what let it."

"Tartaroo," Nate said "home of Echthros. The upheaval begins."

81

John rolled onto his back.

"I'm hungry. We've been watching them for hours."

"How can you be hungry when you can still smell that crap?" Dessa said.

"I don't know." John yawned. "I guess I'm bored and sleepy. When are we going to know something—"

"Do you notice anything?" Nate said to Zack as he stared toward Hahdace.

He pointed to a group of twenty Charis, that were led out of Hahdace under heavy guard. They passed another group, of less than twenty, being led back in, stumbling in from Tartaroo.

"Yeah, I see it," Zack said.

John rolled back over. "Well, I've noticed a lot of people coming and going, but I don't know what that has to do with us—"

"This is the fourth group in two hours that are segregated and led away." Zack said. "And it's the third group that has returned *from* Tartaroo."

"But I don't see—"

"They ain't the same though." Calver shook his head.

"What do you mean?" John asked.

"They don't *all* make it back," Zack said.

"People, time to move." Nate gathered his equipment. "We've got to get at some of them before they reach Tartaroo."

"Good, at least I won't be bored anymore." John grabbed his gear.

"We're going down the back side, opposite Hahdace." Nate started back down the mountain.

"Climb up so we can go back down," John said. "Why didn't we just stay on the ground and cut out the middle man?"

After close to another hour, they reached the base of the granite mountain and Nate gathered them around him.

"Mel and Cal, you keep your company here. We'll continue on down the road to Tartaroo and see what opportunity we can create."

They skirted Hahdace and moved several hundred yards down the path toward Tartaroo. Zack took cover in a cluster of stalagmites and tree roots, the size of his body. Like colossal webbed fingers, he wondered if they were waiting to crush him like a fist.

Nate, John and Dessa crawled next to him.

"Okay, a few things," Nate's voice was low, "a fatal blow to the head or chest will work on the Rawfaw, but the Daemons are a little more resilient."

"Okkayy." John's concern was apparent.

"Well," Nate paused, as if he were grandpa telling tall tales to the grandkids. "Slice them in two and they may have enough fight left in them to get your legs. They'll be shorter, but, you know."

Dessa snickered.

"You're the only one that laughs at his jokes," John said.

"Shut up," Dessa said.

Nate paused.

"So, what takes them down?" Zack glanced down the path toward Hahdace.

"It's got to be a head shot." Nate said.

"You're kidding?" John asked. "You know how bad my aim is. I'm a doctor, Jim, not a sharpshooter!" John tried his best Dr. McCoy imitation.

"Don't ask me," Nate shrugged, "I'm just telling you what we know. Oh, by the way, cutting off their heads seems to work well too." Nate smiled and looked back toward Hahdace.

"We'll grab the next group coming *out* of Hahdace, so let the first group coming *back from* Tartaroo pass by. John, I need you in the forward position, but stay out of sight."

"10-4 or aye, aye, sir or okay, I guess; I'll do my best." John held up his hand making a V with his second and third finger.

"Live long and prosper."

He crawled away.

———

The same tiny, dark haired girl that they had seen drop in, caught Zack's attention a few minutes later. The Charis, dressed in tan, linen tunics, stumbled past.

A Rawfaw guard snapped at the little girl, as she strayed from the path momentarily and she screamed. Zack wanted to bolt right then and cut off its head, but he held cover.

Her mother swatted the creature in the snout and it shook itself and stepped away, growling and hissing as if cursing at her. The little girl's thick curls cascaded down to her waist and Zack wondered how her cheeks could be so rosy and fat when she was dead. He watched her hold her mother's hand as if walking through a cross walk on a green light.

Zack shifted and a dead root snapped.

The little girl turned and looked at him.

He froze.

They were all going to die because of him.

82

Zack put his fingers to his lips. A dimpled smile spread across her face. The little girl turned her head, playing *Hide and Go Seek* and buried her head in her mother's clothing.

Zack crawled into position and signaled Nate that he was ready.

"Good," Nate responded over the headset. "How many do we have?"

"Looks like three Rawfaw and six Daemons and boy, do they stink," Zack whispered into his microphone.

"What did you expect?" Nate whispered.

"Beats me, but they smell like a… sweaty, decaying body that has just rolled in a pile of crap."

"Good description. And you're not too far off."

Zack watched the Rawfaw, former humans who had descended into the underworld in whatever condition they died. One had a cancerous growth jetting out from its face. Zack thought of John Merrick whom they had billed *The Elephant Man*. Another had all the fingers of his left hand mangled and broken. Still another was missing half its head; what was left of its brains hung out of its skull.

Zack witnessed them in their true form, before any undertaker would have worked his magic.

Nate slipped from cover to grab the last Daemon in line. With one twist of the Daemon's head, he popped its neck and sent it convulsing into the dirt. The commotion drew the attention of another Daemon. Nate hit it full force with a body block sending them both to the ground. The Daemon rolled and hissed scrambling to its feet, but Nate was on it. He shoved his dagger deep into its eye socket and dropped the Daemon to the ground, lifeless.

The others fell on the guards with swift precision. Dessa sliced the heads off two of the Rawfaw, so keenly, their faces still had surprised looks when they hit the ground and rolled.

John drove his Baraq sword into a Daemon's arm, pinning it to its body, but the Daemon whirled and caught John in the face, sending him into the dirt. The Daemon struggled to free its other arm as John jumped back up and half sawed, half sliced through his heavy neck muscles with his Mekayraw sword. The Daemon hit the ground and lay still.

Zack pounced, dealing a deathblow across the chest of the last Rawfaw and then spun, driving the tip of his Baraq into the left eye of a Daemon. With a *thwack*, the sword came out the other side of its head.

The rest of the creatures fell without incident while the Charis huddled in confusion.

Nate put up his hands, approaching them.

"I'm Nathaniel Abbeer, don't be afraid. We've come to help you."

"Where did you come from?" one woman asked.

"We are from the World of Light." Nate smiled.

"The World of Light?"

"The surface world," Nate pointed up, "where you used to live. We're here to take you into safety."

"I'm glad of that," the woman relaxed.

Nate continued. "Please bear with me, we don't have much time and I'm going to need your help."

"Now you're talking." A hefty man rubbed his hands together. "Anything you need, buddy."

"I thought you'd see it our way." Nate smiled.

"You can't believe what we've heard," the man continued.

"They say it's like ancient Rome up there." He pointed toward Tartaroo.

"The freaks herd people into arenas, forcing the children to watch horrible atrocities. Unspeakable things." He lowered his head. "I know I did some awful things in life, but—" He shook his head.

"Listen," Nate said, "you're all here temporarily."

The man looked up.

"It'll all be over soon." Nate put his hand on the man's shoulder. "Don't worry."

"I'll help you do anything to get me and my family out of here," the man said.

"Okay, we're going to go back to Hahdace and most of you will stay outside the walls, hidden," Nate explained. "One of our men, Mel Pinkerton, will make sure that you're safe." He turned toward the others. "Zack, you, John, and Dessa will dress in the clothing of the Rawfaw—"

"Whoa," John shuddered. "We have to put on *their* clothes?" He pointed to the carcasses.

"That's not the worst of it," Nate said. "But we're three guys short," Nate pointed at three of the Charis men. "What are your names?"

83

"I'm Ralph Maxwell." He offered his hand to Nate. "At least I used to be. Insurance salesman from up Minneapolis way. Bought it one night leaving work when it was forty below and a gunman tried to rob me. I showed 'em though, died right there on the spot, scared the sonofabuck to death!" Ralph chuckled.

"Nice to meet you, Ralph," Nate shook his hand.

"George Remey," another said.

"Rick Rosedale." The father of the little dark haired girl shook Zack's hand with a cold, strong grip.

"Alright," Nate said, "you three will robe up with us and no one will be the wiser. They won't question why you didn't return from Tartaroo."

Nate squatted in front of the children. "Kids, we're going to play a game."

"What game?" a little girl asked.

"We'll call it, *Don't Tell The Bad Man* and you have to help us play. Okay?"

The children nodded.

"I want you to promise me that you won't let anyone know that we are not the *real* bad men that took you, okay?"

More nods.

"And we're going to help you and your mommies and daddies get to a wonderful place." Nate stood up.

"Mister, will my Nana be there?" A bright-eyed boy tugged on Nate's sleeve.

"Yes, I expect she will," Nate said. "Will you help us?"

They all nodded again.

"Good." He turned back to Zack, Dessa and John. "Now this next part's going to be tricky."

"I knew there was bad news coming." John elbowed Zack. "It's like I have this Vulcan sense about things."

"Follow my thinking here," Nate said. "We don't look like the Rawfaw or Daemons. Not even you, John."

"Ha, ha." John held his stomach in mock amusement.

"I was wondering how we were going to get around that." Dessa said.

Nate took his dagger from its sheath, walked over to one of the severed heads, skinned it and then hallowed out the face. He took off his head gear and microphone and slipped it over his own face, like a mask.

John choked back the vomit.

"We will pull the hoods up over our heads to hide us." Nate's voice was muffled.

"Oh, great!" John turned and couldn't hold it back. He

vomited into the dirt.

"Sorry." He wiped his mouth on his sleeve. "So, not only are we on an adventure in Hell, now we have to wear Daemon faces like some sort of sick Halloween prank?"

"Or you can just smear blood and entrails on your face," Nate said, "instead of the full face."

"I don't know which is worse," Zack gagged and then walked over to a carcass, cut off the head and began to hollow it out. He vomited until he had nothing left in him.

John and Dessa watched Zack and then decided to use the entrails makeup.

Moments later, Zack slipped the head over his own and adjusted the wetness over his face. He breathed in and out of the nostrils trying to calm himself, but made the mistake of sticking his tongue out through the lips. He pulled the chin away from his own and spewed again.

"Control yourself," Nate said.

"I'm trying." Zack wiped his mouth with his sleeve.

"Our success depends on it." Nate touched his shoulder. "You can do this."

Zack nodded and replaced the face, breathing slowly.

84

For the next few minutes, Zack swallowed hard, kept his head down and hood pulled up as they approached the gates of Hahdace and stopped.

Zack glanced down at a shiny object in the dirt. He studied it momentarily and then recognition came.

"Nate." he whispered through the mask.

"Keep it down and don't talk normally," Nate scolded. "We're here."

"But, Nate." Zack caught his arm. "It's Jamie's ring—."

"Not now!" Nate whispered as the Daemon sentry approached.

The Daemon's boot toe came to rest on the ruby with diamonds surrounding it and Zack felt tears begin to well. He remembered the Ole Grist Mill where she had slipped it on her finger and her smile and the tears and the kiss.

The Daemon barked something at Zack in coughs and choking sounds and it brought Zack back.

Zack froze and then nodded, hoping that he was agreeing to the right thing and hoping that the Daemon didn't catch him looking at the ring. The Daemon pushed Zack backward causing the face to shift sideways.

Zack straightened it as Nate stepped forward and shoved the Daemon. Nate spoke to him in a muffled growl. The Daemon lunged toward Nate. Nate drew the Daemon sword he was now carrying and plunged it into its mid-section. The tip emerged through its back. The thrust staggered the Daemon; it looked at Nate, then down at the sword sticking out of its gullet. Nate put his foot on the Daemon's chest and dislodged the sword like steak off a skewer. It stumbled and fell, holding its chest as black liquid oozed through its fingers.

Several Daemons rushed to its side.

Nate stepped back, ready for a fight; but, in an attack of cannibalistic horror, the Daemons dismembered the creature and devoured it.

Zack choked back the vomit once again, scooped up the ring and shoved it in his pocket.

The ranking Daemon approached Nate, surveying him from toe to head. He paused and then slapped him on the back, belching a hideous laugh which triggered laughter from the rest.

Zack sighed and then steadied himself from passing out. The grotesque face, with Nate behind it, glanced at him, winked and then motioned for them to proceed.

They pushed the Charis into the wide opening, and across the expanse, as the Charis guards started toward them.

"Which one of us is next?" one man shouted, with a clenched fist.

Nate and the others ignored them and marched through a gate

in the secondary wall and around the corner of a house.

They pulled off the faces and Zack gulped the air, then spit.

"Nate, Jamie's ring—" was all Zack could say before spitting some more.

"We'll find her." Nate moved back to the corner of the building and peered around.

"Dumb creatures." Nate wiped the blood from his face. "They're not even concerned with us." Then he looked at Zack. "They've probably taken Jamie to Tartaroo."

"What!" Zack exclaimed. "But then we—"

"Listen, Zack," Nate put his hand on Zack's chest, "you've got to keep your head in the game. We'll find her, but first things first—"

"But, Nate—"

"We'll need other clothes to blend in," Nate turned to the Charis, "and something to clean up with."

"Follow me," Rick Rosedale said. "We have extra. Our house, if you want to call it that, is just around the corner."

Zack kept watch back over his shoulder as they navigated the narrow alleys filled with people.

"Don't worry," Rick said. "I've found out already that they never come in here until it's roundup time. Something keeps them away. They run in, snatch us and run back out, like holding your breath to a bad smell. I'm surprised we didn't attract more attention when we just waltzed in."

"Pneuma keeps them out of here," Nate said.

"Pneuma?"

Nate didn't explain.

They turned another corner.

"Here we are," Rick said.

He pushed his way through a simple wooden door and then turned to his wife as she followed them in.

"Marta, those extra clothes you found in the back room, did you do anything with them?" Rick asked.

"No, they're still there."

Rick disappeared down a hallway.

Marta stepped close to Zack and touched his face, with her icy fingers then closed her eyes.

Rick was back with an armload of robes, large enough to fit

over their gear.

"Here, will these do?" He asked.

"Perfect," Nate replied.

Marta opened her eyes and smiled at Zack.

"Thank you for allowing me to remember."

85

Daniel J. Blevins, clergyman extraordinaire, had clawed his way through the small, Midwest churches of his denomination with a degree of success. Finally Joliet, Illinois fell into his lap.

In the boundaries of his association, a pastor was recognized by the number of people that warmed the cushioned seats and listened to him sound off from the pulpit every Sunday. The numeric value, not only produced more *Benjamins* in his wallet, but also gave him a higher degree on the status thermostat.

Amidst the slaps on the back from fellow ministers at their state gatherings and the tailored suits that he received for services rendered, he grew in popularity with the upper crust of the organization as well as his own flock.

The carnivals, food drives, daycare for working moms, help for the homeless and his work with teens, painted "Pastor Dan" as a savior in the community. The front page heralded his name as a spiritual reformer.

His suntan darkened and his credit limit increased.

A knock on his wood paneled office door one day ushered the long legs of Amy Winkler across his threshold.

"Pastor Dan?" she asked.

He put down his pen and flashed the charismatic smile that had become his trademark.

"Yes," Dan answered in his southern drawl.

"I'm Amy Winkler; my father owns KGLW television in Chicago?"

"Oh, yes, my secretary said that you would be stopping by. So very glad to meet you." He came around the large oak desk and pumped her hand vigorously.

"So glad to meet you." He felt stupid for repeating himself, but continued. "Won't you sit down?"

He motioned to one of the tufted leather chairs in front of his desk. He parked himself in the other, remembering that a good counselor never sits across the desk from the counselee, lest he create a chasm between them; and, he certainly didn't want to be too far away from this beauty. He glanced at Amy's form fitting, tailored suit and skirt with the high slit up one leg.

"Now, what may I do for you?" he asked the woman, twenty years his junior.

"I believe that it's more, what I can do for *you*." She crossed her legs.

"You see, daddy, I mean, Leland J. Winkler II to most, owns Crystal Channel Communications. It encompassing twenty high profile radio stations, and a dozen or so television stations, across the Midwest and stretching to the eastern seaboard."

"Oh, really?" Daniel's eyes brightened.

"Daddy," she continued, "has become fascinated." She paused and smiled. "You would almost call him, *obsessed*, with your oratory ability and what has been going on here at your church."

Daniel smiled and brushed back his Grecian Formula, auburn number 3, hair.

"Is that right? Well, I never even imagined..."

On the contrary, Daniel knew the demographics on the upwardly mobile soccer moms and the combined incomes of their husbands, in order to target for maximum potential. For *reaching the lost*, of course.

"Mr. Winkler, Daddy, would like to offer you a time slot."

"Me?" Daniel touched his chest.

"Sunday mornings, 10:30am to 12 noon."

Daniel rubbed his chin and managed a humble look.

"We feel that this time slot will net a maximum return on our investment. We'll break for the local commercials, of course.

Have to get those sponsors in there." Amy flashed perfect teeth.

"Of course we do." Daniel smiled back.

"We figured that the first half hour might be a pre-taped session every week with you, in cardigan, relating to the needs of the people. Real *up close* and friendly. You can have whomever you want on your program as a guest; maybe throw a little music in the mix, you know."

"Oh my, yes, first class all the way." Daniel was already on his way to Hollywood.

"And then the last hour we will go with a delayed feed."

"Delayed?"

"Yes, we do that instead of real time live. That way if something goes awry, let's say someone's hair catches on fire from a candle at a Christmas service, God forbid, we can cut to a commercial and fix the problem. Without anyone the wiser."

"The wonders of the modern media." Daniel feigned simple country boy amazement.

"Well, what do you think?" Amy said, uncrossing her long legs and scooting to the edge of the seat. She placed her hands on her knees, drawing his gaze down.

"Well, I think it will be a wonderful opportunity to further the Kingdom of God." His eyes met hers again and he flashed his bleached teeth.

86

In the dark cell, a rat brushed past Daniel J. Blevins' leg. He recoiled, pulling his feet up to his chest.

—

Rolling between the sheets with Amy had begun eight months

into Daniel's electronic media success. Initially, the guilt of the affair would rouse him in the middle of the night, but he was no virgin when it came to sexual improprieties. He never did quite get it out of his system since Bible College, so the remorse soon faded. The numerous transfers from church to church throughout his ministry weren't always for righteous reasons.

With no personal responsibility for his actions, the affair with Amy continued, as he preached more sermons on understanding and forgiveness.

—

Daniel sat up, blinked and rubbed his eyes, trying to orient himself in the dark. He listened but couldn't tell the direction of the noise. The echo confused him, sounding like someone dragging a bag full of rocks. He shook his head and peered into the darkness. It didn't matter, the outcome would still be the same. He lay over on the cell bed, thinking of the past...

—

After a local headline caught the now famous, some might call infamous, *Pastor Dan* coming out of a hotel room with Amy on his arm, Daniel finally came to his senses. He began the long road back to rebuilding his marriage. The eighteen month affair with Amy ended bitterly and he sat once again in the tufted chair, this time with Shirley, his wife, next to him. A third chair supported a portly marriage counselor. He vowed a fresh start and decided to throw himself on the mercy of the congregation.

After all, he touted God's forgiveness on TV every Sunday with sweat running down his face, so why not partake of a little bit himself?

But even with his repentance, he found himself at a loss to explain to friends, relatives, and his constituents why the white pillars behind the manicured lawn of the Joliet Life Christian Center wouldn't be seen on their television at 10:30am any longer.

With media numbers dropping, as quickly as Daniel's fall out of bed with Amy, Daddy Winkler had lost interest in Daniel's oratory ability.

Daniel J. Blevins' white capped smile wasn't enough to convince anyone any more.

—

The cell door opened and light peeked through. Daniel instinctively scooted to the corner of the slab, that passed for a bed, and rolled into the fetal position.

—

Daniel recalled hitting his head on the oak desk in his office and the liquid draining from his mouth, but he had no conscience recollection of the stroke.

The nurses and beeping machines interrupted his sleep pattern for the next month or so, but he talked to himself and to the Lord quite often. Shirley read to him and kept his lips moist with water, but he only peered at her with sunken, dry eyes.

Then one morning at 3:36 am, the machines stopped beeping and Daniel J. Blevins, televangelist extraordinaire, passed through the veil, never to breathe the breath of life again.

—

The Rawfaw stuck its ugly head in and belched its death stench into the air like a putrid fog. It shoved someone into the cell, blocking the sliver of light and the person hit the floor with a groan.

The Rawfaw slammed the cell door plunging Daniel back into darkness.

Daniel waited, huddling tighter into the corner waiting for a slice or blow to come from the other thing now occupying the cell.

He heard a choke and then a soft sob.

It was a woman, or at least a girl.

"Who's there?" Daniel whispered.

More sobs and then a series of sniffs.

"Who are you?" a girl's voice whispered out of the blackness.

"A friend." Daniel paused. "I'm nothing now, but I'm not going to hurt you. Where did you come from?"

"I don't know," the girl said. "Earth, I guess, if that makes any sense." She snuffed again. "It's so dark, I—"

"Here," Daniel said. "I'll help, they don't know I have this, but I snatched it a few days ago."

He fumbled in the dark and pulled a cluster from under the bunk, struck a match and it chased the darkness to the corner of the rock hewn cell.

"Wait," he said.

In the dim light, he reached into the bundle and extracted a crude candle, made from a bit of dung he had fashioned into a cylinder with a wick in the middle. He held the match to it and the candle illuminated a young girl's face.

Daniel shrank back and grabbed a bit of cloth out of the corner to cover his nakedness.

"Sorry," he said. "They…took my clothes."

"It's okay." She brushed back a tangle, of what was once blonde hair, but was now matted with dried blood.

Daniel looked at her face in the dimness. Her features were soft and pristine, untarnished by the sun's rays or blemishes. There was a smudge of blood across her cheek where she had stanched the gash above her left eye. Her right eye had a swipe of purple under it, high on her cheekbone. Her lip was cracked and out of the corner of her mouth was a line of dried blood. The girl held the neck of her shirt together, where it had been torn from the neckline, and her cut-off blue jeans were caked with mud and filth from being dragged through, God only knew, what. One knee was scraped and scratched and the side of one leg was a mass of grime.

Daniel tried to move closer but his nakedness embarrassed him.

"I'm sorry I don't have any shoes in here for you."

"It's okay." She sniffed again. "I … lost mine somewhere

along the way. They were my favorite slippers."

She wiped her runny nose with her fingers and then onto her cut-offs.

"I'm sorry for asking in this way—" she paused, "but, are you human?"

Daniel smiled a father's smile. "Yes. At least I was once. Sorry." He laid the candle down on the ground and offered his hand out of the darkness.

"I'm Daniel Blevins, call me Dan, if you like. I was a pastor a long time ago…"

She hesitated and then reached out to touch his hand.

"Jamie Watkins."

87

The heavy wooden doors swung wide and two Rawfaw drug Daniel J. Blevins into the sanctuary, naked.

Echthros sat on a tufted, velvet stool, playing a monstrous pipe organ. Daniel would have covered his ears from the fevered pitch, but his arms were captive.

He watched Echthros as his fingers glided effortlessly over the keys, crescendo to decrescendo, to crescendo again; until finally, in a manic spasm of musical climax, he hit a note off the human scale, causing Daniel to slump in pain.

"What do you think, Pastor Dan?" Echthros spun on the stool and stood, smoothing his double-breasted suit and adjusted a blood-red tie.

"It was something Bach was working on when he died, but just couldn't find that last note," he paused, "because it didn't exist!" He laughed.

Echthros sauntered down the polished, black marble steps,

reminiscent of Gene Kelly in *Singing in the Rain,* and onto the cathedral floor. He nodded for the Rawfaw to release Daniel, who collapsed on the cold marble.

"Like it?" Echthros said, turning around with his arms out as if displaying Shangri-La.

Daniel looked up through bloody eyes.

"I thought it a rather good likeness myself." Echthros paused. "Of course, *your* Joliet Life Christian Center had plush carpeting instead of black marble, but I find it easier to clean up the mess if you can just squeegee it into the blood troughs."

Echthros pointed to the small steel ditches running the full length of the sanctuary.

"A neat work area is a happy work area, I always say." Echthros smiled again. "I kind of like my little remodel, even though we made it with you in mind ... I think I'll keep it."

Echthros bent over to look into Daniel's face. "Of course, we kept some of *our* favorite amenities, just for continuity's sake, you understand."

Echthros pointed to the ceiling, where oil soaked Charis hung, suspended from meat hooks, ablaze like Christians in Nero's gardens.

"Guess you didn't use your parishioners to light your sermons though, right?" Echthros smiled. "It *does* save on the electric bill."

Daniel looked back down at the floor, wheezed and then raised his head again.

"You had pews, of course, and we don't—"

"Chairs," Daniel corrected. "Get it right, you freak."

"Ah, yes, I stand corrected, Reverend. They *were* nice, padded chairs, weren't they?"

Echthros's perpetual smile reminded Daniel of the Joker from the Batman comics.

"Couldn't have *pews*, right? Your constituents wouldn't hear of it, because you weren't a 'traditional'," he wrapped the statement in quotes, made with his fingers "church, now were you? No, not in *this* modern age."

He squatted in front of Daniel. "We didn't bother with *chairs*; they take up too much space in such a great room." He stood again. "We *did* have the forethought to bring a few people by though, you know, to help participate in your little, send off, as it were."

Echthros walked back up the marble stage, a place where, in another life, Daniel J. Blevins had plied his trade. He stepped behind an elaborately carved, wooden, high- backed chair, with velvet seat cushions, and opened the double doors that, if this would have been the *real* Joliet Life Christian Center, would have led to the choir room.

Shirley, Becky, Maggie and Danny followed Echthros back into the sanctuary.

Daniel looked up at them, wheezing, and then lowered his head.

"They're not my real family," Daniel mumbled.

"Oh, you don't think so?" Echthros punched Danny in the face and the boy fell to the floor crying. Daniel flinched to make a move toward him, but the Rawfaw knocked him back to his knees.

"And these precious teenage twin girls," Echthros stepped to Becky and Maggie caressing their necks. Terror filled her eyes, as Becky knocked Echthros's hands away.

"Help me, daddy!" she cried.

"You're not real." Daniel didn't remove his gaze from the floor.

"Are you telling me," Echthros continued, "that if a couple of my assistants there," he motioned to the Rawfaw, "were to, say, *have them,* in whatever capacity they are able now, that you, Reverend, wouldn't be moved to help?"

"They're not real." Daniel gasped. "My kids are safe at home."

"Do you think so?" Echthros cocked his head and then stepped to Daniel's wife.

"How about Shirley, here? Your dear, Bible College sweetheart? The one to whom you pledged your heart, mind and your sexual fidelity to? You wouldn't defend her?"

Echthros ripped Shirley's clothes and knocked her to the floor. He jumped on top of her, biting her face and neck and slashing at her with jagged fingernails. He tore at her as Shirley writhed and screamed for Daniel's help.

The auditorium began to pulse and vibrate, like a heavy-metal rock show's sub-woofers, thrumming the lowest bass note ever recorded. Stepping out of the walls, as if they had been chameleons, were Rawfaws and Daemons, chanting in an unearthly tongue.

Several bolted onto the stage and slaughtered Daniel's family while he rolled into a fetal position and screamed.

"You're not real!" He covered his ears and thrashed his head from side to side like an epileptic seizure. "You're safe at home!" His yellow-green vomit sprayed the black marble. "You're not here! You are not here!"

The mania subsided, as the last of the bodies hit that floor, and Echthros sat on the edge of the stage, much in the same manner that Daniel had so many Sundays, to tug on the heartstrings of the congregation. He combed the blood off his suit with his hand and shook it onto the floor.

"What a pain, huh?" Echthros wiped blood from his mouth. "Wondering why you still have the capability of feeling?"

Daniel rolled to a sitting position, clutched his knees to his chest and rocked back and forth.

"Why so much if you are, indeed, dead?" Echthros smiled, crimson outlined his teeth like eating a bowl of raspberries.

"Well, Doc." He spread his arms. "That's what they used to call you in Bible College, wasn't it? Slapped you on the back after a great time and said, 'Great sermon, Doc'?" Echthros stared at Daniel, "Well, Doc, we are all still very much alive here. Don't you worry your pathetic little mind about that."

Daniel sobbed, seeing body parts scattered around the mock auditorium that reminded him of his platform to greatness.

"That tormenting, mind altering, back aching, pain." Echthros shrugged. "Hey, at least you survived the last beating though? Something to be thankful for."

A Rawfaw galloped out of the crowd and tore into Daniel's back, tearing a piece of flesh loose. Daniel screamed in horror, clutching the jagged, bloody hole.

He looked at his blood soaked hand in amazement.

"Yes, Danny boy, very much alive," Echthros nodded. "You know, Reverend, this time I have a special treat for you. A treat for us all." Echthros wiggled his fingers in a *come hither* gesture.

Daniel turned.

From the rear of the auditorium, a woman with long legs and a short skirt, clip clopped in, on spiked high heels. Trailing her was a Rawfaw, leading a bound and gagged Jamie Watkins, on the end of a chain.

As the woman stopped beside Daniel, his gaze started from her feet and continued up her muscular legs.

She squatted and reached out, lifting his chin up so that he was looking into her eyes.

"Yes, Danny, it's me."

"Amy?" He felt his muscles relax and his vision blurred with tears, mingled with blood. "I—"

"Well, not technically dear." She smiled. "Amy. Angie. Abaddon. Jezebel, if you like. It's all the same to me." She tapped him on the nose as if he were a toddler.

"You know, we had a *lot* of good times together, remember?" She reached down and nodded his head for him. "Who knows, you might even like this next part." She looked up. "I know Jamie will."

Jamie tried to pull free, but the Rawfaw tightened the chain.

Abaddon stood and held out her hand. Another Rawfaw placed a whip in it composed of ten leather straps with shards of glass and metal woven into the ends. She drew back and lashed across Daniel's back, forcing him down, pulling shreds of skin and splattering blood onto the marble floor.

The Daemon's screams erupted, in bloodlust, and overwhelmed Daniel's shrieks for mercy.

"You preached about this, didn't you?" she asked. "Quite dramatic and theatrical as I recall." She bent over to look close at him. "Sweat pouring from your throbbing temples. You wiped your tears with your hanky and shook it out for effect. My, my, how things have changed. Firsthand knowledge now, huh?" She stood up, smiling. "It was easy when all you did was pluck those poor, lost sucker's heart strings, wasn't it?"

Again and again she pummeled him, to more chants from the room. He tried to pull himself up, but finally collapsed, gasping for breath and wheezing through exposed lungs.

Jamie turned away, vomited through her gag and slumped onto the marble floor.

Amy stood by his form, breathing heavily; her muscles glistened with splatters of sweat and blood. She wiped the blood from her face and licked her lips.

"Had enough yet, darling?" She asked.

Daniel stared through the blood.

The buzzing cloud, behind the high backed chair, distracted him momentarily from the pain. He followed it, in the flickering light, as it darted back and forth. Hundreds of black flies, as large as bumblebees, swarmed him. They entered his exposed rib cage and stung his lungs, the fire from ten thousand needles gouging his eyes, penetrating his ears and nose, ripping, tearing, biting, and plowing furrows in his skin. Daniel J. Blevins was soon wrapped in a sadistic blanket of agony.

88

Daniel swatted at them. Some would retreat momentarily, but then land again to suck his blood, in long mosquito strokes.

He screamed, waved his arms and squirmed on the black marble. He felt the swarm lay eggs in his gashes. The wounds festered, like a child's science experiment of baking soda and vinegar, and the eggs hatched immediately, the maggots burrowing their way into all of his crevices.

Daniel pulled himself up until he knelt and raised both arms in the air for mercy. Daemons and Rawfaw responded only with screams of mockery. He scanned the platform through blood soaked eyes, but found no pity. He pushed himself up, but slipped in his own blood and collapsed on the floor again.

"I grow weary of this." Abaddon stepped forward and fanned the swarm back to the platform.

She handed the whip to a Rawfaw and knelt beside Daniel, silencing the auditorium. Abaddon took a handful of his hair.

"Did you enjoy that?"

Daniel groaned.

"What do you think, Jamie?" Abaddon smiled at her. "He used to," she glanced at Daniel., "back in the day, when I was just *some* bimbo helping you climb to the top, giving you pleasure and self worth." She pulled his hair harder. "Didn't you!" She screamed. "A little bit of leather on your bare skin?"

"Me, all dressed up in leather and lace, and you promising me that you would leave her for me." Her shrieks echoed from the walls.

"Can you believe this, Jamie?" She shook his head. "This lyin' piece of crap, preacher would tell me that he was going to leave his wife and run off with me. Make me part of his ministry." Abaddon laughed. "I was going to be the next Mrs. Daniel J. Blevins!" Abaddon rolled her eyes. "Men." She winked at Jamie. "Am I right? Or am I right?"

Abaddon let Daniel slump back on the floor, stood and walked toward Jamie.

"I don't think we need this anymore." She reached up and ripped Jamie's gag out of her mouth spraying blood, spit and vomit onto the floor. Jamie coughed.

"Leave her alone," Daniel gasped.

Abaddon turned and walked back to him. "Really, Danny? What, do you have a thing for *her* now?" She wagged her finger at him. "Just because you were cell mates for a little while, doesn't mean... Why Danny, even here you really must control yourself." She smiled. "But I know that was never your strong point. Controlling yourself."

"I, repented—"

Abaddon clamped her hand over his mouth and nose. "Don't even *try* that with me."

Daniel convulsed against her grip.

His eyes bulged and he swatted at her hand.

"I don't think we heard you?" She put her ear close to him. "Oh, sorry, something's cutting off your air." She laughed and released his face.

"I repented of all of that—" Daniel gasped, "and of you."

"Did you?" Abaddon asked. "Did you really repent of me?" She stood again. "Mumble a few words of, *I'm sorry* and everything's all better, right?" She began to dance a jig around the front of the auditorium. "He repents! He repents! Glory Hallelujah, he repents!" She danced past Jamie and ran a sharp nail across her neck leaving a blood trail. Jamie cried out and swatted at her.

The auditorium erupted in laughter.

"Welll," Abaddon stopped in front of Daniel, "sorry, Danny Boy." She put her hands on her hips. "Too, late. You're already dead! No repenting now!"

She reared back in laugher, then walked back to Daniel and spat in his face.

"That's all you're worth!" She screamed.

She kicked him in the face and his nose cracked.

Daniel began to cry like a two-year-old.

"The mighty preacher!" She twirled to the chants of the onlookers.

"Preacher! Preacher! Preacher!"

She stopped and pulled his hand into the air, declaring the winner of a championship fight.

"The Man of God!" she shouted. "His Holiness, the Right Reverend Daniel J. Blevins!"

Abaddon turned to Jamie again and put her hand aside her mouth as if about to tell her a secret.

"Let me tell you, girlfriend, he wasn't that great between the sheets."

She then turned back to the crowd and cupped her hands as if they were a megaphone.

"And NOOWWW, God's Man For The Hour! Pastor Dan! Applause, please, applause. Push that Applause Button! Light that Applause sign!" She screamed. "Isn't that what you used to do, in your *mega-church*?"

"Praise the Lord!" someone shouted.

Her countenance changed immediately.

"I've had enough of you, and your kind, Danny. And I'm sure Jamie will agree." She swiped his blood from the floor and lathered her hands. "We wash our hands of you."

Abaddon grabbed him with one hand and dragged his semi-lifeless form toward a Rawfaw, standing on the periphery. She snatched a club the size of a small baseball bat out of its hand.

Abaddon turned and looked at Echthros.

"Well, Reverend," Echthros said, "at least now you do get to meet your Creator. No telling what *He'll* say. He and I aren't really on speaking terms these days." Echthros paused. "It's really a shame though; we have *so* enjoyed having you with us all this time." He nodded.

Abaddon swung the club. Jamie screamed and passed out.

89

Daniel J. Blevins slumped over, on his own altar, as the room exploded in manic spasms.

"Abaddon, my dear," Echthros laughed, "drop what you are doing and come here."

She walked seductively onto the platform.

"Everything according to plan?" Echthros held out his hands.

"Of course." She plopped onto his lap. "I troll the streets of the surface world, show them some leg, flash them some cleavage and, voilà, they're mine."

"Excellent." Echthros licked her face.

She pushed him away, brushed back her hair, licked one finger and ran it along her eyebrow. "They're tasty."

"Very good," Echthros said. "We'll move in full force and nothing can stop us. And what about our *other* little matter?"

She patted her stomach. "Without a hitch."

He drew a scratch across her stomach.

"Ouch!" She pushed his hand away.

He leaned in and kissed her stomach. "Oh, the possibilities."

"Our ace in the hole," Abaddon motioned toward Jamie who was beginning to stir.

"And James, of course," Echthros said.

"Yes," Abaddon paused. "I've been meaning to talk to you about him—"

"Why?"

"I don't trust him." Abaddon stood.

"So far his intel has been good," Echthros said.

"Yes, but there's more to an operation of this size than just intel," she said. "He's sloppy, his timing's off and he's been wrong before—"

"That's true," Echthros said, "but at least we know they've crossed over the threshold and are on they're way."

"I just don't know." She bowed her head then looked up at Echthros. "What if they've gotten to him?"

"What do you mean?"

"We haven't heard from him for days now," she said.

"It's not like there's a phone booth on every corner." Echthros reached out and brushed her thigh. "Trust me. The heir is on his way and that's all we need."

"I suppose." Abaddon walked down off the platform and over to Jamie. "Here honey, let me help you." She reached out and helped Jamie to her feet and then slapped her hard enough to turn her head.

Jamie cried out and instinctively kicked at Abaddon. Abaddon cocked a fist to hit her.

"Abaddon!" Echthros stood. "Not yet."

Abaddon smiled at Jamie, relaxed her hand and pinched Jamie's cheek. "Soon, dear, and this will all be over and you'll wish you had never met me." She raked her nails across Jamie's cheek and Jamie batted her hand away.

"I'm already there." Jamie said.

Abaddon drew back to slap her again.

"Abaddon!" Echthros called. "We want her in one piece. Let her alone for now, you'll get your chance."

Abaddon didn't remove her gaze from Jamie. "You're right about that." She lowered her hand and stepped back.

Echthros motioned for two Rawfaw. "Drag this poor excuse for a *holy* man out of my sight."

Heavy drapes that hung against the edge of the cathedral parted and they picked up Daniel's flaccid form, dragging him to a precipice a few hundred feet behind the throne.

The first Rawfaw peered over the sharp drop-off and trembled. Black swirls of living darkness engulfed the canyon below. Explosions and implosions collided, boiling and belching black fire, releasing the smell of ammonia, mingled with sulfuric smoke.

The Rawfaw turned back to look at Echthros and a black swirl, like a maimed hand, exploded out of the canyon and snatched the Rawfaw backward into the darkness. His screams echoed through the auditorium and everyone cheered.

Jamie screamed.

Echthros swept his hand in dismissal. The second Rawfaw pushed Daniel to the edge and retreated. Black fire grabbed the preacher and pulled him into the maw.

"Another one bites the dust!" Echthros smiled and shook his head. "Nevertheless, the fun continues."

Abaddon took Jamie by the arm and pulled her toward the platform. Jamie squirmed, but could not free herself.

"Ohh," Echthros said, "don't be that way, Jamie; we have something rather special for you—"

"No—" Jamie twisted.

"Oh, yes," Echthros said. "You're not going to meet the same fate as your friend, Pastor Dan." He patted her on the shoulder. "No, you are our *special guest* and we are going to take real good care of you, Jamie."

Echthros plopped down in one of the platform chairs and pushed Jamie to the ground in front of him. "There's an old friend waiting to see you."

From behind the platform, Milton Drago stepped forward and Jamie recoiled.

Milton's hair was long and matted thick with grease. His dark eyebrows had grown into a uni-brow, furrowing across the top of his eyes. His teeth were yellow rows of grime and his two eyeteeth had grown into canine incisors. His once clear complexion was pocked with erupted pimples and his beard stubble was in-grown, twisting back on itself to penetrate the craters on his cheeks like electrical plugs into an outlet. Milton's chest hair protruded out of his sweat soaked shirt like mange and his overly muscular forearms and claw tipped hands hung down over shredded pants that revealed a dog's leg hair. Shoes could not contain his long toenails that curled around his toes and clicked on the black marble as he crossed the floor. Milton Drago had mutated into the species known as the *DoeRawfaw*.

"Hello, Jamie," he said.

90

Nate and Zack sat opposite Dessa and John, at a rough-hewn plank table, in Rick Rosedale's mud house.

"Rick, may I borrow your fire?" Nate got up and began to dig in his backpack.

"Of course, you can." Marta, Rick's wife, entered with the little dark haired girl trailing behind her. "Need a pot and some water?"

"That would be great, thanks," Nate replied.

"You're the ones we saw," Zack realized.

Marta looked at him quizzically.

"You dropped right in front of us," Zack said.

"Really?" Marta smiled. "I didn't see any of you."

"We were hidden." Dessa offered her hand. "I'm Tredessa."

"That explains it." Marta smiled and shook her hand. "This is

Ricki." Marta pulled the little girl around in front of her. "It's okay, honey, these people are here to help."

"Hi," Ricki said.

"Well, hi there," Dessa smiled. "You're a cutie." She pinched Ricki's cheek.

"I was an IRS auditor." Rick interrupted his contemplation.

"Really?" Nate placed several paper wrapped items on the stone counter top, took some water out of a pail and poured it into a pot. He then grabbed his knife out of the scabbard and began chopping like a five-star hotel chef. In a few minutes a stew was bubbling.

"Hey, Nate?" John asked. "Did you clean that knife?"

Nate looked at the knife, then back at John, shrugged and continued chopping.

"Yeah," Rick continued, "I'm sure my clients didn't care that I bought the big one." He stared through Marta and Ricki. "We were on our way home from my mom's house and I fell asleep at the wheel." Rick lowered his voice. "Head on collision. Next thing I know, we were clawing our way out of slimy body bags." Rick glanced around the room. "But I guess it was good in one sense that we're all here together." He pulled his daughter to him. "Eternity is different than I expected though."

He sipped a drink.

"So this is it, huh?" Rick asked.

"What?" Nate brushed some of the food into a pot.

"The end? The big enchilada? Eternity?"

"Here?" Nate pointed to the floor.

"Yeah?" Rick said.

"Not hardly." Nate smiled.

"You're kidding?"

"No. Most of you slid in here on sudden death." Nate dug in his pack for more food.

"You're like a walking grocery store," Zack said.

"Always be prepared," Nate said. "I was a boy scout." He

winked at Zack.

"What do you mean 'sudden death?'" Ralph Maxwell brought them back to the subject.

"Sudden death," Nate continued. "You know, the accident? All of this here is temporary." He waved his knife around the room. "You're at the airport in a holding pattern right now."

The others gathered around the table.

"We're here in Hahdace." Nate walked over and placed a bowl upside down on the table. He then placed some forks next to it in a square. "Tartaroo is to the east of us and on the edge of that is The Living Darkness."

"Living Darkness?" John asked.

"Yeah." Nate replied. "It takes on a life of its own, almost like some sort of being, and here's the real kicker, the flame's so hot, it burns black."

"Come on," Zack said.

"I know, I know it sounds impossible, but it's true." Nate continued. "Now the only way to Tartaroo is through Gehenna." Nate placed a napkin between the bowl and the forks. "Our plan, Rick." Nate looked at him, "is to get all the Charis to safety here, at the base of the mountain," he put his finger near the bowl, "until we can get you safely to Paradise."

"Okaaay." Rick was hesitant.

"See, you're waiting to move out." Nate said. "The reason you're here is not just your accident, but more because of sudden death."

Rick's forehead wrinkled with curiosity.

"In your case," Nate got up and stirred the pot and sat back down, "death was unexpected. No long drawn out sickness or such. And what is death anyway?"

No one responded.

"It's the separation of the body and spirit. In your case, prematurely." Nate turned to Ralph. "Same with you, right?"

"Yeah, heart attack." Ralph nodded.

"How about you, George." Nate pointed at him. "What'a ya in for?"

"Never saw it comin'." George shook his head.

"What?" Zack asked.

"The L, man." He paused. "I grew up on the south side of

Chicago. Mama always told me as a kid to never play on the tracks. Well, I wasn't exactly playin' on the tracks, but I was late for work and tryin' to catch the L train and I slipped off the platform right as the 8:05 was bearin' down."

"Oooh", Zack winced.

"There you have it." Nate snapped his fingers. "Hahdace is here because of mix-ups in processing, mostly premature death. You're going to a much better place with Lord Pantokrator."

"Whew!" Rick wiped his forehead and flung his hand in the air, throwing imaginary sweat. "Man, I thought that this was all there was. I just knew that we would be spending the rest of our lives in some adobe hut, eating Troglodyte stew!"

The room broke out in laughter.

"So, what's the plan for getting us out of here?" Ralph asked.

"We'll wait for my brother, Mick, and his forces to create a diversion, and then we have another of our colleagues waiting to take all of you to safe haven until we can get you out of here."

"Sounds major," Ralph said.

"It probably will be, but we can handle it. We've done it before." Nate winked. "How many do you estimate are in Hahdace now?" Nate asked.

Ralph looked up at the ceiling and then back at Nate.

"One hundred and thirty five men, women, and children are here. I think there might even be some kind of a dog running around here somewhere, but he's weird looking. Don't think it came in with any us."

"Wow! Impressive," Zack said.

"I'm on the High Council; we keep track of everybody." Ralph grinned.

"Excellent, that'll help us to make sure that everyone gets out," Nate said.

The pounding at the door interrupted Nate.

91

Marta went to the door.

The woman had both arms full and a cloth sack tucked in her mouth.

"Oh, let me help." Marta took the cloth sack.

"Thanks, Marta," The woman smiled. "My hands were so full that I had to kick your door, hope it didn't leave any marks."

They both looked down at the beat up wooden door.

"Guess it wouldn't make any difference." Marta smiled.

Zack watched the commotion.

"I brought you a few things, you know, like a house warming." The woman smiled. "And to remind you about Ann Pink's tonight."

"Ann Pink?" Marta asked.

"You didn't forget, did you?" The woman put her hands on her hips and cocked her head. "The party?"

"Oh, I *didn't* remember." Marta closed her eyes momentarily. "I'm really out of it today, sorry."

"How could you forget?" She waved her hands. "Of course, you wouldn't know what a big deal it is. You haven't been dead that long!" The woman laughed and tapped Marta's arm. "It's the social event of the year!"

"Hmmm, Ann's?" Marta searched the ceiling.

"Well, I guess as social as you can get down here." The woman laughed.

"Now which house is Ann's?" Marta asked.

"The red pots."

"Red pots?" Marta repeated.

"You *are* out of it. Around the corner and down, the place with all the junk out front."

"Oh, the red pots." Marta nodded. "I'm sorry. Yeah, I know now."

"Where she got the pots, I don't know." The woman shrugged. "And the red paint?" She paused. "I don't *even* want to ask." She tapped Marta on the arm again, leaning in as if she was whispering a secret. "Anyway, will you come?"

"Uh, yeah, I guess so." Marta shrugged. "Not like we have anything else to do."

"Well, everyone's going to be there." She counted off one finger at a time. "The Nelsons, Tammy Marin, Ben and Jeff Worthington."

"I don't know them." Marta said.

"Those cute brothers from across the way. Well, they'd be cute if I were younger, and not dead!" The woman laughed again. "No, I'll say they're cute anyway!" She roared and then continued counting. "Renee Manitoba, Nelson Harvis and his daughter. I think her name is Madeline, but everyone calls her Maddy. The Meekings. The Rice's. The Straters are even going to be there. Do you know them?"

Marta shook her head.

"Anyway," the woman hardly came up for air, "I'm trying to round up as many as I can. The more, the merrier! It starts in just a few minutes!"

She was finally finished and slumped over against the wall in exaggerated exhaustion.

"Okay, then, I guess we'll see…" Marta trailed off.

The woman caught a glimpse of the guests.

"Oh, my goodness. I didn't know you had company." She poked her head in, scanned the room and leaned in to Marta. "I *am* so sorry," she whispered. "Why didn't you say something before I made a nuisance of myself?"

"It's okay, Christine." Marta couldn't hold back any longer. "Rick and Ricki were taken tonight."

Christine paused. "Oh, my goodness, I'm so sorry. Are you alright?" She stepped back, "Oh, my gosh, Marta." She hugged her. "And here I am going on about some party and they might have been killed—"

"It's okay, Christine, come in and meet these folks that rescued them." She swung the door wide.

Christine's shiny, brunette hair was pulled back, and secured with two combs, and it caught Zack's attention.

Nate stood and made the introductions of Dessa and John.

"And this is Zack," Nate said.

Christine offered her hand and smiled.

Zack took inventory of her features without reaching for her hand.

"Zack?" Nate elbowed him and nodded toward Christine.

"Hello, Zack," Christine said. "It's so nice to meet you."

"Oh, I'm sorry." Zack finally snapped out of his daze. "Hello."

"Its okay, Zack. It's not every day you meet the dead, right?" She laughed.

"Well, at least not a dead person as pretty as you." Zack studied her hair.

"Well, thank you." Christine blushed. "Hey, be sure and bring *him* to the party too. We can always use more good lookin' guys." She turned to Marta and winked. "In fact, you're all invited!" She spread her arms. "Sorry for barging in."

"Not at all," Marta said.

"Well," Christine continued, "better get going. Lots of folks to tell and it starts here shortly. Wish we still had phones."

She whisked out the door.

92

Nate continued the instructions. "Zack, I'll have you…"

Zack gazed at the door and stood. "I'll be back."

He moved toward the door.

"Be careful." Nate said.

"I will." Zack mumbled and closed the door behind him.

Zack walked into the dirt street. A warm dry breeze brushed against his face. Nate was right, he was getting used to the smell.

He looked up the street and then down again. People came and went as if they hadn't a care. A little brown haired boy ran up to him, paused, smiled and then ran away and disappeared through a doorway.

Zack took a few steps toward the corner and scanned the street. The faces were familiar, but only the sort of familiarity that the human race has in common. They were faces of people he thought he knew or people that could have been twins of others he had met.

He kept walking past city blocks, until he finally stood at an intersection looking in all directions.

A teenage girl sat in the dirt making circles with a stick and a boy watched over her shoulder. A woman talked with two men and they all glanced at him when he walked past. An elderly man leaned back in a chair against a wall. He looked like he could topple over at any moment.

Is that the same guy I saw from the mountain, hours ago?

Zack could have been on his own block, outside of Denver, on a warm summer evening. He circled back the way he came and walked to the middle of the square, turning around a few times. Then he remembered Christine's words: *Anne Pink's house, around the corner and down. It's the one with all the junk out front. The red pots. You know, the red pots? Where she got them, who knows? And the paint? I don't ask...*

The red pots caught his eye. His labored footsteps matched his heartbeat. He approached the pots and stood in front of a red wooden door. A sign tacked above it read: *Be it ever so humble, there's no place like Hahdace*

"It's not pretty, but it's true." Zack spun.

93

"Uh, Sir?"

"My sign." The white haired man, with a three-day-old beard, motioned above the door. "Yup, painted her last week. Mother thought it was silly, but I said, 'what the heck.' Guess we should make the best of it. I mean after all, we're dead, right?" He wheezed with laughter, coughed up a ball of phlegm and spat it into the dirt.

"Don't know why I'm still coughin' like that when I'm supposed to be dead." He laughed again, coughed again, and spat again.

"How long have you been here?" Zack asked.

"Well, I don't rightly know. Let me see." He put his finger on his chin. "Mother and me were on a plane to visit Paris, that's in France, you know." He motioned for Zack to sit on a bench next to the red pots. The old man took out a pipe and a match and lit up.

Zack stared at the pipe and smoke.

The man caught his gaze.

"Yeah, doesn't taste that great any more, but it's a habit and, after all, habits are pretty hard to break." He paused. "Guess they wouldn't be habits otherwise." He paused again and sucked a few times. "Don't ask where I got the pipe, and the tobacco. Well I make it myself out of … Never mind." He winked.

"Now let me see…." He closed his eyes, and then opened them again. "We were on our way to Paris. I was eventually goin' to visit Normandy again. I was there once, you know. Didn't see much the first time. I had my head in the sand on that danged beach most of the time. Dodgin'bullets!" He laughed, coughed and spat once more.

"Yeah." Zack smiled.

"We were gonna make a big wing ding of it," the man continued. "Take Mother to the French Riviera, see the Eiffel Tower and down some of that horrible French cuisine." He let the phrase hang in the air, puffed and exhaled the smoke. "And then, danged if that pilot didn't ditch that aluminum piece of crap comin' off the runway! Went into a danged swamp, for cryin' out loud! I haven't flown in over sixty years and I could've handled the rudder and ailerons better than that, wet behind the ears, kid!"

"Yes, sir, I expect you could have," Zack said.

"Present company accepted."

"Yes, sir." Zack smiled.

"Yup, do you know that we was the only ones on that plane that bought it? The only ones! Me and the Mrs." He shook his head. "What do you think of that?" He slapped Zack on the knee.

"Is that right?"

"Well, it ain't right, but it's true!" He laughed again. "Name's Roy Pink." His hand shot out. "I sure hope when we get to where we're a 'headin' that I get a new body. I figured that at least if I died, and I knew I would sooner or later, that I would get a new set of wheels out of the deal! Maybe look like that Brad Cruise or somethin'." He laughed and smoke puffed out of his pipe.

"Tom," Zack said.

"What?"

"Tom Cruise."

Roy stared at him. "Anyway… I don't know how long we been here." He sat back in silence.

Zack sat for a moment and then looked up at the door. He looked down at the ground, then up and down the street and finally back at the door again.

"You goin' in there?" Roy threw a thumb toward the door.

"Sir?"

"You goin' into the party?"

"Well, I don't—"

"I wouldn't advise it." Roy sucked on the pipe stem.

"No?"

"No. All they do is talk 'bout the good ole days, when we was still a breathin'. It's a real downer. Course they don't call it a party; it's a *fellowship*." Roy wrinkled his nose. "I call it crap!" He laughed again.

"I mean no matter how much you talk about it, it ain't never gonna change, right? We're dead and that's all there is to it. Know what I mean?" He tapped Zack's knee.

"Yeah, I guess, Sir."

"Call me Roy. I didn't catch your name?"

"Zack. Roy, Zack Tucker."

"Well, pleased to meet you, Zack." His hand shot out again. "What tragedy befell a youngster like you to bring you to this place?"

"Well, Roy, I, uh—"

"Oh, come on, Zack. It does help to talk about it, I guess. Don't be shy. We all had to go of somethin', right?"

"To tell you the truth, Roy, I'm not dead."

Roy paused and stared at Zack. Then he burst out laughing, coughing and spitting.

"You got to be kiddin' me?" He laughed.

"No, Roy, I'm not."

"Just visiting relatives?" He couldn't stop laughing.

"Actually, I'm here to see that you get your new set of wheels." Zack smiled.

Roy stifled the laughter for a moment. "Really?"

"Really." Zack repeated.

"Well, God bless ya, son!" He stuck out his hand again and pumped Zack's arm.

"I hope He does, Roy."

94

Zack stood up, opened Roy's red wooden door, and stepped inside.

He noticed that Roy and Anne Pink's layout differed slightly from Rick and Marta Rosedale's, like some dead realtor had made them an *extra special* deal. The Pink's house had a small entryway leading into a living room, giving way to a dining area. In the entry sat a chair, with a cloak draped over the back, and a small table with another red pot on it.

People milled about the house, some sort of drinks in their hands and a variety of food on plates. People nodded at him as they walked past.

Zack pushed the cloak aside and sat down, peering through the archway and past the people in the living room. Christine sat on a chair, in a dining room, facing him, excitedly talking to someone.

Zack fixated on her lips. Her pink mouth opened and closed when she laughed and her dimples moved in and out with each word. Her eyes twinkled, so full of life, and death. He followed her forehead and traced her shoulder length hair with his eyes. Zack watched her muscular arms while she flung her hands in conversation.

Their eyes met. She paused and then waved at him, a young, vivacious wave. She motioned for him to come in. Zack returned her wave, but sat still. Christine jumped up, hurried through the crowd and into the entry.

"Hey, you don't have to sit out here. All the fun's going on in there." She motioned with her head.

Zack looked into her face and she tilted her head.

"Zack, isn't it?" she asked.

"Yes. Christine?" he asked.

"Yes." She smiled. "I'm impressed, you remembered."

"Christine Tucker?" Zack asked.

She paused. Her smile faded and then slowly reappeared.

"Yes. How did you know?"

Zack's eyes welled with tears.

She squatted down in front of him and reached up to his cheek.

"What's the matter, Zack?"

"Were you once married to a man named Jeff? On the surface, I mean?"

Her mouth fell open and she covered it with her hand. She closed her eyes and when she opened them again, huge tears rolled down her cheeks.

"Yes, I was."

Zack retraced all the steps in a smattering of time: The zoo. Running through their little house calling for his mom. A pot of uncooked carrots. The agony of making up for the lack of a mother's love with a knife and fork. Grade school drawings on the fridge, without maternal eyes to view them. One birthday melted into another like the wax running down the candles. No female hugs or good night kisses. Junior High, being shoved around and made fun of. Milton. High School. The conclusion that she was never coming back. Abuse. Milton. The bushes. Mick's appearance. Milton. The movies. Jamie. Her smile. Her kiss. Her love. The job. Gideon. The Gates of Hell. John. His new friends at Gideon. Nate. The mission. Marching through the gates with all of Gideon applauding. The City of the Dead. And finally, Hahdace. Revelation sewed it all up in a neat package.

"I'm Zack... mom." He paused. "I've come for you."

95

"How about this delicacy?" Ophis snorted and nudged Rechlifer. He pulled off a piece of Charis brain and popped it in his mouth.

"Haven't you had enough of that?" Rechlifer stood beside Ophis and jittered like a frightened little dog.

"I'll tell you when I've had enough!" The Daemon snapped. "You don't tell me! I tell you! And address me as, 'sir.'" Ophis growled. "Or maybe even, 'sire.'"

"Why?" Rechlifer tried to get a piece of brain and Ophis slapped his hand.

"Because I outrank you, that's why!"

"Only because you stole it." Rechlifer snorted.

Ophis's eyes widened.

"Oh, yes, everyone knows you killed Magnon and finished him for lunch." Rechlifer darted back and forth. "And then they stuck you here!" Rechlifer cackled.

"This is an honor." Ophis said.

"It *was* an honor until you found out it was the garbage dump that you were guarding." Rechlifer shook with laughter, bobbing up and down.

"Well, I'll tell you—" Ophis stopped chewing and looked up the road. He saw a Charis limping toward them.

"Wonder where the rest of his little band is?" Rechlifer flitted back and forth.

"Must be a stray." Ophis rocked back and forth and finally hoisted himself off the bench.

"Well, any stray is fair game then," Rechlifer growled. "I'll fetch this meal."

Rechlifer trotted toward the Charis, as it stumbled and fell onto one knee.

"Well, little fellow, have you lost your way?" Rechlifer snorted. "You're just in time for our supper."

Calver's broad slash took Rechlifer's sword arm off and it twitched into the dirt.

"Really?" Calver asked. Rechlifer screamed.

"Do ya'll have a turkey on?" Cal stood erect. "Well then, let me carve!"

Another stroke and the other arm joined the first in the dirt. Rechlifer gave a guttural shriek and fell to his knees.

Ophis grabbed for his spear, lost his balance and toppled back onto the bench and into the dirt. He shrieked, rocked back and forth, and attempted to right himself like a beetle that could not get its legs under it. The clamor awakened several gorged Daemons and Rawfaw, sleeping off an earlier kill nearby.

Calver threw off the Charis covering.

"Yee Haw!" he shouted, jumping up and down until the Daemons got a good look, then he sprinted in the opposite direction.

The Daemons leapt up, grabbed the ripples of Ophis's fat and pulled him to his feet. They pursued Calver, tripping and falling over one another, as Ophis jiggled out of camp behind them.

The Daemons rounded the corner and stopped. Ophis ran into one and nearly fell into the dirt. They poked through the garbage and sniffed the air. The arrows pierced all of the Daemon's heads simultaneously and they toppled like dominoes. Ophis quivered and jiggled when Calver stepped toward him. Ophis shuddered again and looked down. He had wet himself.

"Sorry, no supper tonight!" Calver sliced Ophis's head off the rotund body.

—

The Rawfaw at the south gate broke ranks and scattered in confusion. They tripped over makeshift tables and chairs and fled deeper into the garbage dump. A volley of arrows pierced the rest of the Daemons left at the gate. Calver, and his troop, waded into the confusion, severing heads and limbs in all directions.

—

Mick and his concealed strike force, of five hundred, lay on the rise that overlooked the east edge of Tartaroo.

"Dexter, when Calver's forces draw their attention, we will attack," Mick said.

Dexter nodded.

"Here we go!" Mick watched the eastern encampments run south like a swarm of ants.

"Give Cal a little more time and then we will move." Mick touched his throat mic. "Everyone stay alert." Throughout the company people nodded.

"Dex, send one of your men to alert the rest of our company, they are out of my radio range."

"Right, Boss." Dexter crawled away.

Moments later, Mick stood on the precipice overlooking Tartaroo's eastern gate.

"By Pneuma's wrath!" Mick shouted and thrust his sword into the air.

"Victory!" came the reply, and the forces of Gideon threw off their camouflage of roots and dirt and poured down the ridge in a dead run.

Dexter readied his team, which was armed with a nitro-titanium alloy explosive.

"Fire in the hole!" Dexter shouted and the massive marble gates of Tartaroo blew off their hinges and flattened several Daemons, popping them like grapes.

The Gideon storm poured into Tartaroo.

The overwhelmed Rawfaw lifted their swords, but minutes later, severed heads and body parts were the only evidence they had ever existed. Mick and his forces marched around the huge

stone blocks of an aqueduct that supplied water to Tartaroo and
came face to face with a company of Troglodyte warriors.

96

Echthros leaned forward.

"They've broken through?" He spat out a piece of flesh he had
been gnawing on.

"Light Forces, sir. They took us completely by surprise!"
The Daemon messenger was livid. "We received word that they
attacked the south gate and when we went to help defend it, they
stormed the east. They've invaded us!"

"And so quickly." Echthros looked at Abaddon. "Where is
James and why didn't he—"

She shrugged. "I told you."

"What will we do?" The Daemon asked.

Abaddon walked closer to Echthros. "Did you know?"

"I assumed," Echthros said, "but I didn't expect them quite
this soon." He turned to the Daemon. "How many?"

"Thousands." The Daemon dropped to the floor and bowed his
head. "We didn't know how or where they came from, I'm
sorry."

"Oh, we know the *where*," Echthros said. "The *how* might
take some figuring, but nevertheless." He slumped back in his
seat.

"Do you think they're after the hostages?" Abaddon asked.

"Of course, they are," Echthros said, "but they are collateral
damage. Just in case though, we must be prepared."

He turned back to the Daemon. "Send for my Celestine
Guards. We will intercept them when they arrive here. Immolo
are captivitas artis f." He spoke evenly and deliberately. "Death

to the captives."

He reached out and lifted the Daemon until he was face to face with him. "Kill them all."

97

Christine looked at Zack and burst into tears.

"Oh, Zack." She buried her face in his shirt and convulsed with sobs.

Zack slid to the floor and rocked back and forth in his mother's arms. He held her and felt the texture of her hands on his skin. He snuggled close to her breasts and began to sob.

He remembered kicking his legs on a makeshift porch swing as a child, running in the yard, Christine chasing him and laughing, hide-and-go-seek and peek-a-boo and the aroma of cookies baking. He thought of a single trip to the zoo that had opened a void that could not be filled.

Until now.

All of the years of turmoil and teasing, released a gush of emotion that washed down his face, puddling on the floor of an adobe hut, somewhere in the Netherworld. Zack sobbed uncontrollably, as one who had been ripped from his life giver.

"I'm home," Zack whispered.

"Welcome home," Christine replied.

Zack took a few long, deep breaths until he could pull back from her chest. He put his hands on both of her shoulders and gazed into his mother's beautiful, tear stained face.

"Oh, mom." he said.

"Zack," she whispered.

Zack heard his name spoken by the one who brought him into the world and he pulled her close again.

"Don't cry any more, honey. Mommy's here."

"I can't believe it, Mom." Zack's voice trembled.

"I can't believe *you* are here," Christine said. "I don't know how?"

Nate opened the door, with Roy Pink on his heels. "Zack,

we've broken through. We've got to go."

Zack sat up and looked at Nate and then back at Christine.

"Mom, I have to ask," Zack said. "There's so much I need to know—"

"Zack," Nate said.

"But, Nate," Zack's tears flowed again, "this is my mom. Can't I just—."

"It's alright, Zack." Nate placed both hands on Zack's shoulders and energy exploded through him. His emotions stabilized, strength returned and his head cleared.

Zack shivered as if he had come in out of the cold. "Wow!" He said. "What was that?"

"Pneuma." Nate smiled. "Everything's going to be fine; we didn't come *this* far for you to lose her again."

Zack stood and helped Christine up.

"Mom," he kissed her on the cheek, "I've got to help get you all out of here." He wiped the tears off her face. "I'll be back. I promise—"

"I believe you, Son." She hugged him. "I'll be here." She paused. "I love you."

Zack brushed her cheek. "I love you too, Mom."

"Roy," Nate said, "gather everyone that's here and be ready."

"Roger that," Roy said.

Zack followed Nate out the door. "Nate, that's my mom."

"Yes, she is." Nate grinned.

"How did you know?"

"Later. Come on."

They ran back toward the gates of Hahdace and into a mass of confusion. Charis and Daemons were scattered in all directions. Ralph Maxwell ran out of his house.

"Ralph!" Nate yelled. "You've got to find everyone, all the Charis. Get everyone ready to move. Don't leave anyone behind!"

"I'm on it." Ralph ran off into the commotion.

98

The Daemons and Rawfaw stampeded into Hahdace, with Mel's forces on their heels. It was a textbook execution of the Pincer movement, which folded the Daemon hoard back on itself and catapulted them into confusion.

A ram's horn sounded.

"That must be Ralph!" Nate yelled.

Zack shrugged and a Daemon lunged at him.

Zack whirled, caught the upper torso and sliced into the fleshy part of the Daemon's stomach. The Daemon ripped a gash in Zack's forearm. Zack thrust the Baraq into its eye and left it flopping like a fish on a riverbank.

"Help!" A Daemon straddled John with both hands around his neck.

Dessa ran past and hacked the Daemon in half and John hefted the bottom half off and onto the ground.

"Thanks!" he managed, before Dessa rounded a corner.

"You owe me!" Her words faded.

"Hey, hey, what's this!" John yelled at the Daemon's top half, twitching and snapping at him. John kicked it and it latched onto his leg, gnawing at his boot.

"Don't even think about it, you pre-Next Gen Klingon!" John yelled and punched the Daemon repeatedly in the face until it thrashed helplessly in the dirt, like a grasshopper without its hopping legs.

John breathlessly retrieved his dropped sword and walked toward the Daemon, dealing it a deathblow. "Take that, you piece of crap!" He pointed the sword at it. "And yo momma, too!"

Zack saw the Charis pouring out of Hahdace with whatever weapons were available. A man bludgeoned a Rawfaw with a chair, causing the eye to pop out of the socket, and when the Rawfaw turned to look at his attacker, the wooden chair legs finished the job.

A trio of Rawfaw surrounded a rotund little man and Zack

thought of the Triune that had tormented him all of his school life.

"Hey!" Zack shouted and threw a body block, toppling two like a seven-ten split. Zack came up swinging his sword and one head flew one direction and another head in the opposite. Terrified, the third turned to run, when a huge club leveled him.

"Hey, did I ever tell you," Roy Pink stepped forward, "I was senior league batting champion, three years in a row!"

Zack smiled and shook his head.

"Help me, Zack!"

Zack spun and met Kurt Clayton's eyes.

Two Rawfaw wrestled him to the ground, but Zack sliced through one's neck collapsing it in a heap. Kurt threw the second Rawfaw over his head and into the dirt. Zack halved its head with one blow, spilling its brains on the ground.

"Kurt!" Zack pulled him up by the hand.

They stood momentarily, looking at each other without a word.

"Thanks, Zack," Kurt yelled over the commotion. "I don't know what to say." He paused. "I'm so sorry. You can't believe—"

"There's no time right now, man!" Zack slapped him on the back. "We'll talk about it, if we ever get out of this. Come on!"

A rope lassoed Zack's feet, pulling him backward, from Kurt, and his Baraq sword flew out of his hand. Zack twisted back and forth, as Daemons pulled him toward them, his body furrowing the dirt. He slid his Mekayraw out of the scabbard on his back and sliced through the rope, sliding in like a base runner at their feet.

With a single swipe, he cut three legs off two of the skinny Daemons, who tumbled to the ground screaming and holding their bloody stumps. Zack hopped up and thrust a Daemon through, burying the sword to the hilt and teetered on rope-cinched legs.

Zack fell on the one-legged Daemon, seized its head and wrenched it back and forth until it popped off in his hands.

"Holy Crap!" Zack cried. "That's gross!"

He let the severed head fall to the ground. The last Daemon, screaming and pawing away from Zack, met Kurt Clayton's club. Its head exploded, staining the dirt.

Zack sliced through his bonds, as a small Rawfaw jumped him. Grabbing it by the crotch and chest in a bench press, he threw it into the Daemon carcasses. It wobbled to its feet momentarily as an arrow from one of Mel's guys pierced its head.

Mel appeared at the entrance to Hahdace.

"Here we are!" he cried. The forces of Gideon had reached the middle of the battle and had successfully accomplished the Pincer Movement.

"Glad to see you made it!" Zack yelled.

"Wouldn't have missed it!" Mel smiled, wielding his sword above his shiny bald head.

Like a crystal clear note above the carnage, Zack heard a child's voice. Ricki ran past, screaming as a Daemon closed in on her. Zack launched the Mekayraw end over end, and it lodged in the Daemon's back. The Daemon fell to its knees, twisting and thrashing, trying to free itself from the blade.

Zack scooped Ricki up as the Daemon's spear glanced off Zack's vest.

"Zack!" John shoveled the Baraq to him as he ran past.

With the little girl tucked under his left arm, he caught the Baraq in his right and without breaking stride, took the head off the Daemon.

Zack lowered the little girl behind a stone wall.

"Stay here until I come back for you, okay?"

"Okay." She smiled through her tears.

"Don't worry, I'll be back." Zack patted her head.

Zack stood up and felt the rush of air as the spear barely missed him.

Above the battle's roar, Zack heard his mother scream.

99

Christine ran across the dirt street chased by three Rawfaw until one knocked her to the ground. A stick-wielding Ralph Maxwell tried to distract them.

"Help us!" he yelled.

Zack grabbed his Mekayraw, from the back of the dead Daemon, and with a primeval yell, he brandished two swords like a windmill, sending limbs and heads flying in all directions.

Covered in the black blood, he fell on his knees next to Christine.

"Mom, are you alright?" he yelled.

"Yes, I'm fine, Zack." She brushed her hair back from her face. "Wow! That was impressive!"

"I've lost you once, Mom." Zack gulped air. "Never again!" He looked at Ralph.

"Take her to cover."

"I will. Come on, Christine!" Ralph pulled her to her feet.

—

"Come to me, fellas." Nate backed up, smiling at the two Daemons on each side of him.

They circled him like hyenas and lunged. Nate jumped back. The Daemons missed him and collided face first with each other. Nate laughed and brought his knee into the Daemon's chin, dazing it and then kicked the other, knocking it backward. With two deathblows from his sword, he finished them both.

Dessa ran forward swinging her blade. She caught the other Daemon in the forehead, lopping off the top of its scalp.

"Thanks!" Nate said. "Bet nothing like that ever entered his mind before!"

"How long have you been waiting to use that?" Dessa yelled as they ran.

"A while!" Nate smiled.

—

A chorus of howls erupted from the Daemons, and Legions responded, passing it on. In one synchronized group, they all retreated toward Tartaroo. The Rawfaw limped along after them.

"Let's get 'em!" John shouted, pumped with adrenaline.

He led the Charis out the gate, brandishing whatever they could find to fight with.

A fine dust began to settle over Hahdace as the roar of the battle faded toward Tartaroo. Inside Hahdace, the battle-weary soldiers surveyed the weapons and carcasses littering the ground.

Nate sat down on a stone wall. "Any casualties on our side?"

"Not to my knowledge." Zack plopped down beside him with Dessa on his left.

The rest of the troop gathered around them, some on rock walls, some on the ground, some on carcasses.

"Mel," Nate said, "you and your guys police up the area and take your Charis to a safe position. I suspect that Echthros isn't going to take this lying down. He will send reinforcements. I'll take my band, and a group of Charis, with me."

Nate sheathed his sword and stretched, then turned to the group. "We can't let them reach the surface. Do you understand?"

Everyone nodded.

He turned to Zack. "Zack, I'm promoting you. You are my lieutenant."

"Nate. I don't know."

He turned back to the others. "In my absence, he's in charge. Follow Zack's orders."

Everyone nodded.

Mel dug in his pack and produced the salve, Ghil-Awd, and handed it out to the wounded, while Christine and Ricki joined the others.

Zack kissed Christine on the cheek. "We've got a lot to talk about."

"Yes, we do." Christine smiled.

"Mel?" Zack motioned for him. "Mom, Mel is going to take you to a safe place and I'll join you in a little while."

"Be careful, Zack," Christine said.

"We will."

Nate turned to Ralph. "Do you think you and your boys are up for this task?"

"Oh, we're ready. They've got some payback coming for all they've done to us. Besides, they can't kill us twice, right?" Ralph laughed and then contemplated, "Can they?"

100

"Hey, Zack, listen," Kurt said as they marched toward Tartaroo, "I, uh, didn't know. About life. About any of this." Kurt waved his arm.

"It's okay," Zack said.

"No, it's not. I just…" Kurt looked down and shook his head. "No excuses, I was wrong—"

"Kurt—"

"No, really, I was a crap head to you, man—"

"It's okay now," Zack said.

"It was just that I had so much junk going on in my brain." Kurt glanced at a body on the path. "And that chick kept showing up."

"What chick?" Zack asked.

"That Angie chick. She came to the hospital every day. She was sweet to be sure, but there was something that wasn't right. Something behind those gorgeous eyes."

"One of the girls from school?"

"No," Kurt said. "At least, I don't think she was from school." They stepped around a pile of Daemons, all missing heads.

"I never asked her," Kurt continued. "I didn't mind her being there, she was good lookin', but it was one of those things where you think you should know somebody, but you don't want to ask?"

"Yeah." Zack nodded.

"It was embarrassing. She knew so much about me; I didn't know her even after she told me her name, so I just sort of played along." Kurt shrugged.

"I don't think I know her either," Zack said.

"'Till the hospital, right?" Kurt said.

"What do you mean?" Zack asked.

"She was there when, I," he hesitated, "went out the window."

"What?" Zack's eyes widened.

"She was in the room," Kurt said. "You saw her, right?"

"No, I didn't see anybody." Zack shook his head.

"You had to," Kurt panted.

"Sorry, I didn't."

"She was standing in the corner." Kurt pointed as if they were still in the room. "She kept reciting words, like memorized lines in a freakin play! It was crazy."

"Which words?" Zack asked.

"It was a chant. 'Immolo are captivitas atris f, immolo are captivitas atris f'. It's still burned into my brain." Kurt rubbed his eyes with the heels of his hands.

"Those were the words that you said to *me* that night." Zack grabbed his arm and they stopped walking.

"Yeah." Kurt paused remembering the night. "I was just saying them right along with her, like she possessed me or something." He stared past Zack and then mumbled. "I figured you heard her too."

They started walking again.

"No. When I was in your room, there wasn't anyone else." Zack said. "I made sure of that." He paused. "I was checking for Milton."

"I remember her in the corner." Kurt was still looking far ahead of them. "Smiling and chanting. She kept on and on." Kurt closed his eyes and then opened them again. "It was starting to drive me crazy. She finally told me that it was time to join Muriel." Kurt hesitated again. "Those were the same words that Muriel said to me in the cemetery." Another pause. "I guess, I thought she was right." Kurt looked at Zack. "So I did. Just like my big sister."

He looked down at his trembling hands. "I committed suicide."

Kurt's knees buckled and he stumbled for a moment. Zack reached out to steady him.

"Hey, Nate?" Zack called. "Can we rest for a minute?"

"Yeah, it's probably a good idea." Nate stopped. "We can't sit for very long though. Mick needs us." Nate surveyed the area around them. "Let's take a breather everyone."

Zack and Kurt plopped down on a large rock.

"I was so messed up, man." Kurt stared at the dirt. "It was like I was on drugs or something. At the time, it seemed like a logical thing to do. I remember finally making up my mind." He closed his eyes again. "I just wanted her to stop chanting. It was like this thing took a hold of me and started choking me." He opened his eyes and looked at Zack. "That's when I went into the convulsions."

"Yeah, man," Zack's eyes grew larger, "that was freaky!"

"But as soon as you left the room, they stopped. I remember getting up, out of bed, and pulling the IV tubes out of my arm and the little beads of blood; they were *so* red. I took that metal chair from the corner. I still remember every stain on that stupid chair."

Zack listened intently.

"I picked it up." Kurt clasped his hands like the chair was clutched in them. "It was heavy in my hands and I felt so weak. Then I hit the window with it." He swung his arms. "The window didn't budge at first and I thought maybe it was safety glass or something. Angie said, 'Try it again, my love.' She always called me that. It was weird, don't know why. So I did, and the window cracked. Then she said, 'One more time for me?' With that swing the window broke and the chair flew out."

Zack looked at the ground, imagining what Kurt must have seen. He was listening to someone who had actually succeeded in killing himself.

"I put my foot on another chair and grabbed onto the window. It cut my hand." Kurt looked at the scars that were mere bloodless furrows now. "I remember looking at the blood. She walked over by the window next to me, took my hand, and kissed it. I saw this weird look on her face. She had my blood all over her mouth." Kurt waved his hand around his face. "It was this look of satisfaction. 'Go ahead,' Angie said. 'Muriel is waiting and you will finally be at peace.' I took another step onto the sill and felt the cold of the marble on my feet. I was perched like some bird and hanging on to the broken glass with both hands. I felt the wind on my face and saw the lights of the city."

Kurt teared up as he stared at Zack.

"And then I thought of my mom. I saw her face, grieving for me, and I didn't want to do it. I started to take a step back and I felt Angie's hand on me and it was strong, like a guy's. I tried to struggle, it was that *will* to live, I guess, but I lost my balance and went out the window. It happened so fast."

Kurt breathed heavily and bowed his head.

"It was that Angie girl. I changed my mind but," he paused, "she pushed me."

Zack watched his eyes.

"I remember, for an instant, on the way down, seeing the parking lot rush toward me. All I could say was, 'I'm sorry, I'm sorry; please forgive me?' I was out of control and I felt the impact and the pain for a split second and then blackness." He closed his eyes for a long moment and then looked back at Zack. "Until I ended up wandering toward Hahdace."

"Where is she now?" Zack asked.

"Angie?" Kurt shrugged. "Who knows?"

"No, I mean Muriel." Zack said.

"I don't know *that* either. I looked for her in Hahdace. That's why I came with you. I've got to find her if she's here." Kurt scuffed the dirt with his foot. "This is my punishment."

"I don't know about that, Kurt." Zack reached out and put a hand on his shoulder. "But I think you're doing the right thing now."

"Zack, for whatever it's worth. I'm so sorry for the crap I put you through up there." He pointed up. "No excuses, no blaming anyone else this time. It was wrong. *I* was wrong." His eyes welled with tears. "Can you forgive me?"

101

"Time to go, guys," Nate said.

"Everything's cool with us." Zack stood. "Different time, different place. I don't understand it all, but…" He offered his hand to Kurt and then pulled him into an embrace.

"Don't sweat it." Zack released him and clapped Kurt on the shoulder.

"I won't." Kurt wiped away tears. "Tears, yeah. Sweat, no. Not anymore."

Zack smiled at Kurt, seeing him as a person given a second chance at redemption. He had saved Kurt in Hahdace and Kurt, in turn, rescued him. The bond of combat had been forged.

—

Hinnom burned with flames that licked the sky, and the stench of the refuse made Zack gag. Carcasses lay rotting and Daemon and Rawfaw still pawed the landscape, darting in and out of mountains of rubbish. Nate and his forces made short work of those who wouldn't retreat.

The roar of battle magnified the carnage in Tartaroo. Framed by glistening streams of blood, it stood against the blackened sky. Its only illumination being the flames.

"Zack, find John, and take Dessa. Reinforce Mick's flank." Nate said, quickly sizing up the situation. "We have to push through to Echthros's palace!"

They all ran into chaos.

Burning balls exploded around them, hurled from medieval

catapults manned by the Daemons.

"Kurt! We have to take that thing out!" Zack shouted, pointing toward the catapult. "Otherwise they'll keep raining down on us!"

"Okay!" Kurt said. "Come on!" Kurt shouted to a couple of other Charis.

They moved toward the catapult, dodging arrows in the crossfire. A comet tail soared overhead, exploding and showering sparks, like a million fireflies, above them.

Kurt and the others secured the catapult and turned it on the Daemon forces.

Like a sadistic windmill, with razor blades instead of arms, Zack's Baraq sword made short work of whatever Daemon and Rawfaw head it met.

Zack saw John fall to one knee, fending off the attacks of several Daemons. Zack scooped up a medieval mace, wielding it like a helicopter blade and ran toward John. The two Daemons met the whirlwind, one in the face and the other in the back of its skull.

Another ball of fire exploded overhead. On its heels came another, bouncing and rolling, like a mammoth napalm-dipped bowling ball. Zack and Dessa dove behind the same hedgerow, by the steps of the palace. The orb cut a swath through the hedge, setting it on fire.

"Let's go!" Zack scrambled to his feet. In the confusion, he ran into John, just coming to take cover, and sent him sprawling into another hedge. John's arms and legs flailed and he disappeared behind the foliage.

"John!" Dessa cried.

102

Zack and Dessa clawed through the bushes. Zack leaned in too far, lost his balance, and tumbled down a flight of stone steps, landing on top of John, as he lay at the bottom.

"What did you do?" Zack asked.

"Me? You're the one who zigged when you should have zagged!"

Zack stood and pulled John up by the armpits.

"'What a *wonderful* smell you've discovered.'" Dessa came down the crude steps, holding her nose and quoting Han Solo.

"Star Wars, huh?" John asked.

"Better than Trekkie," Dessa said.

"Oh, Captain Kirk could kick Luke Skywalker's butt!"

"Yeah, but not Han Solo's," Dessa said.

"True." John looked at Zack. "Well, now what, Chief?"

John peered into a black tunnel, leading away from them. Another fireball exploded outside the entrance, flashing light down the stairwell.

"I guess we *could* go back up." Zack looked up at the light.

"I doubt it." Dessa said. "That fireball caught the leaves and if we go back up, we'll get roasted."

Zack bent to look. "I guess we *could* follow the tunnel. Of course, the last time I did that, I got us into this mess."

"What other choice do we have?" Dessa shrugged.

"None," Zack said.

They entered the darkness, once again, and their medallions began to glow.

"Even with the medallions, this is going to be tough," John whispered.

"Feel around for some torches," Zack said, running his hands down the wet, rough stone.

Moist puddles dotted the sewage-filled tunnel, sloshing over their boots. After about seventy-five paces, they stopped, hitting a wall at a "T" intersection.

"Well, well, what have we here?" Zack looked both ways. "What's your gut tell you, John?"

John scanned down the tunnels.

"I vote for the light." John pointed down the dark passageway.

The light was a reflection, off a doorway, midway down the tunnel.

"What do you think?" Dessa whispered, as they crept closer.

"From the smell, I'd say Troglodytes." Zack had become a

master sniffer.

"Me too." John paused. "Have you ever passed a pig truck on the highway?"

"What?" Zack looked at him

"A pig truck," John whispered. "Ever had those things pee out the side and it hits your car? Man, you can't even wash that stuff off with a power-washer, why I—"

"John?" Zack snapped him back.

"Sorry." John grinned. "The smell just reminded me of that. Do you want me to…"

"Nah, I'll do it." Zack dropped onto the soggy floor, trying not to think of what he was kneeling in, and peered around the corner. A wooden table with hefty chairs sat in the middle of the room. He could see the legs of a couple of beds and several indistinguishable piles against the far wall; but, there were no legs or feet moving anywhere in sight.

Zack shrank back and slowly stood, peeking around the corner. He stepped in and surveyed the room. Dried blood covered one bed and the heaps in the corner were obviously leftovers.

"I don't want to know what that is," Zack whispered, pointing to the pile.

"Looks like they ate a while ago." John approached the pile and poked it with his sword. He dislodged a few large flies and they buzzed his head. John swatted at them like a little girl.

"Yeah," Zack said. "At least we can use their torches though."

He reached toward the torch and one of the mounds on the floor sprang to life.

103

"I knew it!" John jumped backward.

Zack caught his heel on the table leg and stumbled. The Troglodyte forced him to the ground, its hands around his neck. Zack felt himself begin to pass out as the Troglodyte squeezed. Spots sparkled in his eyes. He slid his hand down to his boot and extracted the knife. In a last ditch effort, before unconsciousness set in, he shoved it into the beast's armpit. It howled and released him. The distraction gave John the opportunity to thrust his sword through its belly, puncturing the sack. Zack and John both heaved, as Dessa backed toward the door.

"Wow! Talk about cuttin' the cheese!" Dessa fanned her nose. "That's about the grossest thing I've ever smelled!"

The Troglodyte laid wheezing and coughing for a few seconds. Blood poured from its mouth. Finally it flopped over, dead.

"Couldn't you have gotten its head?" Dessa pinched her nose.

"Be thankful I got that much," John said. "You know my aim."

"Better get the other torches," Zack gasped. He pointed with one hand as he massaged his neck with the other.

Every step, covering the next hundred yards down the tunnel, was tedious until they stopped at the base of heavy stone steps, spiraling up like the turret of a castle.

"Well, whatever we're after is probably up there." Zack gazed up into the darkness, illuminated only by sporadic torches.

Slowly they climbed, leaving the stench below, until they reached the top and a closed trap door.

"This'll be interesting," Zack whispered as he grabbed a thick, iron ring and lifted.

—

Mick's forces moved up the sprawling steps of the Palace of Tartaroo under its six dark pillars, the size of bridge supports. A blood red portico jutted out from the black marble walls.

"What do you think?" Nate approached Mick.

Mick surveyed the battle.

"The Rawfaw, for all practical purposes, are non-existent, and we are still dealing with the Daemons. It's the Celestine Guard that concerns me." Mick yelled over the carnage.

"I brought reinforcements." Nate stepped close to his ear.

"Good." Mick clapped him on the shoulder. "The throne room is next. The Celestine Guards are backed by the Troglodytes. We're going to have our hands full." Mick scanned the battle again and then turned back to Nate. "How's John doing?"

"I don't know, I haven't seen him." Nate shrugged. "Zack and Dessa are gone too." He keyed his mic. "Zack?"

No response.

"Zack, do you read?"

"We've got to work on the range of these things," Nate said.

"Well," Mick said, "they're resilient kids."

Nate turned to clash with a Rawfaw and splattered its blood against the black marble.

"It's time, little brother," Mick yelled. "Sound the advance."

Nate reached into his backpack and produced his silver trumpet.

104

The blast from the silver trumpet retarded the battle momentarily, but then the roar swelled like a tidal wave and Gideon advanced.

Mick raised his sword.

He and Nate ascended the last steps of the Palace of Echthros, with their forces close behind, like the Mongol Hoards of Genghis Kahn.

Another explosion sent the gates careening off its hinges. Mick, Nate, and the forces entered the Palace courtyard. Troglodyte warriors, flanked by Daemon and Rawfaw, emptied out of every alcove and doorway like water through a sieve. Behind them, shoulder to shoulder, stood the Celestine Guard, clad in black flowing robes with blood red helmets obscuring their faces.

Nate unsheathed his two Baraq swords and carved through the Troglodytes like a lethal ceiling fan. The Daemons, led by Legions, bred especially to guard Echthros, attacked with a vengeance. The echo of metal upon metal filled the courtyard, as

Mick's forces minced through the company sworn to protect and defend the House of Haylel. Finally, the last Daemon head rolled across the floor, against heaps of dismembered bodies.

The captain of the Celestine Guard stepped forward and looked at the slaughter.

"I am Nehfesh, ruler of Echthros's Legion; you are not allowed to enter!" he cried.

Mick stepped toward him, with his bloody body armor gleaming in the torchlight.

"I know who you are, Nehfesh." Mick's eyes tightened. "You don't impress me. We come to you in the Name of Lord Pantokrator, the Almighty." He stared into the blackness of Nehfesh's helmet. "This day your rule is finished here."

Mick swung his sword against Nehfesh, and the Celestine Guard engaged the Army of Light.

105

Zack's movie memories gave him little doubt that something, or someone, covered the trap door and the encounter would not be pleasant. He pushed and the door lifted slowly, allowing light to stream in through the crack. Something hung in front of his face, blocking his view. His heart skipped and muscles strained, as he held the trap door with one hand and his Baraq with the other.

Zack looked closer. He quivered. It quivered. He pushed. It jiggled.

"It's rug fringe." Zack relaxed.

John exhaled.

Zack let the heavy door close.

"It's some kind of room," Zack whispered. "Can you move up

here and help me hold the door open so I can see?"

"Yeah."

John moved up a few stairs and they both lifted.

"Man, this is heavy," John said.

Zack peeked through the crack and scanned the room.

"Okay. You guys ready?" Zack looked back at them.

John nodded and Dessa tightened her grip on her sword.

Zack and John lifted the door. Zack walked cautiously up the steps. He looked around the small room as his shoulders cleared the opening, then his waist. He turned quickly, ready for anything behind the trap door that might be poised to pounce, but nothing moved.

He eased the door back on itself and the rug folded underneath it. Zack cleared the last step and John and Dessa followed him into the room.

"What is this?" John picked up the name plate off the desk: *Pastor Daniel J. Blevins*

"Beats me." Zack snatched a telephone receiver.

"They actually have phone service down here?" Dessa asked.

Zack listened. "Guess not. Dead. It's like it's fake."

Zack ran his hand along the ornately carved oak desk and then twirled a caddy full of pens and pencils. He touched the soft leather of the high-backed desk chair.

Dessa walked to the highly polished office door and cracked it slightly, peering out.

"I hear someone talking," she said.

Zack walked to the mantle, over a roaring fire and picked up a silver framed picture, from a bookshelf, behind the desk. It showed a flamboyant man in suit and tie, drenched in sweat, as he yelled into a microphone, apparently at a church service. Behind the picture was another framed 8 X 10 of a provocative woman, with crossed legs and a short skirt, harboring a seductive smile.

"What the—"

Across her face in black marker was an autograph, "Thanks for all the memories."

Zack stared at the picture. He remembered the waitress in the restaurant and the girl in Junior High.

"Angie?" Zack mumbled.

"You folks made excellent progress."

The male voice made Zack whirl. He dropped the frame and it sprayed his boots with shards of glass.

"Oh," Zack clutched his chest. "Mr. Recent. How did you—"

"Jim. Remember?"

106

"I can hear them." The creature, resembling a Komodo dragon, with the eyes and mouth of a man, slithered away from the throne room doors and slid next to Echthros' feet. "They have breached the outer court."

"Of course, they have, you sniveling coward." Echthros planted his boot into its side and sent it sprawling across the marble floor.

Celestine guards, Daemons, and Rawfaw lined the throne room, listening to the battle outside the doors.

"What will we do, my lover?" Abaddon asked.

"I think we'll handle them like always." Echthros drummed his fingers on the arm of the chair. "We've been through this before and we're still here." He slumped back into his chair, picking lint off the lapels of his suit.

"But they've never made it this far before." The creature rolled over and got up.

Echthros slid a dagger out from underneath the chair and hurled it at the creature, impaling it to a pillar.

"They've done it because we let them," Echthros said.

The roar outside ceased and the throne room held its collective breath. A single fist pounded on the door.

Echthros rose, looked at Abaddon and back at the door. He motioned for a Celestine guard to unlock the sanctuary door.

Glimmering black swords slid silently out of their sheaths. The guard unlatched the locks and gigantic bolts. The huge doors swung open.

Nehfesh entered the room.

"My liege." he said and collapsed. His head fell off his shoulders and his torso convulsed on the floor.

"Guess your best wasn't good enough." Mick stepped over the threshold and into the silent room. Nate flanked him along with Kurt and a battalion of warriors.

Nate keyed his throat mic. "Zack, are you in position?"

Zack, Dessa and John bolted from behind the heavy drapes off the platform to surround the throne. James Recent followed nonchalantly.

"We're here, Nate," Zack said, "and finally back in range."

"Well, well," Echthros rose and bowed, "I've been expecting you. Come on in. Welcome to *my* little corner of the world. We, Band of Brothers, are united once more."

"Band of Brothers?" Zack let it slip from his lips unintentionally.

Echthros glanced at Zack.

"Yes?" Echthros turned back to Mick. "You didn't mention me?"

"Wasn't important." Mick's eyes pierced Echthros.

"No?" Echthros spread his arms wide. "Did everyone hear that? I'm not important enough to mention. The middle child is always ignored." Echthros pouted. "You ask them to give their lives in a conflict that is un-winnable and it's '*not* important'?" Echthros flopped back in his chair.

"*They* are important to me." Mick motioned behind him and then pointed to Echthros. "*You* are not."

"Oh, thanks a lot, big brother." Echthros swiveled again to look at Zack. "I'm the black sheep; everyone's got one. The Demon Seed." Echthros's throaty laugh gurgled. "I was banished a long time ago but funny, it just seems like yesterday. Hah! How ironic." He paused. "It was all because I was just trying to be like *Dear Ole Dad*."

He glanced at Zack, then to Mick, and back at Zack again.

"And so periodically I have to have a," he paused, "spanking. That *is* what this is, right?"

"More like a diaper change." Nate smiled.

"Shut up, Nate," Echthros said, then looked back at Mick and stood. "Dad sends my next of kin to keep me in line. Miykael and Nathaniel Gabriyel Abbeer. Mick and Nate. Mr. and Mrs. Abbeer, for you on the payroll."

Nate's eyes narrowed.

"Or Michael and Gabriel if you must." Echthros waved a hand in dismissal. "But I prefer to not call them *anything*." He wrinkled his nose. "I certainly *hope* they're paying you well for this." He looked at John. "Overtime?"

"They are, actually." John nodded. "And—"

"Good," Echthros said. "You won't be able to spend it when you're dead, but," he shrugged, "it's the thought that counts."

"You are *always* whining." Mick stepped closer to the throne. "Yes, we were sent to clean up your mess, like always.

Echthros turned toward Zack. "The heir apparent?" He hesitated. "Hello, Zack."

It startled Zack so much to hear his name coming from incarnate evil, that the other title didn't register.

"Yes, Zack, I know you. Do you know me?" Echthros asked.

"You're…" Zack's words trailed off.

Echthros smiled. "I'll help you assimilate. I am Echthros the Hateful, of the House of Haylel. One and the same. I was once called Morning Star. Lucifer, if you will." He stood, bowed, and then slumped back in the tufted chair.

"Or, you could call him Luci." Nate smiled.

Echthros shot him a hateful glance. "Watch it, little brother."

"I *am* watching it." Nate smirked.

"Nothing changes does it, *Nate*?" Echthros exaggerated his name. "You're still the biggest pain in the ass." Echthros stopped and straightened his suit and adjusted his tie.

"Bring it on." Nate opened his arms.

Echthros waved again. "Go to hell, Nate!"

Nate glanced around as if to say, *we're already here* and then shrugged at Zack.

"You could've ruled and reigned." Nate stepped closer.

"I rule and reign now." Echthros said.

"On a short chain," Mick said calmly.

Echthros swept his hand. "My people would say different."

"Probably," Mick said.

"Definitely," Echthros responded. "The surface or here, makes no difference and what about Hahdace?"

"What about it?" Mick said.

"Sooner or later they'll see you're playing them for fools, they are only here to feed us."

Mick said nothing.

"And what about poor Zack?" Echthros asked.

Mick was silent.

Echthros stepped off the platform toward Zack, who backed up.

"Did you tell them?" Echthros asked.

"Tell us what?" John glanced around.

"Someday, John-ole-buddy-ole-pal," Echthros paused, "you'll end up like Kurt." He paused again. "Or worse. Maybe, Milton."

"Milton?" John asked.

Echthros turned his gaze to Zack and smiled. "Or maybe even, Jamie."

"What are you talking about?" Zack glanced around the room. "Jamie!"

James Recent stepped forward and put his hand on Zack's shoulder causing him to shutter. Zack looked at him then back to Echthros.

"Milton came to me a long time ago, but Jamie? A recent acquisition." Echthros winked. "Snatched her right out of her lovely little bedroom, all comfy on her down pillows."

Zack cursed.

"Where is she!" he shouted and started toward Echthros. James Recent grabbed Zack's arm. "Wait, my friend. Wait and see how this plays out."

"In due time." Echthros smiled. "Patience is a virtue and from what I hear, you are quite the little virtuous thing. And so is she."

Zack's eyes welled with tears.

107

Kurt moved slowly beside Zack.

"That's her." he whispered.

"Who?" Zack wiped his eyes.

"Me, honey." Abaddon stepped down off the platform and smiled at Zack. "Hello, Zaacko Paacko."

Zack recalled the silver framed picture, with "Amy" on it, in the office behind the platform. He remembered her in the restaurant, and saw her face, much younger as a junior high student. Zack felt his heart flutter and blood rush from his brain. She was the little girl swinging her legs in the nurse's office. Zack grabbed hold of Kurt's arm to steady himself.

"She's the chick that was in my room the night I went out the window." Kurt whispered. "And..." he paused, "the nurse in the ambulance. That Angie chick."

"She seems to get around," Zack mumbled.

"Oh, Zack knows me, don't you?" Abaddon smiled.

"I... *do* know you." Zack's mind rewound.

"I've been in your life for a long time." Abaddon grinned. "Somebody had to take the place of mommy."

Zack's eyes narrowed, as anger churned in his stomach. "You'd never take her place."

"Don't be so sure, Zacko." Abaddon smiled.

Echthros stood. "Did you let them know what they are up against?"

Mick stared at him.

"Like Milton, I mean? No hope."

Zack glanced around for a sign of Milton.

"Only when you and your whore enter the picture," Mick said.

"That wasn't nice." Echthros stepped toward Zack who tightened his grip on his sword.

"Uh-uh-uh, ole boy. Now, take it easy with your toys and remember what I'm capable of." Echthros walked across the stage to a pedestal with a long, black sword lying on top.

He nodded to a Daemon who reeled in a rope, lifting another curtain.

Milton Drago padded out from behind the curtain.

"Ohh," John said, "Milton."

Behind him, Jamie Watkins lay bound and gagged on a granite altar near the chasm of living darkness. It swirled and heaved smoke laden sulfur, like curtains of black mesh. She still wore the same gray, torn T-shirt and blue jean cutoffs, smeared with filth and grime. Terror filled her eyes.

She looked toward Zack.

"Jamie!" Zack cried and started toward her.

A Daemon swung his club catching Zack in the stomach and knocking him to the ground.

Mick's forces stepped forward, swords drawn. The Daemons and Rawfaw unsheathed their weapons, and for a splinter of time the forces of good and evil held each other at bay.

108

"Slow down there, Little Zackaroo," Echthros said, picking up the sword. "You're dealing with a fate worse than death, here."

Zack looked up as James Recent helped him to his feet.

"Live once, die twice." Echthros smiled and nodded. "But one puncture of the Sawtawn blade and..."

He stepped closer to Jamie

"Just one." Echthros continued, looking back at Zack. "Come on. Play along. One Puncture?"

"Leave her alone," Zack hissed.

"A puncture and twist," Echthros said. "And what's left of the ole heart... Well let's just say, no more Hahdace. No paradise." His voice rose. "No more dwelling with Father. No hope. No more nothing!" He screamed.

Echthros calmed and straightened his double breasted suit.

"Jamie is today's winner." Echthros said. "We spun the wheel, we drew straws, and she lost. So she's going to join us."

"No, she's not," Zack said.

"Milton?" Echthros held his hand toward Zack like a traffic cop.

A hideous grin spread across Milton's face.

"My liege." He growled.

"Milton also has made a milestone in his existence." Echthros walked over and petted Milton. "You couldn't really call it a life anymore. He's joined the ranks of the DoeRawfaw and been initiated into our *special* little club." Echthros pushed out the words in short staccato puffs. "No. Redemption. For. Him!" Echthros smiled.

Zack pushed James Recent away.

"Abaddon." Echthros said.

She produced another Sawtawn blade, long, thin, and dripping with oil, that looked like it had come out of a 100,000 mile crankcase.

Mick and Nate stood silent while Echthros continued his rant.

"So, here's the deal, Mick," Echthros said, "you take your forces and back out of here and forget about the rescue of Hahdace. I, being the good natured fellow that I am, will turn Jamie over to you. And we," he pointed back and forth like a playground bully, "will meet on the glorious field of battle at the Gates of Sheh-ole and settle this thing once and for all."

Mick finally smiled and pushed out his own words in short, staccato puffs. "Sorry. Too late. Already. Liberated. Hahdace." He looked at a twin of the creature who had been pinned to the wall. "Guess you had a breakdown in communication somewhere. Aye?"

Echthros's face turned solemn. The arrogant grin disappeared. The creature slinked away, like a dog with its tail between its legs, as Echthros stepped forward and grabbed it.

"I didn't know, Master." It clawed for mercy. "I didn't. Please don't—" Echthros bit his head off and spat it on the floor. He turned back to Mick, wiping the blood off his mouth. "I guess we have nothing to talk about then." He looked at Abaddon. "Take her."

"NOOO!" Zack cried.

109

Nate's dagger flew through the air and caught Abaddon in the back of the thigh, sending her cursing to the floor. The Sawtawn blade flew out of her hand and skidded across the marble, leaving an oil slick as she clawed her way after it.

—

Milton leapt and caught Dessa chest high with both feet, sending them both to the ground.

—

Abaddon jumped up, grabbed the Sawtawn, and hobbled toward Jamie as Zack ran for her. He hit the oil, slipped and skidded past her colliding with the altar. The impact knocked the wind out of him.

—

"Joliet Life Christian Center" erupted as the Daemon forces engaged Mick, Nate and the Army of Light, and the blood troughs began to fill.

—

Echthros slinked behind the throne and watched the mayhem erupt. When it was clear, he crawled across the platform.

"Going someplace?" Kurt wielded a sword toward him, the tip near Echthros's eye.

Echthros rose slowly, hands out to his side.

"Yes, I guess I am. But you can't come." He smiled.

Kurt looked down at his own stomach. Thunder rolled in his ears. Blood began to throb behind his eyeballs, and he couldn't focus on Echthros's face. Oxygen exploded in his head, bubble after bubble. He saw Echthros smile and his lips move, but heard no sound except the roar in his own temples. He tried to grab the object sticking out of his shirt, but it had no handle, only a point. His hand slipped off the surface and he saw the crimson-black spurt between his fingers. He stared at his hand covered in his own blood and felt his knees buckle as he clawed at Echthros's suit coat.

He fell to his knees, all senses keenly aware of the mayhem around him. He noticed the black puddles of drapes, on the floor, as the top seemed to stretch off into nothing. Echthros stood before him in a suit, fit for a head of state, but stained in the blood of his recent victims. The marble platform shown with a mirror image and Kurt wondered if they used some sort of floor buffer and who would operate it and where would they plug in the cord for the electricity?

He saw swords swiping and blood flying and veins spurting as creatures met their demise at the hands of people that he had come to respect and even love. Dessa was locked in mortal combat with Milton who once, an eon ago, he had called a friend, but had turned out to be a sadistic comrade. Mick and Nate, with their forces, had rescued him from certain destruction and for that, he would be eternally grateful. He watched Zack struggle to his feet far across the auditorium by the marble altar. Zack Tucker, who he had once loathed, but now respected and loved like a brother.

Kurt Clayton felt the blade slide back out of him and heard the wet *thwap* as the tip cleared his skin. He turned to see the man, Zack had called, *James,* holding the handle.

Kurt slumped forward onto the floor. He felt James wipe, what was left of, his blood off the blade, onto his back and finally all of his senses faded and darkness enveloped him.

———

Milton scrambled to his feet and lunged at Dessa again. She sidestepped, whirled, and sliced Milton's calf, sending him to the floor shrieking. He clutched his leg, trying to stop the black blood from oozing out.

Abaddon looked into Zack's eyes and transformed herself into Jamie's face and body.

"Zack," she said.

Zack rose slowly, finally filling his lungs again and glanced at the altar, then back at Abaddon.

"I'm here, baby." Abaddon opened her arms. "You found me. You rescued me. We'll be together now."

Jamie writhed on the altar, trying to scream.

Zack didn't take his eyes off Abaddon, as he reached over and pulled down the gag on Jamie's mouth.

"Baby, it's me, don't listen to her!"

"I know it's you," Zack said. Never taking his eyes off Abaddon. He reached into his boot scabbard, pulled his dagger and cut Jamie's bonds.

"It's a trick, Zack," Abaddon said. "It's me, they've tricked you. That," she pointed, "is not Jamie."

Abaddon lunged toward Zack and their swords clashed.

—

Milton was up again and circling Dessa. He bent and picked up the sword of a fallen Daemon.

"You're going down," Milton growled.

"Bring it on, you freak." Dessa said, and swung her sword.

—

Echthros watched the carnage briefly and then skulked into Daniel J. Blevins's mock office, behind the platform, and disappeared through the trap door.

—

Abaddon swung and knocked Zack's sword out of his hand. It ricocheted off the altar and slid across the floor. She slashed again, barely missing his arm and spraying his face with the Sawtawn oil. Zack pounced and they both hit the floor, with Zack straddling her. She rolled, threw him off, and sprang back to her feet.

"Abaddon!"

She turned, Nate stood a few yards away. Jamie's façade relaxed and transformed back into Abaddon.

A grin spread across her face. "Well, well, Nate. Come to

play?" She stepped forward and swung her sword.

———

Like a rehearsed dance, Dessa fought with Milton; swords, kicks, punches and slashes, until they both stumbled onto the platform behind the throne. Milton thrust his sword again and Dessa blocked it, punching him in the face with several quick jabs. The blows forced him backward into the pipe organ bench; his head snapped and he rolled off onto the platform and lay still.

Dessa dropped to one knee beside Kurt and checked him, nothing.

110

Nate clashed with Abaddon's sword, slid down the blade to the guard and drew her in chest to chest.

She snapped at him, fangs laid bare.

He slapped her and she screamed like an insulted woman. "How dare you!" So Nate punched her in the face.

She stumbled back against the altar and Zack grabbed both arms from the opposite side. Nate grabbed her legs and she flailed over the altar, hanging suspended, between the two of them. Abaddon kicked and screamed, with the blade thrashing in her hand.

She wrenched her neck to one side and bit a chunk out of Zack's forearm, slipping from his grasp. She yanked one leg free and kicked Nate in the shoulder, flopping and clawing on the altar in a spasm.

Nate fastened again on the other leg, swung her away from the altar and released. Abaddon slid across the slick floor and collided with a pillar. The Sawtawn blade flew from her hand

and stopped at Nate's feet.

He scooped it up, as she clambered to grab it.

She jumped back; terror and hatred filled her contorted face.

"Guess you won't be needing this anymore." Nate held the sword erect.

"Give it to me," she hissed. "Give it to me or die!"

"Really?" Nate smiled.

He hurled it toward the living darkness at the edge of the throne room. It hit the marble floor and bounced, sliding over the edge and into the blackness.

"Nooo!" Abaddon screamed, while metal thumped against rock as it fell.

Abaddon glared at Nate and shrieked curses. She sprang, wrapping her arms and legs around him, with her fangs gleaming. He grabbed her head with both hands, holding it away from his face and with one powerful twist, snapped her neck. The legs relaxed and she slid down his body and slumped onto the floor.

Nate stepped between the altar and the darkness.

"Are you alright?" he asked Jamie.

"I'm getting there." She glanced at Zack, then back at Nate and her eyes grew wide.

Abaddon screamed again and Nate whirled.

—

Milton raised his sword, with the gleaming point ready to plunge into Dessa's back.

"Dessa!" John yelled and she swiped instinctively behind her, slicing a gash in Milton's shin. Milton screamed and Dessa lunged for him, but he fell backward off the platform and rolled behind the curtains.

Dessa reached the curtains and threw them back, Milton was gone.

—

Abaddon regained consciousness and stood. Her neck was twisted sickeningly, leaving her head resting on her shoulder. She leapt across the altar and caught Nate chest high, sending both of them toward the darkness.

Her head flopped from side to side, out of control, as she

chomped at him. Her nails dug into his flesh and she bit his shoulder. Nate brought his knee up, caught her in the crotch, and threw her over his head. The blow's force sent her legs over the edge of the darkness. Abaddon grabbed the slick marble, her nails scratching, like diamonds on glass.

The darkness shrouded her like a black fog and tugged on her. She struggled, hissing and shrieking while the dark cloud engulfed her body.

"Nate, please!" she cried.

Nate stood watching.

She glanced at Zack.

Abaddon's face transformed into Jamie again.

"Help me, Zack! Please!"

Zack, Jamie, and Nate watched her claw and gasp, thrashing, as the darkness began to suck her down.

"Immolo are captivitas artis f!" she screamed. "Immolo are captivitas artis f!" She paused, then in a whisper, "Immolo are captivitas artis f".

She pawed her way up onto the marble. She hooked one leg on the ledge, as Zack walked over to her.

"Not this time," he said and kicked Abaddon in the face, snapping her head back against her backbone.

Abaddon screamed profanity and swiped at him, latching onto his leg. Zack hit the floor hard as he slid toward the darkness. He kicked with his free foot, over and over, until Abaddon's face turned pale. She looked at him in horror and lost her grip, toppling backward and floundering, as she hit rocks and ledges. Her screams echoed into the canyon and the darkness devoured her.

111

At the mouth of the tunnel, Echthros suddenly fell to the ground and cried out in terror. In his mind, he saw Abaddon plummet into the darkness. He looked down at a wound that opened in his chest and blood oozed out.

Echthros scrambled to his feet holding his chest, blood pumping through his fingers. As he ran, a whine escaped his lips and grew into a full-on shriek that echoed from the walls and penetrated all of Tartaroo.

—

James Recent perched, like a Gargoyle, high above the throne room, and watched the Daemonic forces clashing with the Army of Light. He just shook his head.

—

Zack and Nate stood on the precipice looking into the darkness.

"Wow." Zack said. "I've never even thought about doing that to a woman before."

"She's no woman," Nate said, "so, don't worry about it."

"Zack?" Jamie's voice came from behind them. Both turned.

Milton Drago stood with his arm around Jamie's waist, and a dagger to her throat, backing away from the altar.

"Milton!" Zack yelled.

"You killed mine," he growled, "now, I'm going to kill yours."

Milton took a few steps backward, dragging Jamie with him; while, the carnage continued throughout the throne room. Milton bumped into a pillar, and slid around behind it, as Zack took a few steps toward him.

"You'll never see her alive again, at least in the form that you know her." Milton smiled and disappeared through a concave in a black marble wall.

Zack ran to the pillar, sword drawn.

"Zack," Nate said, "remember who you are and do what you have to. I'll join Mick and the others."

Zack stepped around the pillar and through the concave.

—

Nate rejoined Mick, along with Dessa and John, and began to push the Daemon forces back out of the throne room; while, outside the palace, all of Tartaroo followed suit and began to run. The ground rumbled, and waves of upheavals spewed steam and vapor, as the very essence of Tartaroo rebelled.

The medallions of the Army of Light illuminated all over Tartaroo, at the same instant.

"Mel, are the Charis safe?" Mick keyed his mic.

"We're in place, Boss. The Charis are with us, no worries."

Mass chaos ensued as Daemon factions, pursued by the Army of Light, fell into heaving chasms.

112

Zack's eyes began to adjust, as his medallions glowed red. He found himself in, yet, another underground tunnel, leading him to, God only knew, where. He started down an incline, as he heard the roar of the battle beginning to dissipate above him. The ground rumbled and heaved as if the earth itself was ready to belch up any and all contents of Tartaroo.

Zack stopped, sword drawn, and tried to listen for any sign of Jamie and Milton, but heard only the hiss of gases, rising out of chasms, somewhere in the distance. He saw the glow of torches, a few hundred yards down the tunnel, and he slowed, stepping over cracks in the ground, that oozed liquid and hissed steam. An eerie calm settled over him, as the tunnel finally emptied into a large room surrounded by prison cells, hewn into the rock walls.

The flickering light from the torches, reminded him of a medieval dungeon.

Zack heard the whispers, like the rustling of bats wings in his ears, and he spun to see what was behind him.

Nothing.

More whispers.

Almost like soft singing. Low, methodical, raspy.

Zack scanned the cells. No sign of life, non-life, Milton or Jamie.

But the singing.

Was it singing?

He stepped closer to the first cell and looked through bars, lathed from stone. The torchlight threw dancing shadows across the floor that looked as if it were cut out of large, flat slabs of rock. He saw a simple shelf carved out, like a make-shift bunk, but no occupant.

He stepped to the next cell.

Also empty, but he could tell that a great deal of blood had been spilled in this one.

The next.

And the next.

Empty.

And then the rustle again. The singing. The soft rubbing of bat wings. He peaked around the corner of the next cell and looked in-between the wall and the first stone bar.

A body lay facing the wall on the carved bunk; curled in the fetal position.

A simple shape covered in a garment of burlap; Zack wasn't sure about the garment, but it was definitely a woman's body.

113

Zack stood motionless for what seemed an hour before he heard the body begin to sing again, softly, raspy, like the rustle of bat wings. Zack listened and began to pick up the tune:

Amazing grace, how sweet the sound, that saved a wretch like me...

Zack heard the rise and fall of notes, of what was, in a former life, a soprano, now wrapped in a defeated whisper.

He stepped sideways for a better look and his sword clanked against the bar. The woman flinched, but then lay still.

Why didn't she look up?

What was she waiting for?

Him to enter the cell?

"Hello." Zack said softly.

No response.

A few seconds and she returned to *Amazing Grace*.

Zack looked at the cell door, a key hole, but none like he had ever seen.

Of course, it's not every day he found a woman lying in a cell in Hell, but still…

He glanced around the room.

A few chairs and tables, hacked out of some sort of wood, were scattered around.

"I'm sorry," Zack interrupted the singing. "I'm looking for someone and was wondering if you saw, or heard, them go past?"

The woman paused and then continued her hymn.

"I'm sorry, excuse me," Zack said, "anybody come through here?"

The singing continued.

"I'm Zack Tucker, from the surface world."

Her singing stopped.

More whispers.

But this seemed different; it was a plea for redemption and salvation out of this place.

"Help me."

"Who are you—"

"Help. Me."

The woman rolled over, slowly and methodically. She sat up and swung her legs over the side. Her hair was matted and tangled and she leaned forward, so that it hung at the side of her face like blinders on a horse.

She began to rock back and forth.

"Help me." She whispered.

"Help me." A little louder and more pronounced.

"Can you *please* help me?" She rocked. "Help. Me."

A chant; a mantra of despair.

It grew in intensity until if flowed out of her, in a guttural force, like a woman in child birth.

"Help me."

"You've got to help me!"

She bounded off the bunk and hit the bars so hard that Zack jumped back, and nearly dropped his sword.

She squeezed the bars so hard that Zack could see her pale skin splitting, as she dug her fingers into the rock.

She screamed a maniacal scream. "Help me! Please help me! I'll do anything you ask, please help me! I'll do anything. Help…" Her legs began to give out and she slid down to her knees still holding onto the bars. "Please…"

She collapsed to a sitting position, head down and fingers still wrapped tightly around the bars, and began to sob.

Zack moved toward her and when he was inches from the bars he knelt on one knee, sword at the ready. He looked close, in the flicker of the torches, and saw the bloodless gashes on her wrist.

"Who are you?" He asked.

She slowly raised her head and looked into his eyes.

She snuffed.

"My name was Muriel." She paused as if dredging up a memory long since dead. "Muriel Clayton."

114

"My name is Muriel." A mocking tone came from behind Zack and he slowly rose and turned.

"Milton," he said.

"Milton?" Muriel clambered up the bars. "No! Milton! No! Please." She reached out and caught Zack by the back of his shirt and pulled him into the bars. "Don't let him at me again, don't let him take me! Please!"

Milton stepped from the shadows, of a cell, across the room, with Jamie in front of him. He, once again, had one hand around her waist and the other over her mouth. The gnarled hand around her waist held the Sawtawn blade.

"Sort of like old times, aye, Zacko Packo?" Milton growled. "Except this time, we're not going out to the front lawn and no cops are going to show."

"Milton—"

"And this outcome will be a little different too." Milton smiled.

"Put it down, Milton," Zack said.

"No!" Milton snarled. "You're going to watch her die the same way I watched *my* precious die…"

Zack stepped toward Milton.

"No!" Muriel cried. "Don't! He'll kill you and eat you! I've seen it! I've seen it!"

Zack held up his hand toward Muriel and she stopped.

"Jamie will not die by your hand today or any other day, Milton," Zack said.

"Are you freakin' crazy, Tucker?" Milton said in a nearly normal voice. "Admit defeat. It's over. You're over!"

"Not today, Milton, and not any other day."

"Look around you, Tucker; do you know where we are? Do you have any idea?" Milton chuckled and shook his head.

For a moment, Zack caught a glimpse of the old Milton, without the mutations and the fur; that old Milton shaking his head and mocking him in the hallways of Summit Ridge High. It all came flooding back. Stuffing John into a locker.

Throwing a diaper at Zack in gym class and telling him, "Here's a jockstrap for ya!" while all the other boys laughed at him.

"What, do you think that fat is going to just fall off you one night, Tucker? No, he's thinkin' he'll just jump up and down and some of it will fly up and stick to the ceiling."

Milton Drago.

Harassing him. Laughing at him. Chasing him. Pushing him into bushes. Trying to kill him in the cemetery. Shaking his head at him in that dismissive gesture, letting Zack know how stupid and clueless he really was.

And now once again, with one paw covering her mouth and the other around the waist, of the only girl he ever loved and who loved him back, Zack would be damned forever himself, if he didn't take care of Milton, once and for all.

Zack straightened and inhaled, standing erect.

"I know exactly where I am, Milton, and I know exactly *who* and *what* you are and more importantly... I know who *I am.*" Zack took a few more steps toward him and Milton tightened his grip around Jamie's waist.

Zack looked into Milton's eyes; yellow, like a cat, but vacant and void. Zack's eyes narrowed and Milton's eyes widened.

"You *will* let her go."

Milton made a move, as if to bring the hand up with the Sawtawn blade in it, but couldn't.

"What the—" Milton's hand slid off Jamie's waist and hung limp at his side.

Jamie heaved a cry and rolled away from the hand covering her face. She ran across the room to Zack who embraced her, his large bicep pressed on her back and he never took his eyes off Milton.

"Zack." she said softly.

"It'll be alright, babe."

He shoveled her behind him just as Milton shook himself like a dog and brought the Sawtawn to bear.

115

Zack clashed with Milton's sword, in a death dance, across the room. Milton got a hind leg against Zack's thigh and shoved, knocking Zack backward, into one of the wooden tables. He swiped at Zack, like bringing an ax down on a chopping block, but Zack rolled and Milton buried the sword into the wood. He yanked it free and swung again.

Zack met him, with Baraq, and sent Milton reeling into a torch. The torch jarred loose and landed in Milton's fur, singeing it and catching some tufts on fire. Milton hit himself, with the flat of his gnarled hand, and finally put it out.

He sprang for Zack, on powerful hind legs, driving himself, head first into his chest, and both went sprawling across the floor. Both swords dislodged and slid away.

Milton snapped at Zack's face, with crusted fangs, as Zack held him by clumps of fur, inches away from his throat. In an almost dislocation of his neck, Milton turned his head and bit Zack's hand, sinking one fang deep into a fleshy part. Zack screamed and punched Milton in the side of the head, popping what was left of his human ear. Zack hit him again. Milton shook it off and kept snapping. One more time, Zack punched and his ear exploded, with gushes of black blood.

The impact unnerved Milton and he let out a howl as Zack brought his knee up, into what was left of Milton's genitals, and sent him rolling off into one of the wooden chairs.

Jamie cracked Milton, in the side, with another chair and he screamed profanity at her, as he swiped out with his leg. He caught both her legs and sent her to the ground. Milton was on her, with both hands around her neck.

Zack scrambled to his feet and dove for Milton, knocking him off Jamie and into the wall. Milton clawed at Zack's face, raking his long nails across his neck and splitting the skin. Milton grabbed a shard of wood, that had come off a broken chair, and lunged at Zack, driving it into his chest. The black diamond shirt took the blow, but forced the air out of Zack's lungs and he gasped for breath, as Milton snatched a chair leg and swung. He caught Zack in the jaw and sent him into one of the open cells. Zack collided with the roughhewn bunk and lay still.

Milton stood and looked at Jamie, lying on the floor, and smiled.

"No, Milton!" Muriel was back, screaming from the locked cell. "No, Milton, leave her alone!"

Milton turned and walked toward the Sawtawn blade and picked it up, the blade dribbling oil onto the rock floor. He brought it up, its black mirror finish reflected his distorted, mutated face and he licked some of the oil off.

"Almost as yummy as you." Milton smiled at Jamie, who dragged herself backward into the corner of the room.

Milton took a step. "I'm going to enjoy this."

"Milton!" Muriel screamed. "Stop. Leave her alone!"

Milton snatched a torch off the wall and hurled it toward the bars.

"Shut up you, bloodless freak!" he growled.

The torch hit the rock cylinders, throwing fire and sparks into the cell. Muriel screamed and flailed her hands against the fire until it was out.

He looked back at Jamie, walking toward her, in the bent-over gate of a mutant.

"You, will be joining me soon." He spun the Sawtawn blade like a windmill. "Once and for all, I'll have my revenge on that tub of crap." Milton cursed. "First you, then him." He nodded toward the dark cell.

Milton took a few more steps and Jamie lashed out, kicking with all her might; she caught Milton in one leg. He went down on one knee and quick as a cat, grabbed Jamie by the throat, the Sawtawn blade held inches from her face.

Jamie's eyes bulged and her face began to turn red as she clawed at Milton's arm. He raised the Sawtawn blade to plunge it into her stomach. *Just a poke and a twist.*

The dagger impaled Milton's shoulder and he let out a howl, dropping the Sawtawn blade and releasing Jamie. Milton turned to see Zack Tucker breathing heavy and propped against the cell door. Milton clawed at the dagger and pulled it out of his shoulder just as he felt the Sawtawn blade enter his chest. He looked back at Jamie, whose eyes were narrowed and lips tight.

He grabbed Jamie's hand and the handle of the Sawtawn and smiled. That smile was the last voluntary expression that Milton Drago would have, as Zack swung his Baraq, severing his head from his shoulders. Milton's head hit the wall, like a ripe melon, and bounced onto the rock floor, finally coming to rest, looking back at Zack and Jamie. Milton's body shuddered, fell backward onto the floor and twitched twice. It finally laid still, the Sawtawn blade still sticking out of its chest.

Muriel cheered as Jamie scrambled to her feet and threw her arms around Zack's neck, kissing him long and hard.

"You came for me," she whispered.

"I cannot live without you," Zack said and kissed her again.

116

Echthros watched from the plateau overlooking Jordan's camp. His Daemon forces collided with Gideon's, like a colony of angry ants, stirred up by a child's stick. He saw Nate and Calver, and their force, join the battle from the flank. Echthros shook his head and held his bleeding chest, puffing in and out.

"Will you never learn?"

He recognized Mick's voice from behind him.

Echthros grinned, without turning.

"If I weren't around, *you'd* be out of work." His grin turned into a toothy smile.

The earth shuddered and a crevasse opened, belching smoke and rolling darkness.

"Mick, why do you even try?" Echthros turned to face him.

Mick shrugged. "Like you said, gives me something to do."

"I guess." Echthros shrugged in mockery. "Dad, won't let you annihilate me."

"Not yet." Mick's eyes burned into Echthros's.

"That's right. Not yet." Echthros broke his stare and looked away.

"We *did* wipe out a lot of your force today, though." Mick motioned toward the battle.

"That you did," Echthros nodded, "but there are plenty more where they came from."

"For now."

"They're expendable. Cattle. I'll birth them anytime I need them," Echthros said.

"I would imagine," Mick said.

"Lord knows there are enough people to work with." Echthros laughed and raised his hands. "They're always dropping out of the sky!"

"There will be a day that you will not own them." Mick's eyes tightened.

"But no time soon." Echthros smiled.

Mick raised his Baraq in a symbolic gesture.

"Not yet." Echthros held up his hand like a traffic cop. "Another time, perhaps." He backed away to the edge of the crevasse and stepped off; engulfed by the flaming darkness.

117

The sun cast shadows through fluttering leaves. Red and white-checkered blankets contrasted the manicured lawns of Gideon's park. Under a shaded canopy, employees, and their families, shuffled through a mammoth buffet line, while white coated waiters, with black bow ties, served them.

Under a large shade tree, Zack sat with Christine and Jamie on a blue blanket.

"I can't believe how warm it is for October?" Christine said.

"Yeah, that's Colorado." Zack smiled. "We like the even temperature."

"I had forgotten." Christine smiled.

"Hey, Mom, Jamie's going to be an education major next fall. Going to teach."

"Really? That's great," Christine said. "I taught for a few years."

"Did you?" Zack asked.

"Yes, briefly. They were all dead, of course, but their minds were sharp." Christine laughed.

"There's so much I don't know about you." Zack shook his head.

"I'm going for something else to drink. Do you want anything?" Jamie asked.

"No, thanks." Zack leaned back on the blanket.

"I'm fine, honey, thanks." Christine turned back to Zack. "It was so weird, you know." Her gaze was far away. "You hear about freak accidents, but when one actually happens to you, it's so different."

Zack leaned on his elbow, with his head resting on his hand.

"I just went for a walk." Christine shrugged. "It was so bright and warm. You and Jeff had gone to the zoo. You loved the zoo. Do you go now?"

"Sometimes." Zack smiled, "Jamie and I were going to. I especially love—,"

"The lions and tigers," Christine finished his sentence.

Zack nodded.

"Jeff looked really good that day. Of course, he always did." She raised her eyebrows and grinned. "He was so proud to take you. You were his *little man*." She reached over and punched Zack's shoulder. "You had these little stubby jeans." Christine held her hands apart. "I bought them at Hills." She looked into the sky and closed her eyes. "Hills Department Store. It's weird how much you miss. Just little things." She paused and then looked back at Zack.

Zack waited.

"And a little baseball shirt. You looked like a miniature Babe Ruth." She laughed. "'I'll be right back 'Mommy', you said, and then 'member, I love you,' and off you ran to get in the car, growling like a lion." She turned toward him. "And you know what, Zack?"

"What, Mom?"

"I never forgot that you loved me. Even after all this time." Christine smiled.

Zack's eyes welled with tears as Christine continued.

"I remember the reflection on the windshield as you pulled out of the driveway. I can still see your little hand, out the window, waving." She brushed tears from her eyes.

"You never know what life will hand you." Christine paused, running her hand over the green grass.

"I vacuumed and straightened and picked up a few toys. Remember those little guys that you used to play with? Those little soldiers? They were everywhere; I was forever picking them up." She smiled through the tears.

"I still have them," Zack said,

"Really?"

"Yup, I built a special shelf for them, a few years later. They've been in my room ever since." Zack paused. "I wish you could see them."

"Me too," Christine said. "You know? It's funny how all of those menial tasks, like cleaning, are so important at the time, but in the scope of eternity, they don't even matter." She began to cry again. "If I only would have known? I'm sorry, Zack. I couldn't have known. I didn't know that I wouldn't see my little boy again." She sobbed into her hands.

Zack moved close and put his arms around his mom.

"Until now," Zack said.

"Yeah." Christine took a moment to calm herself and wipe the tears. "Until now." She brushed Zack's face.

"If you hadn't come for me," she paused, "I'd never have seen you again." She cried as Zack held her.

"But it's okay, Mom." He rocked her.

"I'm so sorry, Zack."

"There's nothing to be sorry about, Mom."

Christine dried her tears and composed herself again.

"Sometimes the little things are the most important."

"Yeah." Zack wiped his own tears and glanced at Jamie, by the drink tent, talking to Nate.

"What happened, Mom?"

Christine paused. "You mean that day?"

"Yeah, how did you…"

Christine wiped the last of her tears. "I took a walk."

Zack released her and sat cross legged, opposite her.

"Just around the neighborhood." She continued. "I didn't even think about locking the door. I didn't take my purse. Why would I?" She shrugged. "I wasn't going to be gone long."

"Man, the sun was bright that day." She put her hand up as if shielding her eyes again. "I remember I loved to walk in the sun with my eyes closed. You know, your face up? Just walking." She closed her eyes and lifted her head.

Zack nodded as she went on. "There was this little dirt road by this irrigation canal. I musta' walked for miles? I just forgot about anything else. I figured you and your dad would be gone most of the day, so why not? It was one of those Colorado summer days."

Zack smiled.

"The canal led into a meadow of dandelions, they're my favorites. Sounds weird…" she smiled, "but I love them."

Zack watched her sparkling eyes.

"Well, the canal emptied into a stream. Well, it was sort of a small river, really." She touched his arm. "In the middle of the field was this huge oak tree. I was just going to sit for a minute, but I had to cross the river."

She looked at Zack for mercy.

"I shouldn't have tried to cross it. Somebody put a log across it, but I shouldn't have," she paused "but I did."

She looked down again, shaking her head.

"It's alright, Mom, you couldn't have known." Zack put his hand on Christine's shoulder.

"The water looked so peaceful. I just glanced down for a minute. Just a second. And I slipped." Terror and helplessness registered in her eyes. "It was over my head. I couldn't believe it. I was so scared. I never learned to swim! Did you know that?"

Zack shook his head.

"Of course, you wouldn't." She touched his arm again. "In my mind, I saw your dad, I saw his smile and I saw your little face. I touched your tiny hand and then I saw—"

Christine stopped abruptly,

Zack looked at her. "What, Mom? What's the matter?"

"I saw you."

"Yes?" Zack questioned.

"No, I don't mean when you were little. I saw you now."

Zack saw revelation hit her.

"I just realized." She put her finger to her temple. "You know, when I walked into that house in Hahdace and was introduced to you?"

Zack nodded.

"I knew I'd seen you before. I dismissed it." She waved her hand. "It was so long ago. I just now thought of that. I saw your face. Not what you *were*, my tiny little one, but what you *would become*. My rescuer, oh God... I saw you!"

They both burst into tears again and held each other and rocked back and forth. Christine kissed Zack on the cheek and forehead.

"And then," she pulled back "everything went dark; I was pulled down. I felt myself sinking, like washing something down the drain. When I woke up, I was wet and cold and wandering in some dark place. I roamed for hours, until finally I came upon Hahdace. I didn't mean to go; I didn't want to leave you, or your dad."

She touched Zack's cheek.

"Can you tell your dad when he gets here?" she asked.

"No need." Jeff stood a few feet away, partially hidden behind one of the big oaks. Tears streamed down his face.

Christine jumped up and ran to him. Taking her in his arms, a low guttural sob began from deep inside him and the years of agony finally released. Jeff and Christine stood for an eternity in an embrace. He kissed her, a long, passionate consummation of lost years.

Zack blushed and turned his head.

"I can't believe it," Jeff sobbed. "I thought I'd lost you forever. I'd given up." He bowed his head. "I thought I'd never see you again."

"I'm here now, baby." Christine lifted his chin and kissed him again.

Jamie rejoined Zack, both their faces wet with tears.

"You raised a wonderful son," Christine looked at Zack. Jeff looked down at the ground, shaking with emotion.

"He's got a lot of you in him," he replied.

118

The sun reached high in the sky and Zack sat on the blanket with Jamie, watching his parent's re-acquaintance. There were snippets of laughter, the touching of cheeks and caressing hands, like watching a first date.

Mick stepped to a microphone on the lawn.

"People of Gideon. Once again, you've accomplished your mission and done it well. You've liberated these souls that Echthros sought to destroy!"

Applause erupted and people shook hands and hugged.

Clouds formed and began to swirl until a magnificent tube of light beamed onto the grass.

"Pneuma." someone whispered.

Like gathering for Sunday worship, the former inhabitants of Hahdace gathered around Pneuma's light.

Zack clutched Christine, and Jeff held them both.

"I love you, Son." She brushed his hair off his eyes. "Thank you," she paused, "for liberating my soul."

"I love you, Mom," Zack said, uncontrollable tears rolling down his cheeks. "I'll see you again."

"I'll be waiting for you, Zack."

Jeff looked at Christine.

"I'm so glad we had one last time together. I'm so glad." She hugged him.

"Don't go. Please don't go." Jeff's voice cracked in unabashed emotion. "Don't leave me again."

"I have to, Darling." Christine's tears flooded down her cheeks. "I'll see you soon."

Nate stood on a nearby boulder, the size of a house, and blew a crystal note on his silver trumpet.

Zack glanced around. Everything exploded in color, the azure sky, ruby flowers, emerald lawn and sun-splashed ambers, like a perfect postcard.

Muriel looked at Zack and waved. He waved back.

Ricki clasped Marta's and Rick's hands and Zack remembered that little smile.

He glanced at John trying to help Tredessa make the Vulcan sign to: *live long and prosper.* Zack smiled and shook his head.

Ralph Maxwell stood by the Rosedale family. Roy Pink gave him the thumbs up, his arm around Ann. Others just mingled, like a Norman Rockwell painting of a perfect Sunday afternoon; all was right with the world.

"It's time," Mick announced and the circle of light started to swirl like a rainbow tornado.

Zack felt the heat hit his face; he squinted and then closed his eyes.

There was a flash that electrified the air and it was gone; and, the people of Hahdace with it.

The employees paused momentarily and then turned back to their food and laughter.

"No big deal, I guess?" Zack shrugged, watching the slaps on backs and high five's. His fellow soldiers were animated, as they retold their adventures underground, lunging and slicing as they talked.

Zack kissed Jamie and then they hugged.

"Zack," she said, looking over his shoulder.

"What?" He looked into her eyes and then turned around.

Jeff stood behind them, still holding Christine in his arms.

119

"Mom?" Zack hugged her and felt her warmth. He kissed her cheek, tasting the tears.

"Oh, Zack." She hugged him again. Zack burst into tears again.

"You really did, rescue me!"

"Mom, how—"

"I don't know." She shrugged, looking down at her body and holding her arms out, inspecting them to make sure all was still intact.

"I see you are getting along well." Mick approached, followed by Nate.

"Mick? Nate?" Zack questioned.

"She didn't die, Zack," Mick said.

"What?"

"I didn't?" Christine asked. "It sure felt like I did."

Mick smiled. "Sometimes—"

"Not very often." Nate added.

"There is a," Mick paused, searching for a word.

"A fluke."

"Fluke is a *good* word." Mick pointed at Nate.

"Don't mention it." Nate winked at Zack.

"At times, a person finds their way to the Netherworld, accidentally. With you, Christine," he nodded toward her, "it was through an underwater vortex of sorts. It sucked you down at the brink of death."

Christine nodded.

"See," Nate interrupted, "if you would have found your way

back out," he shrugged, "then no harm, no foul. You would've walked out of some cave somewhere and hitchhiked home—"

"But as it was," Mick picked up, "you made it all the way to Hahdace. Once there, you begin the transformation and you couldn't return."

"Wait a minute," Christine looked around, "you're saying, if I would have turned left instead of right—"

Mick held out his hands, palms up. "I don't make the rules."

Christine smiled and shook her head.

"But I *did* make it out." She stretched her hands again squeezing them into fists and then releasing them.

"An amendment to the previous rule." Nate held up a single finger.

Zack looked puzzled.

"You were liberated," Mick said pointing to her.

Christine nodded.

"Your son, a family member of noble character, had to be contacted when he was of age."

"Which *you* did," Zack pondered.

Mick nodded. "Several times, as I recall."

Zack grinned.

"You could've turned us down." Nate reached out, punching Zack in the arm. "And your mom would've never rejoined you on this earth."

"Why didn't you tell me up front?" Zack asked.

"It had to be of your own free will," Mick said. "You came on the rescue mission after Jamie, but you wouldn't have had to. We would have done it."

"I couldn't have just let you go." Zack looked at Jamie.

"You better not have." Jamie smiled.

"Besides," Zack said, "in the beginning, I really just needed a job."

They all laughed.

"That too," Nate said.

"That's why we never found your body," Jeff said.

"I was still using it!" Christine laughed.

Everyone laughed again.

"You set her free, Zack," Mick said.

"Thank you," Zack said, embracing Mick and then Nate.

"I told you I picked you for a purpose." Mick patted him on the back.

Zack stepped back, watching Jeff and Christine kiss passionately.

"Dad!" Zack flushed.

"Well?" Jeff smiled. "We've got some catching up to do."

Zack turned to Jamie.

"Us too."

120

"Tutoring Mickey Martin in geometry won't be the same," John said as he and Zack stood, looking up at the school on Monday morning.

"That's for sure," Zack said.

John fished out a handful of Boston Baked Beans, popping them into his mouth.

"Thanks for watching my back, man." Zack bumped knuckles with John.

"Wouldn't have missed it." John returned the gesture. "Somebody had to keep your butt out of the fire."

"You're right about that."

"What are you going to tell Mrs. Drago?" John asked.

"Nothing," Zack said. "As far as she's concerned, he took off and never came home again."

"Seems unfair."

"Yeah," Zack said. "I can't hurt her any more than Milton's already done to her, she's innocent."

"True."

They both stood in silence for a moment.

"Hey," John said, "that Tredessa is kinda cute—"

"She's way out of your league man," Zack smiled.

—

Zack and John began skating their way toward graduation without further incident. Kevin Bauer was palatable, but withdrawn; the lack of allies had rendered him impotent. Zack and Jamie kept in contact with Mrs. Drago, visiting periodically, but made a pact never to mention what really happened to Milton.

Zack bounded onto his porch, a few weeks later, and opened the front door to the aroma of freshly baked chocolate chip cookies.

"Guess what?" Christine met him at the door, excited.

"What?"

Christine handed him a travel brochure.

Zack turned it over in his hand. "Australia?"

"Your dad and I leave in three weeks!" She threw her head back and laughed.

"It's really good to have you home, Mom." Zack kissed her on the cheek.

121

Eight months later…

The siren's wail died as the ambulance rolled into the emergency room parking lot. The girl panted and groaned, while the EMT's wheeled her through the maternity room doors.

"What'd ya got?" Jackie Washington, the heavy-set black nurse, asked.

"Pregnant, white female, 18. She's fully dilated and ready to go at any time. ER told us to bring her up here." The EMT said.

"Put her in number 2. I've already got another one in Birthing Room 1. She's havin' this baby!" Jackie smiled, guiding the gurney to the maternity cubicle.

"What's your name, honey?" Jackie asked, grabbing a cloth to mop her forehead.

"Staci Bransen." the girl panted.

"Do you have a husband or boyfriend coming? Mom or dad?"

"No," Staci said. "No one. Just me."

"Well, alright, Staci Bransen, there's nothing to worry about. We, ladies, have been birthin' babies for thousands of years. You're just going to join our little club! Now just breathe with me, honey."

A few minutes later, in Birthing Room 1, the woman in the stirrups panted, through another contraction.

"You're doing just fine." The masked doctor was perched at the end of the table. "One more push and that'll do it."

In chorus both women could hear each other scream, simultaneously, as the final push brought fluid encased life into the oxygenated world. Both baby boys slid into the welcoming hands of the doctor and Jackie Washington.

"Ohhh, how precious!" Jackie smiled, as she placed the little boy on Staci's stomach and cut the umbilical cord. "Picked out a name yet, honey?"

"Kurt," Staci said.

—

"Okay." The doctor in Birthing 1, stood by the warming lights of the incubator. "He's a little jaundice, but that's to be expected." He turned the baby over. "This is weird.

"What's that?" James Recent stepped from the corner of the room.

"This birthmark on his back." The doctor traced the dark pigmentation with his finger. "It's almost like a, worm or something—"

"A snake," James said.

"Maybe." The doctor paused. "Oh, well I wouldn't be concerned, I'm sure it will fade with time."

"I'm not concerned at all," the woman smiled.

"Okkee dokey, Mrs. Recent?" The doctor snatched the chart, looked at Recent and then back at the woman. "Sorry. Mrs. Drago?"

"Yes. Angie." She smiled.

122

"What's up?" Nate poked his head into Mick's office.

"Did you see this?" Mick held up the object.

"No, what is it?" Nate stepped closer to the desk and let out a long whistle. "Is this?"

"Yeah," Mick said. "It is. Zack gave it to me yesterday."

"Zack? What did he have it for?"

"He said he picked it up in that little office behind the throne room, tucked it into his backpack and forgot about it until yesterday. Said he was cleaning it out and it had slipped into the lining." Mick sat back in his chair, hands behind his head. "Thought it was 'interesting', he said."

Nate grinned. "You know Luci's goin' to want this back."

"I would say so," Mick smirked. "I better call Zack and—"

"Oh," Nate's grin turned to a full-fledged teeth whitening smile. "Let *me* call him."

123

The phone rang through a sea of muddy clouds.

"Hello," Zack coughed a sleepy voice into the receiver.

"Zack, its Nate. Hey buddy, get dressed and get down here as soon as you can."

"Why? What's up?" Zack stammered. "Is something wrong?"

"Well, yes and no," Nate's voice betrayed a smile. "Mick and I need to ask you about something."

"Am I in trouble?" Zack's rest was fading.

"Well, not from us but it all depends on the way you look at it." Nate chuckled. "See you in a little bit."

There was an abrupt click on the other end and then silence.

Zack grabbed the clock and then fumbled it back onto the nightstand.

3:33am

"Don't those guys ever sleep?"